THE MATHEMATICS OF CHANGE

THE MATHEMATICS OF CHANGE

A NOVEL BY AMANDA KABAK

THE HELLUM & NEAL SERIES IN LGBTQIA+ LITERATURE

BRAIN MILL PRESS | GREEN BAY, WISCONSIN

The Mathematics of Change is a work of fiction. Names, places, and incidents either are products of the author's imagination or are used fictitiously. Any resemblance to actual persons, living or dead, or locales is entirely coincidental.

Copyright © 2017 by Amanda Kabak.
All rights reserved.

Published in the United States by Brain Mill Press.
Print ISBN 978-1-942083-46-7
EPUB ISBN 978-1-942083-49-8
MOBI ISBN 978-1-942083-47-4
PDF ISBN 978-1-942083-48-1

Cover photograph © Nathan Pearce.
Cover design by Ampersand Book Covers.

A portion of this novel was published under the same name in *Midwestern Gothic*, issue 12, and is reprinted with permission.

www.brainmillpress.com

For Anna,
my number-one lady

THE MATHEMATICS OF CHANGE

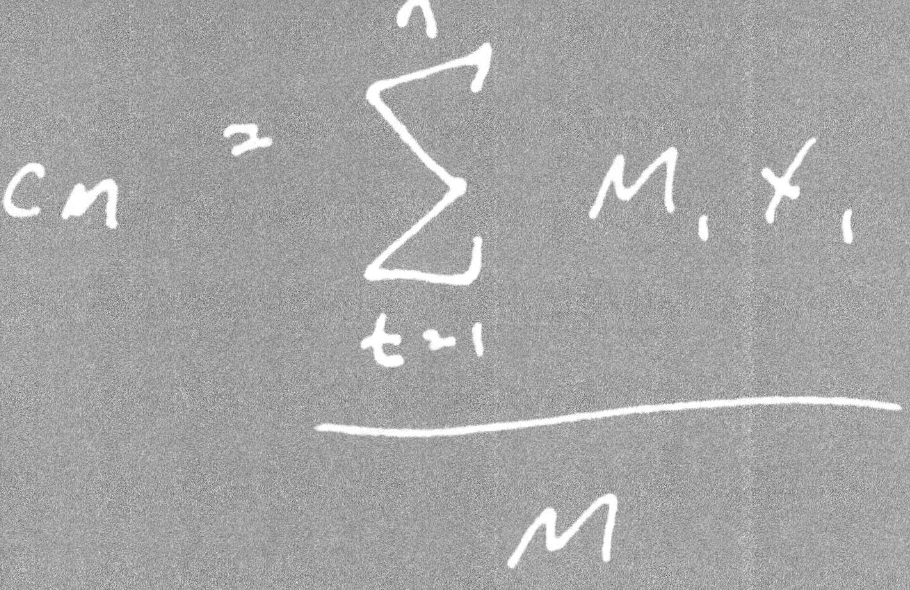

WHAT FEMINISTS HAD TO DOWNPLAY TO MAKE THEIR point was that essential differences exist between men and women. While we should all be equal under the law, we are not all the same in actuality.

–Dr. Abigail Rosen, The F Word: Femininity in the New Century

1

MILLERTON, Ohio, had a certain stench about it. Not egg farm or landfill or even chocolate factory, but college town. Places like Millerton, home of Tilsen University, drew people together not naturally destined to interact, making an aromatic melting pot of school versus town, jock versus brain, science and humanities, silver spoons and charity cases.

Such a morass tended to spark one of two reactions: a sweeping embrace of the chaos or a grueling battle against it. Tilsen University fought the good fight. Though groups self-segregated as a general rule, that small nod toward order didn't satisfy Tilsen. Up went wrought-iron gates between Millerton proper and the university, and even its manicured quad enforced a certain internal hierarchy within the school itself, with the purest humanities highest up the hill to the east and the most applied sciences farthest down the hill to the west. The trek from engineering to philosophy was daunting, to say the least, but close proximity flung people together time and again, and the whiff of those resulting combinations informed Millerton's characteristic scent even more than the skunky haze of pot smoke wafting from dorm room windows.

At Tilsen, the opposites-attract axiom was practically a natural law, a rite of passage as universal as fraternal hazing or final exam all-nighters. It was a perverted gravitational force, a hot stone begging to be touched, a frozen flagpole in search of a tongue, and not only had it left in its wake uncountable broken hearts and wishes to forget, but it was perhaps the only explanation for best friends Mitch Mitchell and Carol Hollister.

Mitch had swum so many miles in lane four of Tilsen University's Olympic-sized pool her name might as well have been lacquered across its starting block. While her way with the 500 free would have been merely serviceable in a Big Ten school, it was sought after at Tilsen and had financed half her undergraduate education while her mathematical prowess had taken care of the rest. She spent hours swimming laps over that fat black line to earn her keep, reaching, pulling, kicking her way through hundreds of thousands of meters. Even after months of twice-a-day workouts, of feeling the rhythm of her stroke in her arms at night, she loved it indecently. By now, at thirty-five, her shoulders had paid a steep price from all that repetitive motion, but didn't everything important have an associated cost?

Ultimate success in swimming came down to who could best cheat the clinging drag of water—a mindset that played right into Mitch's sweet spot, a lifelong obsession with friction in its many forms. Her three Tilsen diplomas stated, in an Olde English font, that she'd studied mechanical engineering, but she'd really majored in friction. Friction was like leaky faucets or opened doors in air-conditioned rooms. It generated noise, ate up power, and produced heat, and Mitch had spent her graduate school years getting intimate with the most insidious types. At the time, if someone told her she rubbed them the wrong way, which wasn't uncommon, Mitch thought about metal against metal, estimated coefficients and loss curves.

She could iterate endlessly over ways to mitigate mechanical friction: cooling, smoothing, buffering with air or water, greasing the proverbial wheels with any of the natural or synthetic lubricants on the market, but her knowledge ended at the boundary between machines and humans, leaving the exercise of reducing friction between people to Carol.

Carol Hollister summed up her solution to this in one word: booze. She was a recognized expert in the subject, a designation reaffirmed every year when Labor Day weekend slapped Millerton awake from its languid summer. For those three days, the last before students arrived, Tilsen became a party school. Each department participated in an unofficial competition for best kickoff event, which had led to the rise of lauded specialties like potato-chip-crusted corn dogs at the engineering party or the way the chemistry faculty rolled out canisters of liquid nitrogen and flash froze everything in sight.

The undisputed king of these events was the sociology-sponsored shindig—due to a punch perfected by Carol, whose husband, Brian, headed the department. Conjecture had it that a single match taken to the cut-glass punch bowl could level the whole neighborhood. Needless to say, the party had gotten so popular it had engulfed most of the other soft-science departments and threatened to overflow the Hollisters' spacious backyard.

< ≈ >

During the Saturday lap swim of this Labor Day weekend, Mitch had the pool to herself except for a very pregnant woman drifting down lane one in a listless breaststroke. The luxury of such quiet water was hard to resist, but in deference to Carol's annual call of party-preparation panic, Mitch stuck to a short set: twenty-five hundred meters in a mix of freestyle and backstroke with just enough butterfly thrown in to keep it interesting. Afterward, she kept her shower short then pulled on jeans and one of her dozen-odd Tilsen T-shirts before driving to Carol's house in a quiet subdivision on the edge of town.

The atmosphere around the Hollister household was exuberant with the smell of cut grass, and Mitch wondered how many of the neighbors had been rudely awakened by the lawn mower this morning. The hedges along the front walk were trimmed to sharp right angles that bristled against Mitch's outstretched palm. She let herself in the open front door and headed through the hall into the kitchen beyond.

Carol set down two trays of cupcakes on the stovetop with a clatter then closed the oven door with one foot. She pushed some curly, bright-red hair off her face with an oven-mitted hand and said, "You're late."

"Late? I thought people weren't coming until one."

At once, Carol was across the kitchen and in front of Mitch. She stretched up, put her nose to Mitch's neck, and sniffed, a move full of accusation. "Mm-hmm. I thought you said you'd be by when you got up."

"I figured the swim was implicit."

Carol blew a protracted raspberry, one of the countless rude noises she'd picked up from her sons, James and Gordon.

Mitch said, "Do you want to argue or put me to work?"

"Yeah, yeah." Carol directed Mitch to her usual station in the kitchen, the deep corner of countertop next to the refrigerator. A large serving platter waited there along with a pile of tomatoes, onions, and lettuce.

"Did you sharpen the knife?" Mitch asked.

"Did I sharpen the knife? Pshaw. When did I ever ask you to wield a dull knife in this kitchen?"

"The last time I was here, I would have done less damage to that tomato with a spoon."

"Yes," Carol drew out the word. "I sharpened the knife. Believe me, this is one area where your anality is a virtue—you make the condiments look like they were catered."

Mitch got slicing while Carol popped in and out of the kitchen around vacuuming, zipping to the store for bags of ice, filling coolers with the party's lesser beverages, yelling at James—her older son—to get off his butt and bring up the folding chairs from the basement. She was a freckled blur while Mitch smiled and worked, a little high on the satisfaction of producing so many slices of uniform thickness. Carol's kitchen was good for small pleasures like these.

Carol finally settled at the sink to wash more produce for Mitch. "This party will be the death of me."

"Where's Brian?"

"Outdoor readiness." Not a trivial task given the size of the backyard and the crowd they were expecting. Carol turned off the water and shook a colander full of broccoli. "I don't know why I even serve this. Who eats broccoli with everything else that's available? Well, maybe *she*…"

Mitch used the front of her T-shirt to wipe away onion-induced tears. "Maybe she?"

Before Carol answered, she piled the washed broccoli in a clear space by Mitch's elbow. "Have I told you about Dr. Rosen?"

"I don't think so, but it's hard to keep track of all the PhDs in this town."

"Oh, you'd remember." Carol leaned against the counter close to Mitch. "She's the department trophy this year—this decade, the way Joe Obermann is drooling over her. He used words like 'monumental,' 'triumph,' and, of course, 'endowments.'"

The academic holy grail. It wasn't all about money and reputation, just mostly. "The dean's happy, huh? What about Brian? Is he all worked up too, or is she competition?"

"He says she's average at best."

There was a point around here somewhere, but it might be a long time coming. "Something doesn't compute," Mitch said, specifically to make Carol smile, which she did before giving Mitch a playful shove and sailing back into motion again.

Mitch started in on the broccoli, raising her voice to carry over running water. "Did they poach her from Harvard or something?"

"No, she was just at City College in New York."

"But Tilsen pursued her?"

Brian asked, "Who did Tilsen pursue?" He walked through the sliding patio door, his tanned arms dotted with cut grass and dirt.

"Dr. Rosen." Carol pulled the colander from the sink, set it on the counter, and moved aside to let Brian wash his hands.

"Pursuit puts it mildly. She passed our tenure review in two weeks, which has to be a new record. In a case like this, I'd usually blame our overactive diversity initiative—"

"She's a lesbian," Carol said. "A smart, beautiful, popular lesbian."

Brian said, "The only kind of lesbian that does any good."

Mitch put down her knife and exchanged a sour look with Carol, who shrugged. Mitch knew she should shrug too, but she didn't have the same peacekeeping incentive—instead of going into business with her graduate school adviser like Mitch, Carol had married hers. When Brian came out with broad statements like these, ones dripping with the weight of his sociological experience, the familial-grade animosity that lurked between him and Mitch flared up into the more vitriolic version that often arose between hard and soft scientists. She said, "Says the incredibly useful straight, white male."

"You know what I mean. This time the diversity was a footnote." He dried his hands on a blue-striped kitchen towel. "There's a book."

Carol said, "A popular book."

"What's it about?"

"How girly girls are going to take over now that feminists have paved the way," Carol said. "It's called *The F Word: Femininity in the New Century*."

Mitch tried not to laugh but failed. "Ah. She's marquee value. How long until Tilsen starts pumping her for the follow-up then punishing her when it isn't as successful?"

Brian put hands to hips and frowned. "How do you live with such pessimism?"

"Ninety percent of engineering is preparing for the worst, which seems like realism to me," Mitch said. She continued to carve out bite-sized florets in case this guest of honor were watching her figure and went crazy on the crudités.

Instead of responding to that, Brian said, "I thought James was going to get the chairs from the basement."

Carol said, "And I thought raising boys was supposed to be easy."

James was fourteen to the marrow of his bones. When he sighed in the new rolled-eyed way of his, Mitch was hard-pressed to keep a straight face and was thankful her role in his life included essentially no disciplinary duties. Carol and Brian were complementary in many ways, not the least of which being their general approach to parenting. While Carol preferred the full-frontal attack, Brian went in for the element of surprise, and he put a finger to his lips before creeping from the kitchen toward the stairway leading up to the bedrooms.

Carol put the cauliflower back in the sink, turned on the water, and said, "Maybe you should ask her out."

"Ask who out?"

"Dr. Rosen. I've seen her author photo, and she's at least as hot as that ex of yours, besides being twice as smart. I mean, Mitch, not only does the woman have a doctorate, but she's got tresses. Honest-to-God dark, curly tresses."

Mitch laughed and kept chopping. "I doubt your Dr. Rosen and I are compatible."

"Compatibility is overrated. No one thought you and the ex were compatible."

"Her name's Kim, and we weren't."

Carol dumped the cauliflower next to Mitch and pinched her through her T-shirt. "You know what I mean. I lost a bet with Brian over that. Fifty bucks. I gave you guys three months, tops, and you went and lasted over a year."

"Such faith. You got off cheap."

Carol laid her hand on Mitch's forearm, not moving until Mitch stopped her knife work. "You know I only joke because you're not heartbroken. Are you heartbroken?"

"No," Mitch said to the broccoli battlefield in front of her. Carol took her by the jaw and pulled her face around so they were blue eye to blue eye.

"Are you telling me the truth?"

"Yes."

She held Mitch's gaze for a moment before smiling. "Well, then. Think about Dr. Rosen. How often does the new person in town turn out to be the only kind of lesbian who does anyone any good?"

Mitch blew a pathetic raspberry, and Carol bounced off to make the beds or polish the doorknobs or something else on her extensive last-minute to-do list. A little of the fun had drained from Mitch's slicing-and-dicing at having let another opportunity go by without telling Carol about someone she'd met at a conference back in July who'd grown into a strange romantic entanglement.

Reginald was English, black, and—as the name implied, though certainly didn't conclude—male, a big man with a popping accent and a coughing laugh. Mitch had lost her mind over him at their first handshake before finding it later that night in his bed, and each week ushered in more transatlantic emails between them.

Her feelings for him were confounding in a pleasant way, and this alone seemed to justify her silence on the subject. But, really, her reasons for not yet telling Carol fell into three distinct categories: her friend's default conversational tactics, which often precluded a word in edgewise; Mitch's initial conviction that time would diminish the affair; and the characteristics of the object of her growing affection.

Certainly in part because of how Mitch and Carol had gotten started—by a short, ultimately doomed romantic "thing" when they'd been undergrads—Carol made the common assumption that Mitch's desires could be pinned down and that she was as gay as James was fourteen. Any mention of Reginald would come to a screeching halt at the wrong part of the story, and though Mitch had misgivings about not saying anything, she wasn't particularly inclined to start talking now.

She kept busy for the next couple hours frosting cupcakes, securing flapping tablecloths outside, moving plastic utensils from bags to baskets lined with a red gingham print, and all other manner of what she considered the remainders—decimal points and fractions of the morning's activities.

When she'd found her way back to her kitchen station and was taking cabbage to task for coleslaw, Carol commandeered the table to make her infamous punch. A profusion of bottles surrounded the big bowl—alcohol, mostly, but also ginger ale and a few different kinds of juice. She poured, stirred, and tasted, and the quiet between them was familiar and easy. Mitch kicked herself for not having ordered "No Smoking / Flammable" stickers from the *Grainger* catalog, wishing she had one to slap on the bowl's side.

Gordon, Carol's younger son, broke their humming industriousness when he thundered down the stairs and slid halfway into the kitchen on the slick linoleum. Gordon was Carol's carbon copy down to his uncountable freckles, and he had a bell-like voice that projected through conventional obstacles to sound. He peppered Carol with a stream of questions about the makeup of the party-going population, the ratio of kids to adults and their ages, and what he might be allowed to do now that he was newly ten.

"Dad told me I could eat two hot dogs and two cupcakes."

"Gordo, if your dad says you can, you can. But if you get sick from all that crap, don't come running to me." Carol pulled him to her and made loud kissing noises against his neck.

"Hey, bud," Mitch said. Gordon teleported across the kitchen to her hip. "Want to make yourself useful?"

"Totally."

"Grab a stool and stir up this coleslaw, okay?"

Gordon erupted in a little-girl giggle. "I don't need a stool anymore."

"My mistake," Mitch said. "You're practically a giant. You must've grown at least an eighth of an inch since last week."

Carol said, "Gordo, honey, don't you think it's time for you to move out and get a place of your own? Now that you're all grown up?"

"Mom," he whined, as if imitating his older brother, but his bubbly laugh undermined the effect.

Mitch finished chopping the head of cabbage and added it to the bowl Gordon was working over. "Looking good, bud. Keep at it, but don't hurt yourself, okay?" Getting Gordon to laugh was as easy and rewarding as making Carol smile. She rinsed the board and knife then wiped errant cabbage bits from the countertop into a cupped hand and dumped them into the sink.

Carol slurped at a shot glass of punch. She smacked her lips, tilting her head back and forth. "So close."

Mitch pulled up her jeans and plunged her hands into her pockets. Around her were trays of food covering the counters, Gordon's body swaying in time with his stirs, and mad-bartender Carol. Everything looked under control. She checked her watch: 12:13.

"Anything else? Or are we good?" she asked.

"You're leaving? You don't have to. Who cares if you're not technically invited? If Brian has a problem with it, I'll pour this punch down his throat until he relents."

"There's a corn dog with my name on it over at the engineering party."

"Right, the corn dog."

"It's not your ordinary corn dog." Mitch rubbed her hands together.

"You can't leave without punch," Carol said.

"I have no tolerance for that stuff."

"I'll fix you some to share with the other engineering geeks."

Carol didn't particularly want Mitch to leave, even though she knew Mitch didn't particularly want to stay, so she made a small production of ladling punch into Gordon's Spider-Man thermos and sealing it up tight. "Give my regards to the corn dogs. May they be structurally sound," she said then pulled Mitch into their usual parting hug. A strange but persistent comfort came from feeling the crazy topography of Mitch's back, the knobs and wings and slats of her sturdy skeleton sliding under Carol's hands.

She handed off the thermos like a football and gave a last little wave when Mitch left the kitchen, trailing Gordo, who had abandoned his coleslaw duty. Though Carol mostly wanted to sit and spend a little quality time with the punch, she limited herself to letting out a James-worthy sigh, picking up two trays of uncooked chicken, sliding the patio's screen door open with her bare, freckled foot, and walking over to Brian, who was scrubbing the rack on a grill he'd borrowed from their neighbors.

He stopped cleaning at her approach. "You read my mind."

"A rare benefit of long association." She winked and held out the trays so Brian could move the breasts onto the heat. Over at their own grill, he arranged drumsticks with surgical precision.

Carol said, "Mitch sure nailed it about Tilsen and Dr. Rosen's next book, huh?"

"Mitch isn't always right."

"No, only ninety-eight percent of the time."

He tossed off a quick harrumph and finished with the chicken. "What do you think, veggie burgers next?"

"Definitely," Carol said. "I don't think anyone eating those will notice if they're a little cold."

"I figured I'd stack them up on some foil in a corner over here to keep them warm."

"Anyone who doubts your genius is summarily uninvited."

"Unfortunately, that would diminish our guest list considerably."

Carol stretched up to kiss the fuzzed apple of his cheek. Brian was dark and broad like James. His graying temples made him look distinguished, not old, but the crepelike texture of the skin at his elbows and in the hollow of his neck had begun to affect Carol's balance. When they'd gotten pregnant and married, their fourteen-year age difference had been the last thing on her mind, but once he'd turned fifty a few years back, it was everywhere Carol looked.

By the time the first people arrived—Dean Obermann and his family—the buffet of meats and salads and Mitch's condiment bar covered an array of folding tables, and the punch was perfect, though that didn't stop Carol from continuing to "taste" it.

Joe and Joyce Obermann certainly looked like the married-to-death couple they were. At a distance, it was hard to tell them apart: two rounded bodies topped with puffs of graying hair who came across as older than they were, more like grandparents than parents to their son, who was James's age and slumping along with them. They scattered halfway across the backyard, each heading to their Hollister equivalent. In Joyce's beeline for Carol, her flower-skirted girth was partially obscured by a massive plastic platter bowed under a saran-wrapped mound of cookies.

If Carol were held at gunpoint and forced to name one thing about Joyce that she didn't despise at least a little bit, she could always fall back on cookies. Joyce made cookies in a clearly compulsive way, and it showed in their deliciousness. Carol harbored a sinking suspicion she would gobble them down even if she knew one of the ingredients was a scoop of dog shit from Joyce's collie, Scooter.

She tried to take charge of the platter, but Joyce swept past her into the kitchen. Carol followed and said, "Do you know what you're bringing to next month's PTA meeting? 'Cause I was thinking of coming up with some sort of cookie appetizer, but that requires knowing the main cookie course." Carol leaned against the counter and watched Joyce struggle with the reams of saran wrap.

"I do prefer to let these things happen more organically, as you might say, but if you want to coordinate..." An unfocused look came over Joyce's eyes. "What would you say to my pretzel-peanut-caramel twists?"

"I would say popcorn, probably cheese."

"Really. What if I said triple-chocolate marshmallow?"

"Cinnamon graham crackers."

"Strawberry shortcake drops?"

"Banana bread."

"Bite-sized puff pastry éclairs with dark-chocolate glaze and chocolate whipped cream?"

Carol smiled. "A defibrillator and extra batteries."

"You're too much." Joyce laughed. But then she said, "Honestly, I don't know how Brian handles you."

Carol and Joyce were nearly a generation apart, and the backward swing of Joyce's behavioral compass showed her age.

She was always saying shit that lit up Carol's whole switchboard of buttons. A lap around the kitchen table revealed only cupcakes, brownies, chocolate-covered strawberries, and an open spot for Joyce's cookies. When Carol realized she was looking for the punch, which Brian had already moved outside, she sidled toward the door. "What do you say to a drink?"

Brian called for her from the patio. Even though his tone was sharp in asking her to help greet some people, beating a sanctioned retreat from Joyce was a relief. The bright sun and smoke-tinged air felt like freedom, but Carol was disappointed at not finding Dr. Rosen in the large clump of new arrivals.

For the next two hours, Carol made inroads on her jumbo plastic cup of punch while she circulated, fielding questions about peanut, gluten, and dairy content, handing out moist towelettes like condoms at a family-planning clinic, and bringing out the second round of cupcakes and burgers. Then, after two cups of party lubricant and no food besides one of Joyce's double-chocolate peppermint cookies, Carol saw Dr. Rosen standing at the edge of the backyard.

Of fucking course. By now Carol was one-and-a-half sheets to the wind and likely to say absolutely anything to this woman. She needed a burger IV with a side of slaw and about an hour to sober up. But, wait. No dark tresses were being tossed about by the breeze. Maybe it wasn't her. Maybe Carol would be granted a reprieve from inevitable embarrassment.

No. It was her. Dr. Rosen took a step back as if to leave, and Carol stumbled forward, sticking out her right hand in ready greeting absurdly early. Had her food / alcohol intake been close to even, she might have been able to tear her attention from Dr. Rosen's hair—or lack thereof—but when Carol's hand finally connected with its target and started jerking it up and down, she was still looking so hard at that almost–crew cut that Dr. Rosen's free hand crept up and touched the side of her head. Carol relinquished her grip.

"Hi," she said through a furious blush she could feel even across her chest. "Welcome. I've evidently had too much to drink."

"I'm sorry I'm late."

"God, don't apologize. Don't you know blushing redheads can spontaneously combust? I'll shut up now."

"Don't worry. It's the sign of a good party. I'm Abby, by the way. Abby Rosen."

"Carol. Resident idiot. Oh, and Brian's wife." While the extent of her lunacy sank in, she contemplated the rest of Dr. Rosen. In a snappy linen skirt and rust-colored short-sleeved blouse, she was voluptuous in exactly the way that most put Carol to shame: curvy yet tight. Carol felt grublike in comparison. The growing pudge around her belly button had appeared in its nascent form the week after her thirty-fifth birthday and, after three years, was officially irreversible. And there stood Abby Rosen with her buoyant breasts, come-hither hips, and a waist that tempted you to try to circle it with your hands even though it was too womanly and mature ever to allow such a thing.

"Dr. Rosen, can I just say—"

"Abby, please. And no."

"No?"

But then Abby shook her head, pushed nonexistent hair from her face, and smiled. "Never mind that. What were you saying?"

Abby had given her a moment of pause, and now Carol was a bit adrift. She looked down at a blade of grass sticking up between two toes on her right foot. Then she took in Abby's lovely smile and said, "Okay, what I was going to say was, 'Wow!'"

Abby jumped.

"I mean, really. Wow. Your hair. I'd been expecting something…but this is so much better. Have you got a set of cheekbones on you or what?"

"It seems I needed a change," Abby said, but her smile had disappeared.

"It suits you. Had to take guts." The stutter between them that followed felt too serious for its own good, and to dispel it, Carol exhaled in a sirenlike stream, clapped, and surveyed the backyard. "Okay, ten-second orientation." Channeling Annie Oakley, she pointed with both hands while she spoke. "Pool;

croquet; tables for the civilized; food for every diet under the sun, though I recommend the chicken; horseshoes in the back over there; and the changing room is through the sliding doors to the left. The only rules are no liquor to minors and try not to injure a child under ten—their screams are too piercing."

Brian must've filled Abby in on the Hollister family tree because she asked, "And your youngest?"

"Turned ten last month. Whale away all you'd like. He's a big boy now."

With a mix of reluctance and relief, Carol went off to pile a plate with food and sequester herself in the kitchen. She had to admit that after reading *The F Word*, she'd indulged in some daydreaming about what Abby's life might be like. She imagined her sitting for a *Today Show* interview, looking and sounding smart, living a life of the mind spiced by just the right amount of glamour. Carol had once contemplated exactly that for herself, eons ago, and Abby made those old fantasies percolate past Brian and the boys, compelling Carol to feel close to Abby in a manner she in no way was.

Later, grounded by chicken and slaw and a handful of baby carrots, Carol reemerged into the hot sunshine. Kids ran around screaming or jumping impressive cannonballs into the pool, and everywhere was a sea of khaki shorts and sundresses. She looked around in a panic until she spotted Abby, eating at an out-of-the-way table, tantalizingly alone and with a pile of used napkins next to her plate. Carol snagged a box of moist towelettes and swooped in.

She brandished the box at Abby. "Wet nap?"

"You certainly thought of everything." Abby took two packets.

"Believe me, with my three slobs, I own stock. Glad to see you went for the chicken. I know law requires us to serve veggie burgers, but anyone who likes those isn't fully human."

Carol hovered behind the chair next to Abby, squeezing and pulling at the cardboard box she held. Abby's face was made up without looking made up, an understated application of eyeliner and lipstick unknown to Millerton, if not the entire state of Ohio. Finally, Abby asked, "Would you like to join me?"

In a blink, Carol was seated and talking. "When I was a vegetarian, which naturally coincided with the forty-two seconds I was a lesbian, I used to wake up in the night gasping for breath, aching for a piece of meat. Any meat. I wasn't particular. I tried to convince myself that it wasn't as good as I remembered, though I practically had to leave campus the mornings I caught a whiff of bacon from the cafeteria."

She had seen Abby's head jerk in acknowledgment of that stupid forty-two-second remark, but she ignored it, made a swooning gesture, and continued. "The meal I used to reintroduce meat into my system was one of those Denny's grand slam numbers sporting half a pound each of bacon and sausage. Let me tell you. I thought I would die of pleasure. I get weak in the knees remembering. I mean, sure, it made me violently ill later, but what the hell is it about pork?"

Abby appeared preoccupied, gazing out across the backyard, but she said, "For half my life, pork was the forbidden fruit. My mother was a pick-and-choose Jew."

"Pick-and-choose? Is that a new denomination?"

"Lois Rosen didn't accept anyone's edict without tweaking, not even God's. I suppose her version of Judaism was no more contradictory than the official one. No pork, but shellfish was okay. Temple every first Friday—when the choir put in an appearance—followed by a late dinner at Howie's down the street. Cheeseburger and fries."

"Mm. Not exactly kosher." Carol played it cool as if she weren't restraining herself from squirming in excitement. Abby's Jewishness and general cosmopolitan aura made her deliciously foreign.

"Not exactly. Eventually, I concluded that my mother forbade pork because she didn't care for it."

"Silly woman. When did you put aside your pork virginity?"

Abby made a dismissive gesture but smiled beautifully, wide and bright and warm. "Oh, you know. Who keeps track of that?"

"Obviously you! I saw that face. Spill it, sistah." In a sizzle of hopefully real camaraderie, Carol nudged Abby with the box of wet naps.

"I was twenty-three and in New York for the first time at a conference. At a fantastic restaurant, this perfectly sized, perfectly pink bite of orange-brined pork roast came floating across the table. So I ate it."

"How hot was the woman holding the fork?"

"Who remembers? No one could compete with that roast." Abby laughed and put up her hand, and the sauced nap it held, to cover her wide-open mouth.

"Well, I doubt that but appreciate the sentiment. After however many years, a spouse can pale in comparison with a well-arranged platter of smoked meats and sausages. But Brian…I swear, every day he ages in reverse, wakes up like cold pizza and sits down to dinner like rack of lamb. I, on the other hand, despite my eternal youth, closely resemble a bulldog by bedtime. I'm sure you have no idea what I'm talking about with that skin of yours."

"No, but I'm wondering what your nefarious purpose is with all this flattery."

Carol whooped and banged the wet naps on the table. "Nefarious! Man! If only I had something nefarious going on. I'm just an outlaw in my own backyard." She pried her ass from the chair and stood up. "I've monopolized enough of your time. I'm sure you'll want to get back to mingling now that you're sauce-free and all. Welcome to Tilsen." She tried to hurry without hurrying back to the kitchen—but not before a detour for some more punch.

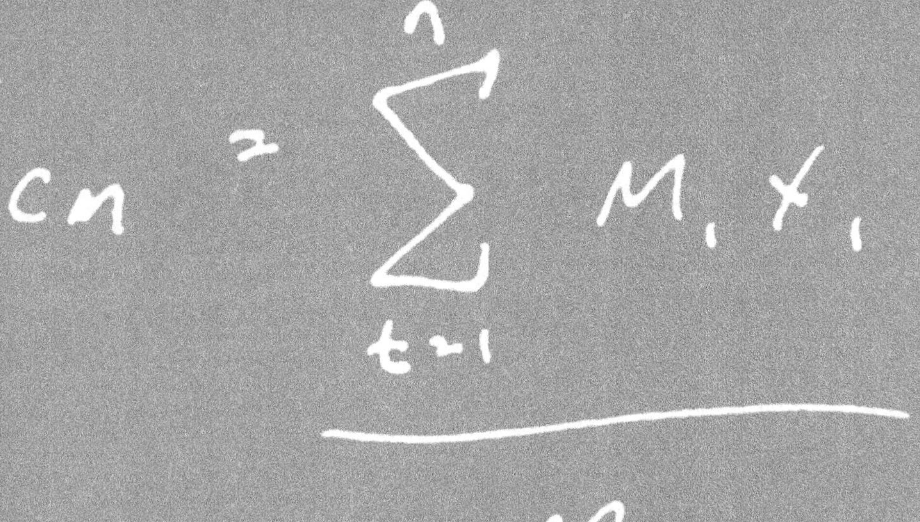

THE NEED TO WORK, AND FOR THE RECOGNITION THAT comes from work, rises directly from living in an interdependent community. The values society places on different types of work—and whether they are done in high heels or steel-toed boots— are not random. We, as active members of our society, have driven these judgments into exis- tence.

–Dr. Abigail Rosen, The F Word: Femininity in the New Century

$$\frac{w \left(R^3 - r^3 \right)}{2^2 - r^3) \, \sin(a)}$$

2

MITCH HAD learned countless life lessons from going into business with Sam Weisenberg, but the most important was never to answer "I don't care" to anything more serious than a question about lunch. And maybe not even to that. Sam had taken that answer literally when drafting incorporation papers, and now their company was named Mitchell Industries. At first, she'd suffered jerks of misplaced recognition at bank statements, software licenses, and business cards, but now Mitchell didn't feel like her last name even when it was jammed up tight against her first.

Although Sam was co-owner and had invested not only money and time but also the uncanny ability to poke holes in Mitch's best-laid plans, he'd stepped back his involvement the last two years, leaving the role of chief-technologist-and-everything-else to Mitch. She'd had to recruit help in her fight against industrial friction, eventually hiring Steve and Eric, who each possessed still-wet Tilsen master's degrees and way more dedication than Mitch had any right to hope for.

For six months after Mitch had hired Steve, they'd worked out of her home office while time-sharing lab space at Tilsen. They spilled over into the living room and kitchen before Mitch would hear of looking for a place to rent, but after scouring Millerton for commercial space, she settled on two basement rooms in the red brick Marketplace building on the south side of Main Street. The Marketplace rented out its aboveground floors to upscale boutiques and gourmet food shops and was a swanky address—one Mitch could in no way afford. But the basement suite, accessible only through a rust-flecked gray door in the alley on the building's west side, had been vacant for a long time, enabling her to bargain a low rent on a two-year lease.

Now, over a year later and deep into this Friday night, Steve and Mitch banged away on their keyboards at desks facing each other across the office, each working on a different section of the same paper. It detailed their system for managing high-volume test data via predictive algorithms, and Mitch struggled with the long-delayed introduction while Steve prepared the data presentations. "Publish or perish" existed even outside academia, a hard truth that made Mitch miss consulting, where only your track record mattered. She spent more of her professional life fumbling with words than finessing equations and materials, which felt as wrong as it sounded.

Without looking away from her monitor, Mitch asked, "Did you get that other graph done?"

"Shit." The word came out in a voice too tired to be vehement.

"I'll take that as a no."

A crumpled-up wad of paper flew past her and bounced off the wall a couple feet to her right. Steve said, "I still need that—"

"I know. I know. I'm almost done."

Mitch stretched away from her keyboard, and her right shoulder popped resoundingly with a sizzle of pain that made her hiss and left her wary of further movement.

Steve looked over at the sound and said, "That didn't sound good."

She massaged the pain away. "It didn't feel good."

"What's it like to be so old?"

"Given the feeble limits of your imagination, how do you expect me to answer with any accuracy?"

Steve genuflected with exaggeration and turned back to his computer. Mitch's so-called advanced age had been a constant topic of conversation since her birthday several months before. Eric and Steve razzed her about her body falling apart. They razzed her about being an old maid. They razzed her about still working in this dump, about not making her first million, about not even trying to make her first million. It was a nice addition to the usual routine.

Besides the low hum of computers and lights, only their intermittent typing interrupted the dragging silence. Mitch made a concerted effort not to look at the clock—any of them. Three were within sight. When she was in the other room of the suite, the lab portion, she could go for hours so occupied that time only returned to her consciousness when her stomach growled or her eyelids started to droop. Here, tonight, she felt every minute.

When the phone rang, she looked first at her watch—8:32—then at Steve, and they both screwed up their faces then rock-paper-scissored for it. Mitch's scissor cut his paper, and he answered. The squeak that emanated from the receiver when Steve held it away from his ear was unmistakably Carol. He raised his eyebrows in question, but Mitch shook her head.

She hadn't been avoiding Carol, exactly, but they'd gone the two weeks since the party without a conversation. Mitch didn't want to see Carol until she could find real determination to come clean about Reginald, but not talking for this long was already notable. Tonight, Carol surely wanted to dish about the party, probably about this Dr. Rosen, who, out of some misguided and certainly morbid curiosity, Mitch had looked into.

Carol hadn't exaggerated the woman's attractiveness, but what Mitch found even more interesting was that Dr. Rosen's first book, obviously based on her dissertation and long out of print, was quantitative sociology complete with charts and graphs, while this latest book was almost completely qualitative, full of quotes and commentary and no numbers besides the ones at the top of each page. Mitch wondered what spurred the change, then wondered what it felt like to be new to Tilsen, not to mention Millerton. Mitch wore this environment like her favorite pair of jeans, couldn't remember when everything had been unfamiliar.

Steve convulsed with strangled laughter, and Mitch grinned at Carol's still audible histrionics. In the distant past, these verbal theatrics used to scare Mitch. They were loud and bright at a time when she swam under the rough, rippled surface of things, when some nights she was driven to tuck her pillow under her arm, shove her travel alarm clock in her pocket, and set off across campus to sleep in the quiet solitude of her hatchback.

Eventually, Mitch applied her analytic mind to the problem of Carol's verbosity, identified patterns in its screeches, stage whispers, and breathless monologues—manifestations of outrage, happy scandal, and wanting something, respectively—and was able to tame fear with understanding. Now, when they were apart, Carol's face or her exuberant gestures weren't what lived inside Mitch but her wide-ranging voice and a huge stockpile of her words.

When Mitch had unveiled a prototype of the wind turbine product to Carol, she had dismissed Mitch's technical explanations and cut to the chase. "So, what, is this device going to make us gazillionaires?" This device became "The Device," and the name stuck so completely that Mitch and the guys used it as a matter of course in the lab and found it difficult not to say to customers.

Steve hung up the phone. "She's going to The Station as soon as she gets her act together, and she expects you to be there."

The Filling Station was a bar a few blocks over on Main, and a drink sounded good. "Let's both go."

"No way am I running interference between you two."

"That's not what I meant." Mitch stood, patted pockets for wallet and keys, and used her wide black belt to resettle her jeans on her hips. "Come on, you know her. She won't show up for a while yet."

Steve ran a hand through already disheveled straw-blond hair. "I'm going to have to work all weekend as it is."

"You need a break."

"I'm serious, Mitch. I can't. Not if you want my part by Monday."

She crossed her arms and frowned. "You're not the boss here. I'm the boss, and I'm telling you that a break is now your top priority. I accept the consequences, so I'm going to get my notebook and will meet you in the alley."

Mitch walked through the open doorway behind her into the lab. The office area was a study in entropy, with its piles of dismembered electronics, tilted whiteboards, stacks of paper, and the disastrous black hole of Eric's space, but the lab was the Jekyll to its Hyde.

Several benches, tables, and portable racks of equipment lined the room. Red and black patch cables sorted by length and connector type hung to her left, and a bank of chests to the right were full of small transparent drawers stocked with electrical and mechanical components: resistors, set screws, capacitors, stainless steel bolts, jumper wires of every length, bread boards, batteries, Band-Aids, and assorted odds and ends that might one day prove useful. The lab's organization was necessary and calming—necessary because experimentation had to be controlled. If why something failed couldn't be identified, any success was essentially accidental.

This neatness and the faint smell of metal and ozone kept Mitch company while she sat on a stool and riffed through her notebook pages, making a flipbook of sketched viscosity-temperature curves, lunch orders, charts of data, and lists of lab supplies to buy. Finally, she heard Steve grumble, his chair squeak, and the glass door to the stairway slap shut behind him. She tucked her notebook under her arm and hit the lights on the way out.

< ≈ >

The Filling Station was Millerton's premium beverage emporium, at least according to Angel Pappas, its proprietor. The Station was situated on the shady south side of Main Street and fronted a heavy door flanked with two large bay windows. In good weather, tables and chairs littered the sidewalk under its brown-and-cream awnings. From six in the morning until five in the afternoon, The Station served up pastries and the best coffee within a hundred miles. But at five, Angel brought the lights down a notch and mixed adult drinks until she got tired and called last round.

When she had opened up shop a couple years before, after having appeared in Millerton from out of nowhere, excited whispers had crisscrossed town for months over her platinum-blond hair, intricate manicures, and apparently single status. Angel let them talk, smiling through it all until her ability to make customers feel instantly welcome silenced judgment and speculation. Mitch, sucker for a good espresso, had been a regular from the start.

When Steve and Mitch arrived, half of the round cocktail tables were empty, but people had begun to gather in the open areas with their drinks. Angel was ringing someone up at the register, and Mitch caught her eye with a wave after sliding onto one of the last two stools at the curved bar.

"Mitch Mitchell." Angel closed the register drawer with a snap of her hip. "As I live and breathe." Before sauntering over, she rang an old-time gas station bell, the perennial sound of her excitement. Her lacquered nails—always painted the green and silver of Tilsen colors for the first month of school—drummed a staccato clacking on the bar top, and she said, "Check your oil?"

Steve let out a short laugh that she ignored.

"Really, Mitch, it's been so long I thought you'd left town. Did you start sending your minions over to get your coffee?"

Steve said, "We don't get her coffee. She drinks the stuff in the lab out of principle."

"Oh, Steve," Angel said, eyes wide. "I didn't see you there."

"Just remember, the minute a place around here starts serving better coffee, the boycott is *on*." Steve slapped a palm on the bar top in emphasis.

"If a place with better coffee opens up, you'll have to beat me to the front of the line. Two beers?"

"I'll have whatever's on special," Mitch said.

"Mitch, you know the way to my heart." Angel's smile was wide and white and seemed to contain more than the usual number of teeth. It brought to mind Dr. Rosen's sparkling author photo, but Angel turned and walked away before Mitch could ask her about being Millerton's newest arrival, how long it had taken to nail down the seasonal hours of the Scoop-A-Rama, to learn the town's unwritten rules.

Steve said, "I'll get back to work after this beer."

"After this beer, you'll have another. Now you're committed. Besides, I know what you still have left to do, and you don't need tonight to get it done." She slid a round coaster over from Angel's side of the bar and occupied her fingers with its shape and thickness and texture.

"You're probably one of those people who never needed to pull an all-nighter."

She laughed. "No. *Never*."

"Yeah, you just don't want me to feel bad. What was your GPA?"

"Are you kidding? You think I remember?"

"I bet engineering was easier back then. The Wheel 101, right? And they even graded on a curve." He put his forehead on his arms and chuckled at his own joke.

Mitch said, "Spear Design and Construction 220."

"Advanced Fire Making 410. I think you remember your GPA and don't want to tell me."

Her GPA wasn't hard to remember: 4.0 over her four years, and not all her late nights could be attributed to insomnia. "I'm not going to help you feel bad about yourself."

He gave her a look that told her she'd said the wrong thing but slid off his stool before she could determine what it was. "Gotta piss."

Mitch dreaded the day when Steve would leave the company. He could dig into the parts of research that drove her batty, the piles of easily overlooked details or hours of thankless troubleshooting, allowing her to take a wider focus. Research, for Mitch, was as physical as swimming. Patterns established through months of examination lived not only as marks in her notebook or bits in a spreadsheet but as a feeling in her body. She knew right away if a result was anomalous even if she couldn't articulate why until later. Eric called her the Data Whisperer, and it was true. When hypotheses were confirmed through experimentation, they settled into gaps in her mind perfectly sized to receive them.

Angel put down a beer in front of Steve's empty stool and a gold-and-tan concoction right into Mitch's waiting hand. "You sure ran him off fast."

"Bladder the size of a pea." Mitch took a swallow, licked her lips for effect, and identified the drink. "Dark and stormy."

"You stinker. No one around here knows that." Then, in a dizzying non sequitur, Angel said, "Speaking of exes…"

"What?"

She erased the distance between them and whispered, "The table by the bathroom."

Like an ass, like she couldn't comprehend Angel's conspiratorial look, Mitch swiveled around and saw Kim. Her straight, wheat-colored hair was caught back behind her neck in a barrette, she had on a deep-red blouse, and the way her face was animated and her fingers strayed across the table meant she was laying some serious charm on the woman sitting with her.

Seeing Kim looking so good was plenty to deal with on its own, but it brought to mind Carol's bet against them and the lurking secret of Reginald. Juggling shit like this made fighting with words back at the office feel downright desirable by contrast. She reeled back and dove into her drink.

"Well, dang, Mitch, I didn't think you'd go and stare," Angel said in a low rush and slapped Mitch's hand.

"Sometimes I'm dumb like that."

"I thought I once heard someone in here call you a genius."

Mitch made a look of disgust and pushed some errant hair behind an ear. "It was a test of your gullibility."

Angel narrowed her eyes. "Why don't you let anyone call you Dr. Mitchell?"

"Because I'm not qualified to operate on humans, only machines."

Steve hopped onto his stool and said, "And she's only barely qualified for that."

"Gee, thanks," Mitch said.

"That's not to say she isn't scary smart."

"When I'm not scary stupid."

"Now that's true." Angel laughed, snapped her towel, and left to serve some new arrivals, an older couple familiar to Mitch in a generic, around-town way.

Two dark and stormies in, Mitch and Steve got to talking about capacitors, and tonight, despite the setting, it didn't take long for them to move from electronic generalities to The Device's controller circuit that Eric had redesigned. In the same way nerves passed along messages to the brain, this circuit transmitted data from the part of The Device installed in the turbine to the processing software outside. When Eric had come on board, a year after Steve, he'd cackled over the state of their electronics.

"I'm surprised you guys haven't electrocuted yourselves," he'd said.

"Oh, we have," Steve said. "More than once."

They had advanced to drawing circuit diagrams in the back of Mitch's notebook when Carol skinnied between them. She was all bounce and energy in her cap-sleeved T-shirt and tidy jeans, and she wrinkled her freckled nose at the page of diagrams. "Ew. Seriously? How has Angel not bitch-slapped you?"

"Mitch started it," Steve said.

"That goes without saying." Carol glanced back and forth between Mitch and Steve. "Whatcha drinking?" Angel appeared, and Carol started in. "All right. I'm tired of everything I usually drink. Seriously, another gin and tonic? Gin and tonic is like white shoes—Memorial to Labor Day only. Maybe a Manhattan? Or a cosmo?"

"Sounds like *you* need a Friday-night special."

"What is it?"

"You'll like it." Angel held up the Girl Scout salute. "I promise."

"Sign me up, then." Carol turned to Steve and said, "I need to borrow Mitch for a while."

He held out his hands. "Be my guest."

When Angel came back with her drink, Carol pulled Mitch off her stool and dragged her to a table in the bay window where it was quieter. Tilsen students drifted by outside, glancing in with clear disinterest. A string of little white lights around the window softened the snap of Carol's hair.

Carol said, "Steve and Angel should totally get together. She's got that thing for younger men."

"Carol…"

"I'm so in love." She yodeled the last word with her chin lifted like she was howling at the moon.

"In love with someone other than Brian?" Mitch said with feigned shock.

Carol looked at Mitch from under her eyebrows and lowered her voice. "Dr. Abigail Rosen."

"I see."

"No, you don't. But I'll tell you. She's gorgeous and brilliant and so sophisticated it's like she's from another planet. One that I very much want to live on. She's all the best parts of Jewish."

"Yeah, you're light-years from planet sophistication." Mitch laughed and nudged Carol's leg with her foot.

"I'm serious. You know how some people get under your skin and make things crackle?"

Mitch answered the rhetorical question. "Yeah, and actually, I've been wanting to tell you—"

Carol made a sweeping motion with her drink, nearly losing some of it in the process. "Well, that's how it is with Abby."

Maybe it was fatigue or the two drinks she'd consumed or some misguided guilt over this Reginald secret, but Carol's statement triggered a gnawing in Mitch's gut. Carol must've seen it, because her goofy grin slipped a little. Mitch didn't want Serious Carol tonight. Serious Carol would keep her captive at this table, rooting around for every last detail about Reginald, would push and press Mitch about her feelings until she got flustered enough to make Carol back off. Serious Carol had her time and place, like those occasional nights when accumulated insomnia and stress broke Mitch down, and Carol could be quiet and calm and just what she needed. But now was not the time or the place.

So she grinned and said, "Abby. First-name basis, huh?"

Carol studied Mitch then gave a motionless shrug. "Mitchy, she's my fast friend and just doesn't know it. I've memorized whole passages of her book. Her office phone number blinks in neon when I close my eyes."

Mitch let the quiet between them stretch before she said, "Sounds like you should call the woman."

"But I can't." The yodel surfaced again.

"Sometimes I think you like driving yourself crazy."

"Then sometimes you're absolutely right."

"Call her. We both know she's been waiting for the phone to ring."

Carol practically laid herself out across the table to loop her arms around Mitch's neck and squeeze. "You're such a catch. You need to find someone who appreciates you." Carol disengaged and flopped back in her chair.

"Like Dr. Rosen?"

"No, silly, like me. Well, me minus the matrimonial entanglement. I mean, come on. You could do a lot worse." Carol gave herself some Vanna White action.

"You're pretty tough to top."

"That's very true, so look for a single me—just one hundred percent lesbo."

Mitch pointed at Carol and said, "Call her."

"Yessir." Carol snapped a salute.

"And go keep Steve company while I hit the bathroom."

"I think Angel's taking care of that." She nodded over at Angel and Steve in conversation, their differing shades of blond dipped toward each other.

"Then rescue him, I guess."

The crowd had swelled since Mitch's arrival, and she threaded through it toward the bathroom. In her peripheral vision, she saw Kim's head follow her, but she resisted the urge to turn and look. In the bathroom, Mitch sat in the last narrow stall and listened to other women come and go.

Carol sometimes claimed that Mitch operated like the FBI, with umpteen layers of security and everything on a need-to-know basis. Sure, Mitch didn't share Carol's compulsion toward confession—she prized privacy and fuss-free quiet—but it would have been easy enough to tell Carol tonight. What really bothered her was that telling Carol about Reginald was in any way different from letting her know, a month into the proceedings, about sleeping with Kim. But it *was* different, and Mitch was going to have to deal with it.

She couldn't find comfort in her body, ached for a pool, any pool big enough to allow a few strokes before turning, to feel the rhythm of movement, of breath, the buoyancy of water just dense enough to cradle her. But at 9:47 on a Friday evening, a swim was impossible, though some relief might come in the drive to her house, the windows open to the balmy early fall night, the familiarity of the wheel in her hands, the forty-miles-per-hour motion.

Outside the bathroom, the dim hallway was lined with bulletin boards hidden under Paleolithic layers of postings. Kim was there, leaning back next to a flier for piano lessons missing half its tabs and looking worse for wear. Her head was tilted so she peered at Mitch down the slope of her straight, fine nose.

She said, "I'm surprised you're not at work. You look really tired."

Mitch felt itchingly awake.

"I mean, but good. You look tired but good." Kim pushed away from the wall and twisted a large silver ring on her right hand with the thumb and forefinger of her left.

"Kim," Mitch said. In every aspect, Kim couldn't be more different from Reginald, but Mitch's attraction to them both felt the same at its root—divorced from gender and appearance. Something inside her had resonated with something in each of them, and that was that. To break the spell, she made herself remember what Kim had said in angry conclusion to their official breakup: "Fuck you and your device." Mitch had tried and only somewhat succeeded in not taking it personally.

Mitch said, "I should go."

"No, wait."

Mitch craved to feel the movements of freestyle and backstroke, the exhausting flailing that was her butterfly. "I really should go."

Kim snagged Mitch's arm. "I'm trying to tell you something." Her fingers pressed into Mitch's bicep. "I know you were just being you, and I thought I'd be okay with that, with you and your work. It's not your fault that I wasn't, but I really, really wanted it to be. Anyway, I shouldn't have said what I did, and I'm sorry."

Mitch forced her gaze from her black oxfords to Kim's face. "I know. It's okay." Kim released her grasp, and Mitch tried to find something else to say. Failing that, she hurried from the hallway, but one step into the main room, assaulted by Carol's raucous laughter, she turned and stumbled out the service door instead.

After walking two blocks in the alley behind Main, she moved to the better-lit sidewalk, keeping her head down amid the steady flow of students while she beat it to her truck. Her house was only four miles west on Route 56, but all that awaited her at home was Chester, an orange tabby more reproachful than affectionate. The way her mind was revving yet disengaged indicated that sleep was long hours away, and so Mitch drove south.

Mitch drew judgments like filings to a magnet. 'Workaholic' and 'compulsive' were a common one-two punch. Then there was 'hard,' which was sometimes a compliment, sometimes decidedly not, and was related to a whole class of similar characterizers: 'driven' (obsessed), 'capable' (know-it-all), and 'focused' (standoffish).

She didn't take them to heart. How could she when she knew how complicated the act of observation was? Quantum physics postulated that probability, not actuality, was king. Left to their own devices, the universe's swarm of subatomic particles existed as a giant maybe: Maybe a particle was exactly here right now and maybe it wasn't. Maybe it was travelling at a certain velocity and maybe it wasn't. If curiosity got Schrodinger's cat and the itch to measure had to be scratched, the natural state of probability collapsed, and what was measured was really only what the act of observation had brought into being in the first place.

A similar quandary existed between people. The force of the observer's history and current emotional state compromised what little objectivity existed around human nature and motivation, and the whole enterprise of understanding another person became hopelessly unreliable.

Long miles later, Mitch pulled over next to a fallow field, cut the engine, and sat in a rich darkness that was absolute until her wide-open eyes adjusted to the starlight. She might have outrun Carol and Kim, but she'd fallen right into the arms of old habit. Not that old habits were always bad. A long time ago, when she was Mitchell but not yet Mitch, she'd gotten used to the huge expanse and quiet of night in the Indiana countryside. Even now, she kept a tight roll of sleeping bag and foam shoved behind the passenger seat for just these occasions.

Her shoulder protested when she climbed into the truck bed but relaxed when she lay down on the unfurled sleeping bag. Under the faint whistle of the breeze, a huge nothingness pulsed against her ears, and she watched the stars move without visible motion while she thought of Reginald.

He'd come up to her after her presentation, when she was putting her laptop and notes into her backpack, that seen-better-days one she'd had since high school. She looked up, and he was there, a tall black man she could describe only as being all smiles. She felt herself grin in involuntary response.

She took his hand. It was broad and warm, and he held on for a beat longer than she expected.

"Dr. Mitchell," he said. "Excellent talk."

"Thank you." Then, on an impulse, she said, "Call me Mitch." Her first name existed as merely an alliterative initial on her publications and the conference literature, Mitch knowing how it generally just confused matters.

"Mitch," he said.

The sliver of a question in his voice made Mitch's delight at his face curdle around the edges. "No, my mother wasn't a sadist."

He laughed loudly, his mouth open with it. "You're lucky. Most mums I've known fit that description perfectly. Mine, for example, named me Reginald, and if that weren't bad enough, she went on and called me Patty for no good reason through most of my formative years."

Later, through more sessions and a buffet dinner she should have skipped, she couldn't quite pinpoint how that innocent introduction had led to a date for after-dinner drinks. Maybe his laugh had done those things or how he used her name at every opportunity. Maybe it was his indefatigable jolliness or the way he asked about her favorite cocktails and her company's work with equally transparent interest. But, that evening, three drinks in, she put her hand on his, and Reginald signaled for the check with such alacrity that he startled people two tables over.

His desire was like his smile, so strong and clear that reciprocation felt wonderfully inevitable. All of the innumerable ways he was different from Kim incited an excitement she had no desire to analyze in the least. She just stopped him outside the door to his room and dug into their kisses, instead.

After they finally made it inside, she watched Reginald work his way out of his shirt and bright white undershirt, belt and trousers, all the while prattling on about tweed. Despite wondering with a throat-tightening want exactly what his skin felt like, Mitch couldn't move. Reginald was down to socks and boxers patterned with screwdrivers and tape measures before he stopped talking and seemed to notice.

"Mitch?"

"Yeah, Patty?"

"Perhaps I got the wrong idea."

"No. I just…Reginald…"

"Patty. Please."

"I kind of have a girlfriend."

"Oh." Reginald sat on the bed and crossed a black-socked ankle over the opposite knee.

"I mean we're basically at the point where we've decided to pull the plug, but no one wants to be the one to do it."

"May I ask if your hesitation is about infidelity or the inconvenient fact of my penis?"

Mitch's hesitation wasn't about Kim or Reginald's penis or even her own ugly face. It had something to do with the inherent unpredictability of people compared to metal and current, with the amount of time it took to suss out someone new, to trace their internal logic—or lack thereof. But there Reginald was, one hand sneaking over to where his pants draped next to him. He wanted her; it was all over the lay of his naked chest. At this moment, it didn't matter that she didn't know why. She trusted her observations, took a step forward, and started unbuttoning.

The last afternoon of the conference, Mitch lay with her head on Reginald's shoulder, watching the digital clock count down to the very last moment she could stay in bed and still make her flight. She'd slept with men since high school, but not many and not with this strange mix of comfort and desire. She thought about rescheduling her flight to the next morning, when Reginald was leaving, then put it out of her mind.

Reginald ran his hand from her shoulder to her elbow. "How many more minutes do I have?"

"I don't know what you're talking about."

"I'm not sure if I'm impressed or dismayed that you can manage to check the time while in the throes. Or maybe you were faking it?"

"I don't fake anything."

"Yes, I got that delightful impression. You never answered me. How many more minutes do I have?"

"Twenty-seven."

"Twenty-seven. Brilliant. I'm less than a half hour from re-maining the dashing, debonair Englishman with whom you had your wicked way at this conference, and I'm quite sure I'm go-ing to blow it."

"Patty, don't." Mitch tried to get up, but he held her tight.

"The problem is that I don't want you to stay just the brash, brilliant vixen I bedded."

"Vixen?"

"It's the closest I can get right now. Don't change the sub-ject. I've never been good at one-night stands, and it's not a skill I want to cultivate now."

"Did you rehearse this?"

"Maybe a little. Is it working?"

"It's splendid. But you still live in London, and I'm…"

Reginald raised an eyebrow. "A lesbian?"

"That's not what I was going to say. You live in London, and I'm a workaholic. I'm not particularly good at relationships, not even local ones." She really hadn't been about to bring up his maleness, though it was certainly hard to forget, but it seemed like such a small thing in the face of the many other reasons why they shouldn't try to pursue this. Despite recent history, she wasn't a lesbian, anyway, not in the narrow, militant, exclu-sive way most people meant when they said it.

"And my penis has nothing to do with it."

"Your penis is delightful," Mitch said and gave it a soft squeeze. "Besides, I'm not gay, I'm…something else." Twen-ty-three minutes. She disentangled herself from Reginald, sat up, and rubbed her shoulder. "Maybe I've convinced you that a relationship with me is all fun and games, but if you don't get sick of me—the insomnia, the smell of chlorine, the T-shirts and jeans—you'll get sick of my work."

She started to slide out of bed, but Reginald took hold of her wrist. "Did you stop to think that if you're 'something else,' which you surely are, I might not be like everyone else either?

It's the something else in you I don't want to give up—your devotion is exciting even if you're clearly not devoted to me."

Mitch looked away from him, not at the clock or for her clothes but at her bare foot against the dark carpeting. Reginald made her feel uncomfortably exposed. He couldn't really know what he was saying—Mitch had heard variants of those words before, though admittedly not so on the mark, and she had still managed to wear out her welcome.

She closed her eyes. "Okay. But email only."

"Are you going to set a limit on word count?"

Mitch smiled. "Knock yourself out." She looked at the clock.

"How many minutes?"

"Twenty."

"Exactly?"

"Exactly."

"That's just time enough," he said and pulled her back into bed.

$$\frac{c_n^2 \sum_{t=1}^{n} M_i x_i}{M}$$

FREEDOM FROM THE NEED TO PROVE HERSELF AS capable leads to the possibility of discovering a true sense of self.

–Dr. Abigail Rosen, The F Word: Femininity in the New Century

$$\frac{w(R^3 - r^3)}{2^2 - r^3)\sin(a)}$$

3

WOMANHOOD found Evelyn

Mitchell in her bedroom on a Saturday deep in her thirteenth year. It met her on a rare morning when she wasn't at a swim meet, practice, or clinic, and it manifested itself as an ache in her back that made her think of endless laps of breaststroke. Coach Smith, with her loud whistle and greenish cast to her blond hair, told her the stroke wouldn't strain her muscles if she did it right, but Evelyn couldn't wrap her body around those froggy motions.

No matter how much she stretched and turned over, a sweet morning dream was elusive, so Evelyn shuffled down the carpeted hall with sweatpants heavy on her bony hips and one hand pressed against a kidney, trying to erase the ache. She could hear her mother downstairs in the kitchen and smelled the sharp saltiness of frying ham. The bathroom Evelyn used was up the hall from her bedroom and hosed down in powder-blue tile, but its hideousness was balanced by the fact that it was hers, alone. A year ago, she'd worked her mechanical genius on the lock, and now it couldn't be picked, jimmied, or forced by anyone—most especially her mother. Evelyn could wile away the time in the bathtub with the flat tables of her kneecaps poking through hazed water, reading a book or magazine until she was chilled through. Even when her mother knocked on the door every ten minutes to check on her, her solitude was guaranteed.

This morning, after putting two and two together and arriving at a dreaded four, Evelyn sat on the toilet for a long time. There had been a lot of locker room discussion about who had it and who didn't, "it" taking on varied meanings as she got older. Hair down there and breasts and menstruation were tallied and measured to enough significant digits a statistician would be proud. They traded horror stories of excruciating cramps and blood-spot embarrassment, rules about white pants and bra straps.

The whole thing made Evelyn nervous. Obviously, all the girls on her team and at school had no doubts she was one of them. With some, she'd horsed around naked since before they had their permanent teeth. The boys, though, were a different story. They knew she was a girl in a manner only half realized, and Evelyn wanted to keep it that easy way. If she suddenly sprouted breasts, there would be no way to navigate among them undetected.

Besides, there was her father, who had taken a giant step back from Evelyn as soon as her twelfth birthday had rolled around. He became distant, closed the door behind him when he went into his den, declared that she was growing too advanced for his home-grown math problems. He'd become only a sharp eye on her grades and a back always receding down a hallway. Evelyn had tried in vain to determine how he'd calculated age twelve as the end of her girlhood, a question her mother answered with, "You're growing up."

"But I was growing up last year, too," Evelyn said.

"Smarty pants. You know what I mean. Who do you think knows more about becoming a woman, your father or me?"

"Yeah, but..." Evelyn said before remembering that phrase held the status of a four-letter word with her mother.

"When you get older, things change."

"But I like things now."

"And why not? When your father and I were your age, we'd already been contributing to our families for years. We've both worked hard so you could be a carefree girl, but you can't be a carefree girl forever. You have to think about the future, and your father's not one for the long view."

"I know, but—" Her mother's look made her think better of saying anything else.

Overzealous preparation had ensured that the cabinet under the bathroom sink had been stocked with pink-packaged feminine products since Evelyn had hit double digits. After dry runs orchestrated by her mother, Evelyn felt like an old hand, but when she was cleaned up and her underwear protected, she stood in the bathroom with a sickening fear of the rest of her life. Eventually, she'd have to go into that kitchen and tell her mother, but whatever would come spilling out of her in response would crash over Evelyn in thick, nauseating waves.

She scrutinized her face in the well-lit mirror for signs of this catastrophe, but the sharpness of her features hadn't changed. Over the last year, the hollows of her cheeks had grown more pronounced and now offered little to counteract the beaklike nose she secretly loved. Her familiar ugliness comforted her, made the relative prettiness of her thick brown hair acceptable. She steeled herself and turned off the light.

Downstairs, the second after words escaped her around half-chewed ham, Evelyn couldn't recall what she'd said. Her mother's delight trampled her back inside herself, and she compressed, her smile tight and fixed around meaty goodness she could no longer swallow. Although much of what her mother shrilled had already made the short journey in one ear and out the other, a new subtext in it made Evelyn feel as if she'd just enlisted in something seriously unappealing.

A knobby hand landed on Evelyn's shoulder, a hand she had inherited in a major way, and her mother's tone turned accusatory. "You're not a child anymore, Evelyn, so you need to stop acting like one. You need to consider how other people see you, start fitting in a little more."

"But—"

"No buts. You're a woman now, and this is something I know a thing or two about." Her mother scanned the cabinets and countertops of the kitchen as if gazing over conquered lands. "And you, my dear, have a lot to learn. We've indulged you long enough in your whims, the sports and those clothes and…and it's past time for you to understand a few things about how the world works."

Evelyn had been told by plenty of adults how mature she was for her age. She liked being around her parents' friends and lurked on the fringes of their dinner parties until she was sent upstairs. A hefty handful of teachers had pulled her aside for praise and projections of a bright future, which, she knew, was going to involve mathematics. Lots of it. Maybe exclusively so. Math was her thing, and it was her father's thing. So, by the transitive property, it was their thing. Or at least had been. When they sat together over a word problem, it was as adults, as equals. She felt appreciated for something she liked being appreciated for. Though she swam circles in the pool, her trajectory in mathematics had a hell of a slope.

But her prowess with geometric proofs was not what her mother's admonishment was about. She had been referencing a softer aspect of her mind—one Evelyn doubted existed. She was talking about the parts of the world that lingered outside stopwatches and black and white, right and wrong, true and false, the vast gray area driven by appearances and opinion that Evelyn had never understood. To her mother, adult life was an endless progression of picking sides, a world where getting what you wanted, what *she* wanted, depended entirely on eliciting the good graces of others.

Now that Evelyn was a woman, her side was picked for her. This side had a dress code and reading list and television preferences. This side had a set of appropriate hobbies, for which swimming qualified only because of its scholarship opportunities. This side had a set of expectations having nothing to do with receiving straight As. Had there been an incinerator in the basement, Evelyn's favorite clothes—her jeans and collection of swim-team T-shirts—would have burned to a crisp that first night her body betrayed her. As it was, her wardrobe soon became unrecognizable.

Evelyn was mute throughout. Her parents *had* given her a carefree childhood, one which had left her ill-equipped for rebellion. She was used to pleasing them, even her mother, and had required so little discipline that a mere look could go a long way. Now, her mother's hand was so heavy with guidance about grace and consideration and endless, stupid patience that Evelyn's cold terror and confusion had no room to push past those years of easy acquiescence, even though her consent had been to conventions and expectations that had made sense. Doubt crept in around the edges of her adamant disagreement. Her mother hadn't been unreasonable before—only somewhat relentless—and Evelyn wondered if maybe her mother was right and being a woman was way more complicated than she had anticipated.

Around wardrobe changes and repeated lectures about how to make friends who didn't reek of chlorine, Evelyn held on to her swimming with a desperate grip. Propelling herself efficiently through a medium 784 times as dense as air—she had looked it up—required an engineering of the entire body that fascinated her. A change of a degree in head position, of a fraction of an inch in the spread of fingers, rippled to measurable effect over two-hundred meters. For every adjustment, there were laps of repetition to commit the change to muscle memory until, now, she could escape into a humming blankness in the pool.

< ≈ >

Evelyn had become exquisitely aware of when she was alone in the house with her father. The hangnail of his proximity invited her worrying attention until it felt red and inflamed. She longed to confess her uncertainty about the path of her life this past year to something besides the thick black line that ran down the middle of her swim lane, but getting her friends to understand was impossible, not with their enthusiasm about her transformation. Makeup smoothed her features into a homogeny almost appealing, and new clothes gave the illusion of a shape that wasn't there. Her naked bathroom reflection retained its hard familiarity but disappeared under ministrations that had become routine.

A bikini with a padded top was what jerked her out of her somnambulance. Her mother had literally squealed over the jungle-print thing when they were out buying new practice suits for the fall swim season, and now it lay balled up at the foot of Evelyn's bed. She seethed in the soft summer air about its purchase, about each horrifying step she'd been pushed down this road she hadn't chosen—the pierced ears and braces, the ballroom dance lessons and Sunday afternoon cooking lessons, the department store makeovers. Nothing in her room brought comfort to her prowling anger, not even her swim medals or the poster of an anonymous butterflier breaking through the water at the start of a stroke—a swimmer so goggle-eyed and swim-capped even gender was buried and irrelevant.

Evelyn sat, trembling with an anger she couldn't quite direct until her mother ran out to the grocery store and left her and her father holed up at opposite ends of the house. She stomped down the stairs to the den off the kitchen then swayed in indecision outside the closed door, trying to determine the exact knock that would bring a spark of recognition. It started out too timid and ended too forceful. Evelyn thought about running away before he answered, but her feet were stubborn. He was still holding the newspaper open in the dusty quiet when she went in.

"Sorry to bother you," she said.

"No bother. Did your mother go out?"

"Yeah. She said we were having chicken tonight and that it'll be ready at six."

He grunted and made a motion toward his paper.

Evelyn dove in with the last of her nerve. "I don't understand what's going on."

"Oh? Perhaps a little precision might be helpful."

Evelyn smiled in relief. This was why her father felt solid and real. The act of digging into her own problems to deliver them to him in an acceptable way had always made them instantly manageable.

"It's about Mom," Evelyn said.

"Well, I doubt I can be much help with that."

"But she's…ever since…it's like she thinks I can't decide anything for myself."

"Your mother has your best interests in mind, Evie. We both want you to be happy. To have a family someday. If your mother hadn't known which way was up in these matters, I could have missed all this." He moved his hands around, indicating nothing in particular. "Her concerns aren't trivial roots."

"Yeah, sure, but don't you think she's…I don't know. Kind of fanatic? I mean—"

His paper crumpled when he leaned toward her. "You listen to me, Evelyn. As long as you live here, your mother and I are the final word. You may not see her point now, sometimes I don't, but we have an agreement, one I still believe in. There's a lot you don't know about a great many things, most especially yourself. You've always been a good girl. Let's keep it that way."

"But you don't know what she's doing."

"What makes you so sure of that?" He turned away, shaking out the newsprint. Evelyn stepped back with a feeling of doom so intense she couldn't bring herself to face it.

Rather than confront her parents with their collusion, she swallowed herself whole and gave in without even internal argument. She wore whatever clothes her mother bought, the lacy bras and cute shoes, and she attempted friendships with girls not involved in swimming. She paid attention to her hair and tried to move with more grace.

At the start of her sophomore year, when her perfectly turned-out self caught the eye of a senior on the boys' swim team, Evelyn knew this was what her mother wanted. Adam

Nutarelli went bare-chested on the pool deck more than he had to, showing off his well-developed body in a jocular, puppy dog way, but his times were nothing spectacular. The flirting began before the team even hit the water that fall. When he caught her alone, his talk was soft and careful. Although Evelyn could see through him, there was just enough substance there that she kept right on looking. But when other people passed them in the weight room or parking lot, he was so completely an ass that she could relax.

He was waiting for her after practice one afternoon, and his smooth talk and lack of regard for her personal space told Evelyn she had two options: reject him without mercy and go home a good girl or accept his advances in a kind of decision that was not her mother's or her own. Evelyn smiled and took his hand, tasting her resolve like metal.

"Mitchell." The hiss of her last name jolted her back into full consciousness. Lauren Tate stood puffed up with her hands on her hips. She swam the one-hundred- and two-hundred-meter butterfly, and her motion in the water was so smooth and strong she was pure pleasure to watch.

Evelyn disengaged from Adam and swayed closer to Lauren.

Lauren whispered, "What're you doing? Adam? You?"

"What do you think I'm doing?"

"Come on, Mitchell. You and Numb Nuts?"

"Hey, didn't you hear? I've changed."

Sex was not what Evelyn had expected. It wasn't demeaning or debasing or even potentially magical. In fact, it was kind of like swimming: a physical act that could take her to a place of mental focus and clarity. Bodies made perfect sense when stripped of clothes and pretensions and dragged down to desire, no matter if laced with embarrassment or pride or silliness. They were predictable and consistent within a certain margin of error. Sex let Evelyn be both exactly who she was and also generic, like that swimmer still tacked to the wall over her bed.

She became as expert in the art of backseat blow jobs and cornfield couplings as she was at trigonometry and the flip turn. Though her mother reached new levels of hysteria, her comments about nice girls, about good girls, proved no match for Evelyn's new maturation. They played the game of groundings and arguments, but Evelyn had honed her skills with locks and no longer needed keys to avail herself of her mother's station wagon. Her father read the paper with religious devotion.

But Lauren Tate was right that Evelyn was losing herself. She could find resonance only at the day's margins. In the early mornings, she felt the pull of her muscles in the churning pool and lost herself in the pursuit of form. The coolness of water against her face made her grateful for an adversary of such known proportions. She could forget her confusions and betrayals, move and breathe as if nothing had changed.

Then, late at night, after her parents had gone to bed, a small pool of white light on her desk illuminated her math homework. Its structure and her ability to see through its mysteries made her feel that real life was possible in her mother's pomp-and-circumstance version of her future. In math, equations balanced, and exceptions were exceptional. In math, concepts were abstract but so closely related to the world—the basis for understanding the world—that Evelyn felt each new nugget of knowledge come to rest inside her body as concretely as her own beating heart, tangible and necessary and perfect.

On a balmy spring evening late in Evelyn's junior year, she and her parents sat tackling a pot roast with a side of zero conversation. The sounds of yelling children and barking dogs that drifted through the open windows provided the only accompaniment to their chewing. Evelyn longed to slide into the front seat of her new junky car and escape.

The shrill of the phone made her father grimace and her mother jump and spill her water. She left the small puddle and rushed to the kitchen to answer. Her father's intolerance for dinnertime calls was legendary. Evelyn shoved an oversized chunk of meat in her mouth and watched a tendril of water from the spill creep toward the table's edge. From the kitchen came only low pleasantries.

Eventually, her mother resurfaced with a dish towel and mopped up the water.

"Who was it this time, another telemarketer?" her father asked when she sat down and resettled her napkin on her lap.

"Actually, no. It was Mr. Nielson from the school. Apparently, they're getting Valley Community College to allow some qualified students to take a calculus class there next year, and he wanted to know if Evelyn would be enrolling."

"Calculus?" Evelyn said around her mouthful.

Her father put down his fork and asked, "Is it during the school day?"

"It would take the place of her final period, but that's beside the point."

Evelyn swallowed with effort and cranked up the volume. "Calculus?"

"Relax," her mother said with a snap in her voice. "You're not taking that class."

"What? But it's calculus!"

"Now, really, Margaret," her father said. He assumed a position of interest Evelyn hadn't seen in years, leaning forward over the arm he'd planted on the table.

"Don't 'Margaret' me, David. We all agreed that Evelyn would be getting a job, and you know my position on that kind of experience."

Evelyn launched to her feet. "What? But I can do both!"

"Sit down," her mother said.

"The hell I will."

"Margaret, the girl has a real aptitude."

Her mother brushed aside an errant hair. "David, I'm quite sure we'd find you had a real aptitude for housework, but that doesn't mean it's the most important thing. Calculus can wait until college, if she really wants."

He said, "This isn't what we agreed on. Not at all."

"It's *exactly* what we agreed on," her mother said in the tone of voice that used to turn Evelyn's blood to ice.

Evelyn clutched the table's edge. "I want to do it. I can do it. Stop trying to make me into some bimbo."

Her mother stared Evelyn down. "Do you think I don't know what's going on around here? People talk, Evelyn. If anyone's making you into a bimbo, it's you."

"Me? Who bought my clothes? Who taught me how to 'walk from my hips'? You might as well charge for my services."

"Enough!" Evelyn's father rose to his considerable height.

"But, Dad, look at me, look at what she's doing. I'm not like this. I'm like you."

"If you were like me, you'd know when to shut your mouth. Get out of my sight."

Evelyn was out of the room before he'd stopped talking, threw herself in her shit-brown hatchback and drove aimless circles until nearly out of gas then spent the darkest part of the night on the edge of the same field in which she'd sloughed off her virginity. She felt dry, explosive. While she couldn't fathom suicide, homicide felt well within her grasp.

She arrived to school an hour early to wait for Mr. Neilson to pull into the parking lot then trailed him to his office, dismissing his news of her parents' decision. Evelyn kept her voice low and practiced the art of persuasion her mother had worked to ingrain in her.

"I understand, Evelyn, but there's nothing I can do. The class is off school grounds, and you're still going to be a minor. The school requires parental consent or you can't attend. I'm sorry."

"Just please call my dad at work."

"They gave me a perfectly clear answer last night."

"It's my mom." Evelyn took a breath and let her voice sink back down. "Please, sir. My dad is a reasonable man—especially at work."

Evelyn listened while he dialed and made his case, but his face told her everything she needed to know. She ran out of his office before he could say it out loud, drove back to that cornfield, and tumbled out of the car, screaming and yelling until her voice failed her. She battered the warm hood past the point when the split skin on her knuckles left red kiss marks, kicked the tires until the impact of her shoe against hard rubber radiated pain up her leg. Then she slumped back behind the wheel and shook with soundless crying.

Later, even though it should have been her father's gray sedan in her sights, she took aim at her mother's station wagon. Evelyn followed her when an inevitable errand pulled her from the house. In the drugstore parking lot, she slashed all four tires with a folding knife her father had insisted she carry in her glove box.

Evelyn returned to the house and loaded her hatchback with everything she could bear to call hers, which besides school books and swim gear wasn't much. She grabbed the cash from her mother's jewelry box and drove two miles to her best friend Rachel Frank's house, where she reclined her seat and waited for school to let out.

The Franks let her stay. They gave her all the space in the universe and were understanding, and Evelyn wanted to punish them. Her rage demanded to be fed. It felt so clean and real that she was powerless to resist. Her sullen silences unnerved everyone, and the clothes she shredded during sleepless midnights made Rachel distant and weird when she found them later in the bathroom garbage. But Evelyn knew that ripped fabric wasn't Rachel's real problem—she could see in the mirror how her face had settled into a hard, twisted ugliness. It scared Rachel, but Evelyn clung to it.

Then, a month into her senior year, Evelyn strayed beyond the reach of the Franks' huge generosity by letting a dinner-table comment about college applications release her ready anger. Her vitriolic screaming felt so good that stopping simply wasn't an option. They asked her to leave, and Evelyn had no place to go. It was liberating in a terrifying way. She scouted for spots on the scruffy rural outskirts of town where she and her car could squat at night. Swim practice would let her shower before classes for several months yet, and if she could get a restaurant job, it would give her a better shot at three squares a day.

Her first night alone, a steady rain pinged off her metal ceiling, and Evelyn curled in the back seat under a drift of sweat clothes and thought about her parents. She calculated the number of days since she'd left their house, the number of hours they hadn't spent tracking her down. Even after everything, she couldn't quite rid herself of an ache of disappointment. She shoved her face against the vinyl upholstery and begged for sleep.

At the start of school, Evelyn had seen everyone catalog her changes over the summer and steer clear. She had lost her allure even to the sex-starved boys who hadn't yet had a crack at her. Now, when the temperature dropped and her old clothes failed to keep her warm at night, Evelyn bought bulky, insulated items from the men's department at Sears that allowed her to sleep off the side of the road or in the corners of empty parking lots. She heard her new nickname when she walked down the halls and secretly, desperately embraced it. *Freak.*

She knew it was true and that her perverse enjoyment of her living situation confirmed it. She knew the differences within her extended hugely in all directions, and she had plenty of time alone to catalog them. Evelyn didn't believe in the distinctions on which her parents—and everyone else—tacitly agreed. Who she was in those long, lonely evenings spilled across boundaries, could not be contained by words or equations, was the swirling mass of possibility essential for quantum physics. Yes, she was a freak.

< ≈ >

In March, on the last day of swim season, Evelyn had yet to come up with a plan to remain clean that didn't involve wet naps swiped from the restaurant. Sneaking into the locker room for

55

a quick shower was proving more difficult than anticipated, and she dithered around after practice, worrying about it. She was tying double knots onto the tops of her work boots when Lauren Tate ambled over. They were alone.

Lauren had grown four inches and found twenty pounds of muscle since her thwarted attempt to come between Evelyn and Adam Nutarelli. Her one-hundred fly was so sublime that several colleges were fighting over her. She was hearty and strong and fit in perfectly where Evelyn protruded like an unruly cowlick. But Lauren had never stopped being friendly, and Evelyn almost found a smile in answer to her lopsided grin.

Lauren motioned to Evelyn's boots. "Those are kind of hot, Mitchell."

"Hot in here but warm outside."

"Not that kind of hot." She cleared her throat. "Sexy hot."

Evelyn let her face go blank and checked the contents of her backpack, waiting for Lauren to go away.

"Hey, do you need a place to stay or something?"

"No." The word snapped out of her mouth right before Evelyn welded it shut.

"It's just..."

Her eyes stayed fixed on her backpack while she waited for Lauren's running shoes to move outside her peripheral vision. She hoped it would be soon because the urge to make Lauren regret this weird overture was becoming hard to swallow.

"Hey, Mitchell. I'm sorry. I take it back, okay?"

The shoes moved closer, and Evelyn's fingers cleaved to the perforated metal bench between her legs. Lauren sat down close enough that their knees touched.

"I know you're genius smart and I'm, like, one-hundred-percent jock, but sometimes you're stupider than I can believe."

Evelyn drew in a ragged breath to end this, but with some trick of fluid motion, Lauren's hand was on her neck and their kiss was over before she even felt it. Her surprise came only at Lauren Tate, of all people, not at her own crawling interest. She'd known since before she could remember that her attraction meandered across swim lanes—being around so much nakedness made certain things very clear—but she had assumed nothing would come of it. These days, the only thing she wanted more than a hot bath was to be touched. Evelyn sat and waited, deflated and hungry and petrified.

"Are you okay?"

No, Evelyn was not okay, not with that hand still on her neck and her face on fire.

"Mitchell." Lauren sighed. "Maybe I'm the dumb one." The hand went away.

Any move to keep Lauren here was irrevocable, would bring into concrete existence what was still safe theory. But mostly, it meant loosening her hold on her anger long enough to touch something lovely. Evelyn didn't know how to be who she was if she wasn't furious and untouchable, but she dragged her eyes to Lauren's face and found a disaster of a smile.

After school that afternoon in Lauren's room, Evelyn pointedly ignored the swim trophies and posters and everything so familiar that threatened to unmoor her studied remove. The only way she kept from crying after they'd hurried out of their clothes and Lauren's familiar body pressed against her, so long and fleshy and strong, was to itemize the differences between Lauren and the boys she'd fucked. There was softness and smoothness and the higher pitch of her sex sounds. But the way desire thickened the air and her throat, the press of fingers against her back, and the creak of springs were familiar enough that Evelyn could abandon herself to pure physicality.

Lauren held Evelyn tight against her side and reminisced about how long she'd liked Evelyn and how infuriatingly oblivious she'd been. Evelyn closed her eyes and luxuriated in the perfect give of Lauren's mattress. She slid closer to blissful sleep, but Lauren pulled her from the brink by asking, "Do you live out of your car?"

"Oh, shut up," Evelyn said with no real force.

"I was so jealous of Numb Nuts."

The hatchback was going to be torture after this bed.

"Mitchell."

"Hm?"

"Nothing. I just like saying it."

"Mitch," Evelyn said. "Call me Mitch."

"Mitch?" Lauren laughed. "Awesome. Mitch Mitchell. Oh, yeah."

A blooming pleasure coaxed a grin to life that felt a little familiar.

< ≈ >

That night, Mitch wound up on the welcome mat outside her old front door. She wasn't sure why she was there, but she couldn't get herself to turn around and leave. Her knock rattled the glass but felt like failure.

Her mother opened the door, and Mitch snapped, "Get Dad." After a start and aborted stutter, she disappeared inside, and Mitch realized that, for a moment, she hadn't been recognized.

Then they were both in front of her, and Mitch knew what to say. "Her maybe I'll forgive, but not you." She stared hard at the bridge of her father's nose. "Never. You knew better and did nothing but bury me. Fuck both of you for thinking—"

Too many words choked her, and she found herself reeling away a step. She hauled herself back in front of them and said, "There aren't any rules to this, don't you know that?" Their faces were out of focus, part of some alternate reality. She was strangely numb. "Do you know I'm homeless?" She hadn't felt it until she said it.

"No one forced you to leave," her mother said. "But you wouldn't compromise. No rules. You listen to me, there are rules everywhere about everything."

"You really don't give a shit about me, do you."

"Don't take that tone, Evelyn. You have no idea."

That name bore no relation to her anymore. "I live out of my car, Mom. I live out of my car, and you think *I* have no idea?" Her mother sucked in a breath. "Shut up," Mitch roared. She wanted to sink to her knees in gratitude that she hadn't lost her rage. Instead, she caught her father's eyes and dared him to say something.

It took several silent seconds too long for Mitch to turn and run to her car.

"Evie!"

She stumbled to a stop with a stupid thump in her chest.

"I'm sorry, Evie, but ... I'm sorry."

From where she stood next to her weathered rear bumper, Mitch could see through the hatchback's dirty glass to the stacks of her worldly belongings. Above her was the window to her old bedroom, and she hated that she wondered if they'd changed it since she'd left or if it still looked like Lauren's. There would always be rules she couldn't stand, and he would never be sorry in the right way.

She walked around the car to the driver's side and put her hand on the handle. Her father hung out there on the front step, open and upset. She looked at him and said, "My name is Mitch, you asshole."

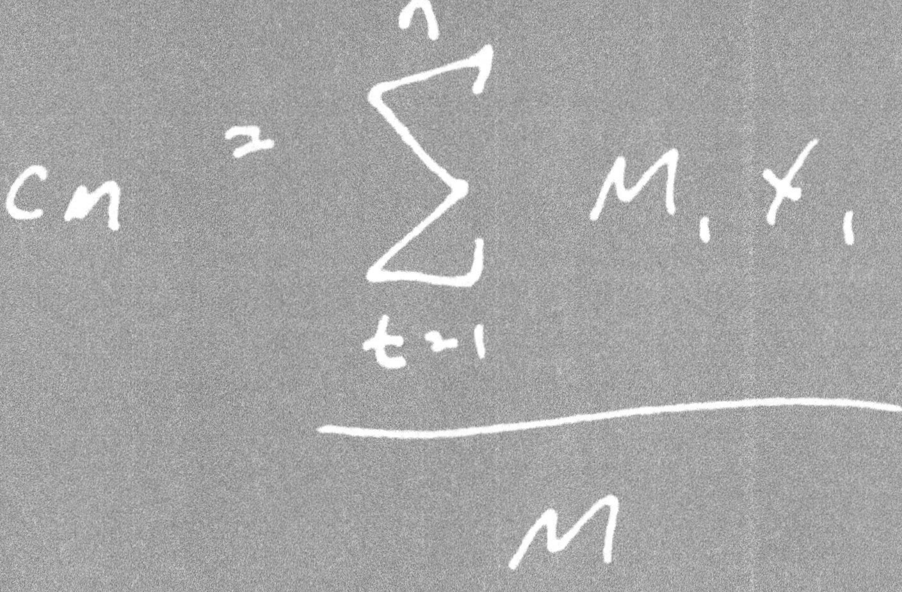

THE KEY TO INTERNAL PEACE AND EXTERNAL uneasiness is learning to think for oneself.

–Dr. Abigail Rosen, *The F Word: Femininity in the New Century*

4

BEFORE taking Mitch's advice and calling Abby, advice which had sounded reasonable and necessary and *easy*, Carol had decided to reread Abby's book. Bad move. She'd spent the three weeks since in chronic hesitation that had kept her from putting finger to phone. And now, with October in full swing, Abby certainly didn't even remember who she was. If Carol actually managed to call, there'd be all awkward pauses and explanations, and Abby would either end up feeling pressured to be nice or hanging up—Carol couldn't decide which was worse.

Besides, who was she to force a friendship on this woman? No one. A deeply flawed mother unable to have a conversation with her teenage son not involving snippy monosyllables. A woman whose most notable skill was matching snacks to cookies. A graduate school dropout who worked part time at a bookstore, a job she'd practically bullied her way into when Gordo had tottered off to kindergarten five years before. After striking out up and down Main Street in a panicked job search, she'd stormed Turning Leaves, her last chance at employment, and peppered the owner with her qualifications in a decidedly rabid way.

Carol suspected that Maggie had hired her to shut her up, but the truth quickly became clear: Maggie was a devoted night owl. Carol worked from ten o'clock until two thirty, and sometimes Maggie didn't wake up and descend the creaky back staircase from her apartment over the store until minutes before Carol left. Maggie claimed she stayed up late reading, and she certainly tore through piles of literature, but Carol preferred to dream up alternate explanations. Mags was a high-priced companion to the older deans at Tilsen. She ran a drug ring that supplied students with contraband in hollowed-out books. Using a high-quality printer and professional adhesive, she pasted subversive messages inside romance paperbacks.

Carol was late to work after languishing in the shower, shored up by cool white tiles while succumbing to tears over a stupid breakfast argument with James that was made worse when Brian swooped in and made her feel ineffectual *again*. But her tardiness didn't keep her from making a stop at Loretta's bakeshop, a fixture on the prominent corner of Main and Ninth just a half block up from the bookstore. Loretta, with her sunny disposition and hands wide and flat as slices of the big loaves she sold, maintained a stranglehold on Millerton's baked-goods market, and Carol had been sneaking out to Loretta's for twenty years.

Loretta was alone behind the counter reading a *People* magazine when Carol came in, tripping over a curled corner of the doormat. The way Loretta sprang into motion with pleasantries and a sheet of tissue paper in each hand made Carol wish she'd hit up the Dunkin' Donuts instead, where she wouldn't be cajoled by a perfectly nice woman to pick out the just-right assortment for the dozen donuts she ordered. Not a dozen, a *baker's* dozen, because that was how Loretta rolled.

Faced with all these donuts, Carol dithered in indecision long enough that Loretta put the box together herself. Maybe she'd gotten a look at Carol's red-rimmed eyes or just wanted to get back to her magazine, but she let Carol pay and escape with a minimum of transactional banter. The wind on Main Street was strong and cold, and Carol wondered what the weatherman was smoking when he predicted an Indian summer starting over the weekend and lasting into next week. She walked across the street to Turning Leaves with the donuts tucked under one arm then unlocked the front door and pushed it open with exaggerated slowness to avoid making the chimes at the top announce her late arrival—not that Maggie seemed to care.

Carol put the donuts on the table in the storeroom, a long, narrow space lined with boxes and shelves and piles of books. She was determined to wait for her boss to come downstairs before taking a single bite of pastry, so she threw herself into re-alphabetizing Medieval History then changing a light bulb in Literature, stocking pens in the writer's corner, and pacing behind the register doing nothing. In between, she found excuses to go back and examine her bakeshop haul, noting any hardening or coagulation, congratulating herself on not letting one pass her lips, and wondering when the hell Maggie was going to emerge so she could stuff herself with a witness. Bingeing alone was one of a whole class of secrets that not only rotted a person from the inside but was also a leading cause of freckles, at least according to her mother.

The store was so resoundingly empty it felt like a morning in July, when Millerton went into hibernation. On the days when her whole shift passed without the door opening, not even nudged by a gust of wind, the urge to swap books between Economics and the Occult or Political Theory and Marketing was overwhelming. Carol would somehow resist and sit on a tall stool behind the register, trying to read, but her interest couldn't hold still for whatever book she'd plucked from the remainders pile—whether Grisham or Faludi. It seemed reading most interested her when she was in danger of interruption, not as an escape in itself.

Noon had come and gone, and still no Maggie. In the thirteen donuts, Loretta had included one of the pink-frosted sprinkled varieties Carol just adored. They made her feel nine years old, made her miss those pigtails she used to have. Her stomach growled with a seismic shift. Did it count as secret binging if she was starving? If only there were customers, but the one person through the door this morning had been asking directions.

Fuck it. A stupid donut wasn't worth this. She could be Mitchlike and eat only one. Actually, being Mitchlike would mean stopping at half, because if Mitch went too far with anything, it was self-restraint—at least around pleasure. Carol lifted the pink-frosted ring from the box, and in a blur, half the donut was gone. She headed back to the register, resolved to chew the next bite at least fifteen times.

At chew eleven, the front door chimes clanged wildly, and Joyce Obermann swept inside on a rush of cold air. Carol swallowed hard, stashed the decimated donut next to the phone under the high counter, and wondered how Joyce always caught her in these "compromising" positions: with pink frosting on her fingers, or dipping into a bag of shaved turkey while wandering the cereal aisle, or even sitting in the minivan in the school parking lot, singing and throwing power chords along with Guns N' Roses.

"Carol, hello," Joyce said. "Don't you look sporty."

Carol refrained from a downward glance at her shirt and chinos. Joyce was poisoned by the extra forty pounds she'd been packing since birth, and she tossed around this so-called flattery all the time. "You're a vision yourself. Did you get your hair cut?" Joyce wouldn't be bad looking if stripped bare of makeup, but the woman did the worst with what she had.

Joyce's mouth compressed, spreading wrinkles into her mauve lipstick. She stood a few paces from Carol, next to the table of large-format photography books. "As a matter of fact, I did."

"Well, it looks nice and fresh." Carol did not like the person she became around Joyce.

"How's James? We haven't seen him in a while."

"He's a pain in the ass and only barely a teenager." Carol wondered if Joyce really was shocked or if she'd just perfected the expression—widened eyes and consternated eyebrows.

"He's fine. I find him and Brian in these quietly heated conversations that stop when they notice I'm within sight."

"Boys that age need their fathers."

"Plenty at our school seem to be doing fine without," Carol said, despite how lost she'd be around James without Brian.

"They may seem that way now, but time will tell." Joyce resettled the shoulder strap of her mammoth tan purse, which must have required the hide of an entire cow for its construction.

"What can I help you with today?"

"Oh, yes. I need a copy of that woman's book. Professor Rosen."

That woman. That woman! And the way Joyce had said it, voice brittle with suspicion as if Abby were a threat. "You know she's a lesbian, right?" Carol asked.

"Who doesn't? She shouts it from the rooftops. Still, a pretty woman like that? Do you think any man has mind enough to care about her *preferences*?"

"I think Dr. Rosen might have something to say about that."

"Yes, she's evidently got quite a bit to say about a great many things. As I'm to find out if you've got a copy of her book to sell me."

"Right. Of course. I think we have a few in the back. Just a minute." Once away from Joyce, Carol demolished an entire chocolate glazed, which instead of righting the world's tilt only underscored how loserish she was for not having called Abby. Yes, Abby was spectacular, maybe even otherworldly, but hadn't she been sitting *alone* in Carol's own backyard? Didn't this town eat newcomers for breakfast? Carol considered another donut but heard annoyance in Joyce's sigh and made do with picking the crumbs from her shirt and depositing them in her mouth. After arming herself with a fake smile and a copy of Abby's book, she walked back to the register. "Anything else?"

"No, thank you."

She rang up the book without further comment, but just before Joyce was safely out the door, she blurted, "You know, we're probably more likely to experience a personal disturbance by Dr. Rosen than our husbands."

"I swear, how you think is beyond me," Joyce said then made the chimes rattle and clank again.

Carol reached for the rest of her donut but made herself hold still and not eat it until she counted to a hundred. She knew that if she finished this donut, she'd make a valiant effort to take down the rest of the box, too, and then would feel bad on every conceivable level. So she counted and gauged the donut's springiness with her fingertips. At one hundred, she counted back down, getting into the rhythm of the two-digit numbers.

Maggie emerged from the storeroom, which connected the main shop to the back staircase up to her apartment. She was one of those older ladies who retained an erect carriage and graceful manner yet couldn't be called youthful. She wore flowing clothes in solid colors that were bold but not bright and had about as many wrinkles as Carol. This afternoon, her long salt-and-pepper hair was piled on her head and run through with yellow pencils.

When she spied Carol behind the counter, she said, "Hello, my beautiful sunrise. I saw the donuts. What's the occasion?"

Carol's finger and thumb pressed into doughy softness. "It's just one of those days." Then, "You get me, right? How I think?"

"What do you mean? How you think is delightful."

"You're only saying that 'cause you've got all that Vegas glitter in your blood. You know, from your career as a show girl."

"See? Delightful. Untrue, but delightful." Maggie made a circuit of the open area in front of the register and ran her ringed fingers over the best sellers and staff picks.

Carol said, "But those gams of yours. Show girl material, definitely. Mags with the Gams. I'll bet you were very popular. I'll bet you're not up late reading but honing your moves with tasseled pasties. Putting a little sumpthin' sumpthin' on your kicks."

"If only I had the colorful evenings you invent for me."

Being considered delightful and colorful wasn't really what Carol was after, were sentiments as common and worthless as a Canadian penny in the cash drawer, and it made Carol feel more distant and small than before. Maggie took her customary glance outside the front door, and Carol pushed the last pink bite of donut into her flapping trap. She chewed and swallowed to the dull clunking of the chimes on the door swaying under Maggie's grasp.

"Any visitors this morning?" Maggie asked.

"One lost leaf peeper and Joyce, who demanded a copy of Dr. Rosen's book."

"Ah."

"What?"

"Joyce always leads you into self-doubt."

Carol had thought she was all cried out after this morning, thought a few donuts between friends would chase away the wrongs nipping at her callused heels, but a sudden thickness in her throat informed her that she was mistaken, as usual.

She took her purse from under the counter and pretended to look in Maggie's eyes. "I need to take off. I forgot about an appointment."

"Carol—"

But she was already past Maggie and hoofing it down the sidewalk—away from the minivan, she realized after two breathless blocks. Not to mention the Boston cream she'd been saving for last. The speed of her flight was cramping her shins, and now she was going to have to sneak back and get the van from behind the store or walk home, which would require all sorts of explanation. But then the cool brightness and the oxygen muscling in and out of her lungs made alchemy in her skull and veered her off down the laughter fork on the road hysteria. She sank down on a sunny bench in the small park across from The Filling Station, giggles escaping between the fingers she'd clamped over her mouth.

Laughing was good. Like nearly equivalent with sex, good. Its rush left her awake and tingling with an unreasonable well-being. She dug around in her purse for her phone and dialed Dr. Rosen's office. Abby answered on the third ring, sounding neither distracted nor friendly, and Carol rushed in.

"So, listen. This is Carol, by the way. Carol Hollister. Brian's wife. Brian Hollister. Anyway, listen. They say that summer's going to come around here one last time, and I, for one, am sick and tired of taking in the sun and watching my grass grow all by myself. What do you say?"

After a long pause, Abby said, "I'm confused but happy, I think."

"Yeah, I've been told those both go away after knowing me awhile. At any rate, I'm proposing you play hooky next Tuesday and keep me company in my backyard. Cocktails and even cocktail weenies will be provided. How's three o'clock for you?"

By the time they'd coordinated, the day's angst was gone. Everything Carol had thought would flatten out her mood swings—Brian, the boys, age—had failed. But given that she lived to be enchanted, subsequent disappointment and despair were inevitable. What else could she do but ride each wave as long as possible?

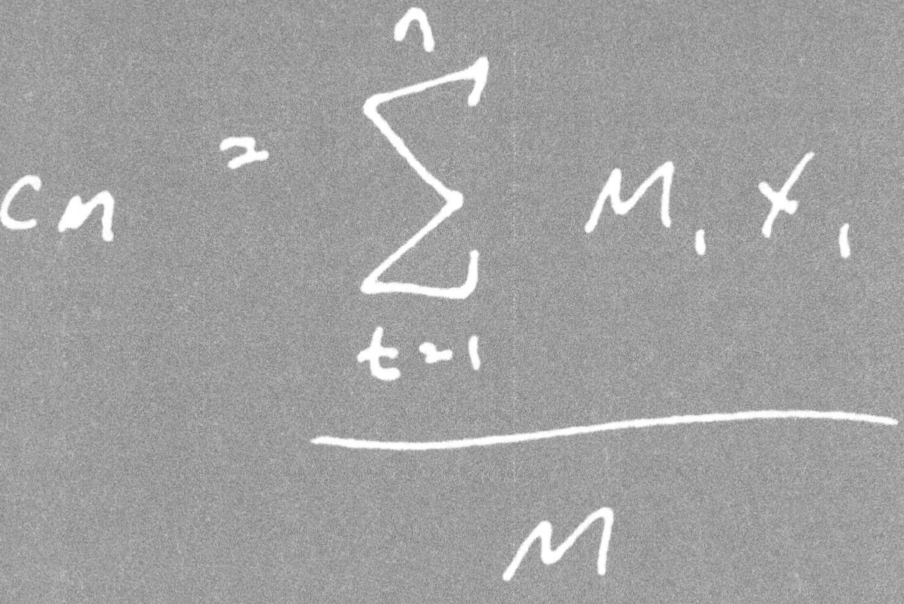

SWIFT JUDGMENT IS A NECESSARY INGREDIENT IN the formation of cooperative societies. Not being able to distinguish us versus them, friend versus foe, led to the fall of Troy and other historical maladies.

–Dr. Abigail Rosen, The F Word: Femininity in the New Century

5

IN COLLEGE, Mitch had discovered many unforeseen pleasures in writing programming code. At its most basic, coding could be distilled down to a procession of orderly and contained logical problems, each of which brought a sizzle of satisfaction when solved. With a few keystrokes, a solution was either verified or invalidated with an addictive immediacy. After a long, productive session, Mitch began to equate the keyboard to those levers in lab experiments that, when pressed, sent bolts right to the test subject's pleasure center.

She briefly considered a career in software development, which was good, lucrative work even though it involved sitting in front of a computer all day. But what didn't? How different was that from what awaited her as an engineer? And coding was much more enjoyable than endless data analysis.

But software development lacked the feel of machined aluminum—cool, smooth, and solid—or powdered graphite's slipperiness. It didn't involve the snap of a toggle switch or the push of resistance when turning the knob of an oscilloscope.

Lab work could be tedious, but it was tactile and tantalizing in its unknowns. Software was just too virtual in the face of such physicality, besides generally not calling upon knowledge of higher math.

Now she knew she'd made the right choice for an entirely different reason: chasing down a bug hidden in thousands of lines of code could be frustrating beyond description. She'd spent the last thirty hours trying to root one out in a cycle of despair rising to elation then plunging back to despair at being proved wrong once again. At least her failures were identified quickly, but she was long past finding pleasure in that.

She reared back in her chair, eliciting a violent squeak. "Motherfucking piece of shit." Nothing brought out the language like software.

Eric said, "I don't think that's proper workplace vocabulary." He sat behind his trash-heap of a desk, cap perched on unruly, thinning dark hair. His round face was both angelic and scruffy owing to a perpetual dark stubble. Steve had once told Mitch that Eric was always crawling with girls, which made a strange kind of sense.

"I don't think I care."

"I'm sensing this is something a fart joke won't solve."

"Is there anything a fart joke actually solves?"

"You'd be surprised." He used his cap to indicate the emptiness of the third desk in the office then resettled it on his head. "You know, you drove Steve off hours ago with the ultimate power of your negative energy. I think he's at the library."

Mitch swore again, and Eric tsked. At once, she was up and out the door without a word. She drove the familiar roads over to Carol's house at top speed. After pulling into the driveway, she took her swim duffel—untouched this morning in favor of a couple short hours of sleep—and hustled to the backyard. But instead of making a beeline for the pool, she headed to the equipment shed and the lawn mower inside.

The shed was dim and stuffy and organized to the nines— something Carol and Brian agreed on. Pool and snow removal equipment on the left, lawn care on the right. One sleepless night, Mitch had come in here with white paint and had drawn outlines around the pool strainer, hedge clippers, shovels—anything that had a place and was hung in it. She meant it as a joke, but Carol was delighted.

Mitch tossed her duffel to the side of the door and approached the mower—a big, red, stand-on-the-back Toro. She stepped on and started it up. The noise shimmered through her, cracking open the top level of her agitation even before she rumbled out of the shed to make broad passes across the yard, starting at the house and moving outward.

Being consumed by vibrations and noise and the lumbering movement of the mower was so delicious after the frustrating silence of the office. This onslaught to her senses made it hard to think in a linear, logical way. All she could take in was the bright sunshine, dense blue sky, and the smell of cut grass. Her frustration shook right out of her.

< ≈ >

Carol careened the 5.7 miles from work to home in record time then almost collided with Mitch's truck in the driveway. Stirrings of dread erupted when she opened the van's door and heard the mower. "Are you kidding me?" She nearly wrenched her knee flinging herself from the driver's seat. Abby was due to arrive in twenty minutes, and now Mitch comes over and mows? Give Mitch carte blanche over the backyard, tell her to treat it as her own, and look what happens. Midnight swims and inopportune lawn maintenance.

Mitch was only a quarter of the way into the proceedings, still at least forty-five minutes from finishing, obviously blissed out, deaf and blind to everything—even her jeans, which were riding so low they seemed sure to end up around her ankles. She looked like a damn hired hand. Carol flailed around for a while trying to get Mitch's attention then checked her watch and gave up—there was barely time to get ready.

Over the next twenty minutes, Carol outdid herself, dragged two teak lounge chairs over to the lawn between patio and pool and settled a low table between them. She rejected several different soundtracks while changing from work clothes and struggling a brush through her tangled hair then mixed up a pitcher of cocktails and set out glasses garnished with little yellow-and-pink umbrellas.

Even after all this preparation, when she stepped out onto the patio from a final trip inside, she was still surprised to see Abby standing at the edge of the yard in almost the exact same position as when she'd appeared in the first place.

"You're here," Carol said. She was carrying a big wooden tray that held a silver bowl of steaming cocktail weenies and small dishes of assorted sauces. When she stumbled over an invisible something on the flagstone, Abby made an alarmed sound and took two quick steps forward.

"Can I help?"

"No. I'm a high-functioning klutz."

"Sure?"

"Come on and take a load off." Carol set the tray on the table, and they regarded each other over the reclined chair between them. "Did you walk here? Brian told me you walked to the kick-off party—five miles, right? I'm positively dumbfounded."

"Don't be. It's a compulsion, and compulsions shouldn't be considered—except when medication might be indicated." Abby put a hand on the back of the chair but made no move to sit. Her fingernails were almond shaped and trimmed short. They shone dully in the sun.

"Still." Carol didn't know why she was insisting on waiting until Abby sat down first, but it was getting uncomfortable. "Still, you know. That's a long way."

Abby finally stretched out and tucked her skirt under her thighs. "I drove. The walking…I've always done it, but it wasn't notable in New York. When I got a car to move here, it took me a minute to remember which pedal was the gas and which was the brake."

"People here go straight from the car to the grave. On particularly lazy days, I've been known to move the minivan from one end of Main to the other." Carol folded herself cross-legged and faced Abby then speared a mini-sausage with a long, cellophane-tipped toothpick. "Weenie? That's barbeque, and there are two mustards—Dijon and honey." She extended the loaded toothpick to Abby but stopped midway and said, "I've never really matured, you know. I'm still totally a child."

Abby studied Carol, a wrinkle between her eyebrows, then took the weenie. "That's okay. I've been an old lady for as long as I can remember."

"Aren't we a pair. A perverted Harold and Maude. Let's get drunk! Or at least tipsy." Carol raised a glass. "This is the more refined older sister of the punch at our party. You must be an older sister."

"Only child, you?"

"I'm flattered you even asked. I've been told I have 'youngest' spelled out on my forehead in freckles. Usually that's my excuse for everything, but at least I can blame the libations for my conduct at the party."

Abby waved in dismissal and chased a swallow of her drink with the offered weenie. The spicy mustard she'd doused it with must've had its way because she sniffed and hummed and wiped a teary eye. She reached up to brush hair from her forehead that wasn't there then turned away and coughed.

Carol said, "But, really, the hair. Somehow I'm thinking there's a story behind that."

"A rogue hairdresser, mostly." Abby fanned the air in front of her mouth.

Staying still and holding her tongue wasn't easy, but Carol had made herself a promise that she would be someone a little different this afternoon. Since this included not prying where she normally would—and not getting tipsy, or at least not *too* tipsy—she concentrated on sipping her drink instead. The drone of the distant lawn mower made each second stretch and bend.

Abby retucked her floral-print skirt and touched the right side of her head over her ear where her hair was its shortest.

"Melanie was my stylist for years and years. All through my thirties. Even so, you should never get your hair cut when you're in mental disarray."

"Guess I'll be growing this out, then." Carol pulled on a red curl then let it bounce back. "I know what you mean. It's like not going to the grocery store when you're hungry. Good-bye waistline," she sang.

"All I said was that I wanted something different, thinking it might mean three or four inches shorter. Or maybe even bangs."

"How much did you get cut off?"

"Almost two feet."

Carol bounced up and down, getting a drop of barbeque sauce on her white shirt. "Holy shit! I've never had half that much hair."

"It was a lot," Abby said and nodded. Then she dipped a sausage into the hot mustard and chewed and fanned the air again.

Carol waited. A lot. Was that it? Abby's reticence made Carol think of Mitch, and she checked on the lawn mower's progress. Finally, she said, "Two feet. Were you drugged? Did your stylist slip you a roofie?"

Abby laughed in a surprised blurt then treated Carol to an author-photo-worthy smile. "Melanie was persuasive, but with the way I was feeling, I was lucky to get out of that chair with any hair left." She sobered and lifted her chin a notch, letting the sun spread over the top of her chest in the open vee of her blouse.

"You'd probably look great with a buzz cut."

"Do you flatter everyone this way?" Abby asked with her eyes closed.

"No." Carol finished her drink with a dramatic upending of her glass. "What were you in mental disarray about?" she asked despite herself.

"It was strange, but I remember a certain euphoria that came from seeing the shape of my head in Melanie's mirror. It faded quickly."

"I can imagine. I've known women to lapse into hysterics over a dye job one shade too dark."

Abby examined her fingernails.

"You lapsed into hysterics?"

"I wouldn't say that. But I cried in my pillow."

"You literally cried in your pillow?" Carol asked then stumbled on, trying to save herself. "Hey, tears are honest. I hope my boys never grow out of them."

"But over hair?"

"Please. You could give a four-part lecture series on women and hair through history."

"All right," Abby said with a sigh. "Hair isn't just hair."

"What did people say when they saw you?"

"The women's voices went up an octave, and the men's went down. Plenty of people were less than thrilled."

"I know that one. I've run into that one my whole life."

"I have to admit you do seem like an outlaw."

Carol impaled two weenies on a single toothpick, dunked them in honey mustard, and said, "That's a common misconception I do everything in my power to perpetuate." This was going so well, Carol didn't even care about Mitch and the lawn mower anymore. It was atmosphere. It was perfect.

Fifty yards away, Mitch mowed to the edge of the lawn and even a bit past into the untended field beyond. When she pointed the machine toward the shed, she realized Carol was on a date. Lawn chairs positioned just so, laughter she couldn't hear. She was going to be deep in the doghouse for trespassing. No matter how much Mitch's assessment of the situation would make Carol scream, the truth was that Carol had wooed more women than Mitch. Courtships full of romance but no sex. The opposite of Mitch and Reginald, though this ratio had shifted with distance.

His last email had been flowers and happiness, comparing her to a Weimaraner bitch he'd seen fetching Frisbees at the park, wondering if she liked mushrooms, imagining what she looked like in candlelight. Candlelight? But she'd reread those three short paragraphs until the words ceased introducing an irregularity to the rhythm of her heart. Maybe their courtship was coming after their sex. Maybe Mitch was going to have to compare Reginald to a summer's day.

Mitch had gotten attached to Reginald's notes, which were full of good humor, London life, and the occasional math problem for her to solve. Sometimes she wished he didn't put so much effort and care into them, but she couldn't deny that she looked forward to checking her email in the mornings. He didn't write every day, and she worked hard at avoiding disappointment when there was nothing from him.

She did her best at responding in kind, though she felt acutely her shortcomings in this area. Words were hard enough when describing technical things, but trying to write about how she felt, about her love-hate relationship to his emails, rivaled debugging in required mental gyrations.

She piloted the mower into the shed and cut the engine. The quiet was deafening, the stillness such a shock that it dislodged a tantalizing idea about her software bug. She froze, even holding her breath in the hope that this was the real thing, a fix that would solidify into something she could retain all the way back to the lab.

When she finally stepped down from the mower, she remembered the swimsuit and towel in her duffel. This had to be one of the year's last beautiful days, and the pool was still filled—the way Carol always enabled a final late-season swim warmed Mitch. She had her T-shirt off and her belt unbuckled before she thought of Carol's date. On top of mowing, jumping into the pool right in front of them surely qualified as a bad idea.

Then again, if Carol were mad already…Mitch gave herself a sniff and wrinkled her nose. She was rank from prolonged frustration. A few laps in the pool would wash off the worst of the stink and get her back to the lab and fixing her problem in no time. She'd be a quick distraction. In and out. The rest of her clothes followed her shirt, and she pulled on her suit.

While she walked across the freshly cut, fragrant lawn, she checked out Carol's object of affection. Dr. Rosen, it had to be, and Carol had apparently won her over quite handily despite her nerves. Carol's reserves of charm were, in Mitch's experience, inexhaustible.

Back on the patio, Carol did her best to ignore Mitch's whip-thin, bathing-suit-clad figure strolling along toward the pool in no hurry at all and continued to yammer on about her mother. Fact: get two women together, and they will inevitably start talking about mothers. Except Mitch, of course, who went tomb-silent on the subject. "My mom babysat. Seriously. Once we were old enough to take care of ourselves—at least mostly—she canvassed the neighborhood for gigs. She put so many girls out of business that half my junior high had a fatwa out on her. But the woman was bonkers about kids. Totally nutso."

Mitch was getting closer, and Carol could practically hear the sucking sound of Abby's attention being drawn away. She scrambled to reel Abby back in. Sure, throw a half-naked woman onto the scene and anyone's going to pay attention—whether lesbian or not. But no one ever just noticed and dismissed Mitch. She inspired fascination despite herself, something Carol couldn't claim even if she tried.

Carol said, "Anyway, being the youngest, I always ended up with the shittiest chores. Never anything nice like folding the laundry. It was all scooping cat litter and dragging trash from one place to another. Having to weed the garden with my mom was a relative treat. Something about that smell of dirt and sunshine and maybe even the pleasure of my company"—Carol snorted—"I was a placid child, if you can believe it—would get her waxing poetic about motherhood. 'Carol,' she'd say, 'just you wait.' Then I ran afoul by not waiting long enough."

Carol swirled her refilled glass, jingling the ice cubes, and kept talking like Abby wasn't fixated on Mitch, who'd finally made it to the pool's concrete apron. "Suddenly I was pregnant with James and ruining my life. I tried to point out the hypocrisy of extolling motherhood as an absolute virtue and then stringing me up because I was pursuing it. Of course, I doubt I was so logical. My placid nature had worn off well before my sweet sixteen. And then, according to my mom, my life was over at twenty-three."

"How long did that last?" Abby asked. Mitch dropped her bag and rolled her shoulders a few times.

"Oh, about six months. Until the bundle of joy arrived and she realized my massive mistake had produced her first grandchild—not that she was old enough to be a grandmother."

At the pool's edge, Mitch adjusted her footing, swung her arms, and dove. She surfaced with a cry half-scream and half-whoop.

"Who *is* that?" Abby asked without shifting a molecule of attention from the pool.

"That's Mitch." Carol watched her best friend's smooth, even strokes.

Abby repeated, "Mitch."

Carol could see her doing sociological arithmetic in her head. As much as she had pushed the idea of Dr. Rosen at Mitch, two ounces of thought would have revealed her mistake. When Mitch had reappeared in Carol's life after escaping from then returning to Millerton, Brian had had a field day trying to categorize her every which way—at least until Mitch's daily proximity had made her bleed like red dye into the fabric of their family and she became…just Mitch. Abby was sure to be no different in her urge to see Mitch as specimen.

"Yeah, Mitch. Mitch Mitchell. Dr. Mitchell to strangers only."

"What's her real name?" Abby turned to Carol as if waking from a dream and picked up her drink.

Typical first question. "Legally? Mitch. It must've been something else at one time, but she's been Mitch forever."

"What's the doctor for?"

Mitch executed a flip turn that was identical to the seventy-three billion others she'd probably done in her life, of which Carol had personally witnessed eighty-two thousand. "Engineering. She's a friction expert. Don't get her started."

They both watched her swim, and Carol wished Mitch were someone else entirely, someone less confounding, someone so normal that, to people like Abby, Carol would appear interesting in comparison. Then she remembered that Mitch was Mitch and that she had loved her in a hundred different ways since before they were fully formed. She pushed past her selfish want to have Abby all to herself.

"Mitch sometimes likes to cut my lawn. She shows up a few times a summer, takes the mower for a ride, and does calculus or something in her head. She's always agitated when she starts and back to normal when she's done. In the winter, it's the snowblower."

"And that sound? When she got into the pool?" Abby did something with her hands at the back of her head that might have made sense if she still had hair.

"Our pool's not heated, so it's unbearably cold this late in the year."

"Oh, so why ...?"

"I don't know. Mitch just has to swim, and chronic chlorine deficiency is the only plausible explanation."

Mitch emerged from the pool, and Abby's drink hovered inches below her mouth while she watched Mitch manipulate a towel over her head and shoulders then wrap it around her waist. Mitch's rush was clear in the jerky way she jammed on her shoes, snatched up her bag, and double-timed it away from them to the side of the house.

Even so, Carol yelled, "Mitch!"

"Gotta run, I'll call you later. Thanks for the water."

"Seriously, Mitch. Come here and meet someone. The Device can wait two seconds."

Mitch reversed course and clomped toward them until she was close enough for Carol to see drops of water hanging off the ends of her unruly hair. The knobs on the tops of her shoulders made her look more naked than she actually was.

Carol asked, "Aren't you going to put some pants on?"

"There are twelve stop lights between here and there, and I always miss the two absurdly long ones."

"Maybe you should show up like that, give the guys something to brighten their day."

Mitch laughed and shook water out of her ears. "Honestly, I don't think they'd be able to compute the fact that I don't have a dick." Her hands searched the front of her towel as if for pockets, and she smiled over at Abby with that crooked, half-dimpled, devastating grin that had gotten the better of Carol when they'd met. Sometimes Mitch's mouth and her eyes, which today looked like hole punches of the clear sky, were so compelling it was easy to forget the urge to strap her to a kitchen chair and feed her until a decent amount of flesh wrapped her muscles.

Carol fought through a spasm of reluctance and introduced them. "Dr. Abigail Rosen, Dr. Mitch Mitchell."

Mitch reached out her hand. "Call me Mitch."

"Abby." They shook.

"Welcome to Tilsen. I see Carol's making you feel at home."

"She's a welcoming committee of one."

"That she is. This backyard is Millerton's hidden gem. Some people spend a lifetime in this town and never land an invitation."

"I consider myself lucky."

Mitch nodded. "I hope you do. Nice meeting you, but I've got to run."

Before Carol could think of something memorable to say, Mitch was hauling ass away from them, calling something about The Device and later and sleep. Carol let her go, makeshift skirt snapping across her legs above those shitkicker black shoes she always wore.

Carol jerked a thumb Mitchward. "Now *that's* a fashion statement."

"You could say that." Abby spoke across the rim of her glass.

She appeared disinterested, maybe a little drowsy, and Carol felt the burning need to dance a jig. Abby not caring about Mitch was frankly unbelievable, but she merely swallowed the rest of her drink, smiled at Carol, and surveyed the backyard.

"Does Brian mow the rest of the time?"

Carol gained control over her dropped jaw. "No, never. I do it. It's fun, but James is on me like a tick to get a turn. If it were up to him, he'd be out here cutting it every time it grew an eighth of an inch, but no way is he going to lose a limb on my watch."

Abby shook the last drop of her drink into her mouth.

"Another?" Carol measured the seriousness of Abby's indecision before she said, "Come on, woman. It's Indian summer, for God's sake."

< ≈ >

That night, Carol's concentration was shot. Every time she looked at the book she was supposedly reading, echoes of weenie victory blurred the words. Brian was blathering on in full lecture mode, but his inflection was so familiar it should have been easy to tune out. Clearly, spending the afternoon with Abby had knocked her filter askew because Brian kept snagging her attention.

So jolly and full of himself tonight, Brian would expound on and on even if Carol were replaced by an inflatable doll. He kept appearing from the bathroom in various states of undress, brandishing a dripping toothbrush or swirling blue mouthwash in a glass too foul for words. After fifteen years, Carol's love for Brian cruised along in the slow lane without flash or acceleration. Sometimes it drifted over the rumble strips near the edge of the road and caused a racket in her heart, but usually, with Brian next to her in the driver's seat, his elbow hanging out the window, Carol could enjoy the scenery for miles without even remembering he was there. Then again, there were moments when her attention fixated on something about him, and she felt that this man wasn't even on the same road, that he existed in a way only tangential to her, that they had built this life together and still remained total strangers.

Tonight, the same distraction that made the page fuzzy and Brian demand her attention also made Carol see the change in how the elastic of his pale-blue pajama pants gripped his hips. A new softness had appeared in the flesh there—not extra weight but a certain *give* to his skin.

In knee-jerk response, she commanded, "Flex. Show me some sugar."

"Flex? What am I, twenty?" He folded his glasses and put them on his nightstand.

"Obviously not, but don't you want me to keep fooling myself?"

"Now that's what any man loves to hear from his wife."

"Your ego's big enough without my padding it."

Brian put his hands on his hips. "Well, as you know—"

Carol finished, "A well-formed ego is a prerequisite for success." He laughed at her insubordination instead of souring. She said, "I may not have been your best student, but I sure paid attention. Are you going to flex, or am I going to have to fail you in the art of husbandry?"

Despite her insistence on this, Carol didn't know if it was sex she was angling for or something less visceral. With sex, they had both mastered the art of skipping over partially true excuses not to—annoyances from the day, tiredness, an ennui of desire—and just getting on with it. The sex occasionally left something to be desired, but it always beat a poke in the eye, and in the breathy afterwards, rumble strips exercised, Carol could easily suspect that fucking was the best thing about their marriage.

He flashed a neatly rounded bicep. "I think you misunderstand the meaning of husbandry." He gave her both guns at once.

She supplied polite applause. "It involves fornication, right?"

"In part." His pecs came next, but he wasn't successful at bouncing them.

"In large part, I believe. Do the stomach thing." She tossed her book on the nightstand's towering pile.

"You're sparky tonight." He rolled his stomach.

"I'm sparky every night. Sometimes I don't show it, and sometimes you don't notice." But he was noticing tonight. His growing erection was poking at the fly of his pajamas. She crawled across the bed and held his hips. "You're such a stud, mister. How old are you, anyway? This is totally the boner of a twenty-year-old."

Even as Brian's age waxed and waned before her eyes, what was hardest to grasp was his urge to fuck her. She couldn't push her suspicions from her mind any longer, but maybe she was wrong this time and the signs she'd read didn't actually point to what she thought. Maybe his hard-on was for her and not some horny first-year grad student in love with his words, his puppy dog brown eyes, and his still-tight ass.

Her husband's belly slid up against hers. Anyone could make a mistake.

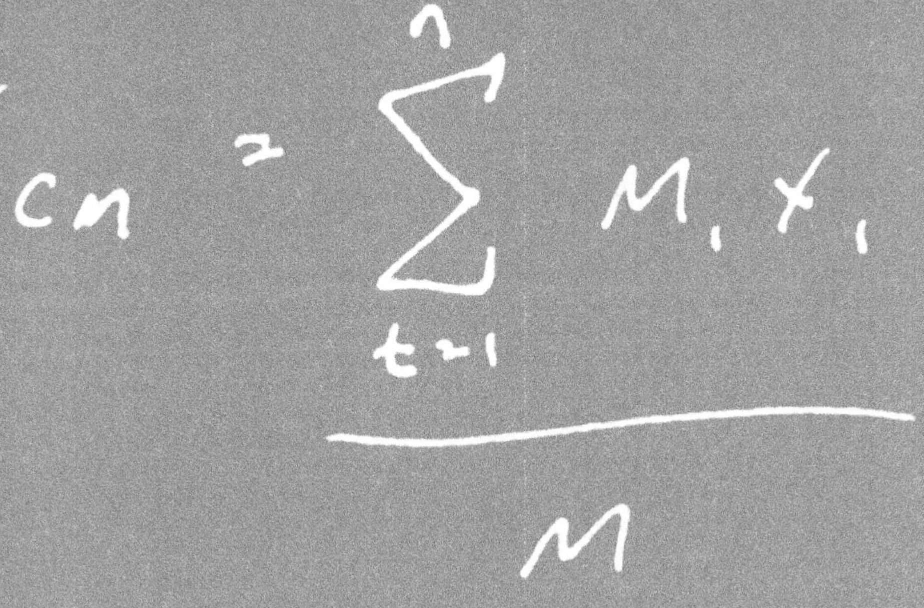

WHILE IDEALISM IS REQUIRED TO INITIATE THE SLOG toward change, without a healthy dose of realism about human nature and the types of societies we've constructed around ourselves, any progress is doomed.

—Dr. Abigail Rosen, *The F Word: Femininity in the New Century*

6

CAROL HAD imagined that starting graduate school would be akin to a major life event like losing her virginity, finding her first gray hair, or finally learning to cha-cha. But frankly, not much changed. She didn't move from her ant-infested apartment two blocks from the social science building, and her roommates, Grace and Dan, were still in a relationship that always struck Carol as having incestuous overtones. They were both short and a bit stocky, had stick-straight hair and faces round as pie plates; they always blew Carol out of the water in Scrabble; and they had a laid-back manner that screamed pothead even though only Grace smoked, and she only smoked with Carol.

Grace and Carol had been no-secrets-barred best friends since their junior year—broken hearts and broken nails and everything in between. Carol had overheard Grace achieve orgasm with three different willowy, effeminate guys before Dan, and Grace had stayed up late with Carol for a week quizzing her on GRE vocabulary words. If they weren't both squeamish, their blood-sisterhood would be literal.

Then, in the depths of Carol's first grad school winter, she met Sasha Ivanov, junior biology major, premed, captain of the softball and lacrosse teams—an intense but charming leviathan with short and messy blond hair, blue-green eyes, and thick, enviable lashes. She trailed a string of moony girls and admiring boys, and the way she brimmed with sexy butchness got Carol on the hot-pursuit bandwagon.

Grace laughed at the idea of the two of them together, compared Sasha to a lithe jungle cat and Carol to something more like a weasel or a mole, but that didn't stop Carol from getting herself in Sasha's way at every opportunity and hoping for the best. At first, Carol lusted after Sasha's legs and the wattage of her smile, but the more she accidentally-on-purpose ran into Sasha on the quad, in front of the life sciences building, in the lobby of the gym, the more she noticed how easily Sasha's laugh interrupted her intense focus or how she had a plan not only for the rest of the day but also for the rest of the semester.

Carol went from daydreaming about Sasha naked and in various appealing positions to Sasha naked and in various appealing positions while asking Carol about her thoughts on gender bias in education. To Grace and Dan's obvious relief, the opposites-attract thing was reciprocal for once—or Carol's status as an older woman was more potent than anticipated—because by Groundhog Day, Carol had caressed every inch of Sasha's legendary body and learned her feelings about animal testing in medicine (conflicted), original sin (um, no), and pistachio ice cream (the best kind of green food, hands down). Still, that body. Those muscular legs and strong hands were one thing, but when Carol first saw Sasha's breasts, her throat closed up at their soft femininity against the broad, strong chest they rode on.

Despite this, Carol's girlfriend managed to infuse more than sexiness into the apartment. Sasha came bearing stacks of textbooks and the desire to study. She came with an easy abstinence from controlled substances, whether inhaled or swallowed, and she came with her foot planted firmly on the gas pedal of conscientious improvement.

Her radiant vitality acted like fluoride in the city water: absorbing it every day affected Carol from the inside out, but instead of stronger enamel and fewer cavities, she felt an assertion
of will, though one still lacking direction.

In May, when the lease at the ant palace was up, Carol and
the Bobbsey Twins moved into a big, clean apartment on the far
fringe of the student ghetto, where they could look out at the
neighbors and feel like they weren't even in school. Everyone
stayed in town to work that summer except for the week in July
when Grace and Dan went to Vegas to blow off steam and came
back having gotten hitched. Apparently, they did it out of sheer
idiocy, high from a good run at the blackjack table. They wore
cheap gold bands and an annoying air of wisdom, and they predicted, based on how much time Sasha spent at their place, that
she and Carol would be next for the altar.

Secretly, Carol sometimes wanted them to be right. Sasha
was quality mate material in many obvious ways—good-looking, smart, driven—but something more subtle about her threatened to undo Carol: Sasha paid attention.

On one in a string of indistinguishable evenings, Sasha sat
at Carol's desk and studied. She wore her usual sweatpants and
Tilsen T-shirt and hunched into a pool of light from the desk
lamp's hot bulb. Behind her, Carol lounged on the bed with a
stack of index cards she was supposed to wrestle into order for
a paper due the next day, but she took frequent breaks to smoke
or bother Grace or let her gaze trace the lines of Sasha's neck
and back.

She broke the studious quiet. "We're our own little microcosm."

After a minute, Sasha turned around as completely as she
could without moving the rickety wood chair. "Isn't 'little microcosm' redundant?"

"Stickler. What I mean is that between the two of us, we've
got a bunch of the melting pot covered."

"Two white chicks, check." Sasha licked her finger and made a tick mark in the air.

"Sure, but we're doing each other, remember?"

"As if I could forget." She stamped her feet like she was on the softball bench, cheering for a teammate at the plate.

"*Anyway*, we've got England and Ireland and Mother Russia. A Catholic family cut short at three kids—the last one a runt—and a couple of agnostics lucky their sole offspring has shoulders big enough to carry all immigrant hopes and dreams—"

"I'm not quite what they bargained for."

"Well, no. Who could dream up anything as fantastic as you?" Carol fanned herself with the index cards.

Sasha put a hand to her cheek, closed her eyes, and smiled. Then she turned serious. "I love our differences, too."

Their differences weren't the only things Sasha claimed to love. They'd been tight with the L-word for six of their nine months together. In part to stop second-guessing Sasha's interest, Carol started applying herself, quit skipping classes, tried for As instead of Bs, and avoided TV like the hard drug it was. Sasha insisted her love was unconditional, but Carol had overheard enough phone conversations between Sasha and her parents up in Cleveland to know where success fell on their spectrum of values. Besides, who wanted to rely on unconditionality, anyway? But the truth was that whatever abilities Carol had were buried under layers of freckles, sexpot ambitions, and the ever-present urge to enjoy herself.

After Grace and Dan had become cosmically one, Carol found herself turning to Sasha with questions of best-friendular wisdom. With Grace, Carol had achieved a certain lack of inhibition due to accumulated past embarrassments, a state she thankfully wasn't close to approaching with Sasha, which meant that as much as she wanted to, she couldn't come out and ask Sasha things like, "Do you think it's a sign that I'm halfway through my master's degree and still don't know what I'm doing?" To find out answers to these unaskable questions, Carol relied on an oblique approach combined with interviewing tactics she'd learned in Soc 201.

Interview tactic one: start with something the subject knows well.

At the end of a preseason lacrosse game where they had smeared Case Western, Carol stood by the Tilsen bench and asked, "So, Sasha. Were you always competitive, or did your parents instill that in you?"

"Instill?" Sasha continued untying the triple knots on her cleats. She was a force on the field, and Carol loved it when she left an opposing player in her wake, sprawled out on the ground with her pleated skirt flung up over her stomach.

"You know what I mean. Nature versus nurture."

"Are you asking if I was born this way?" Sasha's grin was wide and wicked, and Carol gave her a shove that didn't budge her. "Actually, it took a while for my parents to steer me into a more productive direction than trying to steamroll everyone in sight."

"What direction?" Carol gave a finger wave to Betsy Townsend, Tilsen's goalie. Betsy flipped her the bird, proof positive that she still held a grudge over Carol being with Sasha.

"Now I just try to steamroll myself." Sasha chucked her socks and shoes in her bag and zipped it up. "Being that way is more useful and makes it easier to retain a sweet disposition and stay attractive to the ladies."

Carol cleared her throat dramatically.

"I mean, stay attractive to you." Sasha slipped on her flip-flops then picked up her bag and stick, took Carol's hand, and started walking. "Why do you ask?"

"I don't know if I have it in me to try and beat people out for academic jobs."

Sasha stopped them and laid a hot, sweaty kiss on Carol. "I love that about you. You don't have to beat people, but you can try things that are uncomfortable and hard and not let yourself off the hook."

Carol thought about that. She'd always been curious about people and families and communities, enough so that both her parents and siblings had been known to ban her use of the word "why." She'd thought that curiosity was enough. And it was, if all she wanted to do was be a mediocre social worker or research assistant, but knowing Sasha made her think about more.

Interview tactic two: use hypotheticals.

Carol poked her head into the steamy bathroom. Sasha had been in there for so long Carol couldn't even see the goldfish shower curtain from the door. She went in and sat on the closed toilet seat. "Hypothetical question."

Sasha peeked out from behind the curtain. A halo of shampoo suds obscured her cheeks and chin. "Do you think I need a shave?"

"This is serious."

"I thought it was hypothetical."

"I'd say 'fuck you,' but I don't say that to my girlfriends."

"What's the question?"

"*Hypothetically*…do you think interest is more important than aptitude?"

"Depends, right? I mean, who's going to encourage a dwarf to take up the high jump? But in your entirely hypothetical case, my coaches always say that you'll never know until you really try, and they're right. Go for it. Find a mentor. What about that new guy Grace is in a lather over?"

Grace considered Professor Hollister to be a dreamboat. She claimed to be reconsidering her marriage due to his supposedly deep eyes and mouthwatering ass, but the man laughed in a barky, nervous way, couldn't match a tie to a shirt, and pointed with rude abandon. Despite that, consensus was he had a way with words and an attention to teaching that rivaled Sasha's commitment to counting all of Carol's freckles.

Carol usually made an art out of procrastination, but before she'd even run out of excuses, she found herself walking back and forth in front of Professor Hollister's partly open door, summoning the courage to knock. Wasn't being here instead of…*anywhere* else already a triumph of maturity? Did she actually have to talk to the man?

Sasha swam into Carol's imagination, arms crossed and foot tapping in a pose she'd never actually take, but before Carol knew what she was doing, her knuckles had found wood.

"Yes, come in." Professor Hollister's voice was neither high nor low, soft nor loud, and it conveyed the same offhand confidence that oozed from Sasha even in her sleep. Carol had come to the right place. She pushed the door fully open and walked inside.

He was sitting at his desk, chunky glasses slipped down his nose, wearing a pale-yellow striped shirt with a royal-blue tie bearing an orange paisley pattern. The combination was so hideous she wished it had rendered her blind so she wouldn't have to keep seeing it. She focused on his much more pleasant face, like Sasha had coached her, and stepped closer.

"Professor Hollister? Hi. I'm Carol. Carol Mulroney. You don't know me, which is probably fortunate for both of us, but I just started my second year as a grad student."

He stood up, enough of an interruption for Carol to find the brakes on her mouth. "Carol." He stretched a hand across his desk. "What can I do for you?"

His hand was warm and a little moist, and he didn't treat Carol's fingers like they were either glass or overcooked noodles. They sat across from each other.

"I'm not sure, really. What you can do. But I usually don't let that stop me."

He looked at her crookedly, a look so familiar and universal that Carol knew exactly what it meant.

"I mean. Well, what I really mean is that I haven't been a very..." She tilted her head back and forth while she tried to find an accurate word that wouldn't send him running. "I haven't been a very dedicated student so far, but I want to be better. I want to do better, but I don't really know what that means."

He leaned back and crossed an ankle over the opposite knee, affording Carol a good look at gray pants that just made the whole shirt-tie disaster worse. She tried not to hold it against him, which wasn't easy.

"Let me tell you something, Carol. Any teacher given the choice between a student who might not be at the top of the class but *tries* and a slacker genius will always choose the first one."

Carol wasn't sure what kind of compliment that was, but it wasn't one she was eager to hear again.

He untangled his legs and planted his elbows on his desk. "You really want to be better?"

She was flooded with second thoughts but nodded.

"Then here's what we'll do." He laid out a plan for the rest of the semester of biweekly meetings and twenty-page papers, and Carol couldn't believe she agreed to it all. He wrote it up and made her sign it, and when she took ballpoint to paper, she wished Sasha were there. That small thought catapulted her past this meeting and the donut she was sure to have in queasy celebration and through the next eight months to the day when Sasha would power across the graduation stage and out of Carol's greedy grasp.

Being with Sasha kept Carol's future poised to fold back onto the present at the slightest provocation. Just that afternoon, when Sasha had come in from class for a pregame nap, she'd passed Carol on the couch and smacked a wordless kiss on the top of Carol's head. In an instant, Carol was transported twenty years into the future. Sasha would be a heart surgeon, of course a heart surgeon, always a heart surgeon since receiving her first doctor's kit at age six. Well, a surgeon and MVP of her hospital's softball team. And Carol, the Carol this Sasha came home to, would be a scholar and an author and would spend those long hospital evenings of Sasha's sitting at her imposing oak desk surrounded by piles of notes and reference tomes and writing her third—or maybe fourth—book, expertly dissecting trends and gray areas with insight, wit, and compassion. Heart-surgeon Sasha, tired from the operating room and not wanting to interrupt Carol's thoughts, would limit herself to a kiss on Carol's cheek before hitting the shower, and the love Carol would feel from that kiss and its attendant consideration and respect, that fusion of intellectual and emotional passion, would burn with the heat of a thousand suns.

< ≈ >

One late October afternoon, Carol stood in the kitchen with a beer and watched Sasha jog to the wooden back steps and pound up them. When she swung through the door, a deep-pink flush was heavy on her high forehead and cheeks, and she was so drenched with sweat it looked like she'd been dunked into the pond the school used for biodiversity studies.

Right off, Sasha asked, "How was your meeting with Professor Dreamy?"

"Professor Downer is more like it." Carol made a foghorn out of her beer bottle. "How was practice?"

"Brutal. It has no business being this hot." Sasha took one of the slew of mason jars from the cabinet next to the avocado-green fridge and filled it from the tap. She gulped it dry then squared up to Carol. "Why downer?"

"Oh, I don't know. He's so critical, and I totally want to discount him. But then I had a walk and a smoke and looked at my stuff again, and the bastard's right! It's total drivel, and he's actually being kind by not coming out and saying so." Carol toed a peeling corner of linoleum. "Studying competition was a stupid idea. I should look at something remotely familiar. Like underachieving. I'm probably a complete waste of his time. He'd probably rather be bonking a freshman."

Sasha wiped her face with the wet bottom hem of her shirt, which moved the sweat around more than anything. She filled the jar again, leaned back against the farmhouse sink, and took a swallow. "You know, you make me feel stupid."

"Me? What for? You're the one going to med school next year."

"I feel stupid because I can't understand why you think you're such a loser."

"See?" Carol waved her arms, which launched a spray of amber from her bottle. "See?"

"See, what?"

Carol shrugged.

"Anyway, it sounds like Dreamy or Downer or whoever is giving you a challenge, and it's the uncomfortable and hard kind you wanted."

"*You* said uncomfortable and hard, not me."

"You can do it, Carol. This guy might turn out to be the best thing to happen to you at this place. Besides me, of course." Sasha put the half-drunk mason jar on the counter, crossed the kitchen in two steps, and dragged Carol, struggling theatrically, down the hall to the bathroom, threatening to make her wash those hard-to-reach places.

Carol woke at noon the Wednesday before Christmas and wondered how long it would feel good to have the apartment to herself. She'd tried to get Sasha, Grace, and Dan to revolt against family festivities and stay in Millerton with her, but they didn't seem to mind going home as much as Carol did. Ever since she'd succumbed to Sasha's idea of internal competition, she'd been avoiding her parents and the outdated version of her they held on to, but to get out of Christmas, she'd had to tell them about her meetings with Hollister, the mountain of extra work, and this last session with him before the holidays.

Maybe Carol had actually hoped no one else would stay in Millerton. This way, she could reconcile herself to mediocrity without Sasha's relentless encouragement or Grace's easy acceptance. While there'd been progress with Hollister, it had amounted to less than the thunderous sign of the right path. The thought that she would want to mourn her future without Sasha's warm neck to cry in was probably delusional, but wasn't she supposed to be growing up, already?

The apartment's distance from campus had become a liability in early December, when the temperature dropped and never recovered. Millerton was emptied out by the holiday exodus, and on campus, no more than a dozen people hurried through the snowy quad. The elevator wheezed its way to the fifth floor then opened up on a hallway horror-movie dark but for a splash of light from Hollister's open door. She could hear The Beatles' "Yellow Submarine" and Hollister singing along off-tune.

He sat at his desk and tapped his dreaded red felt-tip pen with every beat. Instead of his regular shirt and tie, he wore a green-and-yellow striped rugby top and jeans. An air of sloppy relaxation in him made Carol wonder why he didn't have anything better to do this afternoon than meet with her.

She knocked on the open door. "Don't give up your day job."

Hollister jerked back and clutched his pen to his chest. His eyes were wide, and the pen drew a jagged line of red on the yellow stripe under his collarbone. Carol apologized her way into the warm office, not that it mattered much what she said. Once she'd stopped trying to appear serious in these meetings, Hollister just acted like he didn't hear half of what came out of her mouth.

As usual, he started with a synopsis of her paper, the writing of which had thrown Carol into an unbearable bundle of self-doubt. "In this essay, I understand that you attempted to find trends and correlations in the way different ethnic groups in central Ohio use organized activities to foster competition in their children. First–" Hollister kept on talking, but he'd lost her when he'd used the word "attempted."

He flipped through the paper, which hosted markedly fewer red slashes than usual, but that had to be because he'd given up on her. He talked on and on, and Carol looked at the books on his shelves or the holes in her jeans instead of listening. She preferred to wait to swallow his criticism until Sasha's spoonful of sugar was close by, and so Hollister's positive tone took a while to register. When it did, Carol chanced a look at his face and saw his smile. She burst out laughing. Hollister jumped again, which threw her directly into a full conniption fit.

Only after long minutes and a concerted effort did Carol finally get herself under control. Hollister's face was red, and his lips were clamped between his teeth, but after a moment, he kept talking as if nothing had happened.

"This is what you need to do more of, Carol. What you've built in this paper is a vehicle for your interest, and you did it with constraint and focus. If you can continue to apply rigor like this not only to your research and analysis but to the very task of identifying your thesis, you have the potential to be successful."

Hollister's words were so foreign that his face became unrecognizable, and his dreaminess was revealed in a strong jaw with insistent stubble, warm brown eyes behind his glasses, and hairs on his wrist that curled up over the black leather band of his watch. Carol's sexuality wasn't ambiguous, like Dan sometimes said. Or at least it didn't feel ambiguous. At times like these, it felt like a switch with no off position. She usually knew how to ride things out until her gonads extinguished themselves, but the look in Hollister's eyes triggered a commotion behind Carol's rib cage. She was on a first-name basis with that look. That look was all over campus. The only thing between that look and fornication was the littlest "yes."

Her mouth went dry, and some vital organ Sasha could probably identify dropped between her legs. *Don't be stupid*, she managed to think. "Hollister—"

"Call me Brian," he said and interrupted both her sentence and her resolve.

< ≈ >

Sleeping with a woman gave Carol a passing relationship with her period. She didn't have to monitor her body's every ebb and flow, and a feeling it had been more weeks than usual merited little more than a happy shrug. But one morning in February, Carol consulted a calendar and realized it was eight weeks since her last period and that her itty bitty freckled titties, as Sasha called them, had been tender too long even for the most extended PMS. Considering that the week between Christmas and New Year's had been a haze of extreme student-faculty goodwill, a shrug about her body's tardiness was nowhere to be found.

When everyone was out for a couple hours, Carol ran to the drugstore, bought a home pregnancy test, and hurried back to the apartment, discarding the box in a trash can on the way. She propped herself up against the blue bathroom sink and smoked a cigarette while she read every word of the test's instructions—even the side in Spanish, which strained her meager vocabulary. She burned the accordion-folded paper and flushed the charred remains down the toilet. Out of distractions, she peed on the stick and waited for the bold plus sign the instructions had led her to expect.

The plus sign appeared, and Carol locked herself in her room and propped the test up on a thick textbook Sasha had left behind that morning. Pregnant, it said, and by her hips and family history, spontaneous abortion was probably not in the cards. While panic clambered around in her and obliterated all thought, she sat still and contemplated the pee stick. She sat until her ass fell asleep and then even longer, afraid that any movement would dislodge the impossible truth and make it real. She knew with a twist in her occupied gut that a trip to that family-planning clinic east of town was out of the question, not even with Grace, not even if blubbering and desperation convinced Sasha to go with her.

When Sasha came into her mind's shifty eye, things slid quickly from terrible to unbearable. The thought of having to come clean and see hurt and anger distort Sasha's wide Slavic features was at least as bad as the idea of blowing up like a balloon and giving birth. In fact, it sent Carol jumping up from her numb ass so she could get her hands on every breakable thing in the room.

Later, when the back door banged, followed quickly by the dull clink of one mason jar against another and the kitchen faucet squeaking on, everything in Carol's room aside from the textbook shrine and its positive load was as disturbed as her mind. She sat on the floor and listened to Sasha through the walls, feral as a stray.

"Best girl?" Sasha called.

"Light of my loins?" She was in the living room now.

"Flash?" Right outside the door.

In the pan, Carol thought, but her lips were gummed together. She heard grumbling then the simultaneous rattle of the handle and a shoulder bang against the wood hard enough to shake loose a flurry of paint chips.

"Carol? Are you in there?"

Carol scraped together some composure before answering. "You need to go away."

"Hey, what's wrong? Let me in."

"I said, you should go away."

"Carol, what is it? I'm not going anywhere."

"Sasha." Keeping her voice under control robbed it of its volume. "I need you to leave."

After a long pause, Sasha said, "I don't understand. Did I do something wrong?"

Carol screamed, "Fuck fuck fuck! Just leave, Sasha. Get out!" Still nothing from the hallway. "For Christ's sake, leave me alone!" A shuffle and a sniffle, then receding footsteps. The slam of the back door broke Carol. Her life was over.

She had barely stopped crying before she had to go through the whole routine again with Grace and Dan, only they couldn't be run off. Through the thin walls and the gaps around the door, Carol heard them talking.

"Do you think she and Sasha had a fight? Or broke up?" That was Grace.

"They were fine this morning, cornflake frenching and everything."

"I'll bet you liked that."

Dan said nothing.

"Do you think it's something with her family? Things haven't been right between her and her mom since Christmas."

"Maybe it's PMS."

"You're such a dick."

"Well, sometimes it means you lock yourself in the bathroom."

"Jesus, Dan."

"What?"

Later, Carol tried not to listen to their side of a conversation with Sasha. They talked about breaking down the door but eventually shut up and went to sleep. Carol came out to the quiet living room in the wee hours and watched thick flakes of snow fall with what looked like greater than normal speed, as if they were heavier than regular snowflakes, as if they were little bits of herself plummeting from a height she'd only recently attained.

Then she finally thought of Brian, as she'd indeed started calling him by the end of their tryst. In the new semester, they'd peeled apart with a mutual lack of discussion, not resuming mentoring or even hallway acknowledgment. When she had twirled from Brian's arms into Sasha's—the two of them taking Carol to bed twelve hours (and three showers) apart—the first few minutes with Sasha had burned with involuntary comparison. But by the second hour of their getting horizontally reacquainted, Carol knew who was who and what was what, so when Sasha asked her about that last session with Hollister, Carol could tell her about the breakthrough and nothing else. Sasha worried about the end of the mentoring, but Carol insisted she had a start, the man was busy, and everything would be fine.

Maybe everything would.

Late the next afternoon, when Carol was alone again in the apartment, she bundled herself in a set of Sasha's discarded sweat clothes and stuffed the pee stick in a drooping, fuzzy pocket. She jogged to campus in the gathering winter darkness then up the four flights of stairs to Brian's office, where he sat at his desk with his mismatched tie and red felt-tip poised. Carol skidded to a halt and tried to assimilate this familiar image with the others she'd more recently accumulated. He was playful and shockingly sexy and could talk about research methodology while sitting naked and unshaven in bed. He had enticed her back for ten days in a row, during which they'd wolfed down Honey Nut Cheerios at midnight and had a lot of sex she hadn't expected to be so good.

Carol stepped past the threshold and closed the door behind her. His pen remained frozen in the air. "I'm knocked up," she said.

Brian dropped his pen and pushed back from his desk as if the miracle had happened right there, which maybe it had.

"What? What do you mean? Are you sure? Are you sure it's mine?"

"For the past year, I've been exclusive with the captain of the women's lacrosse team. She's butch, but not that butch." Carol realized she was being unfair, and Brian's ashen face cautioned her not to be a dumbass.

She shut up and watched him stagger around the office and look anywhere but at her. When he settled against the dusty windowsill and set his shoulders in a take-charge way, Carol knew she couldn't let him take charge. Decisions had come to her in the night, and she had to get him to go along with them. She started to talk, nerves forcing out the words in an irrepressible stream.

"I know that you've got fourteen years on me, all of them really important nonchildhood ones, but I feel I'm in a better position to think clearly about this, considering how long I've already been freaking out. I can't get an abortion." She blurted this last part. "Believe me, I know that isn't what you want to hear. Me neither, but there it is. I'm going to have this baby and get hormonal and even wackier than I am now. It's not going to be pretty. I mean, really, I'm going to have baby up to here"—she motioned across her neck—"and ankles as big as my head and a bunch of other ailments you surely never wanted to experience, even secondhand. I mean, those freckles on my belly are going to become life-sized constellations."

Carol wished to God she could tone it down. She had watched Brian make gestures of intent to break into her flow of words, but she had been effective at shutting him out. His face wasn't warm and attentive and had none of the serious affection of their work together. Fear rose like bile, and she said what she had come here to say but never thought she actually would.

"Brian, will you marry me?"

"What?"

"Now, wait. Before you get mature and logical, you have to know, I have to say, this isn't crazy, all right? We might not know each other in the traditional nonbiblical sense, but listen to me. We've spent some time together. With our brains. You must know by now how I think and that I *try*, and I know that you're honest and kind and helpful as hell. Sure it's your job and all, but you seem to like being around me, and you make me feel…anyway, before you even start to think about it, there are some things you should consider."

She held up her hand and ticked these things off on her fingers.

"I'm young. This kid probably won't completely ruin my body. I'm relatively intelligent. I wouldn't be an embarrassment at a party with the dean or the provost. I'm tidy. I really like a clean house, and one of my roommates is a guy so the whole toilet seat is a nonissue. And my mom is nutty about kids and only a three-hour drive away. I think you'd be a good and patient father, which, God knows, this kid will need with me as a mother."

Carol's one wish was that she could see Brian's face, but the thick dark hair on the top of his lowered head blocked the sight. He really did have nice hair. She imagined for one sinking, useless moment that Sasha was the kid's father and that this was a conversation about love's strength and not its potential for existence. She could always read Sasha's face, even when she couldn't see it.

Time stretched, and the cacophony of fear and determination and sickening shame inside her gave way to a gut-rumbling, shaking hysteria that wandered her body like a Freudian womb. She clamped her lips shut but could feel her nostrils quiver at this effort of containment.

When Brian looked up, the blankness of his face let loose her laughter.

She laughed so long and so hard that she had to find escape from the deafening interior of Brian's office. The door gave her trouble, but once she was past it, she ran through the hallway and down the stairs then landed on her back in the quad and shrieked with laughter into the cold air, eyes watering and abdomen cramping. Perhaps a hilarity-induced miscarriage would end this all. The image of Brian stuck to his windowsill in rejection of her felt a little like salvation, but peeing in her pants did not. She tried, between peals, to remember what breathing felt like.

When she found control, her cheeks and stomach ached, and Brian stood in the shadow of the building's doorway. She looked up through her plumed breath and the soft campus light at stars still so brightly sharp and numerous they appeared fake. If she stopped to think about the future she'd imagined—Sasha in her scrubs and those books she was going to write—she would cease to function in this nightmarish present. This plan of Hollister domestication was probably as stupid as the decisions that had gotten her to this point, but it was the only plan she had.

He walked across the quad to her. She wiped her eyes and got up on one elbow to greet him.

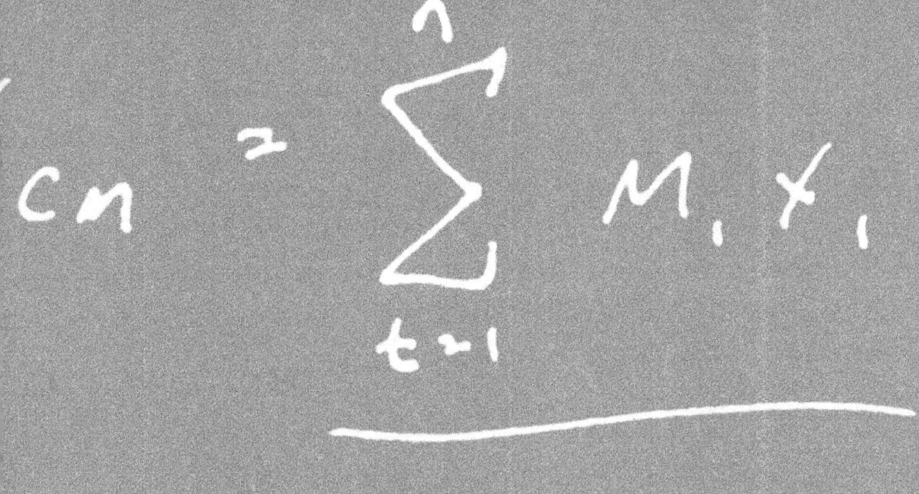

IN OUR CONNECTED WORLD, WE ARE BOMBARDED BY prepackaged judgments and values. Freedom from them requires not only a desire to be free but a change in thinking equivalent to being retroactively raised by wolves. Which, of course, would leave one conditioned to think a certain way about wolves.

—Dr. Abigail Rosen, *The F Word: Femininity in the New Century*

$$\frac{w(R^3 - r^3)}{(z^2 - r^3)\sin(a)}$$

7

BETWEEN Reginald's dinner and bedtime, he'd begun to write short notes to Mitch that arrived in her inbox in the meat of the afternoon. They were usually welcome interruptions, but this afternoon's email gnawed at Mitch during her walk across campus to Tilsen's machine shop, located in the basement of the engineering building. She usually savored the time alone and the cool tendrils of air sneaking down the back of her neck, tried to deconstruct the dead-leaf smell of fall, but the text of his email refused to give way.

I'm afraid I might have forgotten your voice, not its pitch and those stunning vowels of yours, but the exact amount of gravel in it. Somewhere between one and two packs a day, though you've supposedly never had the pleasure of a fag. I remember it really rumbling when I had you close in the middle of the night, but that could be the romantic in me. Or the lack of sleep in you. I keep trying to picture you at fourteen being smart and sassy in your husky voice. I'd give a lot to hear you again, though that might make our current setup even more intolerable. Still, maybe we'll speak soon.

In the meantime, attached is a little something from my commute home.

The picture was of a tangled, rain-soaked intersection ringed with gray stone and neon, an absolutely foreign landscape—at least until Mitch descended into the machine shop, which was shades of silver with odd splashes of color and made the photo resonate and the loose ends of her life snap together.

The air down here was heavy with a metal tang peppered with scents of oil and wood and Old Spice cologne. To Mitch, the smell and the shop's cool atmosphere—not much warmer than the chilly November outside—was the perfect complement to its drone of compressors, the sharp squeals of drill presses or band saws, or the beeping of a forklift in reverse. The machines, some bigger than Mitch's kitchen, had strips of yellow-and-black caution tape decorating the floor around them in square-cornered polygons, and their operators wore safety glasses and orange ear protectors. Although the workspaces were swept clean, every crevice and corner was grimy with sawdust, metal shavings, and dirt trapped in machining oil.

The shop worked on projects for Tilsen students, cutting forms from aluminum sheets or blocks, rendering plastic models via 3-D printer, or running computer schematics through its laser cutter to create pieces too time-consuming or intricate to craft by hand, and Sam Weisenberg's position as a Tilsen insider and Mitch's business partner let her sneak in a few pieces to be machined at a reduced cost.

In the grubby shop office, she pushed Reginald's email aside to focus on her new chassis design displayed on a smudged monitor squatting on a too-small desk. Gary, who had been the shop foreman since before even Mitch's time, manipulated the model, his hand engulfing the mouse.

He sighed. "Mitch, come on. Haven't you learned anything?"

She laughed and leaned over his shoulder. "What'd I do now?"

When he rubbed his cheek with his free hand, the silvery gray stubble made a metallic rasp. "Total disregard of the KISS principle. Is this even structurally sound?" The silky looks he gave the monitor undermined his gruff tone.

Gary had taught her the Keep It Simple, Stupid principle when she was twenty, and she'd been an avid adherent ever since. If Occam's razor were a foundation of inquiry, how bad could it be to apply it to design? Yet, through the years, she'd also learned that sometimes a little complexity was called for.

She said, "There's one more file there. You'll like it. All straight lines and right angles."

"You should respect your elders."

"I completely respect your need for an occasional challenge."

"Your challenges are the cause of too many of these gray hairs," he said to her diffuse reflection in the monitor.

"I'll pick you up some Just for Men next time I'm at the drugstore."

"You're lucky I like you."

He *did* like her, always had, as far as she could tell. The other female engineering majors used to bitch and moan about coming down here, but Mitch had felt at home in this noise and grit, knew what of the machinist's banter to take seriously and what to ignore. A certain kind of joking jocularity colored so many of her professional relationships, and she knew that wrapping her always serious intent in that lightness was an important element of her success with these guys—and many others. Somehow, the more she showed she didn't take herself seriously, the more seriously she was taken.

Today, feeling this comfort made her unable to ignore her discomfort from Reginald's email. Sure, she wanted to hear his voice and his own stunning vowels, but where could they go from there? He made it sound easy, but anything other than emails, and kiss the KISS principle good-bye.

She and Gary confirmed materials and tolerances and timing and then she lingered, talking about carbon fiber layups, aluminum alloys, and predictions for a snowy winter. This office felt removed yet familiar, and she was reluctant to leave.

When a phone call interrupted their camaraderie, Mitch shook his hand then headed slowly back across the quad, cutting over the grass and the scattered fallen leaves, listening to their crackle under her shoes. Back at the office, Steve was saying, "That's just pandemonium. Pure and utter pandemonium." Early in the morning, the guys had declared "pandemonium" to be the word of the day, and they'd been throwing it around incessantly with predictable results.

"Look it up." Eric moved around his desk to the back side. He wore a dark-green T-shirt depicting a hookah-shaped bong with the word "oHIo" written on its bulbous base.

"Look *what* up?" Mitch asked.

Steve said, "Nothing. He doesn't know what he's talking about."

"Whatever," Eric said. He crouched under his desk, probably to adjust one of the thousand-odd cables and cords down there. In the process, he exposed a not insignificant amount of ass crack, and Steve hurried behind him, carrying a tape measure.

With a silent flourish, he extended the tape and eyeballed it against Eric's backside. "Four-and-a-half inches," he shouted. "Plus or minus a hair."

"What?" A bang sounded from the underside of Eric's desk, followed by a mutter. "Pandemonium." He crawled out and rubbed his head. "What?"

"That was four-and-a-half inches of pure, unadorned plumber's crack. A new lab record, right?" Steve asked Mitch.

"We'll have to check the spreadsheet, but that's up there." She sat down at her desk.

Eric hauled his jeans up as far as they went, almost to the barrel of his chest. "There, you guys happy?"

"Dude." Steve snapped the metal tape in and out of its casing. "That's just…"

"Pandemonium," Mitch said, which caused a cascade of laughter.

Steve and Eric had regressed to making obscene gestures with extended tape measures when a kid in a sharp gray suit stepped through the glass door and looked twice at the wrinkled piece of paper he held. "Um, hey. Is this Mitchell Industries?"

Steve whirled around. "Sure is." He and Eric stared at the stranger.

The kid cleared his throat. "I'm looking for Dr. Mitchell?"

The guys hooted. "*Dr.* Mitchell!"

Not until Mitch heard that name and looked at the closest clock did she realize who this kid was: Sam's nephew. Sam had cajoled her into hiring a contractor to fix up the controller code that had given her fits a few weeks back. After she agreed, he casually mentioned that he had the just-right candidate.

"He's good," Sam repeated like a tic until Mitch laughed and promised an interview.

"That's me," Mitch said over Steve and Eric. "Come on over and have a seat. Guys, this is Ryan. He might be helping us with the controller code."

Steve said, "Ah, finally someone to get the wife in line." He called this program "the wife" since, in his words, it was not only bossy but had once been thin and was now bloated and a little ugly.

Ryan slumped into the empty chair next to Mitch's desk then almost immediately sat up straight. "Did you find the place okay?" she asked.

"Oh, sure." But then he ducked his head and looked down at his hands, one of which clutched the wadded paper.

"Don't worry, no one expects this office, but it keeps costs down."

Eric said, "In other words, she's so fiscally responsible it's like Scrooge come to life."

"I'm pretty sure you have something to do," Mitch said. She watched him give Steve a complicated handshake and go back to his desk.

She spent the next half hour grilling Ryan on aspects of the existing code she knew needed work, mostly around handling and reporting errors and other self-monitoring tasks. Talking with him made Mitch agree with Sam that this work wasn't the best use of her time, but delegating things she enjoyed doing so she could do things she didn't enjoy—like writing grant proposals or responding to requests for information—was becoming all too common.

The more questions Mitch asked, the more animated Ryan got. He shifted back and forth in his seat, jiggled his knee, and finally hovered a couple inches over his chair. "What I mean is…" His fingers flexed in the air. "If you, well, can I just show you?" He leaned toward her computer.

She asked, "Did Professor Weisenberg tell you the terms of the position?"

"Um, no. He said that was up to you."

"It'll be a part-time contract, and I plan on getting you cheap because you're still a student. Are you interested?"

He blinked a few times, then a few times more. "You mean I'm hired?"

Steve busted out laughing, and Eric said, "Don't be so flattered. We're not all that pandemonium."

"He means we're not that great," Mitch said.

Ryan said, "But, no, that's not what Uncle Sam says."

"Uncle Sam?" Steve asked in a squeal.

"Hey, guys. Zip it," Mitch said.

The kid leaned in and whispered, "Seriously. The way he talked, I was afraid to even come here."

She sat back and tried to hide a smile. "If that means you're interested, you can make your own hours, but I'm not kidding about taking you for a ride on salary. There's a firm deadline for the project, and I'll break it down into four or five milestones so we can keep an eye on progress."

"Where do I sign? I won't let you down, Dr. Mitchell."

"I'll draw up something before the end of the week. Our lawyer will insist on a dozen nondisclosure forms, but for now we can shake on it. And call me Mitch." She put out her hand.

The small hesitation before Ryan shook it was only visible because Mitch was so used to seeing it. Past experience had taught her that people hesitated because they didn't really notice she was a woman until they had to touch her. Encountering someone—either professionally or personally—who was so incredibly tactful or completely immune to her that their reaction was imperceptible was rare. Abby's calm, appraising look by Carol's pool came to mind before Mitch dismissed it out of hand.

She walked with Ryan up the stairs. "I'll be in touch when the paperwork's ready for you. Then we can get our hands dirty."

He took the steps so slowly they were practically standing still. "Dr.— Mitch…Uncle Sam made me expect to be sliced and diced at this interview."

"I'm satisfied you can do the job."

"You don't understand." He stopped and turned back toward her. "The way he talks, everyone in the family is either crazy jealous or wants to kill you. Or both."

Mitch jerked a little in surprise. "Well, don't tell the guys that."

"I ruined it with them, didn't I? With letting it out that I'm the nephew and all?"

"Ryan." Mitch got them moving again. "They'll have a field day with you no matter what." She opened the door to the alley and held out her hand. "We'll talk soon."

This time Ryan shook it eagerly then left Mitch leaning against the door, half inside and half out in the heavy early darkness. This small pause in her day and the ashy light of the alley felt both delicious and somehow dangerous, and Mitch was relieved when the office door opened downstairs and Eric shouted, "Oh, Dr. Mitchell. Phone call. Muy importante."

"Carol?" Mitch asked and headed back down.

"That woman's on fire."

"Don't you have a girlfriend?"

"Yeah, yeah." Eric held the door open for Mitch.

"How'd you ever convince her to date you?" She thought that maybe Eric cleaned up nicely, but she'd never had an opportunity to confirm her theory.

"I was the one who needed convincing. It was pure pandemonium, baby."

"I'll bet. I've seen her, you know." Mitch settled into her chair.

Eric pulled up his jeans with one hand and pointed at Mitch with the other. "Hey, don't go working your voodoo dyke magic on her."

Mitch picked up the phone at her desk. "Do I have voodoo dyke magic?" she asked Carol.

"You're still a dyke?"

Steve snorted, and Mitch saw that he was listening in on his extension. To Eric, she said, "According to Carol, I'm steeped in the stuff."

Steve laughed louder.

Mitch looked at Steve. "If you know what's good for you, you'll hang up that phone. The fridge needs to be cleaned out, and I think you're just the man for the job." Steve slammed down the receiver. "What's up?" she asked Carol.

"You know, if you're reconsidering the lesbian thing, you could do a lot worse than Steve," Carol said. Gordon's sing-song voice was loud in the background.

"Carol, seriously."

"We both know Kim's moved on. For once you should take a cue from her."

Mitch's sigh pushed Steve and Eric back into the lab. "I really don't want to talk about this. Besides, I *have* moved on," she said before she knew what she was saying.

"Oh, yeah? In what way?"

"I'm…forget it. I said I didn't want to talk about it."

"Fine. That wasn't why I was calling, anyway. Come over for dinner. Please?"

"Gordon driving you crazy?"

"And then some. Besides, I thought an ambush invitation might get you out from under your rock."

"I'm not under a rock."

"Right, you've moved on. Don't argue, just come."

"Okay." Mitch checked her watch and her computer. "I'll be there at 5:32, 5:36 if I miss those lights."

"Roger wilco, Mitchy-poo."

Mitch hung up and took her coat from the back of her chair. "I'm heading out. Call if you need anything."

Steve appeared in the doorway to the lab. "Eric and I have been talking, and we agree."

"Is this about Ryan?"

He made a dismissive noise. "Hell, no. He's going to be fun. We agree with Carol."

Mitch closed her eyes and groaned.

"Now that Kim's gone, there's a distinct lack of hot women popping in and out of here. You need to get out there again."

She shoved her arms through her jacket sleeves. "Who's to say I wouldn't bring a man around next time?"

Steve grinned smugly.

Mitch said, "Besides, when's the last time *you* contributed to the girl situation?"

Eric whistled in appreciation.

Carol sat at the kitchen table, the phone rocking on its back between her and Gordo. She had to make it through another twenty minutes with him. Not even doing homework could stop Gordo from talking. He was completing an assignment on ancient Egypt, yet he rambled on, examining the relative merits of spaghetti versus various short pastas. Carol felt like strapping his mouth with duct tape.

Not ten minutes before, Brian had called for the second time in as many weeks with a vague excuse for missing dinner. The thought of spending the evening alone with the boys and conjecturing about what—or whom—Brian was doing was unbearable. Thank God for Mitch's calm quiet and level head.

They were a comfort, though her refusal to pass judgment only made Carol see more clearly the countless ways she deserved to be judged.

Twelve minutes more, maybe sixteen. Gordo dissected the sauce-catching capacity of rotini. Mitch had had a way with the boys from the very beginning. Before Gordo could even wrap his pudgy fingers around a Lincoln Log, Mitch sprawled out with them on the floor and overengineered with whatever tools were at their disposal: Froebel blocks, Legos, Erector Sets, and, on one memorable occasion, every toilet paper roll in the house and most of a giant bag of balloons. Mitch was designer and project manager and Gordo and James her willing workforce.

Several years before, Carol had been in the kitchen, as always, when she'd overheard a conversation between Mitch and the boys. They were erecting a scale-model limestone quarry on the living room floor using Legos and leftover materials from the flagstone patio in back when Gordo asked, "Mitch? Are you a boy or a girl?"

James said, "She's a girl, stupid face. That's why we call her 'she.'"

Mitch said, "Hey, what's this 'stupid face' business? No one who asks an honest question is stupid, and only stupid people think they know everything. Which would you rather be?"

James was conspicuously silent, and Carol laughed into her arm.

"That's what I thought."

Gordo said, "But is he right? Are you really a girl?"

"What do you think? In science, we observe then conclude." There was a pause. "What I mean is, based on what you see and hear, tell me what you think." Another pause. "Okay, just, well, tell me something you know about me for a fact."

"Your name is Mitch!" Gordo shouted.

"That's right."

"You like to swim!" he shouted again.

James said, "You're good at math and stuff."

"I do like math," Mitch said.

"Yesss!" James said then added, "You're skinny, and you have pretty hair."

"But she doesn't dress like a girl," Gordo said.

"She's friends with Mom."

"She doesn't have a husband."

Mitch raised her voice. "Okay, okay. I think that's enough."

"But which are you?" Gordo's wail rattled the dishes in the cabinets.

"Listen, I'm going to tell you guys something. All that stuff you're talking about, the math and the hair and the name, they aren't boy things and girl things. They're person things. You can be a girl named Mitch or a boy with pretty hair who hates math. You can be any kind of person you want, okay? You don't have to confine yourself to those kinds of expectations, and whatever anyone else tells you is bullshit."

Carol heard nothing more for long seconds.

"That means you're a girl, right?" Gordo asked.

Mitch heaved a sigh. "Yes, I'm a girl, Gordon."

"I told you she was a girl, stupid face."

Witnessing Mitch love the boys made it even easier for Carol to love her. Sometimes, when Mitch came for dinner and propped herself up in a corner of the kitchen to eat carrot sticks or grape tomatoes or almonds, Carol imagined being married to her.

"Hidey ho," Mitch called from the front door.

Gordo threw down his chewed pencil and scampered from his chair. Carol could hear him talking a blue streak in the hall. "Did you know that ancient Egyptians mummified their cats sometimes? And they wrote without paper? They used triangle-shaped sticks and clay. *Styluses* and clay." His words got louder again when he arrived back in the kitchen, orbiting Mitch. "And they were smart and knew that the Nile would flood every year."

"Gordo," Carol repeated with increasing volume until he stopped talking. "Sit down and finish your homework. Then we can make dinner."

He slumped in his chair. "That means you're going to hog her, and she never comes over. She's my friend, too."

Mitch said, "Hey, bud, how's this? Your mom gets me before dinner, then you get me for at least, um, thirty-seven minutes after we eat and clean up. Deal?"

"Well ... okay. Deal."

"Shake?"

"Shake." They shook with solemnity then Carol and Mitch retired to the living room. Carol curled up in a corner of the overstuffed couch and watched Mitch consider and reject the empty cushion next to her before kicking back in the recliner.

Gordon's low mumbling drifted in from the kitchen, riding on the thumping bass of James's music upstairs. A deep quiet settled between Carol and Mitch. Carol usually found something to fill such gaps, but now that Mitch was here, she didn't feel like talking.

Mitch stretched, exposing a slice of pale skin between undershirt and jeans. "I gather James is upstairs."

"Making himself deaf."

"When's Brian due home?"

"Late."

"Late? What's he doing?"

Carol allowed herself no hesitation when she said, "Dinner with Joe, he claims." It had felt easy to say until Mitch's thin eyebrows pulled down and she met Carol's gaze fiercely.

"He claims?"

Carol looked away. Telling Mitch about Brian was a given, but sometimes Carol wished it weren't. When Brian got fast and loose with his fidelity every couple years, she always went running to Mitch, and while she felt more resigned every time, Mitch's fury continued unabated, a wild anger so out of character. Like now. She was staring at a point on the ceiling, her mouth clamped so tight her lips were white. Maybe she was trying not to bother Carol, but who wouldn't be bothered by something it took such effort to hold in?

"Bastard," Mitch whispered. She huffed out some breath then sat next to Carol on the couch and put her hand on Carol's arm. "I'm sorry. Eric knows someone who knows someone who breaks kneecaps."

Carol slid away and moved to the recliner. "I had coffee with Abby Rosen last week. This time, I managed to stop babbling long enough for her to get a word in edgewise. You know, she won't talk about her book. She dances around and changes the subject, and the next thing you know, you're off again on power struggles in the PTA. Anyway, this time I at least got her to tell me about earning her degrees and working her way up."

In the kitchen, Gordon sang something about the Nile and the pyramids.

"It made me think of grad school. Fuck, you know when you're a kid, everything's about the future. Everything you're going to do and how you're going to be this whole new breed of adult. You were never the starry-eyed type, so maybe you don't know. But, believe me, one day I was drunk on all that and the next…" She shrugged.

"Sometimes you do what you have to, and there's no getting around it." Mitch sat forward on the couch, elbows on her knees, her face turned toward Carol.

"That doesn't mean anything. It's not like 'have to' is this immutable thing. Life isn't engineering. It's all multiple solutions."

"I know that. I was just—"

"—trying to make me feel better. I know."

"Brian's in the wrong, not you."

Carol ran her fingers up and down the recliner's microfiber arm. "You think I'm not in the wrong?"

"Not in this, no." Mitch's hands hung limply between her legs, and she looked at the carpet and shook her head. "Will you come and sit over here?" She indicated the cushion next to her. "Please?"

"You don't get it."

"What? What don't I get?"

"Anything that's not black and white." Mitch frowned, and Carol rubbed her forehead, hard. "I didn't mean it like that. I just mean that it's complicated, and it's not like I don't have a hand in what happens in this marriage."

"Carol. Are you going to come over here, or do I have to get in that chair with you?"

Instead of answering, Carol got up and walked across the room and back. Gordo wasn't singing anymore, which meant he was listening to this conversation.

She sat on the coffee table, leaned close to Mitch, and whispered. "I roped him into marrying me, and that puts a different spin on things."

"That doesn't justify his actions fifteen years later," Mitch whispered back.

"I'm just saying that it's complicated."

"Complicated, my ass," Mitch said at full volume.

Carol shushed her. "Stop it. Stop trying to make me feel better. I don't want to feel better, Mitch. Feeling better is just naive. I got him to marry me then went and fell in love with him and James, and he never got a say."

"He was a grown man, unlike you. He had plenty of opportunity."

"Listen to me. I'm trying to tell you something. This is all my doing. I got pregnant and married and fell in stupid love—maybe out of sheer panic, who knows. When James was old enough, I could have gone back to school. Brian was fine with that, but I—" Carol looked at the kitchen doorway and listened. Gordo was humming, and she could picture him sitting on the edge of his chair, chest against the table's edge, drawing a sarcophagus.

Mitch took Carol's hands, and Carol let her, liked the feeling of those warm, rough fingers despite herself.

She said, "Sometimes I don't know if I really wanted a second kid or if I was just scared." Mitch's face was too covered in well-meaning to look at directly, and Carol closed her eyes against it. "I just couldn't get myself to go back for my degree after how I'd left. I burned that bridge hard, you know? I didn't have it in me to take classes from all those people who *knew*."

"None of this excuses Brian."

"Well, it doesn't excuse me either. You're the one who always says that nothing's free. Maybe this is the price of my choices."

"You don't deserve this, and that's not how it works."

"That doesn't really matter, now, does it?" Carol opened her eyes to Mitch's face, screwed up tight, and she gave in and sat down next to Mitch, who scooted over so they were jammed together, shoulder to thigh. They sat like that for a long time, listening to Gordo amuse himself in the kitchen.

Mitch took Carol's hand again. "What can I do?"

"Nothing. Just keep the boys busy tonight."

Mitch gave her fingers a squeeze and got up. "Bud. You and me. Dinner."

Carol said, "Mitchy."

Mitch stopped in the doorway. "Yeah?"

"Come around more often."

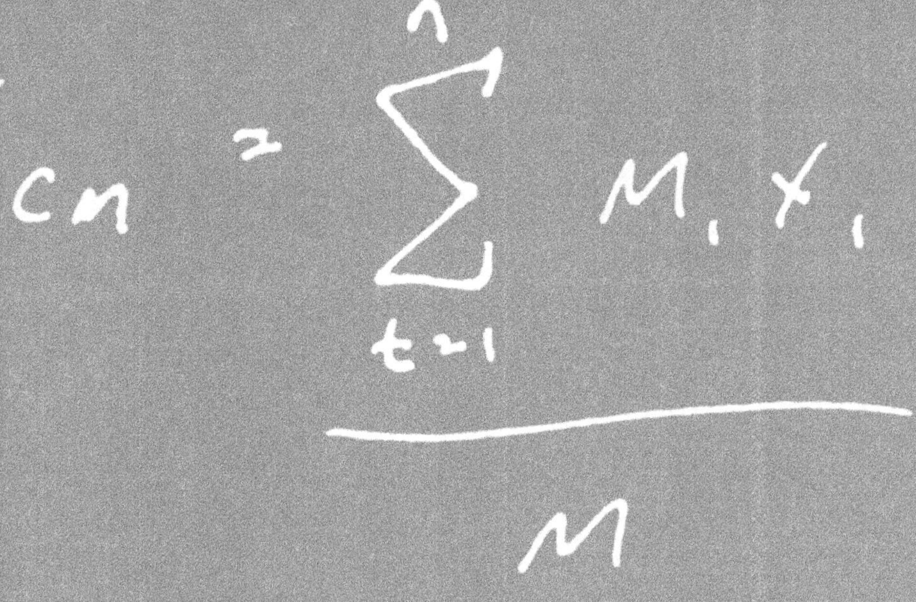

$$c_n^2 \frac{\sum_{t=1}^{n} M_i x_i}{M}$$

IT HAS BEEN PROVEN, TIME AND AGAIN, THAT WE seek out the confines of roles, definitions, and labels within a larger societal construct.

$$\frac{w(R^3 - r^3)}{z^2 - r^2) \, \sin(a)}$$

8

MITCH WENT over to Carol's for dinner, for dessert, or just to watch TV with the boys. When Brian was there, it taxed Mitch not to lay into him. He and Carol pretended like neither knew anything when both knew everything, or maybe he was deluding himself that Carol didn't have him pegged this time.

During these weeks of pretending to be nice while quizzing Gordo on multiplication tables or sipping coffee with a slice of cheesecake in the kitchen, Mitch plotted retribution against Brian, most variations of which revolved around a small collection of novelty items she kept in the bottom drawer of her desk at work—not flowers that squirted water or glasses with an attached nose and mustache but a darker version: lifelike spiders and slugs, a shocking buzzer that delivered a real kick, and various silicone versions of bodily excretions.

She waited to act until the day before Thanksgiving. The guys were so intent on getting their work done so they could leave early that they didn't even look up when Mitch slipped a coiled piece of silicone shit into the pocket of her hooded sweatshirt and jammed a worn Tilsen cap on her head.

The quad was in deep shadow and practically deserted. She passed only two people on her way to Brian's office. Thanksgiving was a short break, and Tilsen insisted on holding on to its students until the very last minute so that, when they were free, everyone scattered like buckshot—the Hollisters included, off to Carol's parents. Mitch had always felt this weekend's exodus as a bleeding out of something vital in her. Even the pool closed for the four days.

She climbed the flight of stone stairs to the entrance of the Ira Thompson Center for the Humanities and let herself in one of the heavy doors. The dark, empty hall yawned in front of her, confirming that this was the perfect time to break and enter—late enough for people to be gone but early enough for the buildings to still be open. Up on the fifth floor near the end of the hall, Mitch knocked softly on Brian's office door before fishing a single key from her pocket.

Inside, she considered lines of sight and turned on various combinations of lights to see where the shadows lay. She stood and squatted and looked at the snapshot on the desk of Carol squinting and laughing in bright sunshine. The shit glistened when she took it from her pocket, and she brushed it frcc of sweatshirt fuzz then settled it into the perfect spot behind the desk—in sight but out of range of all but the most intrepid vacuum. She admired it for a moment then shut the lights and let herself out into the hall, making sure the door locked behind her.

"Hey!"

The voice was loud and reeked of authority. The Tilsen Police. Despite herself, Mitch froze. A shadowy figure moved closer with purposeful steps that made hollow bangs on the linoleum.

"Mind telling me what you're doing?"

Mitch made herself relax, put her hands in her pockets, and leaned back against the wall. Then, in a show of deference, she took off her cap. At the same time, her accuser stopped close enough to an emergency light for Mitch to see that this wasn't the Tilsen Police at all but Dr. Rosen.

"Mitch?" Her voice was strangely shrill and loud. "Hi. Abby Rosen? We met—"

"Yeah, at Carol's. I remember."

Abby stepped closer. She wore a long coat that hung softly in the dim light. "What brings you to campus?"

Maybe because of Mitch's relief at not being busted, or maybe because Abby being here alone so close to Thanksgiving made Mitch feel a sort of kinship, she smiled. "Can you keep a secret?"

"I'm like Fort Knox."

Mitch assessed her. "Oh, all right. But you're in serious trouble if you blab."

She held up the key with a flourish then unlocked Brian's door. After waving Abby through, she gave the hall an unnecessary once-over before shutting them inside. Though the office was roomy, it felt claustrophobic with both of them standing there in the dark.

"Over here," Mitch said and led Abby behind Brian's desk.

The two of them were less than a meter apart in the space between the desk and the credenza behind it. Mitch could smell Abby's perfume, a deep, musky scent, and it hit her like a drink on an empty stomach. Abby really was good-looking, her face open and radiating with it. Mitch was close enough to snake an arm around her waist, and that thought snapped her back to reality.

"There." She pointed to the shadowed corner she'd painstakingly selected. "Can you see it?" Mitch waited then laughed and bent over, picked up the shit, and held it out in front of Abby.

Abby flinched.

Mitch pushed it an inch closer. "This is high quality. You'd be appalled at how expensive this was." Then, after she was sure Abby'd had a good look, she placed it back in the shadows.

Abby said, "Freud would have a field day."

All Mitch could do was shrug.

"Okay, so, why are you putting that in Brian's office?"

The truth was that she was crazy angry and made nervous on top of that by Carol's calm calculations of fault, but she just said, "Oh, he's such a prima donna. All sorts of stupid things scare him, then he walks around and pretends that everything's fine. When I find something I think would be disturbing, I plant it in here."

Abby looked around the office as if she'd never seen it before. "Is Carol in on it?"

"No way. The point is to get Brian worked up. Carol would prompt him, which would let him divulge, which would throw my investment in top-notch novelty items out the window." Abby was still close enough that Mitch, despite the darkness, could see the faint shine of her lipstick. Mitch wondered why she wasn't with family or at least heading in that general direction.

Abby fidgeted with her hair. "You do this to make him suffer?"

"He wouldn't suffer if he weren't such a baby."

"How do you find out about it without Carol?"

"I don't, but I have a good imagination." Mitch smiled and rocked back and forth on her feet a little. This was not how she'd imagined her errand playing out.

"You and Carol are quite a pair. A couple of children." Abby's smile didn't look friendly.

"You underestimate Carol."

"But not you?"

Mitch folded her arms but resisted taking a step back. "I don't pay attention to what people think of me."

Abby raised one perfect dark eyebrow. "What do people think of you?"

So many sociologists tallied and boxed people using subjective measurements, thought a person could be mostly known from a few key indicators, and considered the unknowable rest to be unimportant. Understanding this about Abby would normally make it easy for Mitch to bail on this conversation, but they stood here together on the precipice of the loneliest weekend of the year, and by some transitive property, Abby Rosen brought Carol back within reach.

Still, she couldn't be trusted. "It doesn't matter what people think," Mitch said.

"Of course it matters. Maybe not to you, but in the scheme of things."

"Yeah, well, people think all sorts of unfounded crap."

Abby put a hand on the edge of Brian's desk and leaned forward. "I thought you science types valued precision." She touched Mitch's forearm then jerked away as if shocked. Her eyes flicked to the side then back.

"I'm an engineer, speaking of precision." Mitch felt a hint of her old fury. Abby was poised there like a predator, but something about her short, disheveled hair and the smooth curves of her cheeks undermined Mitch's habitual reticence. She said, "I'm ugly. I'm cold. I'm an unfeeling robot. I hate men. I hate women. I hate myself. I don't love or need or understand people. And I'm a…you get the idea." Mitch immediately regretted letting out that litany. She felt suffocated by it. The piece of silicone shit was no longer funny, and she gave Abby the best evil eye in her arsenal.

Abby just touched her mouth and cheeks then dropped her hand to her side and smiled. "Seems to me like you pay attention. If that's wrong, what's right?"

"I don't think that way."

"What way?"

"Who are you, Columbo?" Mitch said, unable to come up with a better dig.

Abby ducked her head and eased back an inch or two. "Questions are my thing."

Mitch answered despite herself. "Labels are coarse and loaded, and I can't stand them. They're useless for real people, even when I try to apply them to myself."

"Do you consider yourself butch?"

Mitch rolled her eyes. "Does having short hair mean you're not a femme anymore?"

"That's ridiculous."

"It's *all* ridiculous. What good is being a lesbian if you believe the same old stuff?"

"The two have nothing to do with each other. I'm a lesbian because I'm attracted to women."

"Yeah, as long as they wear dresses and makeup, right?"

Abby put her hands in her pockets and studied the pictures on Brian's desk. Then she looked right at Mitch and said, "Mostly. Yes, as a general rule." She brushed past Mitch and slid into Brian's chair. "You know, most people who claim that labels are useless tend to be wedded to the ones they've secretly adopted."

Mitch thought that was probably true, but Abby's assumptions were typical and smug. She turned to leave.

"Where are you going?"

But Mitch didn't feel like answering. She left, strode down that long hall and the stairs to the crisp outside, where she took a shortcut to the lab to drown her bitterness and spoiled fun in the guys and work. Letting Abby Rosen get to her was her own damn fault. Mitch chastised herself into the alley and down the stairs and was grumbling when she gripped the handle of the lab door and pulled.

Her arm nearly came out of its damaged socket when the door didn't budge. Eric and Steve must've staged an uprising, and she didn't blame them. Suddenly she felt like a freak—the very thing people thought of her that was hardest to ignore. She might have refrained from telling Abby this particular judgment, but it had lodged in her mind, regardless.

The most hated weekend of the year had officially begun, and her life looked as ugly and lonely as the person she had described to Abby. Escaping the bits of sticky truth in what people thought was impossible—they tarnished whatever she looked at. All she could see of her truck was the crooked tailgate that latched on only one side. Out Route 56 to her house, the road's emptiness had a menacing quality that dogged her with every mile.

When she pulled into the driveway, her headlights transformed her home into a peeling, spotted hunk of neglect, obliterating its many welcoming traits: the blue door and matching shutters, the towering oak, the wink-and-smile of the roof and windows. Tonight, it felt like the kind of house that knows being caressed with police lights and dressed in caution tape, the kind of house with a history. A past. A dead body or two.

The engine was still running, and she thought about backing the hell out of there and finding a nice quiet field to spend the night by, but she'd be too cold with only the midweight sleeping bag she had in here. Surely she wasn't freak enough to go inside only to grab a blanket or two and leave. She cut the engine.

Inside, she turned on every light in the five rooms, blasting brightness into hidden corners and making Chester skitter from sight in an orange blur. All around her were the possessions she had finally begun accumulating—the large, glass-cased Atmos clock on the mantel and the leather sofa opposite it, the ancient yellow enamel stove that glowed like a sun under the kitchen overhead, and the Technicolor bedspread Kim had particularly liked. These things were evidence of the life she'd made for herself. Maybe it was lonely, but it was hers. This house, the lab—they were proof that her jumbled self amounted to something not only tangible and measurable, but substantial.

She filled the old claw-foot bathtub to capacity then stripped down, turned off the light, and sank into sizzling hot water. The heat loosened her joints except her shoulder, where it magnified the slow throbbing that jerk on the lab's door had set off. Halfway through graduate school, this injury had started as an almost imperceptible pinch in the pull portion of her swim stroke. It had gotten worse each year until, now, the pain was as likely to appear outside the pool as in, which was all the reasoning Mitch needed to keep swimming. Carol had stopped badgering her about it a couple years before, but everyone had to try at least once to convince her to have it looked at, thinking physical pain was the worst thing when it was far from it.

During her first night with Reginald, she'd propped herself up for a better angle of attack and had been unable to suppress a yelp at the pain. He'd initially mistaken it for a sound of pleasure then had laughed at her terse explanation of the injury and meandering justification why she hadn't had it checked out.

"Mitch, you get better every hour," he said, and she scowled at him. "What, hasn't anyone ever told you how delightful contradictions can be?"

To Reginald, Mitch's contradictions and ambiguities were sexy, inescapable fact, but Abby had no room for these differences. The data in sociology represented great aggregations of individuals, and lines were thrown through those forests of points to put the pretense of order to something disorderly by nature. These distributions hosted means, medians, modes, and, Mitch's favorite, oxymoronic standard deviations. When a point fell far off to either side of average, it was barely noticed before being discounted. Abby surely saw it as her job to dig through Mitch's pockets so she could throw loose change and almost-lost buttons on some graph paper and discover a hidden vein of normalcy.

Mitch clambered from the cooling water, begging for a cracked skull or broken leg to go with her ruined shoulder. Her maroon flannel robe stood in for a towel, and she skidded into the hall, frantic until she found her laptop where it tempted fate half off her nightstand. She sat cross-legged in the middle of her bed and started an email to Reginald.

Clearly you're as disturbed as I am. A problem solver by nature who does not see me as a problem to solve. For that I ought to marry you. It seems impossible that we could meet and know each other without exchanging user manuals or at least a tear-out page of high-voltage warnings. Well, let me warn you now. All the things you've managed not to ask me are banging around in my head waiting for a faulty gasket. My mother named me Evelyn. She named me with a fucking vengeance I didn't even see for years. But when she laid her entire inventory of expectations on me—

Mitch stopped. She played with the individual beads of water clinging to her shin then shivered and sighed. Wet, curled ends of hair poked her neck, and the pipes churned out heat.

She pressed and held the delete button until the message was blank. If only self-pity didn't require acknowledging the piteous things in the first place. She longed for company, Carol's chatter or the guys' easy camaraderie. This loneliness could become a problem. Mitch curled on her side next to her humming laptop and, with every light in the house burning, closed her eyes.

< ≈ >

At the office the next day, the phone interrupted Mitch's attempt at finessing a grant application that was due in a week. If only Sam had a nephew who could take *this* off her hands. The phone rang again, and Mitch's annoyance surged before she remembered it was Thanksgiving and no one was around to answer it.

She unearthed it from under a pile of paper. "Mitchell Industries, this is Mitch."

"I was informed that today is some sort of Yank holiday, so when I thought about where you'd be, your office sprang immediately to mind."

During the time it took Reginald to spit out that sentence, Mitch exhausted her anger at his breaking their agreement and moved into a pure, undiluted happiness. "Patty."

"Mitch."

"I thought about you last night."

"Brilliant! It's my evil plan to be on your mind every waking moment. And some sleeping ones as well."

"Your plan is progressing without impedance."

"See? This is rather nice. Why on earth do you want to exclude this from your life?"

Mitch wrapped two loops of the coiled phone cord around her index finger. "Don't talk about that, Patty. I don't want to think about it."

"What would you like to talk about? Your every wish is my command."

On the top shelf of the cabinet in the back of the lab was an industrial glue that came packaged in two adjacent tubes connected by a single plunger and nozzle. Each element of the glue was inert on its own, but when they combined, they formed a bond not to be fucked with. When Reginald's voice mixed with the collection of his emails already lodged in Mitch's mind, her guts cramped. All her worn memories of their now-ancient sex and midnight conversations were eclipsed, and Mitch didn't know the right thing to say. Instead, she said, "Tell me what you're working on."

Reginald sighed. "Do you really not have a romantic bone in your body?"

"Evidently not."

"No flutter of sweet nothings? Mutual assurances of utter fantasticness? Transatlantic sexual doings?"

"You want to have sex with me at the cost of an international phone call?" Mitch tipped her chair back and laughed. "We'd be much better off setting up webcams."

"That's a fantastic idea!"

"Reginald, I'm not going to have virtual sex with you."

"That's okay. I'd much rather have the real thing so I could see your beautiful face during the act."

"Are you trying to get me to hang up on you?" Mitch immediately regretted not only her words but the honed edge to her voice.

"You know, Mitch, thinking you're ugly is one thing, but impugning my taste is something else. For the last time, I don't date ugly women!"

Mitch let the silence spin out before she asked, "We're dating?"

"Damn it!" he roared. "You're so far under my skin, I'd need a transfusion to be free."

The way Reginald surfaced in her thoughts over spreadsheets of data, during a Saturday-morning swim, or while unloading hot clothes from the dryer, Mitch had to admit to him that his predicament was mutual. In their subsequent breathy quiet, she wondered about last night's aborted email and who she trusted less, Reginald or herself.

He said, "Come to London. You'd like it here."

Mitch leaned forward and put her head in her hand. "Be serious."

"I'm utterly serious. How much vacation time do you have?"

"I've never taken a vacation, so a lot, I guess."

"Great. You're coming here for Christmas and New Year's and the whole next week."

"Reginald—"

"Don't start, Mitch. Don't even start with work and the guys and Carol. Don't say anything unless it's about me."

For most of the last decade, Christmas had meant the Hollisters. It meant shopping for parts in supplier catalogs to build something for the boys. It meant setting her alarm for an ungodly hour so she could creep into Carol's kitchen to make thick French toast and a pile of eggs then a pound of bacon and coffee to wake everyone up. And, of course, it meant a morning of torn wrapping paper, bows pasted to foreheads, and general good cheer.

The idea of missing that—not to mention abandoning Carol to Brian—made sweat spring up between her shoulder blades. How could she not think of it? But she didn't know how to quantify Hollister comfort and joy in order to measure it against this growing desire to see Reginald's face and feel the width of his hands with hers.

Calculated risks she could do, but this went beyond the realm of pros and cons, error bars and projections. The fact was that rational decision-making seemed to be impossible around Reginald, and when Mitch combined that observation with the memory of deleting last night's email, she sat up straight and said, "Okay. I'll come."

"Did you just say 'okay?' Unconditional and everything?"

"Yes."

"And I don't even have to bribe you with the ticket I already bought?"

"I want to see you so much, I'm not even mad about that."

Reginald was quiet. Then, "I feel it's only fair to tell you that I'm very much in love with you."

Mitch's sweat spread to her upper lip and lower back, and the phone creaked in her grip. She pictured Reginald in his silly novelty boxers and thought of how he seemed incapable of lying to her—not even by omission. But this, this was too much. She pulled at her shirt to let in cool air. When she wiped at the sweat on her face, she realized her cheeks hurt from smiling.

The rumble of Reginald clearing his throat filled Mitch's ear. "Just didn't want you to come all that distance and be surprised by the size and scope of my crush."

His tone made her wish she could have responded in the expected way. Reginald's love squeezed her ribs like the last ten meters of a hard hundred-meter fly.

He said, "You drink tea, right? Are you still coming?"

"I don't scare away that easily."

"You know, cohabitation with me is so endlessly delightful you won't want to leave."

"I find that hard to believe, but I'm looking forward to being proven wrong." Mitch played her fingers over the phone's keypad.

"Considering I have a month to plan and lay in supplies—"

"Supplies?"

"You don't stand a chance."

They filled the next several minutes with logistics and inanities. Hanging up wasn't as hard as she'd imagined it would be, maybe because she'd be seeing him in less than a month. The silly grin she knew was on her face resisted her attempts at removal, and she vibrated with energy, unable to concentrate on anything but her own exuberant happiness. This basement could not contain it, and she had her jacket on and was up the stairs in a flash, hurrying toward The Filling Station out of habit before deciding that Angel and coffee were just the thing.

She hummed a tuneless nothing of a song. The sharp, unseasonable cold that had come in the night couldn't penetrate her, and the bright sunshine felt like a personal gift. Her strides brought her to The Station in no time, but when she pulled at the door, it didn't budge, just brought another yelp from her shoulder. Not again. She tried with her other arm then stepped back.

Mitch was slow to consider that The Station might be closed, but when she did, she got up tight to the window, cupped her hands around her eyes, and peered into the darkened interior. Chairs and stools upturned on tables, the coffee-of-the-day board wiped clean, not even a mop bucket in sight. They'd been closed for a while, then.

Mitch checked her watch. Only barely past lunch. Maybe Angel was sick? Then she remembered that it was Thanksgiving and sagged against the locked door. She laughed at the empty street, at the feel of the cold air against her teeth, at nothing in particular. Her laughing was fueled by her own silliness and relief and joy, and it was only starting to taper off when she noticed Abby Rosen standing up the sidewalk, staring at her.

The day's improbability increased dramatically. Not only did Reginald love her, not only had she agreed to fly to London to see him, and not only had she momentarily forgotten this loneliest holiday, but there was Abby Rosen with her nightgown looking like it was caught in the car doors of her jacket. Mitch couldn't imagine a scenario in which Abby would be out in public looking like she did. On one side of her head, her hair swirled around itself, simultaneously matted and spiky. Her eyes blinked behind thick-framed glasses, and she was silent.

Because of the last, Mitch smiled and said, "Happy Thanksgiving."

"Happy Thanksgiving." It came out as a croak.

"Hope you weren't looking for coffee. It seems everyone's closed but me." Mitch couldn't help but wonder what had happened to Abby since yesterday. The descent from proud predator to this was breathtaking.

"Carol was right about your work ethic. It's legendary." Abby's voice was rich with an up-all-night quality.

"I'm sure that wasn't couched in a wholly positive light."

"She's proud of you." She cleared her throat and coughed.

"Yeah, well, sometimes she's proud in public and impatient in private about the exact same thing." But Mitch smiled when she said it.

"Friendship is complicated."

"*Everything* is complicated, but you didn't seem to think that yesterday."

"Yesterday." Abby shrugged and cleared her throat again. "Yesterday, I was—" She dissolved into a coughing fit.

After it had gone on for a while, Mitch put her hand on Abby's back. "Are you okay? Do you need some water or something?"

Abby eventually nodded.

"Come on. The lab's just a few blocks."

Abby walked a half step behind Mitch's right shoulder. After each of her rattling, choking coughs, Mitch chimed in with the time and distance remaining in their journey. Abby seemed even worse off than Mitch usually was on this holiday—resoundingly alone and beat up. Why wasn't she enjoying some turkey and football? Why had she seemingly been up all night, and why was she out wandering in this cold? Mitch said, "One hundred feet."

When they got to the alley, Mitch noticed Abby taking a good look around and saw the windblown litter and flecked paint on the steel door through new eyes. A little seedy. She let them inside, and when the door banged shut behind them, Abby jumped.

At the bottom of the stairs, Mitch waved her into the warmth and light of the office. "Water's over there to the right. If we're out of cups, just drink from the spout. We've all done it." Mitch grinned.

She sat down at her desk and listened to the gurgle of the water cooler. Everything was so strange that she wondered if this intensely good feeling that filled her might become permanent, if she might find some traction with her fingers and be able to hold on to it. In her inbox was an email with the flight information. She felt an irrational desire to shout the news to Abby.

The water cooler gurgled again. When Mitch felt how Abby looked, if she couldn't be alone or swim, she wanted her condition to go completely unnoticed. A small part of Mitch wanted to repay Abby for her questions of the day before with some tit for tat, but her good mood dissolved the urge.

After Abby's third drink, Mitch called out, "We charge after the fifth cup."

"I'm good for it."

"You'd be surprised at the going rate. Now that everyone's allergic to tap, it's like liquid gold."

"Well, it was a lifesaver. Thank you." Abby emerged from the closet and hoofed it across the office. She put a hand on the door before she said, "I can see you're busy, so I'll let myself out."

"I'm not busy. Just killing time." Mitch tipped her chair back. "Don't you want a tour?"

Abby hesitated. "I should probably get back to my walk."

"Your walk."

She didn't move.

"You don't look nearly as awful as you think." In fact, now that some color had returned to her cheeks, she had a certain fragile appeal, looked like a possible ally instead of an adversary.

"That may be the most comforting thing anyone's ever said to me." She pushed the door open a crack but didn't appear as if she really wanted to leave. It was a coy move that usually would have annoyed Mitch, but she let it slide.

"That's not what I meant. Most people in your position wouldn't look half as good."

"Marginally better."

Mitch let her chair fall forward with a bang and leaned across her desk. "Christ, Abby. What do you want from me? You look like you've been through the wringer and might want some company."

Abby studied Mitch for a long time before she let the door close. "I only have five dollars. Will that cover both the water and the tour?"

"I'm sure we can make an arrangement."

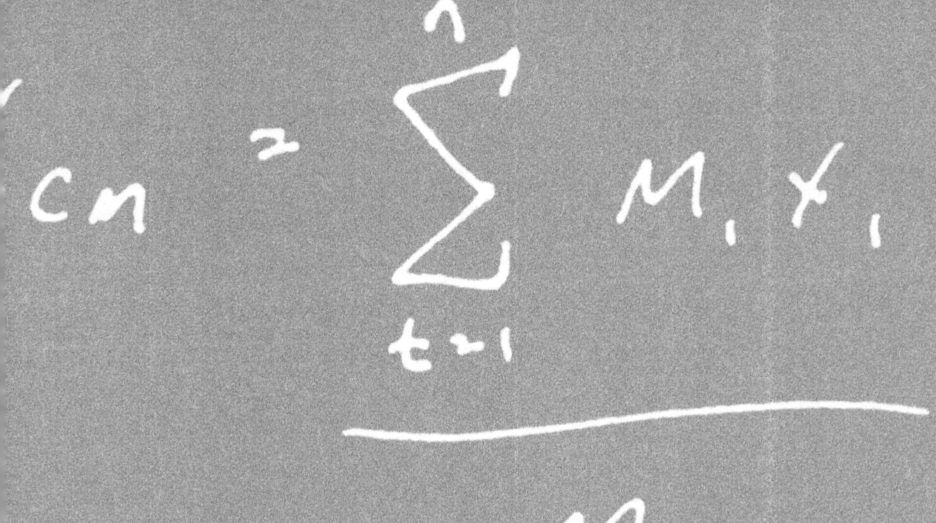

HAVING TO EXPLAIN OURSELVES MAY SOMETIMES feel like an unnecessary burden, but doing so illuminates us not only to others but to ourselves. Lacking an answer to the 'why' behind who we are and what we do is indicative of one thing and one thing only: we are brainwashed.

–Dr. Abigail Rosen, The F Word: Femininity in the New Century

9

CAROL WAS slow to get rid of sweaters she never wore—the once-favorite argyle, that cozy cardigan that was now a hair-and-fuzz magnet, a roll-neck that looked good in the store and nowhere else. While this tendency was a major contributing factor to her chronic lack of drawer space, the deep folds of wool were excellent hiding places. Old love notes from Sasha nestled in the scratchy sleeve of a black turtleneck sweater, a blue angora acted as her piggy bank, and for years, a bulky cable-knit had played host to a two-foot-by-four-foot piece of plotting paper origamied into a small, thick square.

When this paper was unfolded, it revealed a chart riddled with points and lines that sported a large legend in the upper-right corner to decipher it all—a little something Mitch had compiled that tracked Brian through the six months he'd first had his shorts on fire. She called it an "event graph" and had been so scientific about the whole thing that Carol had screamed with laughter, at least until Mitch had left her alone with it.

A green line traced out Brian's mood, a mountain range of ecstatic peaks and miserable troughs that jittered back and forth over the bolded baseline. Most of the jagged shifts corresponded to one or another of the made-up milestones marked by blue diamonds: first kiss, first gift of flowers, first fuck, first fight, first make-up sex. All those firsts when Carol hadn't had one with Brian in longer than she could remember. At least if she didn't count first affair.

Other different-colored lines tracked Brian's weight, his paranoia, and his patience with the grad student's immaturity (low after the fight, high after the make-up sex). Dotted vertical guides delineated the months, and the axis marking his mood ranged from wild euphoria at the top all the way down to existential despair.

Carol was nowhere on this chock-full chart, which was such a massive oversight it had to have been purposeful. All these lines and points excluded Brian's random gifts of cards or saltwater taffy or fresh gnocchi from the Italian place thirty miles away. Nothing indicated family game nights or the afternoon he spent smoking ribs enough for an army or, thankfully, when he crossed the equator of their bed without Carol managing to resist him.

When Carol had first pored over this chart behind the locked bathroom door, her already tenuous grip on rationality loosened, but this artifact had turned out to be rather useful, allowing her to follow these affairs from a certain remove and sidestep the urge to learn more about the girl-women Brian screwed. The first of them, Bonnie Brightman, a bouncy bobbed brunette, had sparked an obsession in Carol, and she couldn't keep from imagining the co-ed's well-behaved, conditioned hair flying when she ran after Professor Hollister to ask one last question, her ample chest heaving in not-really-restrained excitement. Researching Bonnie Brightman uncovered cheerleading squads and high school honors, and Carol envisioned Bonnie's oblique approach, her shocked-yet-titillated reaction to Brian's proposal. By all objective measures, Bonnie Brightman put Carol to shame. Her fashion sense, endless legs, and remarkable grade point average were so threatening, Carol waited for divorce papers that never came.

Over time, the chart's accuracy was verified—big surprise—but it failed miserably in capturing the awful shape of each day. The mornings, especially, which started with the alarm clock set forty-five minutes earlier and the treadmill in the basement thumping and vibrating clear up to the bedroom. Then the long shower and the thick haze of aftershave that rode on its dissipating humidity. But the worst was how he strolled down the stairs, yelling for breakfast requests from two sleepy, grumpy boys. Carol wished she could remain fused to the bed so as not to witness how much he loved James and Gordo when he was fucking around on her.

In every affair, Carol had moments of wondering why she got upset at all. So he was fucking someone else, sampling the tight, twentysomething wares. So what? If he hadn't left her for Bonnie Brightman, he wasn't going to leave. Why couldn't she accept her self-made lot in this marriage, enjoy his extra, guilt-induced family love, and get on with it?

She would try, pull him into deep kisses and hanky-panky for a few nights running, but her resolve never lasted. Even though she had effectively railroaded him into these affairs, she still wanted him all to herself, wanted to sidestep feeling absolutely irredeemable and questioning everything.

The week before Thanksgiving, Brian traipsed around the house, whistling and accenting his many bad jokes with a series of sharp finger snaps. His levity induced a corresponding heaviness in Carol, who wasn't remotely in her acceptance phase of this latest go-around. While he loaded the van for the drive to her parents' house for the holiday, she slipped upstairs, unearthed the chart, and squinted at the legend. There it was, seven weeks into the proceedings, the most dreaded milestone: the co-ed had professed something more than intense admiration, than desire, even than infatuation. She had professed love.

Carol made herself fold the plotting paper along its creases and slide it back into its hiding place with exaggerated care because she very much wanted to rip it to bits or maybe set fire to it and the whole house in the process. Maybe the girl hadn't really said those three little words, but she might as well have.

The drive was exquisite in its discomfort. Carol closed her eyes even before they were fully out of the garage and feigned sleep for the three hours of Brian herding them along like an old chuch while forcefully eliciting conversation from the boys. The distance between the front seats wasn't nearly enough to keep her from feeling his physical existence as a pulsing, sweetly malevolent force.

Pretending to be asleep for three hours was exhausting, and crabby barely scratched the surface of Carol's mood when they arrived. She grumbled then mimed the slow waking that comes after such a long nap. When she opened her eyes, Brian was already out of the van, and her mother was patting him on the arm. Fawning.

Brian opened Carol's door. "Hey, sleepyhead."

She looked past him. "Hi, Mom. Where's Dad?"

"Oh, he's inside tearing his hair out over a new computer game he bought for Gordon."

Brian laughed. "I've seen Herb at the keyboard before, and it's not a pretty sight."

"He's convinced he gives off some kind of energy field that fouls up those machines."

This exchange was giving off an energy field that nauseated Carol.

"Why don't I go help him?" Brian asked. "Before he tears out what little hair he's got left."

"You're bad," Carol's mother said. "But a dear." She gave him a squeeze then practically slapped him on the ass when he turned to jog into the house.

"Hell, Mom, at least play a little hard to get." Carol climbed out of the van and twisted the kinks from her back. She felt ancient.

"Look who woke up on the wrong side of the car," her mom said and laughed.

"Mom, really." Carol's fleece did nothing to temper the late November cold, but she had no desire to follow Brian and the boys inside. She leaned back against the van. "Go on in. I just need some air."

Carol's mother eyed her. No matter how adult Carol might get, which was debatable, her mom maintained certain voodoo powers over her. To escape her gaze, Carol walked around to the back of the van.

"Carol."

"Mary," Carol said to get her mom's goat.

Mary tsked, which was totally satisfying. "There's no law that you have to come here for Thanksgiving."

"Really? Could've fooled me." Carol opened the hatch and surveyed the luggage inside.

"Well, you don't have to come *every* year. Not if it's so distasteful to you."

"For Christ's sake." But Carol was at least a little relieved that Mary's voodoo needed adjusting. "Coming here is fine. Better than fine. I'm thrilled to pieces to be here. Honestly."

Mary's eyes narrowed. "What's going on?"

Carol put the heel of a hand to her forehead then dropped it just as quickly. "Nothing. Really just…nothing. Want to help me with these bags and show the guys how it's done?"

She made herself busy with backpacks and suitcases then, later, with cooking and washing dishes or arguing politics with whomever was in range. She kept herself in motion to hold Brian at bay and outrun thoughts of the girl who had the audacity to think she knew what love was, let alone that she loved Brian.

Through the four dragging days of the holiday weekend, she kept it together, didn't rise to looks from her mother or affectionate touches from her husband. She remained stridently zen, but then, when they at last started their drive home and Brian backed out of the driveway in a sluggish, lazy way, Carol had to clamp her teeth together to keep from screaming.

Once they were down the block, she let herself say, "Take your time, now." She adjusted the vents to catch the miserly heat.

"Thank you. I believe I will." He practically crawled through her parents' subdivision, and Carol wished she'd eaten enough turkey at lunch to induce a coma.

From behind her, James asked, "Can you turn on the radio?" That he used a voice he probably thought was polite and that he'd waited until they were actually in motion to make this request showed atypical restraint. Still, Carol and Brian rolled their eyes at each other with such automatic coordination that it pissed her off to no end.

"Let's play a game instead," Brian said.

James and Carol groaned, though Carol at least swallowed hers into silence.

Gordo cheered. "Twenty questions. Can I start? I have a good one."

Brian swung onto the highway and accelerated barely up to Sunday cruising speed. "Gordy can start, and James'll be next."

James sighed with such insolence he deserved to be left by the side of the road. "Can we at least have some background music? I mean, if I have to play this stupid game and all?"

Carol snapped on the radio, tuned it to one of James's presets, and adjusted the volume a couple notches too loud. She felt an urge to flip down her visor and find James in the mirror on its underside, but she was afraid to see more than the usual sullen adolescence in his face. The thought of him knowing what was happening between her and Brian was worse than living with her own twisted gut over the last four days.

Carol's love for James had always had an uncomfortable sharpness at its center as if in cosmic retribution for her feelings during pregnancy. She had never expected to love him with such desperation, and she strove to hide that unseemly excess from everyone. This love made the awful teenaged version of James that much harder to swallow and the vast distance he now insisted on maintaining between them unbearable.

She didn't look at James, just turned down the volume and got into the game.

The instant the van pulled into the garage, Brian and the boys emptied out in a chorus of shouted dibs on the downstairs bathroom, but Carol stayed back, dug her keys out from the bottom of her purse, and climbed over the center console and into the driver's seat. She backed out with the whine of high-speed reverse.

With every block that opened up between her and Brian, her lungs eased. She drove for a while with no destination in mind, turning left or right at random in a doomed effort to get lost, the tightness inside her loosening while the odometer clicked over. When she could consider rehashing the weekend—or at least deflecting related questions—she picked up her phone. Mitch sounded happy to meet at The Filling Station for coffee, which enabled Carol to take her first deep breath in days. She parked across two spaces right on Main just because she could and felt almost herself again.

Mitch sat at one of the coveted window tables, sipping from an extra-large mug. The Station served their beverages in a vast constellation of mismatched drinkware, and Angel kept that mug just for Mitch. It depicted a cartoon version of Mitch's elusive cat: dripping wet with milk and sitting over the caption, "A little coffee with this?" Mitch loving that mug did more to confirm her status as a cat person than the very fact that she owned a cat. Carol waved, and Mitch grinned.

The only other customers were a young couple completely engrossed in each other, their legs entwined under the table. A bored, pierced boy served her. Carol took plenty of time doctoring her coffee with heavy doses of cream and sugar while she savored Mitch's happy-to-see-you smile and prolonged the anticipation of feeling loved from right across the table.

In a sort of Escherlike optical illusion, Mitch always looked thinner after Carol hadn't seen her in a while—her eyes set a shade deeper, the hollows of her cheeks an even greater contrast to her elastic mouth. Worrying about her was easy but useless since change and Mitch weren't well acquainted. Besides, with Mitch's overdeveloped sense of responsibility, anything Carol could think of to worry about had already been monumentally handled.

A wayward lock of Mitch's hair tempted Carol into tugging on it before she sat down. "What's the news?" she asked.

"Did you know this place is closed on Thanksgiving?" Only Mitch's raised eyebrows were visible over the rim of her mug when she tipped it back for a drink.

"Why were you wandering around Main Street on Thanksgiving?"

"I wanted coffee."

"I should have brought you to my parents'."

Mitch brushed that off. "I was fine."

"No, really, I should have brought you to my parents'," Carol said in a voice that was way too serious.

"Not good?"

"So not good it could be a popular country song. But enough of that." Carol watched Mitch's eyes crinkle and saw something like color in her cheeks. She looked less like death than usual. "Got some sleep, huh?"

"Oh yeah. I didn't work Friday. Between Thursday night and Saturday morning, I took two baths and slept twenty-four hours." She put her hands behind her head and leaned back, but the picture of relaxation was marred by a wince. That damn shoulder of hers.

Carol ignored it. "Count yourself lucky. Brian and I were on the living room pullout—full, not queen—and turkey gives the bastard gas. I'm telling you, I was almost overcome. I was tempted to sleep out in the van."

"That's funny, the night before Thanksgiving, I almost—"

"Actually, with the third row folded away, it'd be pretty nice in there. Not that Mom would let me live it down if she caught me, no matter how noxious the prodigal son's farts."

"The prodigal son?" Mitch leaned forward on her elbows.

"Brian was busy charming the pants off my mom. I swear, you and Abby are the only people with tits who are immune to him."

"Yeah, speaking of Abby, when I was looking for coffee on Thanksgiving—"

"I took a page from her and went on walks like you evidently took baths. That woman is a walking fool. Sorry, you were
saying something?"

Mitch buried her gaze in her mug. "I'm not going to be able
to make it for Christmas."

"What?" The three other people in the shop looked over in
reaction to Carol's shrillness.

"Or New Year's."

"What fucking conference happens over the holidays like
that?" Carol tempered her voice enough so only the counter guy
kept staring.

"It's not a conference."

"What, some deadline? Am I not going to see you until
March? You can't spare even a day for the boys?"

"Listen. Don't. Come on, Carol. Don't you think I want to
see you guys?"

Carol was slam out of benefit of the doubt, which Mitch
should've known, so she just folded her arms and sat back to
wait for an explanation.

Mitch shifted around and looked outside, and her mouth
lost its hard edge. "I'm taking a vacation, okay?"

"Good one. What's really going on?" The smile fell right off
Mitch's face. Sometimes Carol wished Mitch had the decency
to disguise the worst of her emotions because the pinch of hurt
in her features made Carol feel like a jerk. But, hell, what did
Mitch have to be upset about? She wasn't the one with the jack-
ass husband and unbearable kids and a future that was nothing
but more of the same. And now she was taking a vacation when
Carol really needed her, when she supposedly wanted to help.

But no one liked being the cause of disappointment, so Carol said, "You're not kidding? I'm sorry. I am. But...so where are
you going?"

"London."

"London? What's in London?"

"Lots of things. Big Ben, double-decker buses, Notre Dame,
pubs with bad English food. I don't even know." The way Mitch

dragged her mug back and forth across the table and the grating tone of her voice made it clear she didn't want to talk about it.

Carol didn't care. "Notre Dame is in Paris."

"Whatever. I'm going for two weeks, and I'll bring back something delightful for everyone. A replica of the Rosetta Stone or something royal."

They stared at each other.

"Who is it?" Carol asked.

"Who is what?"

"Who's in London? Some mystery woman?"

Mitch's blush was ferocious. The only other time Carol had seen her redden like that was when her college roommate had walked in on them. Whatever Mitch was hiding was serious. Anger at being not only abandoned but deceived by her rock of a best friend stampeded Carol and flew right out of her miserable mouth.

"I can't believe you're lying to me. How could you lie to me? We don't lie to each other." Carol watched Mitch's frown curl down to her chin. What a fucking disaster. "How long has this been going on? What am I asking—probably years for you to do this. What else aren't you telling me?"

"Hey! What's wrong with you?"

Mitch didn't reach out and touch Carol's hand, didn't see through the flimsy excuse of that outburst to how much Carol needed her. Without stopping for the smallest thought, Carol said, "It's been a long time since you were really a friend."

There went Mitch's face again, even her witchy nose participating. "Is that what you really think?"

"Yeah, that's what I really think. You and your device. You're just the same. Cold and hard and bound to fail."

Once the words were out, Carol would have given anything to reel them back in. Mitch's fingers whitened around her mug before she lurched to her feet, mug jerking up along with her, coffee splashing from it across the table and trailing her in spattering drips when she ran outside. She strode back and forth on the sidewalk before stopping and hurling the mug against the wall to the side of where Carol sat. Then, clutching her shoulder, she walked away with short, stiff steps.

Carol burst into tears. It felt like her whole body participated. She expected to find her sleeves wet, the legs of her jeans drenched. The Station bystanders were certainly having a show, but she was as incapable of stopping as Mitch was of love. The untruth of that last bit blurred her eyes even more but at least got her staggering to the exit.

She felt short of breath, faint, leaned against The Station's window until she finally noticed people noticing her, which prodded her into a run to the van then past it, wanting literally anything but to be the bereft middle-aged woman crying in her car, probably over a two-timing husband. The few blocks to Turning Leaves went by in a lumbering, ever deepening embarrassment.

Once inside the store, she sank down under the rattling chimes, never so happy to be here. Waves of nausea came and went under her tears, and she was sure they would never stop. When they did, she wasn't quite ready for the hiccupping stillness and faint shame at being sprawled out on the floor of her workplace. Her breath came wetly through her stuffed nose, and her eyes, under the probing tips of her fingers, were tender and swollen.

Her lungs felt as junked up as her nose, and Carol wanted very much to avoid thinking about how much of that was Mitch and how much wasn't. She went to the bathroom to clean up—keeping the lights out so her wrecked face was nothing more than a head-shaped blur—then blew her nose into a growing mound of tissues until she could breathe normally again.

Carol and Mitch fought, but not often, and it was always so disconcerting and uncomfortable that it never lasted long. Given what Carol had just said, she should march herself to Mitch's office and grovel right through Mitch's mad, but by the way she was prowling the store, looking for work to do, she wasn't going to be the bigger person this time.

Why didn't Mitch know that Carol didn't always want to pry out information, didn't relish having to make Mitch uncomfortable to get at emotional truth? Didn't she know that Carol would normally be overjoyed to see Mitch flush with happiness—even though it meant Carol would have to share, even if it were the worst time to have to share?

No, she wasn't going to be the bigger person this time. At least not right away. At least not for a while. Instead, she dusted the fiction shelves and replaced the receipt tape in the register. She swept up the break room and straightened the piles of books on the remainders table. Then she called Abby Rosen. Why not? Odds were against Abby answering, let alone being available and willing to keep Carol company.

But Abby answered and wasn't busy. Abby was happy to come see Carol at Turning Leaves. Abby, in fact, would be there as soon as she found her shoes and walked over.

Carol hung up and succumbed to a mortified stillness until Abby knocked "A Shave and a Haircut" on the front door. Carol fantasized about slinking into the back and not answering, but she bucked up and let Abby and the harsh outside light into the gloom.

She didn't even look at Abby after she flipped the lock and went to lower the already lowered shade, just drifted behind the register and lifted herself onto the stool there. "Maggie's gone until tomorrow night. There are some brownies or something in the break room, but…forget it, they're stale by now. Feel free to browse. Or leave. I don't know why I dragged you out here."

"I'm guessing Thanksgiving wasn't so great." Abby wandered back into the store.

"Thanksgiving was a laugh riot compared to what came after." Carol tried to leave it at that, but no matter how horrified she was at having called Abby, she'd made that call for a reason. "You have no idea. I'm surrounded by infuriating schmucks I insist on loving. I mean, really, you have no idea."

"If I have no idea it's because I'm always the infuriating schmuck in the situation."

Carol laughed. "Now that I don't believe."

"Take my word for it. What happened after Thanksgiving?" The swish of Abby's pants receded another stack or two.

"If anyone thinks you're a schmuck, it's probably because they're jealous."

"Believe what you want. What happened after Thanksgiving?"

"You know what happened? Fucking Mitch happened. You remember Mitch, right? From my pool?"

Carol expected immediate and hearty recognition. Instead, she heard only the faint flipping of pages, a bookstore's ubiquitous background noise. Just when Carol was going to jog Abby's memory with a battering of description, Abby said, "Mitch, sure. From your pool."

That was all Carol needed to go off and running again. "She's fucking impossible. Really just…impossible! I mean, she's my best friend, and I'll say it: I'll probably love the skinny bastard past death, even. I know it might not seem possible when you look at her, but sometimes there's nothing more comfortable and easy than washing dishes with that woman or watching her delight your own fucking kids. But today—" Anger and hurt, as fresh as when she'd sat across from Mitch, choked her off.

She struggled with it. Hadn't she come in here to avoid witnesses? But her sinuses weren't very obedient and filled up despite moderate success at holding in the tears. She snuffled and blew her nose as quietly as she could manage. Calling Abby had been a huge mistake. The distance between them was not just the physical one of bookcases and scuffed wooden floors. Any possibility of understanding was marred by Abby's very nature. What could she know of betrayal as a matter of course? Of monumental and chronic failure? Of being impossible to be taken seriously?

During those walks Carol had taken over the weekend, she'd thought about Abby, fantasized about what her life was like—a still-unfocused image partly informed by things Abby had said but mostly by that old dream of the future she'd had with Sasha, a life so different from what she had now, a life tantalizing in its foreignness. It had felt so real back then, and it felt real again with Abby here to give it focus in her mind.

Carol knew how childish and futile these fantasizes were, and that fueled her shame at being the one who made the choices that put this imagined life out of reach in the first place. She blew her nose one last time, and it echoed in the store. "Sorry. Just pretend I'm not a mess."

"You're not a mess. In fact, weren't you the one to educate me about tears?"

"See? You're too nice to be a schmuck." She sniffed hard. "You know how when you've been with someone a long time—whether romantically or not—you get this expectation of an implicit understanding? That communication of wants and desires should be unnecessary? Or at least really, really easy?" Carol slammed the counter with her open hand, making a gratifying bang. "Where the fuck did that idea come from? Because, man, sometimes it's so wrong it just about kills me."

"The media." Abby's voice was strong and steady. Reassuring. At least until Carol listened to what she was saying. "Popular media tells us that love is real when it's easy and wrong when it's not. That what is effortless is right and that happily ever after means not just forever happy but always happy."

The shock of being so neatly reduced pinned Carol to the stool. Abby had the same power as Mitch, that remove of objectivity coupled with a deft scalpel of long observation. Being the one dissected was no fun and made Carol want to turn the tables in a way completely outside her capabilities.

For now, all she could do was let her futility in the face of popular media cascade through her and erupt in something between a giggle and a sob. She clapped a hand over her mouth and closed her eyes against the sight of Abby hustling up the main aisle. If only Abby didn't have to see her like this to offer the comfort Carol was sure was now coming.

"I'm sorry," Abby said. "I told you I was a schmuck." She reached across the counter to touch Carol's arm.

"It's okay. You're not. Or maybe you are. But you're the kind of schmuck I wish I could be."

Abby laughed, so Carol did, too, and it cracked something open in her chest that hurt and freed her in the same breath.

$$cn^2 = \frac{\sum_{t=1}^{n} M_i x_i}{M}$$

DON'T FEEL TOO BAD ABOUT BEING BRAINWASHED.

–Dr. Abigail Rosen, The F Word: Femininity in the New Century

$$\frac{w(R^3 - r^3)}{z^3 - r^3)\sin(a)}$$

10

MITCH'S shoulder radiated pain when she moved her arm in any of a half dozen habitual directions. Throwing that mug had felt like a shining burst of perfect clarity, an action she deemed worth the subsequent hours of discomfort. She winced with each shift of her truck's stiff gears while she drove over hell's half acre trying to burn off her mad.

It didn't work. Midnight found her prowling around her house, hungry but with a taste for nothing in the fridge, spoiling for a fight with anything she could convince to get in her way. But nothing was getting in her way—especially not Chester, who'd had the good sense to hide even before she'd finished getting the front door open.

She paced around her small office, leaving a trail of paper bits torn off a succession of sheets, the confetti showing white on one side and a jigsaw of text or charts on the other. Even though she kept it up until her fingers ached, it provided no relief. This room was stuffed full of her things—desk, books, laptop, chair, a trash can she hadn't had to empty in months—and it was no better elsewhere in the house. Pots and pans, the bed, rugs, silverware, even a goddamned fireplace poker.

How had this happened? Going into a rage had been so much easier when she'd had nothing. Anger was the perfect complement to abject solitude. But now? It felt all wrong, was too big to exist in her life with everything else.

She slumped in her desk chair and examined the plaster above her. At one time, she'd made an inch-by-inch survey of the upholstered ceiling of her hatchback, learned every wrinkle, pill, and water stain and could recall them in the cafeteria at lunch or when hanging out near the dumpster during her fifteen-minute break at the restaurant. That intimacy had been so clean and solid, but she couldn't recapture it now.

Sometimes when Mitch thought of that year, she wondered about who she was then versus who she was now. Lately, despite a continuing pride in her old fury and crushing independence, she'd felt a twist inside at how hard and unforgiving she'd been. Back then, she'd done what had been necessary to find the kind of congruence she'd needed so badly, but what about now? Did she still have to be so forbidding? Did she really have to put Abby in her place for those questions? Or be too rigid to correct Carol's assumptions?

If she were so secure in who she was, wouldn't that mean she should be able to find some *give* in herself? Strength without flexibility belied an internal brittleness, and brittleness was the enemy of real strength. Lauren Tate had swayed her, Serious Carol moved her, and these exercises in creaking shifts were necessary no matter how scary they could be.

Accepting Reginald's invitation and his long-distance love rocked her so deeply that she wanted to deny it, and the hugeness of that denial, of having completely erased him from her conversation with Carol, made her scoot her chair up to her desk and her keyboard. Her first attempt at writing to Reginald was three screens of incoherence that she deleted as soon as she finished, and she had to fight to remain in her chair instead of flying off to her truck again. In a new email, she started with an outline:

Told Carol about London
Carol freaked out and decided I'm having a secret affair
with a woman out there
I didn't deny it
It ended badly

But these facts were too pale to become a framework for continued thought. There'd been a whole lot of failure on both sides of that table, but what Carol had said—

Mitch picked up her wooden cup of pens and pencils and threw it across the room, with her left hand this time. The satisfaction in it was hollow, and she knew this night was going to take its own sweet time ending.

Later, in the black predawn, she sat outside the locked natatorium doors, getting stiff with the cold waiting for Jerry, the usual morning lifeguard, to show up and unlock the doors. When he arrived two minutes late, swaddled in sweat clothes and half asleep, he grunted at her, and she grunted back. Even before he had all the lights on over the pool, she dove into lane four, shattering the placid surface of the water. Her shoulder complained loudly, which was fine with her, something to pay attention to that was unequivocal. A small, thin pleasure hid inside the pain, and Mitch hung on to that as long as she could, through thirty-five hundred meters of mixed strokes, until her range of motion became too constrained to allow her to get down the lane and back.

She took her time in the sauna, then the shower, then finally drove the mile to work. When she stomped through the door, Steve and Eric looked up from their computers.

Steve said, "Hey. How was your…Thanksgiving?" He petered out by the last word and cringed.

Eric said, "Dang, Mitch. Lose a fight with the bottle?"

She had no idea how she looked, and she didn't particularly care, which felt almost as satisfying as throwing things.

"Just drop it," she said in a snarl, the beginning of indulging herself in her anger, saying whatever she wanted, being tough and unreasonable, riding Eric about his mess until he took to working in the lab part of the suite, pushing off grant-writing tasks to Steve that he wasn't equipped to do, and driving Sam's nephew right into silence with the unrelenting negativity of her code review.

It felt good to be a bitch, or a dick, depending on who was asked. Every day Carol didn't call or Mitch failed to divulge the fight to Reginald was another that justified remaining at a simmer, ready to be an asshole at the slightest provocation.

Over a week into this, she was alone with Steve in the office long after Eric had cleared out for the day. The tiniest groove of normal concentration coursed through her, and she wanted to succumb to it and feel something a little familiar and good.

But Steve asked, "Mitch?"

"What?" It had too much of a snap to it, and Steve said nothing. She felt that bit of happy calm evaporate. "What?"

He heaved an exceptional breath in and out then got up. Bright red spots rode high on his cheeks. "Get your coat. We're going to The Station."

Mitch laughed. "Have fun."

"Listen. Fuck. You either come with me or I quit."

A scared seriousness was evident in Steve's stance—feet widely planted, hands at his hips, and eyes circling the office. Mitch's annoyance percolated, but she put a lid on it and got her coat.

The Station was crammed with both patrons and holiday cheer, and Mitch wound up at the end of the bar, sandwiched between Steve and a Christmas tree heavy with ornaments. The sleeves of her chamois shirt sparkled with glitter from the bar's garland, her thigh was pushed up against Steve's in the crush, and all evidence pointed to this being a bad idea.

Steve's confidence had suffered on the silent walk over, and now he seemed to be pretending she wasn't there. She knew she should apologize and tell him it would be over soon, but she didn't. He drained most of his beer and said, "Man, did you and Carol break up or something?"

"I don't want to talk about it. Why'd I come here? You weren't going to quit."

"You came because something happened, and you *do* want to talk about it."

"Tell me. How did you manage to get your psychology degree while working fifty hours a week for me?"

"Okay, see, listen to yourself. You're so wrong. I put in sixty hours a week, easy." He smirked.

"And I'm supposed to feel bad about that?"

"Mitch. Man, just stop."

Mitch swallowed the last gulp of her old fashioned. "You're right. Carol and I aren't talking."

"Don't worry. She'll come around." Steve smiled, activating the small dimple up by his right eye, and she wanted to punch his cherubic face.

"Why do you assume she's the one who has to come around?"

"Well, what did you do?"

"I didn't do anything." Her voice was loud enough that Angel glanced over from where she was making change at the register. Mitch ducked her head and went on more quietly. "All I did was tell her I was going on vacation, and she flew off the handle."

"Really? You going on vacation *is* pretty shocking, but that doesn't sound like Carol."

Mitch couldn't decide which was worse—that Steve doubted her or that he was right. "Let's drop it," she said.

"I'm just trying to help."

"I know. I'm being an asshole. I'm sorry." And she was.

Steve pointed the neck of his beer bottle at Mitch. "If you were a dude, I know what I'd say."

"Try it. I'm dude enough."

"You need some distraction. You need to get laid."

Angel appeared with her ever-present bar towel. "I completely agree." She replaced Mitch's empty drink with a full one. "Sex rebalances both the physical and mental. It's as necessary to the body as alcohol."

"And, what, that's one of the major food groups?" Mitch asked.

"The way you're drinking tonight, it looks like it. What is it you so loudly didn't do?"

Steve said, "Mitch and Carol are fighting."

Angel lifted her hair away from her neck. The flush on her face from the room's heat was clear even through her make-up. "That explains everything. Carol was in here the other night crabby as hell, too. You guys should give it up already and sleep together. Solve all your problems. It wouldn't surprise me if Carol could lean your way."

Mitch set down her drink. "That's enough."

"My knees are quaking. Can't take some friendly advice?" Angel drummed blood-red fingernails on the bar top.

"Carol and I tried that in college. Believe me, we're much better as friends." Angel and Steve shared a comically stunned look. A little-known benefit of playing one's past close to the chest: letting the truth out at moments like these stopped conversation cold.

Finally, Steve cleared his throat. "In that case, have you thought about apologizing?"

"What for? I told you I didn't do anything."

"Chicks go for it, especially when they're to blame."

Angel laughed and took Steve's empty beer. "How in the world are you single with an attitude like that? What a catch. Another?"

When Angel left, he said, "I'm serious. Even if you're in the right, maybe you should make the first move. If only out of consideration for Eric and me."

Mitch leaned back and felt a flare of irritation at the Christmas tree bristling against her. "I'll think about it."

And she did—all night and into the morning, through hours draped across her couch with eyes helplessly open, during three thousand meters at the pool, over coffee and an egg sandwich with the other early risers at The Station. She sequestered herself behind computer and headphones and watched the office clocks until they agreed that Carol was at work. Then she started down Main Street.

At the first opportunity, still blocks from the bookstore, Mitch turned off Main and traversed the hill to campus, where she walked a lap around the quad then sat on a bench in front of the life sciences lab building, cold hands between her thighs. Unless she took Steve's advice and went in with apologies blazing, nothing good would come from seeing Carol, and she just couldn't do that yet.

When Mitch got up, she followed an even less likely approach. The humanities building was ninety degrees clockwise around the quad, and she headed that way then took the stairs to the fifth floor. For the first time in years, Mitch walked to Brian's office with no subterfuge. She strolled along under the blazing hallway lights with the innocence of someone not carrying a vile novelty item in her coat pocket.

Her knock on his door jamb sounded like gunshot, and Brian jumped.

"Damn, Mitch," he said and clapped a hand to his chest.

"Hey." She closed the door behind her. But inside, with just the two of them, she didn't know what to say. She hovered in the empty space between the bookshelves and the chairs in front of his desk and looked at him, sure he was somehow to blame for this.

He said, "Carol says it's taco night. You coming? If you bring Corona, don't forget the limes."

That Brian didn't know she and Carol weren't talking was interesting but not really surprising. Mitch didn't stop to consider if maybe Carol wanted to keep it that way before she said, "We're fighting, so I doubt I'm invited."

"Fighting? Since when?"

"Thanksgiving." Mitch put her hands on the back of one of the chairs and leaned in.

"Really. Carol hasn't said a thing." He shrugged as if Carol's ways were perpetually inexplicable then glanced over to his computer.

Mitch refused to take the hint. Thanksgiving felt like ancient history, but she suddenly realized there was a chance Brian hadn't yet confronted the silicone shit she'd left in here. She stood on her tiptoes for a better look at where it would be, but his desk obscured the spot.

Brian said, "So...what can I do for you?"

She didn't have an answer, not only to his question but for why she was here.

"Do you want me to tell Carol something?"

"No. In fact, don't even mention I stopped by."

He put an innocent look on his face and said, "I was alone at my desk all morning, officer."

"Good man." She got as far as the door then said, "Brian." She didn't know what she wanted to ask about more, Carol or the piece of shit. "Never mind. Enjoy the tacos tonight."

Getting that close to Carol put Mitch at odds again. She shoved her hands deep in her pockets and made herself take the hallway slowly, reading the names next to every door and peering into the offices. Kennedy, Regalis, Donnelly, Rosen.

She stopped. Abby's door was closed, and Mitch thought about knocking, pictured Abby at her desk, reading a book or journal, thick glasses slipped down her nose. But Abby didn't normally wear glasses, did she? Mitch sifted through her memory. No, she didn't normally wear glasses.

Mitch turned an ear casually to the door and tried to hear inside then wondered what she was doing. On Thanksgiving, once Abby had gotten over her self-consciousness, having her in the office had been almost cozy. It had changed the atmosphere, made the holiday feel different from other days, as holidays should. Well, Abby and Reginald, both, but the excitement about seeing Reginald that had been there before telling Carol was replaced by an unshakable trepidation, and the ways Carol was right about her, her lies of omission, her pushing people aside, would ruin everything unless Mitch found a way around them.

Mitch pulled herself from Abby's office with reluctance and continued down the hall.

< ≈ >

In the back room of Turning Leaves, Carol teetered on the very top of their tallest step stool and ran the duster across the overflow books. She was sure Maggie was keeping mum about these last weeks of most uncharacteristic industriousness for fear of jinxing it. On a piece of notepaper grown ratty with age and tacked to a big bulletin board over the snack table, Maggie maintained a running wish list of things she wanted done around the store. She called them pipe dreams, referring to how rarely any of them got accomplished. The list could languish for months without activity, but Carol had finished half of it since Thanksgiving.

Young adult reading corner? Cue beanbags and a short shelf of the latest tween fare. Map of the store color-coded by subject? Done, laminated, and posted around with red "you are here" stickers. She cleaned up the customer database and rearranged plants, reformatted their lists of recommendations and now dusted the back room—though this one made Carol fear a broken neck from her zealousness.

She obliterated the just-completed item on the list with a fat marker and was taking a good whiff of the beveled tip's sharp intoxicating scent when Maggie appeared from upstairs. Her loose black pants were paired with an orange top that wrapped around her in complicated ways.

She put a hand on Carol's shoulder, her fingers digging in. "All right. I give up. You're telling me what's going on with you."

Carol broke free. "I don't know what you're talking about." She made tracks into the store proper and took up her seat behind the register.

Maggie followed her. "You know exactly what I'm talking about. You've been upset for weeks, and frankly, everything you're getting done is unnerving me. No offense."

"None taken."

She settled across the counter from Carol. Next to her right hand was a mug full of blue ballpoints, and she took one and added it to the two chopsticks already in her mass of a bun. "I'm not going to make you tell me, but I'd appreciate if you'd volunteer."

"You know, one morning I called all the biggest hotels in Vegas to find out which one you danced at."

"Are you kidding me?"

"They were surprisingly nice, but no one claimed you. That's not definitive, though. Some of the old famous casinos aren't around anymore, and you might have changed your name. Did you change your name?" Carol hit the sale button on the old register a couple times to hear its money-tinged ring.

"Maybe we can stay on topic."

"Fine. I guess Mitch and I are fighting." It seemed wise not to mention Brian's affair, the other source of her efficiency.

"You guess?"

"Have I ever told you that you remind me of my seventh-grade English teacher? As if sentence diagramming weren't bad enough, the woman was precise and picky as hell."

"What happened?" When Maggie got inquisitive like this, her eyes went wide, showing white all the way around her dark-brown irises.

"I said some things I probably shouldn't have, and she flipped out, hasn't talked to me since."

"What did you say?"

"I don't want to talk about it." Carol hopped down from the stool and went back to the break room, but Maggie tailed her. "She asked for it, okay? Well, maybe not all of it, but sometimes she's such a tight-lipped fucker. I mean, here she is, flying off to London, of all places, and leaving me alone for the holidays, and does she have a word to say about why?" Carol stopped, but Maggie didn't take the bait. "Of course not! Only a mythic creature could have the power to compel Mitch across a thousand miles at the cost of two weeks of work, but no, not a word."

"Mitch doesn't strike me as a forthcoming person, in general."

"Maggie! You're supposed to be on my side. I'm her best friend, for Christ's sake."

Maggie held out her hands in supplication. "Don't bite my head off, but have you tried talking to her? Or even…apologizing?" She half turned away as if expecting a blow.

This deflated Carol. "The thought crossed my mind. But it crossed too fast to do anything about. Maybe I'm in the wrong, but I don't care." She straightened some stacks of books. "That sounds awful, doesn't it."

"All's fair in love and war," Maggie said.

"I know you don't believe that."

"Just because I don't believe it doesn't mean it's not true."

That thought trailed Carol for days. Maggie was right that truth didn't depend on belief, just like sometimes desire might as well be piss in the wind of reality. So, forget about right and wrong. Carol couldn't blame Mitch for not calling, but she couldn't quite blame herself either. With so much history between them, casting stones became problematic.

Maybe that was why Abby's appeal had bloomed far beyond what was rational for everything admirable about her. Carol was still patting herself on the back for how quickly she'd gotten over losing her shit in front of the woman, how she'd made sure that embarrassing afternoon at the bookshop led to a series of nonembarrassing encounters that now, a few weeks later, had become a routine of regular dinners. Seeing Abby was a minivacation from real life.

It was her turn to bring dinner to Abby's, and she decided on cold sesame noodles and moo shu pork from Yang's. She thought the pancakes would be fun, not to mention slow down the progression of food from plate to mouth (and thighs). Chopsticks used to accomplish that, but she'd become too adept for them to be a handicap.

The front door to Abby's rented house was open when Carol arrived, and she let herself in. At times, the only indication that Abby lived here was her briefcase flung over a random piece of furniture. The place had come furnished, and Abby hadn't changed or added a thing. When she wasn't in the room, the sterility of the place was unnerving.

"Herro? You ordah Yang's?" Carol said with a thick Asian accent. She heard Abby laugh from somewhere in the house. "You want I come in?"

"Yes, come in. Get comfortable. I'll be out in a minute."

Carol shut the door behind her then dodged the couch and recliner on her way to depositing the food on the dining room table and searching through the kitchen cabinets for dishes. She wasn't sure what Abby ate when they weren't together, but there wasn't a whole lot of cooking going on in this kitchen. The sink was dry, and not a single dish graced the drainer. Carol barely resisted the urge to snoop in the refrigerator or freezer—the public version of the medicine cabinet—before she carried a stack of plates and bowls back to the dining room and then, on a whim, past it to the coffee table.

Friendship meant holding a plate in your lap and risking the cleanliness of your shirt to chat across a couch cushion, and Carol was ready to declare it. She set out the dishes and opened each white cardboard takeout box. The smell was heady—sweet and savory, both. She ran to the kitchen then back with a roll of paper towels she'd found under the sink.

Where the hallway emptied out into the living room, Abby appeared with wet and newly shorn hair and bare feet. Carol silently cheered her long toes. Abby wore a moss-green sweater and faded well-worn jeans, which was something new, but those feet said it all.

"Okay if we don't sit at the table? We can use these as bibs." Carol held up the paper towels. "Have I ever seen you in jeans before?"

"Don't make a fuss."

They busied themselves with plates and food, trading commentary about smells and all-time favorite Chinese restaurants until they were both settled on the couch, backs leaning against opposite corners, each with one leg tucked under the other.

Carol started assembling her moo shu. "Sometimes you gotta love food that asks something from you beyond just forking it in. Not enough plum sauce, and you think ol' Yang's lost his touch. Too much filling, and it won't wrap right. Too little, and you run out of pancakes."

"The art of moo shu."

"Some books are like that." Carol took a bite of the rolled pancake.

"What, have too little plum sauce?"

Carol smiled around her chewing then swallowed and said, "No. Ask something of you. I wouldn't make a steady diet of it, but I like it when a book has me dipping into the dictionary every few pages, especially if it's that unabridged monster on the stand by the register at work with those onionskin pages."

Sesame noodles dangled from Abby's chopsticks. "What's the last thing you read that required a reference book?"

"Oh, I don't know. Probably something about particle physics. Or maybe neuroscience. I don't remember."

"Particle physics?"

Carol shoved the rest of her moo shu in her mouth and made a big production of chewing, holding up first one index finger then another in a plea for patience. Finally, she said, "There's a method to my madness. I don't know if I thought it would help me with the boys or something—with discipline or homework—but not long after I started at the bookstore, I decided to use my employee discount to learn about something new every three months. Whatever the subject, I read a bunch of books about it before moving on to the next thing on my list." She used her thumb to mop up a drop of sauce from her plate. "I know. It's kind of weird."

"It's not weird," Abby said, and Carol snorted a laugh. "Okay, it's a little *unusual*, but in a good way. What are you reading about now?"

"Polar exploration. You know, Shackleton, Cook, Peary, and those guys."

"What's next?" Abby stretched out her legs and sank back into the couch.

"Ghandi and Indian independence."

"There's some light reading."

"I doubt it'll be as bad as when I read about agribusiness and factory-farmed animals like the poor pig we're eating right now."

Abby looked at her plate.

"Sorry. Forget it. Let's talk about literally anything else." But Carol didn't allow more than a second to pass before she said, "I know that might have sounded like I was bragging, but I wasn't. I'm just a dabbler. All surface knowledge and no depth."

"Maybe one of these quarters you can read about healthy egos and how to obtain one."

Abby had said it breezily, as if it were a common offhand thought, and the sting of it shut Carol up for a while. Abby unveiled her completed moo shu wrap, and Carol roused herself to a polite golf clap at its neat construction.

Instead of taking a bite, Abby said, "I didn't mean that."

"Yes, you did."

"Not in a hurtful way."

Now there was a cop out. When did someone's good intentions ever make anything hurt less? And yet, at least Abby was telling her the truth. That's what friends did. Even if it hurt. *Especially* if it hurt. It took a monumental effort not to unburden herself about Mitch and her asshole nature and the ongoing status of their fight, things she'd managed to keep quiet recently.

Abby put her plate with her uneaten moo shu wrap on the coffee table and squared up to Carol. "I told you I could be a schmuck. I'm cruel and self-serving on several counts, and not just with you."

"You were being honest, which is more than I can say for—"

"Stop it," Abby said and got up. "Christ." She walked across the room and talked to the terrible landscape painting on the wall. "Before I came here, I cheated on my partner of three years with over a dozen one-night stands. I kept it from her that I intended to come to Tilsen if I could, then I broke up with her in the most heinous way."

Carol was, at last, speechless.

"I told her I didn't love her, swore up and down that I'd never loved her, then refused to talk to her again. Want more? My mother's always been my best friend, and I haven't spoken to her in eight months."

"I thought she was dead. Didn't you tell me she was dead?"

Abby spun around. "That's what I'm saying. I lied. I lie all the time. She still writes letters to me. I get them every couple weeks in my department mailbox, and I throw them out without reading them. See? I'm poison. Stop admiring me." Abby came back across the room and got right in Carol's business. Carol could smell sesame noodles and Abby's coconut-scented shampoo. Her face was squinched up, unattractive for the first time. Mean. "You know that book you love so much? That everyone loves so much? Well, I wrote it out of spite, for revenge—"

"Stop," Carol yelled and pushed her away. "What's wrong with you?"

Abby shrugged, her mouth set in a crooked grimace. "Everything, I guess. And I let you think I'm so together, so *perfect*. Don't let the door hit you on the way out."

Carol was stunned at how much Abby's twisted expression resembled Mitch's face when she'd thrown that mug. She should find Mitch and pour herself into salvaging the friendship with someone merely flawed and not evil, but she didn't move. She believed Abby. Lying could never look so raw—the hurt in her features indicated layers of truth below this surface venom. Abby muttered and wandered into the dining room and back. Carol helped herself to more noodles.

Abby said, "What're you doing?"

"Finishing dinner. Keep confessing if you want. Don't let me stop you. Did you fake your doctorate, too? Tamper with your glowing student evaluations?"

"If you think what I said about your ego was mean, I can do much worse."

"Be my guest."

"There's something seriously wrong with you. Fuck." Abby disappeared into the kitchen.

Carol remembered back to that Indian summer afternoon and what Abby had said about cutting off her hair. Mental disarray, she'd said, which now seemed like a massive understatement. Maybe she'd been lying then, but it hadn't seemed so, especially with her admitting to crying in her pillow. If Abby were all about hurting others, why cut her own hair? Why exile herself to this godforsaken town?

Besides, something delicious wound through Abby's fall from grace and the clarity of her fucked-upness. Even though these declarations shattered Carol's fantasy of her life, they opened a sliver of hope about her own future. Maybe Carol could have something that was not the imagined bliss with Sasha or the evidently false exaltedness of Abby's position but something uniquely Carol's. Just what that was remained to be seen, but she could feel it in her trembling fingers, and it pressed her to the couch with its tangible weight.

After several minutes, Abby came back with an amber drink in a thick highball glass. "Why are you still here?"

"The way I see it, I'm not a professional rival or your mother or lover, so I might be safe." Carol slurped some noodles.

"Your optimism is astounding."

"I prefer it to the alternative. One thing, though. I'm not taking too kindly to people screwing with me lately. Just, you know, FYI."

Abby sat down and set her plate on her lap. "I'll do my best. I'm not proud of those things, you know."

"I sure hope not." Carol rummaged around at the bottom of the takeout bag and found cellophane-wrapped fortune cookies. "Take a chance?"

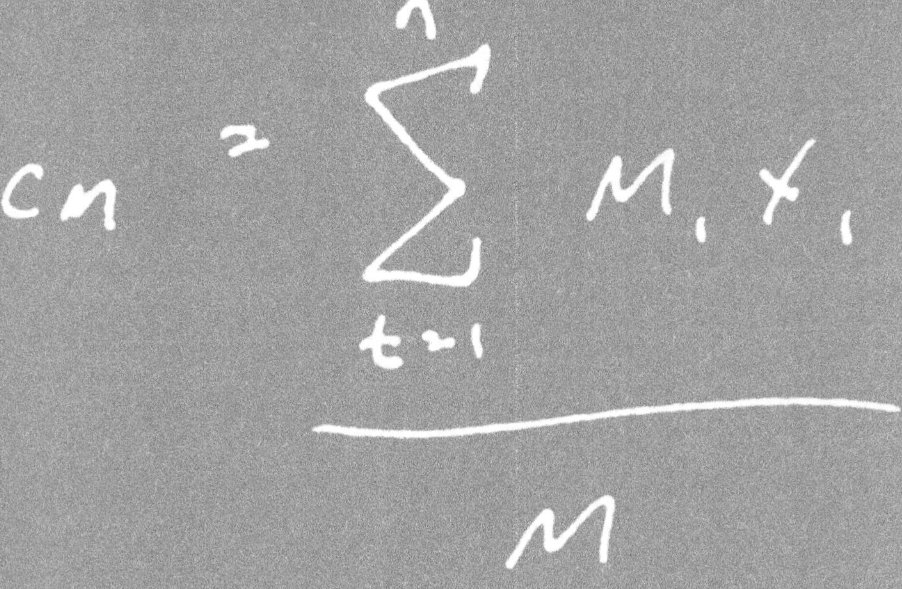

$$c_n^2 \frac{\sum_{t=1}^{n} M_i x_i}{M}$$

$$\frac{w(R^3 - r^3)}{z^2 - r^2)\,\sin(a)}$$

11

CAROL maintained that the only good thing about washing dishes was the hot-steam facial that went along with it. She'd heard other women claim doing the dishes gave them time to think or was a meditative stress relief or other such bullshit, but that was trying to find a bright side that didn't exist. One member of the PTA—who shall remain nameless—went so far as to say it made her happy because it gave her time away from her family.

Unlike that woman, Carol's husband and kids had no problem finding the right side of a sponge, and recruiting help for after-dinner cleanup went down via the finger-on-nose method, which left her paired with James more often than not. But tonight, she'd wanted to contemplate the grease-ringed suds alone, which she did with a grim determination. Though she and Brian had settled into this affair of his with only minor fanfare, Carol wasn't aching to spend more time than necessary around him pretending everything was fine. Add to that the looming specter of Christmas, and some time alone with dirty dishes was just the thing.

Carol was trying so hard not to think about anything related to the birth of Christ that she'd almost forgotten to buy presents for the kids, let alone anyone else on her list. Like Abby. But what did you get for the woman you once thought had everything?

Some of the bravado that had surged in Carol that night with Abby had ebbed away, leaving a flotsam of mixed emotions. She knew thinking herself immune to Abby's destruction was ludicrous, yet she couldn't rouse herself to either fear or judgment, maybe because along with Abby's implosion, a seed of possibility had begun germinating in Carol's gut. This little bit of hope was surely what allowed her to feel so easy about the way Abby had shed her old life in one massive, violent shake—not to mention that Carol had made her own fair share of suspect decisions.

Even so, the sheer magnitude of Abby's destruction inspired wonder. At least some of Carol's enormous change in plans had been due to simple accident. She tried to imagine being cruel not in knee-jerk reaction but with premeditation, maybe having an affair herself. Or a dozen. Well, really, who wouldn't want to sleep with Abby?

After setting the pot roast pan in to soak, Carol considered the winter landscape visible around patches of steam on the window over the sink. She didn't judge Abby, but she judged the hell out of Mitch, who had proven her love for years. The groggy morning after that dinner with Abby, Carol had come closest yet to seeking Mitch out to apologize, but it hadn't been quite close enough. The bottom line was that empathizing with Abby held a certain appeal, but she didn't want to put herself in Mitch's clunky shoes, not anymore. She'd tried and failed to understand, really understand, Mitch from the beginning. Why waste her time again?

When the doorbell rang, she cursed softly then waited to see if anyone not up to elbows in dishes would answer. Of course not. She dried her hands on a dish towel slung over her shoulder, walked up the hall, and opened the door, expecting the UPS man or her neighbor to the right, who never failed to inform her when she'd left the light on in the garage.

Mitch stood outside. The ages since their fight peeled away layers of familiarity and let Carol see her sharp cheekbones and crow's-feet and obvious exhaustion with a renewed clarity. Underneath the tiredness, Mitch's feverish handsomeness made Carol remember seeing her for the very first time, so young and with such a bad haircut, and suffer again the pull she'd felt.

At the same time, having Mitch right there made their history—especially the bruising recent stuff—thickly present. Carol considered channeling Abby's brokenness and slamming the door on Mitch. But it was two days to Christmas, and Mitch was both here and leaving, which brought a wave of desperate sadness that Carol rode out onto the cold front porch.

"For the boys," Mitch said and held out a plain brown box. "Sorry it isn't wrapped. I ran out of time."

"Mitch," Carol said while she tried to figure out what she actually meant to say.

"What? What do you want now?"

She'd really done it, then. Done a number on Mitch. Gotten inside and hurt her. While that was actually a little thrilling, it was mostly so intensely horrible that all Carol could do was examine her worn slipper socks.

"Aw, that's not right," Mitch said.

Carol leaned back against the door and took a deep shuddering breath.

"Come on. Don't."

"I'm sorry." The words were choked and muffled and strangely difficult to say.

"All right, okay." Mitch's hesitation was so huge that Carol could count the seconds of it, but she finally put the box down and pulled Carol into a hug. "It's…I know I've been unfair. I don't understand why everyone but me gets to be unfair all the time. It's fine, just relax. But, listen. I can't get into this. I'm on my way to the airport…"

Carol burrowed closer and talked into Mitch's shoulder. "Everyone gets punished, right? For all sorts of different things." Being tight against Mitch undermined Carol's desire to school her about how unfair she was in general. Carol held on long enough to feel Mitch's breath move in and out, to smell chlorine and fabric softener, to hear the low hum of a sigh. She pulled back. "I know. You have to leave."

"I'll call you."

"Don't call me, you moron. Just go vacation yourself into a stupor." Despite her words, Carol couldn't quite let go. Then, faster than the speed of thought, she stretched up and kissed Mitch. Oh, yes. That's right, the real reason their coupledom had lasted as long as it had. No matter how unyielding Mitch was, her lips were soft. Downright womanly.

Mitch was too paralyzed with surprise to lurch back, which not only would have sent her tumbling down the porch steps but certainly would have derailed this budding reconciliation. The anticipation of Reginald's quite different lips coupled with the instantly rehydrated memory of those college nights with Carol made feeling her best friend's mouth against hers more scientific observation than participatory act. And yet her mouth was there, and Mitch could feel it in a weird, complicated, stirring way.

Mitch let Carol press her advantage long enough for some noise to start up in her gut then peeled away and danced down the steps behind her. Once safely in the middle of the driveway, Mitch said, "I suppose you're going to want to talk about that later."

"Don't count your chickens." The orange tint of the porch light made Carol's curls wink with current.

"Well, ooh la la!" Mitch said and opened the passenger-side door of Steve's Corolla, which was idling at the curb. "I'll see you in two weeks." She waved and got in the car.

She and Steve had patched things up enough that he'd offered her a ride to the Cleveland airport, almost two hours away. She fastened her seat belt and nestled her feet in a drift of gas station receipts and parking tickets.

He leaned over the gearshift. "Um."

"Just drive. I don't want to be late."

He pulled out, but not two blocks later, he said, "I guess you guys made up, then."

"This isn't some game."

"I don't know. Looked a lot like tonsil hockey from where I was sitting."

Mitch snorted then let herself laugh for real.

"If that's Carol's way of ending an argument, I'm going to pick a fight next time I see her."

"Okay, that's enough," Mitch said, still laughing.

"At least you're in a better mood and can go on your vacation happy. What's in London, anyway?"

But Carol had exhausted Mitch's meager supply of tact. "Jesus Christ, not you, too. What's the big fucking deal about London?"

"It's not London, it's everything," Steve said in an echo of her exasperation. "You're the original man of mystery. For all I know, you could be going over there to interview for a job."

"Why would you think—? That's ridiculous. Is it so impossible to believe I might want some time off?" Mitch sat up and tried to turn to him, but the seat belt wrestled her back in place.

"Honestly, yeah it is. But that's not the point. I mean, I know you're my friend, right? You hauled me to the hospital when my appendix burst. Stayed all night and made sure they billed my insurance that I had because of you in the first place. You know the last time I got laid."

"Everyone knows that. You practically broadcast it over the FM dial."

"You know my baby sister's major."

"Misguided though it may be."

"You know that I played the trumpet and right field—neither very well."

"Yes. I could write your biography. What's the problem?"

Steve slapped the steering wheel. "The problem is I don't know a thing about *you*. You might be my friend, but I've never been yours."

While he went on to list the many more instances when Mitch had been unforthcoming, she felt the truth of Carol's kiss—that it was not an end but a means to a temporary truce. Everyone was suddenly interested in the minutiae of her life, and Mitch hated it. What was wrong with privacy? What was it about this trip that got everyone fired up? Were it not for going seventy-five in the middle lane, Mitch would have gotten out of the car.

When Steve finally stopped talking, Mitch said, "What do you want to know?"

"That's not the point." He glanced at her. The oncoming headlights washed him out and made Mitch see how angry he actually was.

"I'm well aware that's not the point, but I'm making an effort."

"Just forget it."

"Last chance, Steve. Tell me to drop it one more time, and I'll drop it."

"You can be a real ass sometimes."

Though he was right, his peevishness was doing little to put her in the mood for intimate disclosures. Mitch turned her face to the window and watched the darkened landscape slip by.

He asked, "Where were you born?"

"Indiana. That's what you wanted to know?"

"In a city or what?"

"A smallish town."

"What were your parents like?"

"I really don't have time to pull out my knitting and tell you a story." She was so close to the window that her breath fogged the glass.

"Fine. Why are you going to London?"

"I needed a new stamp in my passport, and they speak with a pleasant accent."

"Be serious."

"Seriously?" She looked at Steve. "None of your fucking business."

Each interminable second, they covered 110 feet of asphalt with only the wind and road noise for accompaniment, and Mitch wished she had spent her life's work on the problem of teleportation rather than industrial friction. The heaviness between them was suffocating. Mitch wanted to break it with a hot harangue, but what she'd already said was bad enough. Being pushed was no excuse for pushing back like that. Questions about her parents notwithstanding, it was Mitch's problem that she wouldn't give Reginald the light of day in any reality but her own.

But there was more to this than Reginald and his penis and everything that entailed given rampant assumptions of a previously penis-free existence. Disclosing him, Mitch assumed, would open a groundswell of curiosity about everything else she had held close to her flat, flat chest all these years. She felt claustrophobic just thinking about it.

She said, "I'm sorry."

"Don't. You're right. It's none of my fucking business."

Hearing those words was worse than saying them. "Steve."

"No, don't. Just treat that whole conversation as an experiment and draw conclusions. Then make adjustments and move on." He didn't even shift his eyes to look at her.

"You sound like me."

"You're a good teacher."

"I sound like an asshole."

He said nothing in a resounding way.

"One failed experiment isn't conclusive," Mitch said.

"There's no such thing as a failed experiment."

"Jesus, Steve, stop quoting me and accept my apology. What I said was out of line. I know I'm difficult, and I hope you'll continue not to hold that against me."

"I'll think about it. A raise might help."

"What?"

Steve smiled and smacked her shoulder, a shade harder than friendly. "Kidding."

The white noise of their travel modulated, acquired a different, softer quality. Mitch counted off ten mile markers of quiet between them. Then she said, "I think I might be in love, and I'm going to London to find out."

THE MATHEMATICS OF CHANGE

< ≈ >

On the flight, Mitch tried hard to think about Reginald, but what she mostly thought about, ached over, were those seats in first class that unfolded flat into beds. She was so far beyond tired that sleep was both a distant memory and a present long shot, but lying down would still feel like a dream. She'd once succumbed to the siren song of a sleeping pill, and the blissful nature of the ten hours that had followed had shaken Mitch so much she never took another one, though she'd trade a kidney for one now.

Her attempts to occupy herself were pathetic, and she kept coming back to her lack of nerve with Steve. After she'd let out that in-love business into the hushed car, Steve hadn't asked, and Mitch hadn't volunteered. That sentence was a missed burr on a surface otherwise polished smooth—a lone, sharp nub impossible to keep from touching. On so little sleep and in this limbo high over the Atlantic, Mitch could run her fingers over the words without having to feel the meaning underneath.

When she'd finally written to Reginald about her fight with Carol and her failure not only to reconcile with her but also to tell her the truth about this trip, she'd sat at her computer for five late-night hours, waiting for his response. She sat as if strapped to the chair, denying her body's impulses to sleep, eat, even stretch, doing penance in advance of Reginald's sentence.

His email arrived at three in the morning, absolving her of any wrongdoing and taking her side absolutely. She reread her confession to see where she'd been less than honest, to try and understand how Reginald could have possibly missed her meaning, but the truth was there. Reginald just chose not to see it. In a maneuver that only compounded things, she went to bed without making him face it.

By some miracle of aerodynamics, her leaden limbs didn't drag the plane out of the sky before they landed at Heathrow. She shuffled along with everyone else down corridors and through slow, snaking lines and hoped excitement would materialize at the sight of Reginald. Her shoulder ached under the strap of her heavy duffle, and she let the bag rest on the linoleum in front of her. As much as she told herself to snap to and pay attention to her first trip out of the country, the yearning for a shower consumed her. She hoped Reginald wasn't waiting out there crazy with ideas about having sex this morning. A shower, some coffee, and they could talk.

At the end of the line, a man behind a tall desk creaked open her rush-ordered passport, and she answered questions she had a hard time understanding out of both fatigue and accent. He smiled then pointed, and Mitch followed a rotund couple who'd sat a few rows ahead of her on the plane. When the couple veered right, Reginald was straight ahead. Even through his thick sweater and behind the jacket he held, it was unmistakable how much weight he'd lost since the conference. Gone was the layer of softness to his cheeks and neck, and his belly had diminished significantly.

Mitch dove into his arms. She didn't know what it was about him that struck a vein of desire, but it had persisted through the last desolate months. People trickled around them, but Mitch was so comfortable against him she could feel sleep within reach.

"We should probably get moving," Reginald whispered, his breath tickling her ear. "Where's the rest of your luggage?"

"This is it."

"This is it? You had more at the conference."

Mitch stepped back and grinned. "I spent most of the time at the conference fully clothed."

"I see. Well, then. Shall we?" He took Mitch's duffle and her hand and started walking. "Tell me everything."

"Carol kissed me." That was not at all what Mitch had planned on telling Reginald. Something about work, something funny about the flight, something about his bicep that seemed permanently flexed. But now that she'd said it, she realized exactly how strange it had been.

Reginald stared at her and drifted enough off course that Mitch had to keep him from walking into a door jamb. "Wait, is this the same Carol who gave you hell about this trip?"

"That's her."

"And the same Carol married to that bloody fool of a husband?"

"Yes. But, see, I may have neglected to mention—"

"I don't doubt there are many things you've neglected to mention." But he squeezed her hand when he said it.

"Anyway, we sort of dated."

"Prior to the marriage and children?"

"Oh, yeah. We're talking a whole different Paleolithic era. Carol was mostly into girls in college. I think they call people like her LUGs."

"LUGs?"

"Lesbians until graduation."

Reginald guffawed, and it galloped through Mitch, shaking loose her exhaustion. He said, "What will you Yanks think of next? But the lug nut kissed you recently."

Mitch checked her watch, which she hadn't yet set to London time. "About eleven and a half hours ago."

"Right, so, maybe not just until graduation."

"Who knows what goes on in Carol's head. It has nothing to do with anything. I mean, it's not like she suddenly wants to be with me again after all these years."

"Carol broke up with you?"

"That's not the point."

"I'm just trying to understand why this woman laid one on you eleven and a half hours ago."

But Mitch wasn't sure *she* wanted to understand or even let this conversation continue. She stopped at the side of the corridor and struck a mock sexy pose. "You don't think this is reason enough?"

That laugh again. "Well, sure. I don't know how you make it through the day without being molested. What I was I thinking? Speaking of," he said and pulled her to him.

Mitch didn't know what kissing Reginald was like when not bookended by the feel of a woman's lips. First Kim then Carol. Kissing was kissing, sure, but he was so vastly different from Carol that comparison was difficult. After reminding herself that comparison in these matters was, in fact, useless, Mitch let go.

They rode the Tube, then a bus, and finally walked, most of which wasn't conducive to talking or kissing. Mitch spent the trip leaning against Reginald's firm shoulder, floating in the gray area between sleep and wakefulness that matched London's steely sky and stone architecture. She dragged herself up the stairs to Reginald's flat and wondered how she was going to stay upright for the shower she longed already to have taken.

Purely on the basis of its size, the apartment reminded her of his hotel room at the conference. Galley kitchen, living room barely big enough for the couch and TV, and two doors she hoped to God led to bedroom and bathroom. Reginald motioned to the couch and told her to sit, and Mitch said, "Don't bother with the tour. I think I've got it."

"You're a laugh riot. Now, stay there."

He disappeared through one of the doors—the bathroom, judging by the almost immediate sound of running water. She shrugged out of her jacket and closed her eyes then kicked off her shoes and lay down.

"Do you want to sleep or have a bath?"

Her eyes refused to open at Reginald's voice, and she let him interpret her moan without further context.

"Mm-hmm. Very interesting," he said, and then she was aloft in his arms.

"Show-off."

"Well." He maneuvered them into humid warmth then set her on her feet and held her upright. "I did some calculations recently. Arms up." He pulled off both her thermal top and flannel shirt. "By my figures, I've put in close to two hundred hours in the gym since we last met, so I'm entitled." He unbuckled her belt and undid her jeans. They fell to the tile with a clatter.

He laughed and said, "Oh, Mitch," presumably at the boxers she'd bought specifically for this moment—ones that looked like a blueprint with measurements next to the seams. He slid them down around her ankles. "Step out."

After another short trip through the air, she was up to her neck in perfectly hot water. "This tub must be the biggest thing in your apartment. I hope you're planning on keeping me from drowning." Her eyelids felt melted together.

"Your perfect health is integral to my plans."

She heard Reginald drag something over to the side of the tub and knew when he sat next to her by the displacement of the air and the sound of his breathing. He wet her hair then massaged in shampoo that smelled like almond cookies.

She said, "You weren't kidding about laying in supplies."

"Keep still and enjoy. You're on vacation."

"That is absolutely true." He completed the rinse and moved on to repeat. Mitch was usually good at leaving things well enough alone—at leaving things alone, no matter well enough or not—but she said, "It didn't mean anything, you know." He kneaded away. "The Carol thing."

"That might be up for debate."

"I mean to me, Patty. To me it didn't mean anything. Not in that way." He rinsed her hair then kept his hands to himself. Mitch managed to unstick her eyelids, sit up, and turn around. "What?"

He looked at his wet hands instead of her, but he answered. "Are you sure I'm what you want?"

"What do you mean? I've told you, I've said…don't you know?"

"I told myself to assume you wouldn't be on that plane."

"Why? I said I was coming, and here I am."

"When you tell someone you love them…"

Mitch kept her mouth shut.

"It's not that you didn't reciprocate, that's not what I'm saying. But Carol thought she could kiss you because she doesn't know about me."

Mitch sank down and pressed her knuckles against her eyes until she saw static. "Carol kissed me because it was her way of dealing with my being an asshole. She kissed me because she's confused about her life, and I haven't been helping her. I don't know, maybe she kissed me because she can't kiss Brian. Or maybe because she knows I'd rather spend my Christmas with whoever is in London than with her."

The slow dripping of the tub faucet kept the beat of their silence. She dropped her hands back into the hot water but left her eyes closed. Why couldn't she say it, tell Reginald what he wanted to hear? After a long while, a splash above her chest preceded the sharp smell of lemon soap being worked into a washcloth.

He said, "Sit up so I can get your back."

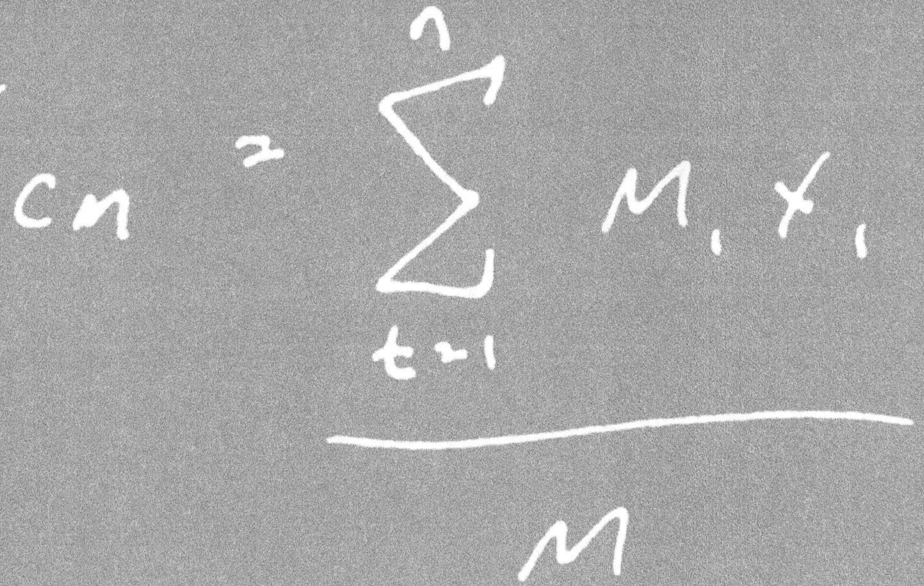

IS EVERYONE PARADING AROUND IN THIGH-HIGH boots and short skirts an automaton just following orders passed down by high fashion? Maybe most are, but some have led an exhaustive search through the mall and have determined that wearing these clothes makes them feel good, look good, and be absolutely themselves.

12

EVER SINCE that kiss with Mitch, Carol had been happy in a way she refused to examine—for fear of it either evaporating under scrutiny or revealing its truth, which was surely murky and complicated. The kiss hadn't been either one-sided or reciprocal but somewhere in the middle; only Mitch could calculate exactly where.

Regardless, that lip lock had enabled her to float through Christmas and the following week, humoring everyone in the process. It had even gotten her to the afternoon of the Obermanns' annual New Year's Eve party without the usual dread and angst. Being "the wife" around Brian's colleagues was one thing in her backyard when she was in charge, but having to flit around on the uninvited fringes when she was just an ornament was downright intolerable.

But this year, she felt sexy and vibrant. For the first time in a long while, Carol was happy about the party's "dressy" designation, which allowed her to honor her out-of-season happiness with a new ensemble: a deep blue, knee-length number that matched the silver-and-lapis-lazuli barrettes Brian had given to her on their fifth anniversary, a set far too pretty and dear to hold their origin against them.

Since the invitations for this party were more edicts than requests, Abby was sure to be there. Carol had caught her on the phone a couple times since their last dinner, but they hadn't gotten together. She understood. Who wouldn't need a little space after all that disclosure? Hell, Carol probably wouldn't even answer her phone for a month if she were Abby. When they had spoken, Abby's voice held a trepidation Carol hadn't heard before but had felt in the dark recesses of her own mind countless times—a lack of surety fueled by a deep distrust of another's regard. Abby didn't believe Carol still wanted to be her friend, and if Carol were clearheaded, she probably wouldn't.

By the time she and Brian drove across the subdivision to the Obermanns' house, the party was already in loud swing. Joyce ushered them in, flushed and babbling about coats and the open bar and the layout of the place as if it weren't built on the same exact floor plan as the Hollisters' house, though Joyce's decorating sense sparked disorientation. Everything was hosed down in various pastels, and the floral-printed furniture was plump yet strangely firm. In the dining room, two small paintings hung close together on the pink wall above the buffet-laden table. They looked like the beady eyes of a piggish man surveying the food right under his nose—a spread of smoked meats and cheeses and a half-dozen varieties of both olives and Joyce's cookies, including massive peppermint wheels in the green-and-silver Tilsen colors.

Joyce steamed to the kitchen, sweeping Carol along in her wake, then seemed hell-bent on pinning her there with talk about the school board and adolescent boys. Only when the dean poked his head in and said something excited and unintelligible did Joyce reclaim her hostess duties and leave Carol alone to find a drink before going in search of Abby.

Abby was nowhere to be found, and Carol redoubled her efforts at making full use of the open bar and pretending to mingle. Among easy conversation about the holidays, the weather, and the five to ten pounds everyone had to lose, Carol drifted in and out of pockets of shop talk.

"Did you hear about that study…"

"There's an article in JSTOR I think you should read…"

"She got an intern from the computer science department to help with the data modeling, and you should see…"

Carol hung on the edges of these conversations for only so long before she reeled off to the bar so she could temper the tantalizing idea that she still had it in her to be one of these people, that her future was big enough to contain real possibility. She'd been unable to squelch the strange hope that had bloomed with Abby's confessions, the idea that something different could await her, that the hard work it would surely require was not impossible, just merely excruciatingly difficult.

A hint of determination had woken in her with that hope, and she leaned on it tonight to use her position as an outsider not as a reason to feel bad but as an opportunity for empirical observation. She made an informal survey of people's drinking habits, of the way groups formed and disintegrated, of who deferred to whom. Doing so was a revelation. Suddenly this party was fun instead of horrible obligation. Carol felt her juices flowing, and not just from the booze.

When Abby finally arrived, snazzed up didn't even come close to describing her. She had gone above and beyond in a dark-green dress that showcased her shapely arms and gave lingering looks at her thighs with every step. Carol could only conjecture about how much the dress had cost then had to double the estimate when she saw the matching emerald pendant and earrings that topped off the outfit.

She intercepted Abby and said, "Dang. You're totally wasted on this crowd. I mean, dang. Really. Are you for real?"

"Too much?"

"If you didn't already have tenure, I'd think you were trying to lay someone to get it. Give me a twirl. Come on." Abby turned around with obvious reluctance. "God, you look as good from the back."

Carol steered them toward the bar, which was set up in a corner of the crowded dining room. "I don't know how this kid is mixing the men's drinks, but he's giving the women alcohol in proportion to their bust lines. I've had to have four or five to get any kind of buzz on, but Darla over there hasn't even finished her first drink yet." She indicated a heavy-breasted woman laughing hysterically by the melting ice sculpture of Tilsen's insignia.

They took their glasses to the living room and settled next to a large fake fern. Joyce had gotten her carpet cleaned for the event. Carol could see the tell-tale lines disappearing under the couch and was happy not to be the one to host this party.

The air was hot and moist from endless pontificating. Brian was usually right in the fray, but Carol didn't see him on the curving sectional or in the group milling behind the loveseat. Carol imagined Mitch in this crowd. Forget trying to figure out what Mitch would say, Carol didn't even know what she would wear. Sure, Carol had seen Mitch pull herself together and look nice in a snappy androgynous slacks-shirt combo, but nothing on the level of Abby, who made a face at the first sip of her Manhattan then seemed to treat it like doctor-ordered medicine. She was surveying the room and swirling her drink with a dark intensity, and Carol feared losing the last merry parts of herself to the brooding quiet next to her.

She tried to corral her amateur observations from the evening into some semblance of order so she could find a tasty tidbit to share with Abby and lighten the mood. But before anything came to mind, Abby leaned close and said, "Have you ever tried to peg someone based only on their appearance?"

"Sure, but it's not much fun around here. Hick, town, or Tilsen about cover it."

"Not broad categorizations. I'm talking favorite food, greatest fears, and relationship with their mother."

"What do you take me for, a sucker?"

"I'm not kidding." Though Abby smiled, she didn't look happy. Her features were too controlled, her fingers tight on her drink.

"Prove it."

"Pick someone in this room you know and I don't."

Carol raised an eyebrow then perused the people mingling around them. When she saw Dr. Barbara Treacle in all her quirkiness, she pointed. "Her."

"In the cardigan?"

"Yep. She's—"

Abby cut her off. "Don't tell me anything." She sipped her drink and watched Dr. Treacle, the anthropologist who always raved about the veggie burgers at Carol's barbeques.

Carol shifted her weight to her left foot and slipped the other half out of her shoe. She tried to see Dr. Treacle as Abby might, the strawlike hair harnessed by a chunky wood barrette and a gray cardigan covering a sleek black dress that showed off pleasant calves and ankles. But there were those habitual Birkenstock clogs. Did she ever wear anything else? She stood with two men from her department, her whole body engaged in the conversation. Then she laughed, a full bray, and raised her hand to cover her mouth. Even after the laughter choked off, her hand still hovered there, her engagement ring catching the light.

Abby said, "She's on sabbatical from the anthropology department."

"How'd—"

She put up her hand. "She's engaged to a shiny, successful lawyer. He lives in Cleveland or New York, and he was supposed to be here tonight but something came up at the last minute. She used to wear glasses and have bad teeth, but he made sure all that was fixed before he proposed. She's spending most of this sabbatical at his place, but she wanted to be home for the holidays. He's probably screwing his city girl while we speak." Abby sighed. "You know what happened? She'd gotten so used to being considered smart but homely that when he laid on the charm and she felt pretty for the first time, she went and got stupid about it."

Carol stared at her.

"Well, am I right?"

"Are you right?" Her voice turned to a fevered whisper. "You're scary right. The fiancé's from New York. I don't even remember how they met, but she's been his project ever since. How'd you do that?"

"Observation. I haven't seen her around campus, but she's obviously professionally close to Rick and Jeremy, so…sabbatical. She touched the bridge of her nose twice while I was watching, pushing up glasses that weren't there. That rock speaks for itself, but the way she covered her mouth meant she used to have bad teeth—or maybe she does it because of her unladylike laugh. I guessed there. I also guessed the fiancé's profession, but when I think rich manipulative bastard, lawyer comes immediately to mind."

"You're my new hero. I am wildly impressed."

Abby shook her head. "It's a parlor trick." She took a gulp of her drink then looked at the last smear of liquid in the bottom of her glass. "T and I played it like a game. Therese. My ex. We called it Strip Tease."

"Therese." Carol tried to keep the interest out of her voice.

"T was really good. Better than I was, not that I'd ever admit it." She muttered something Carol didn't catch, though she swore it included the word "asshole." Then Abby huffed a breath and spoke out of the corner of her mouth. "Once, T picked apart one of my colleagues so completely, down to his penchant for reflective aviators and the reason for his last breakup, that I literally swooned."

"T," Carol said then succumbed. "What did she look like? Butch or femme?"

Abby closed her eyes. "Femme." The word rode on much more breath than necessary. "Crazy femme. Four-inch heels all the time. Gorgeous. We had the same coloration, but she turned it into something smoky." Abby swallowed the last of her drink and grimaced.

"Miss her?" But Abby didn't answer, and Carol hurried to change tracks. "Well, you're an asset to have at a party. This evening is now officially worth the hour of negotiation James put me through before he'd stay home and watch Gordo. I swear, that kid makes me feel like a failure as a mother. When you were fourteen, did you give your mom a mouthful of trouble?"

Abby tipped back her empty glass. "Rebellion is a necessary component of adolescence."

"Believe me, when you're on the side of the establishment, it's suddenly not so simple."

"I can't imagine."

"I mean, really. What the fuck? How did I end up here? I had perfectly attainable dreams. I didn't want anything excessive or crazy, or at least not too crazy. And even though I'm suddenly sure I've had too much to drink, I'm going to keep talking. Here. Come here."

She pulled Abby upstairs and to the end of the gloomy, cool hallway where the party sounds were muted by distance and thick wall-to-wall carpeting. Every door was closed, and a smoke detector's red light stared, unblinking, like an evil eye. Or maybe a warning sign she wasn't going to heed.

As soon as her ass hit the carpet, Carol started talking about Brian—or Brian via a long Sasha introduction. The way Abby had said Therese's name…it had embodied exactly how Carol felt whenever she thought of Sasha. Love all but obliterated by stifling regret. She talked about Sasha's drive and her honesty, her humor and her way with a lacrosse stick. Sasha had made being an adult seem interesting for the very first time, and Carol had gone and ruined it by being an irredeemable adolescent.

Not that she said that to Abby. But when she couldn't spin out the prelude anymore and had to get to Brian, she spared no detail. She talked about that week with him, getting pregnant, and leaving Sasha and town without her degree or telling anyone the truth, but she did so without a glance at Abby's neatly crossed ankles, let alone her shadowy face.

"The whole pregnancy was a blur of terror, but the birth— Abby, don't let anyone tell you birth is beautiful. If the top layer of its horribleness didn't get worn away by immediate sleep deprivation, no one would have a second kid. But, then, I don't know. We were a family, and there was love and caring and shit.

A lot of that. I mean, sometimes I think it would be easier if I didn't love them so much."

Abby had slipped her feet out of her heels and was making divots in the deep carpet with her toes. "Love and caring and shit sound good."

Carol groaned. "They *are* good." She rolled the back of her head against the wall. "And for a long time, they were good enough to let me forget that I wanted something really different. Wanted it bad. Not bad enough to save me from my own idiocy but enough that I could almost choke on it. You know, right? You've wanted like that."

"Yes. I used to want like that."

Carol ignored that statement being in the past tense. She had to. She had an agenda. "Anyway, now that I've already embarrassed myself..."

"You haven't embarrassed yourself."

Carol folded her hands in her lap so she wouldn't fidget. "Hold on to your hat, then. I know it's too late for me, but I was thinking of trying to, you know, pick up where I left off. Not go back to school officially, but maybe do some reading and a little research and just, like, remember how to think."

"Sounds like a good idea."

"Yeah, well, here's the thing. I wanted to ask if you'd consider helping me. Just around the edges. Suggesting books. Maybe someday reading something I put together. Please don't feel bad about saying no," she said in a rush.

"I'm not going to say no. I work at a university. I'm supposed to like teaching, right? Tell me what you want, and we'll figure something out."

They were quiet enough that Carol could hear Dr. Treacle's doomed donkey laughter. She swiped at her teary eyes and said, "You're lucky I can't give you a hug right now because you'd have to pry me off."

"It's my pleasure."

Neither of them made a move to get up and rejoin the party. Carol's overwhelming thankfulness took a while to recede enough for renewed thought, but when it did, she remembered something she'd been meaning to ask Abby since before they'd even met. "Do you really believe that 'freedom from the need to prove herself as capable leads to the possibility of discovering a true sense of self'?"

"What do you mean?"

"Page 213. When you're talking about Title IX and everything. Because I think it might explain Mitch. At least a little."

Abby's silence had an impenetrable quality to it that very loudly told Carol she'd said something wrong. Too late, she remembered Abby's professed reason for writing that book and realized that talking about it was probably not high on her list.

Carol was about to sweep the question under the wall-to-wall when Abby said, "Mitch? You haven't mentioned her in a while. Does this mean she's no longer persona non grata?"

"No. She's persona something else entirely." Carol considered mentioning their kiss and seeing if it got traction, but she refrained. "I've been wondering about what you wrote. It's really smart. I don't know if I completely understand it, but I thought of Mitch right away. She seems simple and straightforward, you know, with her 'I don't care' butchy clothes and her obsession with work. But once, when we were dating—"

"You dated her?" Abby's question was the most alert-sounding thing she'd said all night.

"Why does everyone find that so hard to believe? Granted, we were children, but Mitch could be charming in a disastrous kind of way, and she's more attractive naked than you'd think. You look at her and picture a skeleton, but it all comes together well. Not as well as Brian, who's downright elegant naked. You probably look really good, too. Proportionate and tight and everything." Carol paused. "Yeah, definitely. Anyway, this one night, Mitch and I were crammed together in her extra-long twin, and she starts to talk about how she's confused."

Even in the dimness, Carol could see Abby's hand float up and touch her hair above her ear. "Was she…what was she confused about?"

"Exactly, right? I mean, I was a whole twenty years old, and I have no idea it's possible to be confused about anything other than your major or your sexuality. But Mitch wasn't talking about being torn between me and the wide receiver down the hall, and she certainly wasn't talking about her major. Christ. If anything broke us up, it was differential equations. I still don't know what a differential equation is, but Mitch kept me up one night too many sitting at her fucking desk with the light on going over and over those things."

Abby broke in. "What was she confused about?"

"I don't even know. She talked about traits and gender and who knows what else in circles I couldn't really follow. She must've said 'who we are' about a million times. Things like, 'Who determines who we are?' and 'How much of who we are relates to what we're called?' I don't even know. Eventually I kissed her to shut her up, and she's never mentioned it again."

"Was she talking about not wanting to be a woman?"

"Who knows? It was a long time ago, and honestly, it scared me. She kept saying that she didn't want to be anything at all, didn't want to play like that, but how can someone not be anything?"

What had made Carol keep Mitch from talking that night hadn't been a lack of desire to know Mitch but, instead, a quaking fear. What Mitch was trying to say felt too big for Carol to understand—was clearly too big for Mitch to understand—and knowing something like this lurked inside Mitch made Carol suddenly certain that her failing Mitch was inevitable. And though that fear now spent most of its time deep underground, Carol sometimes still felt a shiver of it in her bones. Mitch would say it was stupid, but as much as Carol wished she could agree, she never quite could.

Abby said, "Mitch is fascinating. I mean, she sounds fascinating. She works in friction? Friction. Interesting." Abby's voice was soft, as if she were talking to herself. "Never mind. I can dig up some good books for you to read about roles and labels if you want. Or something else. We can do anything you want, Carol."

"Now that's not a common sentiment. I'd buy you a free drink for that if the bar weren't all the way downstairs." Carol struggled to keep herself from lying down on the soft carpet and luxuriating in this unexpectedness.

Later, when they rejoined the party and made a circuit of the downstairs, the women seethed in jealousy over Abby—except Jane Truman from the psychology department, who spent her summers competing in adventure races. Carol was so enamored of being Abby's friend, she wasn't even jealous of the attention, just basked in the secrets between them.

Abby made a quiet exit not long before midnight, and Carol finally found Brian out on the snowy back patio in his loafers and sport coat, laughing into his cell phone. Anger and hurt flambéed the alcohol in her system. Witnessing this chuckle Brian was having with his Bonnie Brightman right after she'd spilled her guts to Abby made Carol find an answer to her old question about Mitch: she wanted desperately to be nothing that she currently was.

She stuck her head out into the biting cold. Before she could hear a single word of conversation, she said, "I'm going home."

Brian held the phone away from his ear. "What? Wait, what do you mean you're going home? Just hold on."

"I'm walking. You can drive home later."

"Are you sick? Should I take you?"

Carol laughed, her breath pluming like smoke. Then she ducked back inside and closed the door. She stopped to unearth her coat from a pile on the bed in the guest room and had only made it to the end of the driveway before Brian came stumbling down the front steps in pursuit.

"Carol, what the hell?"

"I need some air."

"You could get it on the patio like me."

She blew a raspberry. "You were getting more than air out there."

"What're you talking about?"

"You were practically getting a blow job through your phone."

Brian stood right next to her. His voice was low and serious, like it always was when he was lying. "Is that what this is about? I was talking to my brother, wishing him a happy new year."

She kept her words quiet, too. "Just because you're smarter than me doesn't mean I'm a complete moron. I don't know who, but you've been fucking someone else for two months."

In the place of more denials was a long muted roar from inside the house. It was the new year, and Carol wasn't going to leave things at resolutions.

She said, "Sometimes it's worse that you don't go ahead and leave me. After what you put me through. You'd think it'd make me feel some kind of loved that you always come back, but it doesn't."

Brian's hands drifted up then back down.

"And it doesn't make it easier that I should've expected it. You were the one who was fully formed when we met. I was the one who was nothing and malleable."

"Where's this coming from?"

"You sure formed me. Molded me right into the long-suffering wife."

"I didn't mold you."

"Yeah. I did it all by myself."

"All I did was love you."

She shouted, "Don't you think I fucking know that? It's killing me. *You're* killing me."

He took her by the arm. "Keep your voice down. Those people in there are our lifeblood, Sparky."

"Oh, I've heard that one before." She wrenched herself from his grip. "It was the whole chorus line of our beginning. We sure saved your ass and your career. Saved it by sacrificing my whole life."

Brian was washed out in the streetlights, but she could see the red flush to his ears and a shiver run across his shoulders.

He said, "I didn't have to marry you. There were plenty other options."

"Like what? Don't you think I spent some time hoping to come up with something better?"

"I'm trying to tell you something."

"Well, let me abase myself into an empty vessel for your thoughts. I've gotten really good at that after fifteen years."

He clenched his fists and growled. "Hell, I was clueless back then, too. I wanted it to go away, but I don't know. I didn't want you to go away along with it."

"Yeah, I imagine it's nice to have adoring students underfoot."

"Listen," he yelled. Bits of spittle shot through the air, spotlit by the streetlight. He shuddered. "You just listen to me. I know you're upset, but listen. The first year was a blur. A panic. But you and the boys have made me happier than I deserve."

Carol laughed. "I'm really fucking glad to be of service."

"That's not what I meant, and you know it. I meant that I love you."

"Yeah, well *I* don't love *you*." She walked away faster than she wanted, but she couldn't keep the hurrying clatter from her steps.

"Carol!"

She heard a few of his scuffed strides.

"Let me get my coat. We can't leave the car here."

By the time she got to the sweeping curve at the end of the block, she was running as fast as her heels allowed, a stuttering, stilted jog that didn't affect her wind, and its inherent silliness may well have been the only thing keeping heaving sobs at bay. Her eyes felt steely, and her face had none of that congested gunk that went along with her tears. The air's crisp cold filled up her sinuses.

After two blocks, Carol slowed to a walk. She still had most of the subdivision to cross before getting home, and she felt full on those in-between streets, the neither-here-nor-there avenues. Even though the cold ached in her feet and fingers, she slowed down even more to make it last.

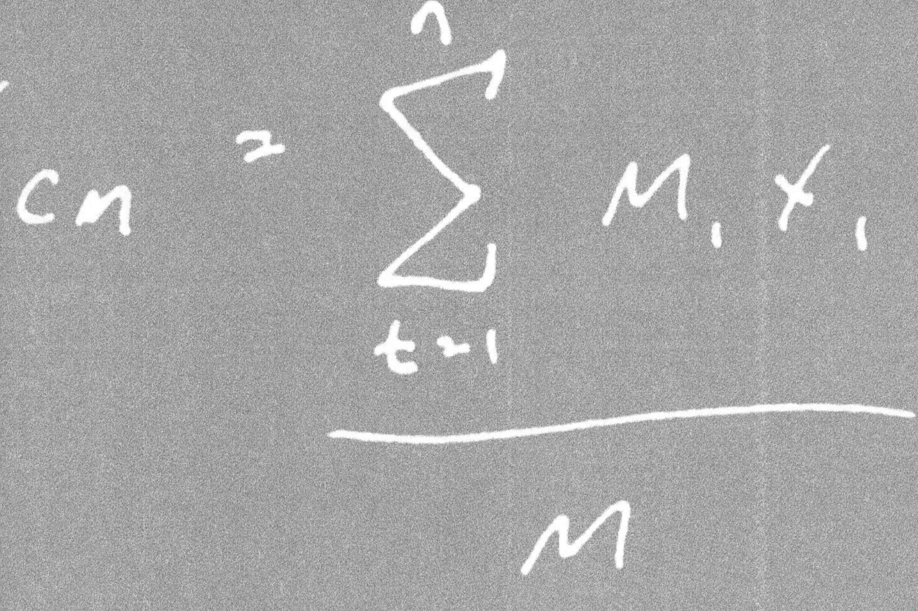

SOMETIMES KNOWING YOU'VE EXAMINED YOURSELF
and your place in the world and have
made decisions based on that examination is enough. Sometimes it's not.

—Dr. Abigail Rosen, The F Word: Femininity in the New Century

13

LONDON sunlight was deceptive. When filtered through low clouds and intermittent precipitation, high noon masqueraded as dusk or dawn. When Mitch woke, the light that made it past the drawn window shade was gray and weak and hinted at early morning, but the stiffness in her back and shoulder said otherwise. For the last week, she'd slept like she hadn't believed possible. Eight, nine, even ten hours at a stretch, waking only to turn over and consider getting up to pee before being consumed by sleep again.

When she surfaced from these marathon nights, she kept still and felt Reginald's old flannel sheets soft against her back, her knees, the tops of her feet, listened to the rhythm of his breathing. This almost-solitude seeped into her skin and made her cells expand a little. No matter how genuine she felt around Reginald, Mitch was wholly familiar to herself only during these rare moments outside his influence.

They woke up late, ate at odd hours, fell into having sex with the same ease Mitch used to drift into thinking about work. Not that she thought about work here. The closest she got to engineering or mathematics was categorizing the different types of bridges over the Thames and observing the small adjustments required for her stride to stay in rhythm with Reginald's.

This trip felt like a dream, though not any kind of dream she'd ever had. In moments when she felt practically overcome with happiness, she wished for an injection of dreary reality. Back home, Reginald was an illusory pleasure tacked onto the side of real life. He would never stand to be designated an illusion, would bellow on about how he was no figment, but wasn't he? At least a little? And didn't this whole magical vacation perpetuate that?

Mitch craved an intersection of these worlds—an appearance by Eric and Steve in this London flat or the sight of Reginald walking through the glass door of her office. She wanted less magic here and a little more at home, and she had no idea how to calculate the probability of that happening.

Long past midnight on New Year's Eve, Mitch sat across from Reginald on his bed, the London edition of Monopoly in midplay between them. Reginald wore a light-green robe that made him look like an Andes mint and loomed over Piccadilly, Trafalgar Square, and King's Cross Station. He rattled the die through a complex series of maneuvers before letting it fly only to have it skip across the board and into Mitch's lap.

She laughed and searched the soft folds of the long-sleeved T-shirt and sweatpants she'd borrowed. "I think you put a little too much English on that one."

He rolled his eyes. "Going big has its risks, you know."

"If you think some fancy dice work is going to save you, you've had too much of that champagne." She found the die and passed it back to Reginald, who huffed on it then polished it on the sleeve of his robe.

"Imagine, we could be wading through crowds of rat-arsed people."

"What were you thinking, making us come home after dinner?"

"I was thinking two hours with my friends was quite enough. Any longer, and they'd succumb to a group swoon over you."

Mitch still hadn't gotten used to Reginald's offhand compliments, but at least she'd learned to stop arguing. "Chuck *was* making eyes at me when you were in the bathroom."

"Now that's low. Flirting with a mate's girl while he's in the loo. And in front of his own wife."

"It was brazen."

"Still, can't blame the man." Reginald waggled his eyebrows.

"It was good to meet your friends."

"I only agreed to go because there've been rumors in the ranks that you were an imaginary girlfriend, and some proof was in order. I thought it'd be torture to have to share you with them, but it was actually quite pleasant."

"I must be wearing out my welcome," Mitch said with a chuckle.

"Never. Don't think I'm not turning the ol' gears over how to see you again."

Mitch took his hand. "Just be happy about now. I am."

He kissed her knuckles, letting his lips linger before he dropped her hand and went into his windup. This time, Reginald's roll stayed on the board, and he moved his top hat past Go and to Whitechapel Road, a rare square free of houses or hotels. He counted out two hundred pounds from the bank and said, "I've been thinking about tomorrow."

"You'd be better off rethinking your strategy here." Mitch riffed her thick stack of money.

Even his hands, broad and dark on his mint-green knees, were disapproving.

"Sorry. I told you Monopoly does something to me."

He hummed. "Monopoly?"

"All right. Games of all sorts. What were you thinking?"

"I was thinking Paris."

"Paris?"

"Or at least the closest thing to Paris in London: the best pastries in town then evensong at St. Paul's."

Mitch turned the die over in her hand. She'd seen the Rosetta Stone and the earliest evidence of a man-made tool at the British Museum, braved biting wind and spitting rain at Stonehenge, viewed the city from the top of the London Eye, had a traditional English breakfast at Regency Café. Now Reginald wanted to go to church? Was there anything less inspiring than sitting through a church service? But this week she'd learned what that flare of his nostrils meant and how to see the restraint in his smile that identified his true desires. Just because they'd run in perfect parallel until now didn't mean that would always be the case.

She said, "Whatever you want to do is fine with me."

Reginald raised his hands in surrender and beseeched the ceiling. "I want to win this frimpin' game, is what I want. Will you still have me when I've gone bankrupt and lost all self-respect?"

Words, *those* words, bubbled up from Mitch's gut so fast she almost couldn't stop them. But she did. And then she wondered what was wrong with her. The corners of the die were pressing into her palm. She looked at Reginald—smiling, jolly, and so dear. She loved him, was *in love* with him. What should be easier to say than that?

He asked, "What? Is that a no?"

"It's a 'let's call this a draw.'" She shoved the board off the end of the bed and tackled him. Mitch loathed using their sex as a way to change the subject, but that didn't keep her from succumbing to its delights. Somehow, in bed, Reginald remained Reginald, and Mitch stayed Mitch. Reginald's laughter in no way undermined the seriousness of their pleasure. In fact, it knocked Mitch off balance enough that she twirled in a sort of freedom she'd rarely experienced in sex, into a place separate from expectations and roles and pressures.

Getting intimate with Reginald made her remember those high school conquests—if only because of how different they were: cramped, rushed, full of feigned power. She'd had lovely, satisfying sex since, but this was the first time she was affected by it, the first time she felt well and truly naked, and the first time she wanted just that.

Later, with Reginald turned away from her, snoring softly, Mitch lay awake and considered what was broken inside her. She loved Carol and the boys, an insistent, piercing emotion that had come about from a deep spasm of belonging. But had she ever told them? She'd had a couple romantic relationships long or passionate enough to bring about a profession of love from her partner, though she'd never reciprocated. Now here was Reginald, making her reconsider her entire internal landscape at the same time the bedrock of her emotional existence, the Hollisters, was eroding beneath her.

A yawn caught her by surprise, and thinking about this suddenly seemed like too much effort, not to mention pointless. Her containment reflex around those words approximated a force of nature, and worrying about it would be like worrying about gravity or the charge on an electron. If she needed something to worry about, there were always the four thousand miles between here and Millerton or what she was going to tell people there when she got back—Carol, especially. But she fell asleep without worrying about that either.

The next afternoon, they crossed the churchyard spread out before St. Paul's cathedral toward a Parisian-style pâtisserie aptly named "Paul," which Reginald had been describing in great detail since his eyes had opened around noon. While he ordered, Mitch headed upstairs to secure a table for them, comparing the actual café with his description of it. Smells of butter and chocolate and tea rose on toasty humid air. Compared to The Station, this place felt distinctly European, with furnishings on a smaller scale that wore the patina of age with pride. Reginald had been spot-on, even to the warm color of the walls. Despite never having been to Paris, she could feel the idea of it in this place. She wondered what the City of Light was like and considered suggesting they skip church and hop the high-speed train under the channel to find out.

Reginald traversed the obstacle course of tables to where Mitch sat in the back corner then set down a tray full of enough pastries for four people. "I've been dreaming of this through these months of deprivation." Half a chocolate croissant disappeared in a single bite. "My eyes are probably bigger than my stomach," he said around the mouthful, "but who cares."

"I hope you didn't deprive yourself on my account." Mitch plucked a blueberry off the top of a fruit tart. It burst with tangy sweetness between her molars.

"Even if I did, I'd never admit it. I'm still a proper man in most respects." He thumped his chest. "Not that that seems to matter to you."

"You being you is all I ask."

He smiled a Cheshire grin then proceeded to taste each of the different pastries. The croissant was his favorite, but he deemed the éclair to be a close second. That didn't stop him from eating everything else, including the rest of the tart Mitch left on her plate. He was so buoyant with happiness, Mitch almost held her tongue the second time he checked his watch.

But she couldn't. "Do we really have to go to church?"

"It's not church. It's evensong at St. Paul's."

"Are there pews and crosses and people talking about Christ?"

"Sure, but it's a real experience." He dropped a wadded napkin on their pile of empty plates and scooted his chair back.

"Why don't I wait here for you?"

He stopped pulling on his jacket. "What do you mean?"

"I mean that I don't want to keep you from going, but I'd rather not."

"Why didn't you say something earlier? I'm not going to make you do something you don't want to do, but I assure you it's not your ordinary church service."

For the first time, Mitch realized what an admirable poker face Reginald had. She wasn't in the habit of doing things just to please other people, but if anyone were exception-making, it was him. She said, "No, you're right, and if you think I should see it, I should probably see it." Mitch got into her jacket for the walk across the churchyard. "Ready?"

"What? No! I'm not ready. Sit down." Mitch did. "What's going on?"

"Nothing. I'm still a *proper* woman in most respects." She patted her hair dramatically. "Can't I change my mind?"

"Absolutely not."

"Come on, Reginald. I'm trying to be open to new things."

He narrowed his eyes. "It feels suspiciously like you're humoring me."

"Do you want to fight or go see this incredible church?" She got up, took his hand, and pulled until he acquiesced, but instead of his usual running commentary, he said not a single word all the way across the churchyard and up the stairs to the entrance of the cathedral. They settled into a pew without talking—or even looking at each other—and waited for the service to start.

The cathedral was a study in awesome geometry, with lines that drew the eye upward toward repeated circular motifs, intersecting arches and rings and carvings that became increasingly complex and beautiful in a way that made fractals rise in Mitch's mind. The gleaming vertical shafts of the pipe organ were like uniform slices of the main dome's gold leaf brought down with perfect precision to almost human scale. But the sheer loftiness of the space, the massive but balanced scale that made the details of the ceiling's many mosaics impossible to discern, pushed aside analysis and invited ideas of rapture and elevation, feelings that made Mitch wonder if this infusing of the divine in its visitors had been the architect's intent. Most churches seemed aimed at making God big and the parishioner insignificant in comparison.

The last time she'd attended a religious service was twenty years before in Indiana. That church had accomplished the diminution of humankind with a low-flying ceiling and a distinct lack of grandeur, helped along by the preacher's endless repetitions of sin and unworthiness, and when everything in Mitch's life fell apart and she stopped going from one Sunday to the next, she felt free and light—not unlike being in this tremendous structure with the organ breathing out notes that ricocheted every which way, that propagated through her like normal sound waves but set up a resonance under her skin that prompted her to gather Reginald's hand in both of hers and squeeze so hard he flinched.

She hadn't missed God in those decades away from the church, had found the something greater than herself in science and preferred the connections in her life to terminate at the mortal world. But how could she not be affected by this space and the still-vibrant belief of the men who built it? Of the countless people who had sat where she was sitting and reverberated with their own thoughts and feelings, whether they offered them to God or not?

Reginald was avoiding her gaze, but she tugged on his arm until he leaned down to her. Under the echoing voice of the priest, she said, "I do, you know. A lot. A lot plus or minus no more than a very little."

He laughed without sound then laced his fingers through hers, and Mitch let herself be dazzled.

Carol greeted the new year repulsively early with a screaming headache and a mouth that tasted like ass. The crustiness of her every pore reminded her how much she'd drunk at the party, a fact her scene with Brian had made her conveniently forget. She was twisted up in the sheets, dressed in nothing but a throbbing blister on the heel of her right foot. Although she desperately needed a shower, she also desperately needed to get out of the house without encountering anyone.

A bracing dose of Listerine would have to do, and she swirled around a mouthful while hurrying into jeans and her favorite thread-worn sweater. She crept downstairs and passed Brian, who was snoring on the couch, only marginally covered by an afghan. On her way through the kitchen, she eased some crackers from the cupboard and filled a thermos with water, wincing at the squeak of the faucet when she turned it on. Then she was safely in the van, the garage door rumbling open and probably waking the whole house, but she was already backing out of the driveway. Advil and saltines kept each other company in her stomach while she heavy-footed the gas out of town then south on 77 toward the general vicinity of West Virginia.

Everything she'd said to Brian on that cold sidewalk was true and not true. A small measure of comfort came from knowing what she'd said couldn't be taken back or pretended away. Granted, that also meant she and Brian were going to have to have a real conversation at some point, but not while she was out here in the boonies.

Already, the crackling high that had come along with getting angry and saying whatever she wanted was draining out into the winter landscape buzzing past her windows. As terrible as that exchange had been, she'd felt one-hundred-percent alive while it had happened. She couldn't remember the last time she'd felt so individual. Independent. It made her understand Abby a little more.

Carol spent the daylight hours driving loops across the Ohio border, first speeding away from home then meandering back on narrow country roads that cut through either winter forest or barren fields where crop stubble poked through a thin layer of sparkling, icy snow.

When the sun grew thickly orange on the western horizon, Carol found herself on 77 again, rocketing north toward Millerton. In town, her nerve proved not to be as steady as her lead foot because, instead of going home, she ended up piloting the van to a stop in Mitch's driveway next to her snow-crusted truck. The walk to the front door was covered with an inch of crunchy snow marred only by small boot prints from Freddie down the block, the boy Mitch always hired to feed Chester when she went to conferences—or far-off trysts, evidently.

The house was dark and cold, and Carol doubted her choice of destination until she got some lights on and set the heat to somewhere near tolerable. While the place warmed up, she took the opportunity to poke through the drawers and shelves in the kitchen, living room, and office. She contemplated extending her curiosity to the bedroom but managed to resist that temptation. In all those nooks and crannies, the only interesting thing she found was a fancy wine opener in the kitchen junk drawer. A whole system, really, and news to her that Mitch even drank wine, let alone owned such a contraption.

Carol searched the cabinets for coffee but found only a confusing stash of tea—black, white, and seemingly every color in between. Mitch hated tea, called it watered-down water, probably because her taste buds had long ago been blunted by a steady stream of bitter black coffee.

Wine and tea? What was going on here? Clearly it had been too long since Carol had visited, but Mitch hadn't mentioned anything about it, let alone complained about always going to Carol's. Then again, Carol couldn't remember the last time Mitch had complained about anything besides maybe a late vendor or parts screw-up. No, Carol shouldered the burden of bitching and moaning all on her own. This was supposed to be easier than going home, but not being able to find the damn coffee inundated her with everything about Mitch she apparently didn't know.

She brewed a mug of tea and took it with her to the living room where she settled back into the couch. Every move she made on the well-worn black leather released a whiff of Mitch's hair. The coffee table hosted a collage of engineering journals, well-used coasters, and the mystery novels Mitch read to pass the hours of her insomnia.

A pile of wood and kindling was stacked next to the fireplace across the room. Carol left her tea and walked over there, hoping matches weren't as elusive as the coffee, but she was distracted from her purpose by three pictures on the narrow wood mantle.

In the first, Mitch and Sam stood next to the huge, bullet-shaped body of a wind turbine, mad smiles on their faces, thumbs jerked toward it as if to say, "It's in there." The next was an action shot of the boys an instant before they hit the pool in twin cannonballs. The green swim trunks Gordo was wearing told her the picture had been taken this past summer.

Seeing the kids gave Carol pause. Getting up and leaving them this morning had been easy. She'd been so consumed with the need to escape that their general health and welfare hadn't even crossed her mind, and she wondered if she should feel shame or liberation in having put herself so far ahead of them. Before she'd learned how much it really did change things to have a kid, Carol had thought she might be able to bail as soon as Brian could manage the baby on his own. But then, after terminal hormone poisoning had set in and all clichés became true, escape was not only impossible but undesirable.

Last night had apparently wiped her system clear of survival-instinct love, and the last picture on the mantel told Carol at least one place where this more independent, liberated person she wanted to become would be welcome. The snapshot was in black and white, and the Carol in it had been caught looking off to the side of the camera and smiling. She didn't appear goofy or confused or sure she was fat / silly / a clown. Even her eyebrows looked serious and substantial, set firmly under a smooth forehead. Her neck and shoulders were unabashed around the straps of a tank top. In this picture, Carol was young and hot and firmly rooted, and she wondered not only when it had been taken but how she'd never seen it before.

If any version of her could be at home on Mitch's mantel, this was it. The woman in that picture seemed capable of putting together a life as deliberately as Mitch had. Not that Carol desired the same work-obsessed existence as her best friend, but she envied the way it was exactly what Mitch wanted.

Carol picked up the phone and called Brian.

The door from the garage opened into a quiet so deafening Carol felt like she'd just left a long, loud concert. Obviously, Brian had done as she'd asked and cleared the boys out of the house, and she could well imagine how this must've gone down with

James, who acted like he would self-immolate if forced to cross the threshold of his room against his will.

Carol was disproportionately pleased about the long, hot shower she'd taken at Mitch's, the new toothbrush she'd found in the nearly empty medicine cabinet, the unscented lotion and deodorant. She felt clean and put together and not entirely herself.

"Carol?" Brian called from somewhere deep in the house. "That you?"

"Yeah," she said and put her keys on the hook by the garage door. She watched them sway there for a moment then snatched them off and dropped them in her purse instead.

She and Brian found each other in the hallway outside the kitchen. They stood a few feet apart and didn't say anything for too long until they both blurted out something at the same time. The awkwardness was so painful it nearly overcame Carol's resolve.

Brian turned and walked toward the living room, and she followed him for no good reason. He said, "We can sit in here if you want."

Carol stood in the doorway and took in the couch and recliner, the television and the print that hung above it: a long-exposure shot of a large, brightly lit Ferris wheel. "No. Absolutely not."

"Okay. Maybe the dining room?" Brian turned and collided with Carol. "Sorry. I'm sorry."

"Forget it. Let's sit in the kitchen." Home-field advantage. She led the way, seizing the opportunity to take a deep breath to calm her suddenly noisy heart and try to squelch the doubt surfacing in her thoughts.

She sat in her usual spot and looked at Brian across the table, fidgeting into place, gazing at the kitchen like he'd never seen it before. His face was creased with raw fatigue, and the cowlick at the crown of his head stuck straight up, something that usually made Carol imagine him as a boy but now made him seem disheveled. The sleeves of his Tilsen sweatshirt were stretched out from age, and they drooped over his hands while he toyed with the plain, diner-style salt and pepper shakers on the table. His wedding ring was dull and dinged, and seeing it made her spin hers around her finger a couple times.

Carol alternated between anger and fear. What was he waiting for? Why wasn't he talking, throwing vocabulary around to razzle-dazzle her into submission? He sat there, head bowed and back bent, communing with the salt shaker with such intensity that it robbed her of her usually ready words. She squeezed her hands into fists under the table. How could it be that now, after all these years of mindless verbosity, her mouth refused to cooperate?

She forced herself to say the first thing that came to mind. "If you're thinking reconciliation, you can forget it."

His head bobbed up and down. "I know I'm in the doghouse."

"The doghouse?" Carol laughed and felt the ground beneath her become solid again.

"I broke it off with her," he said to the top of the pepper shaker.

The only thing that statement deserved in response was a dialogue-ending outburst, and containing it felt like swallowing a volcano. Her hands trembled when she released them from their clench. She waited until words could come out in anything other than a scream then said, "I can't even look at you," which was true. She could study his fingers all she wanted, but she avoided his eyes, his stubbled cheeks, the hollow in his throat.

"I don't expect you to understand. I don't even understand. I was up all night going over it—"

"I'm not feeling very sympathetic." This time she glanced up as far as his mouth, which was clamped together in admirable restraint. "All right. I'll try to behave. But multiply your last night by ten years, and you'll have some clue."

He sat up straight then leaned into the table, pushing it an inch closer to Carol. "Can you just admit that most of what we have is good? Because"—he cut her off before she could say anything—"because, if you can't admit that, I don't think we should try to talk until you cool off."

"You don't get to make the rules here," she yelled and scooted back from the table with a big shove. She felt an inexplicable embarrassment at the move and scanned the kitchen ceiling until it passed. Where had the ferocious woman from last night gone? What had happened to the Carol on Mitch's mantle? "I counted six. Was I right?"

Brian's answer followed a long, squirming pause. "There were eight."

"Last spring?"

He nodded and sagged back in his chair, tugging at the neck of his sweatshirt.

"How can you sit there and pretend not to know why I can't stand the sight of you?" She lowered her voice and continued. "Don't ever fucking condescend to me again."

"I'm sorry." When she didn't acknowledge that, he shook out equal piles of salt and pepper onto the table then mixed them together with an index finger. Contriteness radiated from him like body odor, infused his slow, heartbreaking movements.

Carol gripped the edges of her seat. "There's nothing to talk about here, not really. One of us has to go, and I think it should be me."

His head jerked up, and his hand went to his sweatshirt's stretched-out neck again. "What?"

"Don't worry. James won't even notice, and Gordo's malleable. He'll probably talk nonstop for a couple weeks then will be fine." Carol felt a little sick at having said those ridiculously untrue words and made herself put her hands on the table, made them appear as relaxed and easy as she could.

"I wasn't—" Brian pressed his palms to the table as if he were going to get up but then froze there. "Isn't this—" He frowned then grimaced, and Carol thought of Mitch for a split second. Then he captured her hands before she knew what was happening. "Carol." His palms were hot and damp, and his grip offered no possibility of escape. "Think about what you're saying." He closed his eyes and shook his head. "I didn't mean that. I meant, don't you want to work on this?"

Carol wrenched her hands free. "*You* can work on this all you want. I really don't need to supervise."

"You want to separate? Flush fifteen years down the toilet?" He flung his arms out then slapped his hands on the table, scattering grains of salt and pepper there was no way in hell Carol was going to clean up.

"Come on, Brian! You're the one who screwed around on me *eight* times." She lurched up and crossed the room to the sink where she noted the pile of dirty dishes before she leaned back against the counter. She refused to be swayed by his down-turned head. "Just let me have this one. You get to be you all the time, as eight lucky girls know. It's my turn."

"What do you mean I get to be me?"

"Do whatever you want. Make decisions. Traipse around. Screw graduate students."

"Come on."

"What?"

His mouth moved for a moment before he spoke. "Can't we figure out a way for you to 'be you' here?"

"What about 'my turn' don't you understand? Because it doesn't have a thing to do with what you want. I guess that might take some getting used to for you."

"Do you have to be so nasty?" The corners of his mouth drew in and hardened.

Carol took a big step toward him and leaned even closer. "Yes." It came out low and loud, with a hint of gravel. "And you're still getting off easy."

"Okay, I get it," Brian said. He looked at her with bloodshot eyes.

The fact that she held her tongue made her feel almost unbearably adult. She retreated to Mitch's corner of the counter and jammed her hands in her pockets to deny their shaking. The kitchen was so quiet that she jumped when the refrigerator clicked on.

True and not true, she thought. She was being her and not her, and the pervasive dichotomy of everything felt absolutely genuine. Being so nasty was both easy and hard, as was contemplating this great escape, and Carol supposed she was going to have to get used to this yin-yang version of things.

Brian said, "Are you going to stay with Mitch?"

"None of your business."

He sighed and rubbed a hand across his cheeks. "Would you consider holding off a few days? To let the boys get used to the idea? I'll stay on the couch."

A strange relief bloomed in answer to the thought of delay, but Carol kept it out of her voice. "Listen, I know you want the best for them. I just don't believe you want the best for me."

He stood up, his hand creeping across the space between them. "I may be a jerk, but that doesn't mean I don't love you."

Carol scooted past him to the hallway. "That's enough. We can talk about the boys later." She took the stairs two at a time, which left her winded. In the bathroom, she tried to catch her breath, and when she couldn't, she turned on the shower then sat on the toilet and keened under the white noise of the water.

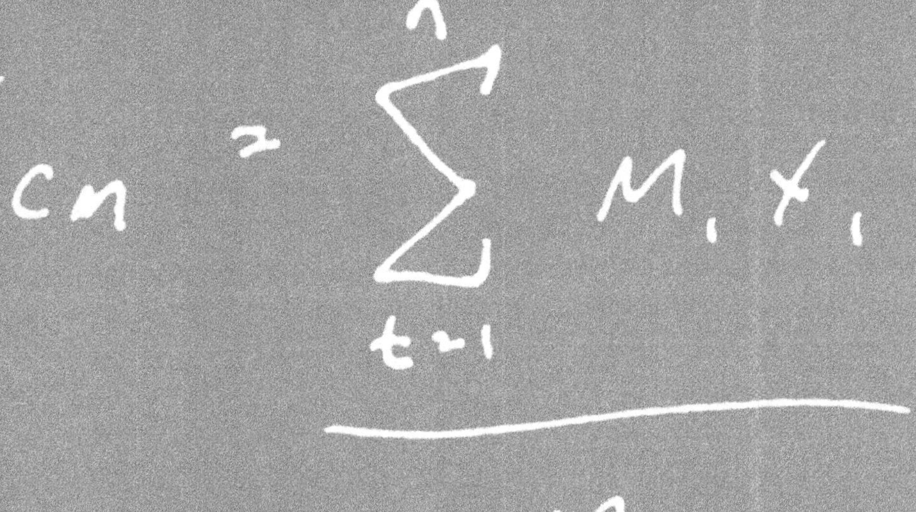

THE TRUTH IS THAT UNLESS YOU MANAGE TO LIVE an entirely unexamined life, one day you will encounter your own fundamental self. The magnitude of the disruption this causes will be in direct proportion to how close your fundamental self is to the person society has always said you should be.

–Dr. Abigail Rosen, The F Word: Femininity in the New Century

THE 5:48 Greyhound local from Cleveland to Cincinnati (stop six: Millerton) had a funky, overripe smell that made Mitch wistfully recall the sanitized air on her flight over from Heathrow. Besides this one difference, the two conveyances were strikingly similar in that they both lacked leg room and Reginald.

Tall dingy humps of snow half obscured the breakdown lane, and Mitch let her sight coast over their uneven outlines caught by the bus's headlights. Her knees ached to be fully extended, and she tried to focus on that one discomfort rather than the legions of other discomforts associated with leaving Reginald, the abrupt way she'd said good-bye, how she'd refused his company to the airport, practically pushing him away, then throwing herself down the stairs from his flat so fast her feet touched only one or two steps every flight in her attempt to outrun her sadness.

While Mitch watched the mile markers count down toward Millerton, she kept hearing Reginald say, "Marmalade, my dear?"

in his best top o' the morning voice. It played on repeat like the refrain of a catchy song overheard at The Filling Station. Why this particular phrase looped in her head was a complete mystery, but her efforts to trick herself out of it were undermined by a fear that she'd succeed and lose his voice completely.

She shifted in her seat, which only made her knees complain more loudly. That smell must be a long-discarded banana peel. Or maybe the whole banana. Carol could have picked her up at the airport and spared her this, or even Steve if Mitch didn't mind owing him favors for a good long while. Truthfully, she hadn't thought of it, and if a few hours on a noxious bus were the cost of delaying the full reality of this trip's conclusion, it was worth it. She breathed through her mouth for the last forty miles.

The Millerton bus station was out by the McDonald's on the other side of town from Mitch's house. The cab she took home reeked of pine from tree-shaped air fresheners hanging off the rearview mirror, and the driver acted like he was on a mission from God to transport Mitch in record time. He rocketed around corners blind from high piles of snow and put his antilock brakes to the test several times before depositing her at the foot of her driveway and peeling away, fishtailing on a patch of ice.

Mitch stood next to her bag and breathed in the dry, cold smell of winter. The only disturbance in the blanket of snow around her house was a thin trail Freddie had beaten from the front door to the street. She looked at the trail while she twisted her torso first one way then the other, eliciting pops up and down her spine.

The driveway was blocked by a berm of icy snow reaching to above her knees, and Mitch climbed neatly over it only to plunge into the drifts beyond, six or maybe eight inches deep, a big accumulation for Millerton. She waded to her truck and the snow shovel that rattled around in its bed all winter. Her hands already stung from the cold, but they'd go numb soon enough.

She shoveled outward from her truck to the edges of the driveway. The snow was wet and heavy with a thin crystallized crust, and pushing it around was a struggle. Her biceps and lower back burned with exertion, and she shed her jacket in no time. When the driveway was clear and her truck was swept off and scraped, she hacked at the plowed, packed ridge by the street, keeping at it until her arms trembled and her thermal top clung wetly to her back. She persisted until every bit of the icy snow was relocated into chunky piles on either side of the driveway.

When she stopped, she was breathing hard enough that each exhale's vapor plume merged with the one before. Chill sank in while she stood at the end of her driveway, gazing around like an amnesiac, and she finally picked up her duffel and went inside.

She'd gotten from London to here without emotional incident through intense focus on logistics and deadlines, which had let the reptilian portion of her brain that handled those sorts of things expand and push complicated, conscious thought from her mind. But now the lack of motion was having its way, and she could feel herself toeing the edge of thoughts that branched and twisted like a nightmarish maze, that led nowhere and solved nothing. She dropped her bag at the foot of the coat rack, sank down to the floor, and shivered. Her back found the closed front door, and she enumerated natural laws, axioms, and absolutes as an antidote to distress. The measured pull of gravity. The speed of light. That an object in motion tends to stay in motion. That entropy increases.

That she and Reginald would talk. That they would email. That, if he had his way, they would put web cams to illicit use. But, oh, were her baths going to be lonely.

Chester appeared from around the far corner of the couch in a puff of orange fur. Mitch sat still and watched him creep toward her as if he were preparing to pounce and sink his teeth into the bit of ankle exposed above her sagging sock. But he didn't. He bumped his head against her knee then settled in next to her, purring. Mitch buried her fingers into his soft fur. Was this all she had to do to acquire the pet she already owned? Become a little more accessible? Be at home in his domain?

This cat's-eye view made her whole house look different. From the unobstructed sight of dust bunnies under her couch to the looming coat rack, the strangeness of the familiar was helping ease this transition home. She looked at her watch then checked again in a double take, having forgotten it was still set to London time. The pool wouldn't open for hours and hours. In fact, she'd missed the evening lap swim not long before. The desire she felt to pull on her suit and experience the drag of water played like a compulsion, to grit her teeth when her shoulder seized up, to match her breath to her stroke. Would her catch feel the same? Her kick? Or would they have changed, too?

Her ass and Chester were both sound asleep on the hardwood floor. He was warm against her leg, and she thought about closing her eyes and seeing if she would fall asleep now that she was back in her natural habitat and if so, how long it would take for discomfort to wake her, but such experimentation had to be done with an open mind, which Mitch had temporarily misplaced. Tomorrow would come no matter whether she slept or not, and no matter where.

She struggled to her feet, which sent Chester darting for cover and a cascade of pins and needles down her legs. Her clothes stuck to her. She shivered violently and went to run a bath.

The next morning, Mitch got to work before the guys and spent that quiet time taking inventory—not only of the new calendar depicting a leggy blond draped across the hood of a red sports car but of the way opening and closing drawers and turning on machines filled her with satisfaction. She felt whole and functional here in a way that she hadn't at home.

An email from Reginald was waiting when she booted up.

I knew it would be too much to ask for you to call when you got home. I knew you'd sound reasonable in your unreasonable refusal, and I'd go along with you and be back in this exact position, sure some great disaster has snatched you up.

Maybe things like this are why you are suspicious of love. But after a day full of tensile strength and load, I look forward to a bit of irrationality in my off hours.

Tell me you've made it home safely.

Patty

She replied, *I've made it home safely*, then stared at the thin slip of blinking cursor, searching for words that might describe how she could feel empty and full at the same time, trying and failing for a long time until she was filled with a deep unease and sent that inadequate sentence if only to stop thinking about it.

When Eric and Steve arrived, they were bickering and carrying three cups from The Filling Station. Eric elbowed Steve and said, "Ha. I told you. Pay up." He held out a hand in front of Steve's chest.

"Now, wait a second." Steve pushed the hand away and put a cup on Mitch's desk. "Hi. Welcome back."

"Thanks." She took off the lid and looked inside. Large espresso.

Steve turned back to Eric. "I didn't say she wouldn't be here before us. I said she probably wouldn't need coffee because she'd get in early enough to have made some here."

"Revisionist," Eric said. "When did you get here?" he asked Mitch when she was in mid-sip.

"Six. But I haven't made coffee. Call it a draw. But you can give me the money. The dollar was down against the pound, and I'm tapped out."

Before they could even ask about the trip, she dug their presents out of her bag—a five-pound block of otherworldly chocolate for Steve and assorted Jermyn Street handkerchiefs for Eric, who claimed that tissues were for girls. Once they got going on the chocolate quality disparity between the US and England ("Do you know how much *wax* is in our chocolate here?"), Mitch knew she was safe even despite the way Steve studied her when Eric wasn't looking.

She took detailed status reports from both of them and was organizing the information for a meeting with Sam when the phone rang. Eric answered.

"Mitchell Industries, Eric here." He leaned back and listened, smiling. "Carol. I thought we were friends. I thought you liked us."

Mitch felt anxiety settle in her joints, and yet she grinned. She and Reginald hadn't talked about Carol after that first night, but that didn't mean Carol hadn't lurked around the edges of the last two weeks.

Eric folded and unfolded a purple-and-green-striped hankie. "Being in your top twenty-five people is supposed to make me happy? Why not top ten? Is that why you didn't call at all when Mitch was gone even though she's by far the least appealing person here?" He winked at Mitch and swung the handkerchief in a circle over his head. "What's the magic word?" He waited. "That's the one!" He pressed a button on his phone. "I warmed her up for you."

"Just what I needed." Mitch picked up the receiver. "Carol."

"Welcome home. And happy New Year."

Mitch couldn't quite peg Carol's voice. Its cadence indicated excitement, but her intonation had a flat, unhappy edge. "Hey, thanks. Same to you. I'd love to talk, but I'm only halfway through my emails and am already running late for a meeting with Sam."

"That's okay. I only wanted to invite you to dinner tonight. Just you and me. Chill, I promise."

Mitch let go of any misgivings. "Now *those* are the magic words. I'll be there."

The day passed in one big heave of catching up and assuring everyone that her vacation was great and had left her well rested and ready to get back at it. Despite the proliferation of clocks, dinnertime crept up on Mitch. She wanted to stay here at work until after the guys left, recover the solitude of this morning that had carried no trace of loneliness, but she reminded herself of how long it had been since she'd seen Carol without distractions. Mitch had accepted the two of them alone without a second thought this morning, but now it made her wonder. What about the rest of the family? She had presents for everyone, even a set of cufflinks shaped like pence pieces for Brian. And with Thanksgiving and the fight, Mitch hadn't seen the boys in too long.

Carol had something up her sleeve, but conjecturing about it was useless.

When she pushed her chair back to get going, the phone rang, and she snatched it up. Carol started talking even before Mitch could spit out her name.

"Mitchy? Oh, good. You haven't left yet."

"Just about to. Need me to pick up something?"

Carol laughed, but it didn't sound amused. "Yeah. Abby."

"Abby? As in Dr. Rosen?"

"Yeah. I'm an idiot. I just…my calendar…I'm an idiot."

"You're not an idiot." Mitch stood, wedged the phone between ear and shoulder, and got her jacket on.

"I forgot we made plans on New Year's for her to come for dinner tonight, and to make things worse, the woman decided to walk over here. With all this snow! What was she thinking?"

Mitch sat back down. "Do you want me to come another night?"

"No no no. No. I mean, no. But can you pick her up? She said she's somewhere near Grove and Chestnut, and I swear she's asking to be killed." Carol sighed. "I'll have to share you."

"Somewhere near Grove and Chestnut?" Mitch got up again.

"You'll figure it out. Just hurry."

She got going after bidding a hasty good-bye to Eric and Steve, had her truck in gear before it was even properly warmed up. The intersection of Grove and Chestnut was devoid of human life, and Mitch drove around in an approximation of widening concentric circles looking for Abby on roads considerably narrowed by banks of snow. This part of town was lacking in streetlamps, and the only illumination besides Mitch's headlights came from a bright half-moon reflecting off the snow.

Eventually Mitch spotted Abby a block or more ahead, wearing the same light-colored coat as Thanksgiving. What Mitch remembered most about that strange day wasn't the mess Abby'd been but the glimpses of relaxation in her, especially the sparkly smile she'd worn when she'd asked, "What's your real name?"

The question hadn't even made Mitch mad. She'd smiled right back and said, "My name is Mitch. You can look it up."

She pulled the truck alongside Abby, who was staring straight ahead like she was on a death march. Mitch kept pace until Abby looked over. Her face was twisted in one big scowl, which made Mitch grin. Abby stopped. Mitch put on the brakes, wished for power windows, and mouthed, "Get in."

Abby opened the passenger-side door, and Mitch said, "Fruitcake." She was inexplicably merry.

"You're Carol's help?" Abby leaned partway inside.

"Knight in shining armor and triple-A all in one. Come on, get in. You know you want to." Mitch waited until Abby was settled and seatbelted before driving again.

"I'm grateful, I am, but what are you doing out here?"

"I was heading over to Carol's for dinner when she called and asked me to pick you up on the way like you were a head of lettuce she'd forgotten."

"Who knew you were so obedient." Abby tucked her hands under her thighs.

Mitch turned up the heat and directed one of her vents toward Abby. "I'm obedient when it suits me. What're you doing wandering around in the cold?"

"Habit." The word was an almost-whisper.

"Apparently. Do you wander around in the heat, too?"

"I have a strict nondiscrimination policy."

"Well, at least about the weather." Mitch looked over in time to catch the nod that went with Abby's chuckle.

"That's true." Abby turned to the window, making her next words soft and muffled. "Carol didn't mention you were coming to dinner."

"Carol…it's my fault. I got her confused, I think. I'm just back from a vacation, and I guess me on vacation is enough to confuse anyone."

"Considering you were working on Thanksgiving, that's not surprising."

Mitch took the opportunity of a stop sign to give Abby her full attention. The pale dashboard lights did lovely things to Abby's cheekbones and chin. "Why don't I drop you off at Carol's and visit her another time?"

"No," Abby said with a snap in her voice. She touched her mouth, and her tone changed. "Don't be absurd. Besides, I've never really seen you two together, and I'm interested."

"Great, an evening as a lab rat."

"You act like I'll be taking notes. Where did you go on vacation?"

The shift in topic surprised Mitch, but she answered without hesitation. "London." They were getting close to Carol's house and an end to this conversation if Mitch wanted.

"And you just got back yesterday? You must be exhausted."

"I'm fine. For now, at least. Traveling in this direction should mean I can't wait to get to sleep, but my biorhythms aren't big rule followers in general."

"London's fantastic. Did you have a conference there?"

"No. It was personal."

"Visiting friends?"

"Not exactly." Mitch swung into Carol's driveway and rolled to a stop. "Not friends. More like a boyfriend. Reginald." It was easy and good to say. She covered Abby's seatbelt buckle with her hand before Abby could move. "Listen, don't tell Carol. She's kind of mad at me about the whole thing."

Mitch was out of the truck and halfway to the house before she heard Abby pop open her door. Regret might not travel as fast as light or even sound, but it was plenty fast enough to have flattened her by now if it were going to.

Inside, what felt like utter chaos was only Gordon with a little Carol around the edges. The first minute was a blur of hugs and a stream of questions and high-pitched laughter impossible to untangle from each other. Mitch watched Carol try and fail to wrangle Gordon into submission and finally felt truly home.

This, Carol thought, was why they didn't have a dog. She willed Gordo to put a sock in it long enough for her to ask Mitch what she'd done with Abby, but the not-so-good doctor walked in just when she'd given up. She flashed Abby what she hoped was a look more self-deprecating than deranged.

Gordo finally settled on a single comprehensible question. "Did you drive on the wrong side of the road?"

Mitch said, "I rode on the top of a double-decker bus on the wrong side of the road. Does that count?"

"Was it red?"

Carol said, "He's been Googling since you left."

"It was red, and I sat in the very front row."

They were jammed in the small foyer, and Carol felt like an idiot no matter what Mitch thought, especially given that she was all neat and put together like this was a date or something. She was even wearing new earrings and a satin headband.

Gordo said, "Cool. Mom said you'd have presents."

Mitch put her arms out, her left hand brushing Abby's shoulder. "Do I look like I have presents? Do you see any presents on me?"

"No." The word was low and drawn out.

"That's because I left them at home. I didn't think you'd be here, but I'll bring them by this weekend, okay?"

To no one in particular, Carol said, "He was supposed to get picked up twenty minutes ago."

Gordo pulled Mitch behind him down the hall, saying, "Come and see what we did with your rubber-band cars."

Carol was left alone with Abby. What with preparing for Mitch, Carol hadn't considered what she would and wouldn't tell Abby about all the shit that had blown through her own personal fan since their New Year's Eve tête-à-tête. Despite how good it had felt to get so reliably angry—channel her inner Abby, she'd considered it—confession was not remotely an option, not with everything ripped open but unsettled.

"Mitch and the boys have a special bond. Here, give me your coat. I don't know what I was thinking, inviting you both on the same night," she said into the drapes of wool and Gore-Tex in the front closet.

"I don't mind. Mitch offered to bow out, but I told her the more the merrier."

Carol closed the closet door and rested against it while she looked at Abby. The tips of her ears were a red echoed perfectly in her thin V-neck sweater. Her corduroys were tucked neatly into fur-trimmed boots still wet from her walk. She was always a sight—thoughtfully assembled and feminine even if barefoot and in jeans or just after tromping through the snow.

"Come on. Let me get you a drink while Gordo monopolizes Mitch. It might be a while." Carol led the way into the kitchen.

"She doesn't seem to mind."

"She loves it. She's their all-time favorite adult, hands down."

Abby wouldn't know, but the kitchen was in full-blown Mitch-seduction mode—not sexual seduction but emotional. If the way to a man's heart was through his stomach, then this was one area where Mitch landed squarely in male territory, and Carol had spent the entire afternoon cooking her favorite foods.

They'd start with a spinach and bacon salad Mitch had gone wild over the first time she'd had it then move on to ribs from the summer that Carol had vacuum-sealed and frozen. Vanilla pudding, chunky with Nilla wafers, was chilling in the fridge for dessert, but the pièce de résistance was a batch of Grandma Arlene's macaroni and cheese finishing up in the oven. If anything were a tip-off of the impending asking of a major favor, this mac and cheese was it. The recipe existed only in Arlene's grave and on a yellowed three-by-five card Carol had spirited away from the woman's recipe box at her wake, and the magnitude of its deliciousness was matched only by the labor required in its preparation.

Carol checked on its progress through the dirty oven window then got two beers from the fridge, setting one in front of Abby. She slid into the chair to Abby's right and nodded her head in the direction of the living room. "Sometimes they get going on something, and Mitch forgets what she came here for. And I'm beginning to wonder if Gordo's ever going to get picked up."

"Have you two been friends since college?" Abby pushed the sleeves of her sweater halfway up her forearms.

"No, not really." Carol belatedly realized how nice those conversations with Abby had been when lacking any mention of Mitch. Still, she answered obediently. "After we broke up, we never really saw each other. Different circles, you know? She graduated the year after me and took off. By the time she reappeared, I was the exact opposite of the person she'd known."

"I doubt that's true. Your circumstances were different, sure, but do any of us ever fundamentally change?"

"God, I hope so. Don't you? Of course, your fundament is a lot nicer than mine, so maybe not."

"My fundament could use work, but don't change the subject."

"Well, I certainly *felt* different. And having a baby velcroed to you makes an impression."

Abby tipped her bottle in acknowledgment.

"I mean, isn't it true that if you take a woman strolling around town alone and toss a couple kids into the picture, all you see is a mom?"

"So, Mitch saw you as a mom?"

Carol considered claiming that the salad needed to be tossed or the ribs monitored just to get away from Abby's insistence on this story—on all things Mitch, she imagined. Instead, she drank some beer and succumbed to the inevitable long night ahead.

"I don't know how Mitch saw me. But one afternoon, there she was, storming her way across the quad to the engineering building, and I hauled jiggly ass to intercept her, dragging James and Gordo with me." She twirled her beer, remembering. "At first, Mitch had this blank-faced stare she gets when she's interrupted. But then she really looked at me, at James, at Gordo in the stroller, and at me again. Then she gave me the kind of smile she reserves for total eclipses of the sun. She hugged me hard and squatted down to talk to James, and she never said a word about anything, not even after she met Brian and heard the whole story."

"She sounds like a good friend." Abby flicked her eyes toward the living room then returned to picking the label of her beer to tatters.

"She's both irreplaceable and impossible. Mitch accepts you so viciously for who you are that it sometimes makes her blind to the possibility that there might be room for improvement."

"What's her mother like?"

For once, Carol understood Mitch's annoyance at these questions she deemed to be obvious and pointless and nearly entirely confined to practitioners of the soft sciences. At the same time, it hurt Carol a little to admit that she didn't know.

"You've never met her?"

Carol threw up her hands. "Me and no one else in this universe, apparently. I don't think she exists. In fact, I'm convinced the stork dropped her off at the gates of campus fully formed. If you ask her about it, she goes quiet as death and not only do you wish you hadn't asked, you wish you were never born."

A horn honked outside, and Gordo blazed through the kitchen and down the hall. Mitch appeared seconds later, all grins and insistence that Carol get up for a proper greeting. Mitch's smile and the tiredness evident both underneath it and in the deep wrinkles in her white button-down shirt made Carol forget Abby for the long moment of their hug.

When Carol stepped back, she said, "You look—"

"I know," Mitch said.

"I was going to say good."

Mitch hitched up her jeans. "You were going to say tired."

"Well, that, too." Carol pushed her toward the table. "Take a load off. I'll get you a beer."

Mitch sat down to Abby's left, collapsing into the chair in a way that made Carol imagine she could hear the clatter of her bones. She asked, "How was Christmas?"

Carol opened another beer and put it in front of Mitch. "Christmas was fine."

"James okay?"

Abby's observation felt like a heavy blanket, and Carol turned away from it. She was trying to woo Mitch, and she needed Abby around like another hole in the head. She peeked in at the mac and cheese and deemed it done then slipped her hands into oven mitts. "James is fine." She pulled the casserole dish out and set it across two burners.

A chair shifted behind her, and Mitch said, "Is that—"

"Yep."

"Maybe I should start going away more often."

Carol looked back at Mitch. "Funny."

Abby leaned closer to Mitch. She rubbed the short hair on the back of her head. "Tell us about your trip. I haven't been to London in years, but I'd love to compare notes."

"I don't know that I have many notes. I wasn't a very good tourist."

"When people say that, it usually means they spent all their time in the pubs, but I doubt that's true of you."

Mitch was sprawled in her chair, the very picture of relaxation. "No, though I managed to drink plenty of Newcastle. I went to the British Museum three times. I can't believe that place is free. I would have paid good money just to see the Rosetta Stone."

The label of Abby's beer lay in ragged pieces on the table. She asked, "Did you go to Westminster Abbey? Evensong with all those dead kings? US history is so paltry in comparison."

"I know. I went to St. Paul's, and I could feel it there, the continuity. Then again, I could've been high from the pastries I ate right across the courtyard. Paul's? Have you been there?"

They talked London while Carol put the finishing touches on the salad and waited for the mac and cheese to set. Keeping busy allowed Carol to let Abby and Mitch's conversation pass by her without comment and refrain from throwing something at Mitch for being such a consummate liar. The way Mitch told it, she'd spent those two weeks in London alone, spent her evenings drinking Newcastle and thumbing through her copy of *Lonely Planet*. She could have been bunking in a hostel with

Helga from Germany rather than getting boinked half to death by her mystery woman.

A small comfort came from knowing that at least she, alone, recognized Mitch's lies for what they were, and Carol could even feel a squeeze of pleasure at imagining Mitch in love. Mitch's capacity for passion was enormous. In ways, passion was her natural state, and witnessing it directed not at The Device but at another actual human being would be a vicarious delight. The closest Carol had seen Mitch get to this was with the boys, with whom she was not only completely herself, but had a certain openness around her that let her love shine though.

At the same time, the idea of Mitch's love filled Carol with a sharp but undefined fear. She was used to sharing Mitch with Steve and Eric and The Device, but if Mitch were in love, would there be any room left for Carol at all? It was a stupid fear—love didn't obey the laws of mathematics—but Carol couldn't shake it. Even if Mitch hadn't yet totally forgiven Carol for acting like a selfish wretch after Thanksgiving, she would, if given enough time and close proximity. But if she'd gone and lost her heart to someone, finally fallen in love on Carol's watch…who knew what that would mean?

Abby and Mitch were swapping bus lines and bridges when Carol set out the food. Abby left off her incessant questioning of Mitch to ooh and ahh over the meal, and Mitch half got up, offering to help. Carol swatted her down.

Mitch filled her plate with some of everything the way she always did, then went clockwise around the foods, tasting a single bite of each. Each elicited a nod or an "mmm," but when she got to the macaroni, she made Carol get up for a brutal hug.

"My God," she said while squeezing the life out of Carol. "I'll need supervision or I'll eat the whole batch."

While they ate, Abby dropped London but not Mitch. She questioned Mitch about her work and her history with Carol, over which Mitch frowned, kicked Carol under the table, and refused to answer. Abby periodically swayed toward Mitch then away, and her hands seemed drawn to her hair and cheeks and ears, empty of adornments tonight but still pink at the tips. Her questions were nothing, really, but this body language completely contradicted her aloofness that afternoon out by the pool.

Maybe Abby was a better liar than Carol had thought, though she obviously wasn't trying very hard tonight. What was Carol thinking? *Of course* she was a better liar than Carol wanted to admit. She'd needed to believe some good of Abby so she could have an ally in her mental reawakening. She still needed to believe, just not tonight. All tonight required was a whole bunch of getting through.

Besides, how could she blame Abby for finding Mitch several times more interesting than herself? She had nothing to offer Abby tonight besides a deteriorating marriage and a knockout recipe for macaroni and cheese. Mitch was scintillating in comparison. She wished she could say that her marriage was over or something equally dramatic, but she and Brian hadn't even told the boys yet, though they'd had two more short but tortured conversations. Brian's continued apologies were infuriating, especially when added to his deer-in-the-headlights manner. Why couldn't he be an asshole about the whole thing?

Later, Abby put her spoon down in a definitive way and pushed her empty pudding bowl an inch away from her. "If I knew my way around a kitchen, I'd ask for the mac and cheese recipe. Incredible. I'm beyond stuffed."

"Grandma Arlene. Her cooking made the rest of her bearable." Abby and Mitch laughed, and Carol said, "She was horrible. My father surviving to adulthood despite her sharp tongue and strict belief in corporal punishment was a miracle. She could've made a stew out of him, easy. Really. You could see her doing something like that."

"Carol's dad is a sweet man," Mitch said to Abby.

"All the better to eat?" Abby asked.

Carol said, "She'd age him down in the cellar first. Not even my brother calling me chicken nonstop for three whole days could get me to go down there alone. Spiders as big as my face and a chest freezer that could hold a couple bodies, easy. My dad got trapped down there overnight once and claims he's never been the same since."

Mitch laughed through a yawn. "Carol, you believe everything your dad says."

"Why would he lie?"

"Because he's so good at it." Mitch stood up and started to gather plates and silverware. After a look at Abby, she said, "He's got a cherubic face and a soft voice, and he uses it to his advantage."

Carol said, "Mitch! Next you're going to tell me that Santa Claus isn't real, but I saw the man not two weeks ago, milk mustache and all."

Mitch glided to the sink, balancing a tall stack of dishes. "Santa Claus isn't real."

"You're evil." Carol sighed. "And you look beat. What time is it for you, midnight?"

"Something like that. My internal clock is somewhere in the mid-Atlantic."

"You should go home and get some sleep. Give Abby a ride while you're at it."

Abby said, "Let us help you with the dishes."

"Nope. This is why God invented dishwashers."

Abby argued to no avail then excused herself and went to the bathroom. When she'd left, Mitch intercepted Carol between the table and sink, laying a hand on her arm.

"What's going on?" Mitch put more pressure on her fingertips.

"What do you mean? Nothing's going on."

"Nothing's going on?"

Carol shook off Mitch's hand and put dishes on the counter. "Don't repeat me. You sound like Gordo."

"Grandma Arlene's—"

"What the hell, Mitch. So I made some mac and cheese." Carol gave Mitch a withering look, arms folded, cheeks flushed.

"Is this because of Abby? She won't be back for a minute. Just tell me."

"I don't know what you're talking about. Here." She rummaged around in the Tupperware drawer then slung some mac and cheese into the container she'd dug out. "Take this and

Abby and leave. You're practically sleepwalking. Whatever I supposedly have to say can wait until tomorrow."

Mitch tried to dodge the full container, but Carol finally pressed it against her belly. "Carol."

"Just go, Mitch."

Out in the truck, Mitch waited for Abby and tried to sort through the dinner. Carol used Grandma Arlene's macaroni and cheese like a fat stack of currency, never made it unless she was preparing to ask for something significant. Hollister folklore had it that she'd made a double batch for Brian when broaching the subject of a second baby. This time, it was a bribe for something Carol couldn't bring up with Abby around, not even when she was in the next room.

So far Mitch didn't regret telling Abby about Reginald, though the inquisition at dinner had gotten her pretty close. It had felt like a test on a subject she hadn't studied, and she didn't know if she'd passed or failed.

When Abby climbed in the truck, Mitch got her address and didn't waste any time pulling out. They weren't even to the end of the block when Abby asked, "Is Brian cheating on Carol?"

"Looks that way," Mitch said then wondered if she should have sidestepped the question. Was Abby someone Carol trusted? Maybe not as much as Mitch had thought. Something had happened to Mitch in London. That backward traffic had unwound something in her brain.

"What's Carol going to do?"

"I don't know. It's not the first time. I usually hear all the gory details..." Mitch trailed off, not wanting to get into it, especially without knowing what Carol had been fixing to ask for tonight.

"I don't see how anyone could put up with that."

"She loves him."

"Still." Abby shifted in her seat to face Mitch, bracing one hand against the dashboard. "Would you sit around and let Reginald step out on you?"

"No, but I'm not Carol, Reginald's not Brian, and I don't have to worry about two kids and a lot of years of marriage."

"Are you always so rational?" Her eyes were dark sockets under her full eyebrows.

Mitch felt crankiness scratch at the underside of her skin. "Of course not."

"How did you meet Reginald?"

"At a conference last summer."

"What's he like?"

"What're you getting at? What do you want from me? Why are you always digging around for dirt?" Mitch knew Abby's questions might be perfectly innocent, but they didn't feel innocent. They felt purposeful in a way Mitch couldn't stomach.

"Mitch, I'm not—"

"Right. Questions are your thing. Well, here's some dirt for you. Reginald came up to me after my presentation on continuous data integration. He's English and black, and I fucked him after dinner and drinks I'd rather have skipped." The words came out sharp and loud, and she didn't know why she was telling this to Abby when regret had finally caught her and sat heavy on her chest.

"Hey." Abby put her warm hand on Mitch's thigh, and Mitch remembered how to shut up. She wanted to get home and write an email to Reginald that exposed some part of herself he hadn't seen, but she knew she wouldn't.

A couple miles passed without further comment, but Mitch knew Abby wasn't sitting back and enjoying the ride, the moonlight on the snow, the velvet darkness of the sky. No, Mitch could feel her thinking.

They turned onto her street, and Mitch wasn't surprised when Abby said, "Would you like to get together not by accident sometime?"

Just as Mitch wanted to grant Reginald more than a peek into her innards, she wanted not to be afraid of Abby, wanted in her a friend she could clearly never be. Being around her was appealing in the same way running for one's life brought with it the thrill of immediate existence.

Mitch said, "I don't think so, but thanks. Have a good night."

Abby slid from the truck without a word.

When Mitch got back to Carol's, she knocked and let herself in. Even in the foyer, she could hear the grumbling swish of the dishwasher under the higher-pitched spray of the sink faucet. Carol's back was to her when she reached the kitchen doorway, and Mitch hesitated, not knowing how to avoid startling her.

"Hey," Mitch said. No response. She walked closer and repeated herself. Nothing. Braced against what was sure to happen, Mitch closed the rest of the distance between them and touched Carol's shoulder.

Carol screamed and jumped, which sent soapy water spattering out of the sink and onto the window above. She turned around and braced herself against the counter. Her face was splotchy with crying.

"What the fuck?" she yelled. Then her hands covered her face, and she was jumping and shuddering and making indecipherable noises behind her red, wet fingers. But when she uncovered her mouth, she was howling with laughter.

Mitch took her shoulders, directed her staggering, lurching steps to the living room, then sat next to her on the couch, thigh-to-thigh, shoulder-to-shoulder. She waited through the hoots and the wails, the gasping for breath, and finally the hiccups.

Carol sighed and trapped Mitch in a sideways hug. She put her face in Mitch's neck. "I'm leaving Brian. It's all done. We talked about it. He's staying here with the boys, and I'm leaving."

Mitch wrapped an arm around Carol even though she very much wanted to slip off the couch and out the front door. Yes, she wanted Carol to be happy, but what she wanted even more was for everyone to behave and stop rocking the boat.

"Anyway," Carol said, "I'd planned to have more wiles about this—or some wiles, at least—but Abby…I know I'm naturally as subtle as a bullhorn, and I know this is ridiculous, but hell, I didn't make all that food for my health. Can I stay with you? I promise it won't be for long. I'll sleep on the couch and won't make a mess and will stay out of your way. I'll—"

"Carol, it's fine. Stay as long as you need."

Carol's hug went uncomfortably tight. They'd had that whole exchange without looking at each other, for which Mitch was thankful. She could feel dismay in her features, and she didn't want Carol to see. Her trepidation had so many parts that she didn't know what to try to eliminate first. For now, she just ratcheted her arm tighter and let Carol talk while she leaned back and worried at the ceiling.

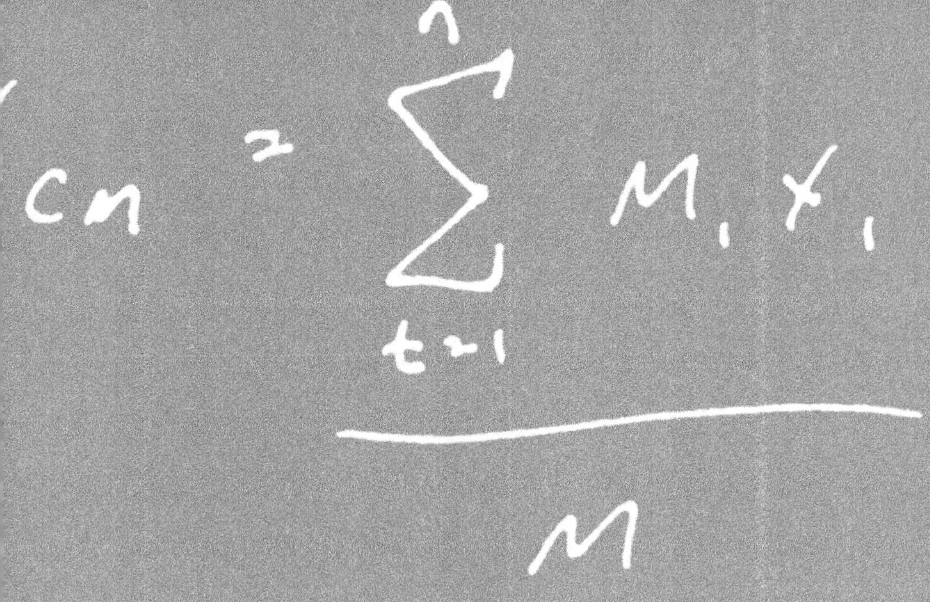

ONCE YOUR EYES ARE OPEN TO YOUR FUNDAMENTAL self, the temptation is to assume everyone else is still blindfolded, that the very feminine woman you just passed on the sidewalk is wearing that skirt because society zipped her right into it. While you may be right, this feeling of superiority and accompanying disdain only perpetuates the problem.

–Dr. Abigail Rosen, The F Word: Femininity in the New Century

15

CAROL DIDN'T move to Mitch's that night or even the next day. She did, however, put the rest of Grandma Arlene's mac and cheese to good use, feeding it to the boys until they were narcotized and docile enough that she and Brian could spit out the news of their impending separation. Stock, hackneyed phrases cushioned sharp bits of truth.

"Your mom is moving out."

"Dad and I need a little time apart."

"We love you kids like crazy, and nothing will change that."

"We're not sure what's going to happen."

"This has nothing to do with you guys. It's just complicated."

"Adult complicated."

James slammed himself in his room and turned his music to window-rattling levels. Gordo cried then followed Carol around the house, peppering her with questions she didn't let herself hear. She answered them with variations on the theme of "I don't know" until finally taking refuge in the bathroom.

After the boys were asleep, Brian barely had to ask before Carol caved and postponed her move for an unspecified while. Just until things calmed down, until the boys got used to the idea, until James came out of his room. Brian's utter transparency and the flapping open end of this decision should have made her start packing right then, but she agreed, promising herself she'd delay maybe a day. Or two. Certainly not more than three.

A week later, Carol woke and stretched luxuriously, straying well over to Brain's vacant side of the bed. The sheets over there were cool and retained their fresh-from-the-dryer smell. This was the first good night's sleep she'd gotten this year, and all she wanted to do was lie in bed, breathing in and out and thinking of nothing.

These walls were the perfect shade of blue—dark enough to inspire relaxation, light enough not to shrink the room, gray enough to feel soft, blue enough not to look gray. The perfect color to lie in bed and stare at. Mitch's place had nothing like this color, not to mention any of the comforts Carol took for granted here. Moving there was going to be so... When the full shape and size of that thought asserted itself, Carol scrambled to her feet and started emptying the closet of her clothes.

She filled a medium-sized suitcase to bursting with toiletries and other necessitics then shoved everything but the kitchen sink (including her favorite skillet) in a beige behemoth of a bag she had insisted on buying despite Brian's doubts as to its practicality. Practicality? What could possibly be more practical than consolidating both their shit in one bag when traveling? But he turned out to be right. The thing was too massively heavy to maneuver and usually sat in the back of their basement storage area.

Despite a long break in packing to go to work, Carol still managed to finish with a few minutes to spare before James was due home from school. She bumped the huge, musty-smelling bag down the stairs in a hurry, doubting James wanted to share some heartfelt moment at her departure. She wouldn't mind avoiding it either.

Out in the driveway, she strained to heave the monstrous suitcase into any part of the vehicle equipped with a wide-enough opening. Her attempts were so frantic and herculean that she was sweating and shaking before realizing that James stood at the foot of the driveway, staring.

He was Brian all over again, only with Carol's blue eyes and a curl to his hair that he wore much too long. When he let his wide-open face escape his hat or his hair or his sour demeanor, he was a good-looking kid. A small spray of acne dotted his forehead, and the bright winter light brought out a dark haze on his upper lip that had recently appeared.

Neither of them moved, and squeamishness rose in Carol. She felt delinquent, caught in the act, and at the same time, unbearably sad.

"Hey," she said.

He didn't reply, just shoved his hands deeper into his jacket, a brown Carhartt with a fluffy sheepskin lining they'd given him for Christmas.

"James."

"What?" His voice cracked, but it was still sharp.

"I'm sorry. I am. I could say phony adult stuff to try and make it better, but I don't do that, right?"

He squinted. "You do it."

"Well, I try not to, okay?" Carol's hands had crept to her hips before she knew it.

"Yeah."

"Listen, there's nothing I can say besides that I love you but have to leave, no matter how lame that sounds."

"I get it." He swiped some hair from his face. "But The Gord doesn't."

A freight train of grief barreled through Carol, which made breathing hard and her vision blur. She propped herself up on the van's bumper. "Jimmy, you take care of him. I know he's your kid brother, but be nice."

"Don't call me Jimmy."

Carol hadn't, not for years. "Sorry. Extenuating circumstances."

"Yeah." He indicated the suitcase with his elbow. "Do you need help with that?"

"I guess I do. If that's okay."

He shrugged but came over and helped her hoist the bag into the back of the van. Carol could tell how much stronger he'd gotten in the last year.

"Jeez, Mom. Is there anything left in the house?" He dusted off his hands.

Carol grabbed him and squeezed hard enough to keep from crying. "We'll figure it out," she said into his shoulder.

"Yeah." Then he went into the house without looking back.

Carol drove right to the twelve-screen movie multiplex two exits down 77 and sat through the first movie playing that would carry her through the rest of the afternoon. She didn't want to call Mitch and inform her of this belated, creaky start to her plan and have it sound like an emergency or desperation. The whole situation needed to feel normal even though it very much wasn't.

After the movie, when Carol finally called Mitch from the theater parking lot, Mitch played her part perfectly, claimed to be at a good stopping point, confirmed that Carol had the spare key, and said she'd meet Carol at the house. All with an opaque cheerfulness.

The house was quiet and dark when Carol got there, and she left her crap in the van and parked herself at the kitchen table, feeling a little shy. Time slowed nearly to a stop. Each thwack of the large classroom clock mounted on the wall over the table felt completely distinct from the ones both immediately before and after.

Mitch arrived not more than ten minutes later, but Carol was half-crazed with the waiting. "Sorry I'm late," Mitch said. "I stopped to pick up dinner." She deposited a large paper-wrapped package on the table and gave Carol a rough one-armed hug. By the size and smell of the bag Mitch had brought, Carol knew it was a two-foot toasted Italian sub—the house specialty of Mr. Tony's in town. "Do you want to eat or get settled in first?"

Carol's missing appetite reappeared with Mitch's smile and matter-of-fact ease, and she said, "Are you kidding? Get the plates."

Mitch gathered silverware and cups. "I cleared out a couple of drawers and part of the closet for you. And we can find more room if you need it."

Carol laughed and unwrapped the sub. Smells of pepperoni, mozzarella, and pepperoncini were swoon-worthy. "Did you get a load of my bags in the van? You might have to move out entirely before everything'll fit."

"I saw them. How'd you get the big one in there?" Mitch sat across from Carol.

"Don't ask."

Carol polished off her half of the sub while Mitch kept up a stream of conversation about the weather, her intern, and an invitation she'd received to present at a conference in Toronto over the summer. Mitch's talk, though lulling in a way, was as foreign as her kitchen, and Carol felt again how little time she'd actually spent in this house. At Carol's place, Mitch had always seemed perfectly comfortable, but tonight an extra relaxation showed in her face, and a lack of tension graced her movements when she tipped her chair back to reach into the refrigerator for a bottle of hot sauce.

When their plates were empty but for toasty crumbs, Carol said, "I don't want you to feel like you have to tiptoe around me in the mornings or anything. I've got a set of earplugs to die for. They can drown out Brian's hay-fever snores, which means I can pretty much sleep through the coup of a small country."

"Don't worry. You won't need them." Mitch wadded up their discarded paper wrappings then shot the ball at the open garbage can in the corner. She missed. "I'll take the couch. I'm out there at some point most nights, anyway."

"No. I'm the one imposing. I get the couch. No argument."

But Mitch argued, went into detail about how long she'd spent at the furniture store picking out the couch (hours) and how long she'd lain on this particular couch before buying it despite the salesperson's best efforts to dislodge her (forty-five minutes) and how the couch was sizeable enough (six feet, even) for her to stretch all the way out. By the time she finished laying out her points, she'd cleared the table and bullied Carol into submission.

"Well," Carol said, "if you ever want a break from the wonder couch, I'm conditioned not to take up much room in the bed."

"I'll keep it in mind."

Carol felt guilty the first few nights, especially given how Mitch's splendid mattress induced a comalike sleep, but she got over it. Whenever the need to pee forced her from her dreamless slumber, if Mitch wasn't at her desk, she was on the couch with all the lights blazing, reading, sleeping, or just staring at the ceiling. By the time Carol put bare feet to cold floor in the mornings, Mitch was gone for the day, piling up laps in the university pool, never mind that she had more ice packs than food in her freezer.

Gordo called Carol four times each of the first three days, James refused to talk to her, and Brian sent nightly emails assuring her how fine and under control everything was, how she could take all the time she needed because they were hanging in. Missing her but hanging in. He was anything but reassuring, especially when the school called a week into the proceedings to inform her that James had done his level best to beat the shit out of a boy almost twice his size. He was lucky to come away with only a split lip and the start of what promised to be an impressive shiner.

Brian was too furious to deal with James, so Carol had to give him the "you're grounded and don't be a dumbass again" talk alone. At the end, they looked at each other, and she felt like the blind leading the blind.

"I don't know," she said. "You're not going to listen to me, and I'm tired of being reasonable, anyway. If you have to act out, don't do anything that'll land you in the hospital or jail or that you'll regret too badly when you're my age."

"So, I can get a tattoo?"

"That would probably lead to regret. Unless you get 'Mom' big and bold over your heart. Best not to do permanent things before you know what permanent means. And I'm just learning that now."

When Carol had come up with the wise idea to bunk with Mitch, she should have known better than to imagine evenings of talk and understanding. That first dinner together proved to be an anomalous high point. If she hadn't had some idea of Mitch's lifestyle before, the full ugly extent of it was laid out all around her now. Carol didn't know what Mitch actually did with those hours at work, but she couldn't imagine what could take so long.

While Mitch worked in the evenings, sometimes at the office and sometimes at home, Carol tried to pin herself down on the couch with the ultimate Gandhi biography she was reading—it was certainly heavy enough to keep her physically still—but her concentration scattered like buckshot in the quiet of Mitch's house. She tried to channel her inner Gandhi, but she was pretty sure she didn't have one, not his patience, vision, or conviction. Certainly not his loyal spouse.

Nearly two interminable weeks after James's schoolyard brawl, Carol met Abby at The Filling Station for coffee. Carol hadn't exactly been avoiding Abby since that accidental dinner for three, but she hadn't been making her usual effort either. There was no telling what would come out of Carol's mouth around her, whether by prompt or her own stupid volition, and she wasn't ready to dig through this mess with an outsider. This afternoon, she was hoping for distraction without dissection, though Abby was far from the best choice for this.

When Carol arrived at the coffee shop, Angel was chatting with Abby, who was clearly in her usual questioning mood. Great. Carol wasn't as good as Mitch at evasive conversational tactics—who was?—but hopefully she'd learned something over the last ten years.

"Hola," Carol said then slid into the chair opposite Abby.

Angel glanced back and forth between Carol and Abby, adjusting the white towel slung over her shoulder. "You two know each other?"

Abby said, "I work with her husband."

"But we're friends despite that," Carol said.

Angel slapped her forehead with her hand. Silver glitter on her nails caught the light. "Duh. One plus one, Angel. Small latte, skim?" she asked Carol.

"Make it a medium mocha, and don't go skimping on the chocolate."

"Just for that it'll be practically solid with the stuff. Skimp on the chocolate. Ha!" she barked out then headed back behind the counter.

Carol smiled at Abby. "How's tricks?"

She asked Abby about the new semester, about how her walks fared in the mild temperatures they were having, about where she'd gotten her blouse, a nondescript blue cotton with bone buttons. When she stopped to take a sip of the drink Angel had brought over—the best mocha she'd had here, she should give Angel a hard time more often—Abby butted in.

"Did Mitch get over her jet lag?"

Mitch wasn't the last thing Carol wanted to talk about, just really, really close. But she answered anyway. "Sure, not that it slowed her down. If she were married to an actual woman instead of The Device, that would be one lucky wife."

"Has she ever been in a serious relationship?" Abby scooped invisible hair behind her ear, a move Carol was starting to understand in a way she wished she didn't.

"She has occasional flings that last until the chippie gets tired of Mitch's work ethic."

"Chippie?"

Carol rolled her eyes. "They're not the pick of the litter, if you ask me. The last one had the intellect of a paper bag."

Abby peered into the depths of her coffee mug and said, "Guess she's looking for something other than brains."

"I prefer that side of Mitch to remain a mystery." Carol wondered why that made Abby look particularly interested. Instead of finding out, she changed the subject to the deplorable state of Tilsen's basketball team.

That night, she woke in the wee hours to find Mitch curled up on the other side of the bed, breathing deeply and evenly. When Carol got up on one elbow, she could see Mitch's profile, her cheeks hollowed out and ghostly in the nighttime shadows. With great stealth, Carol lifted the covers between them and moved closer to Mitch's sleeping warmth, which was gentle, so unlike Brian's blast-furnace heat.

The hard curve of Mitch's back had no answers about her taste in women but was comfortable in a way Carol had forgotten about after she'd dumped Mitch in college, the slow rustle of her breath and the vulnerable spread of her ribs under her T-shirt.

After that night, Mitch started showing up in bed regularly, and Carol scooched closer each time until at the midnight end to another interminable, tedious, worthless day, she closed the entirety of the gap between them and looped her arm over Mitch's thin side. Mitch shifted, but her breathing didn't change. Carol pressed closer, finding the back of Mitch's neck with her nose.

This move evoked a grumble, then, "Carol? You okay?"

"What did you see in Kim?"

"What?" Mitch half turned.

Carol kept her arm locked in position, firm against Mitch's belly. "I mean, was it just her body?"

"It's the middle of the night."

"Not really, not yet."

Mitch sighed.

"Kim. Tell me."

"Why? I know you hated her. What does it matter?"

Carol tightened her grip. "Just tell me, all right?"

Mitch turned her face away but said, "She was warm and easy. Easy with me, I mean. There was the physical stuff between us, yeah, but I could relax around her. At least for a while. I knew it wasn't going to last, but it was … nice."

Carol couldn't tell which started first, the painful thudding of her heart or the play of her fingers over the hills and valleys of Mitch's ribcage. She had a hard time swallowing past the beating that filled her throat, yet that proved no impediment to speech.

She said, "I think we should sleep together."

The laugh she got in response spurred her fully into motion. It was easy, even graceful, to throw her leg over Mitch's and slide herself up and over so they were chest-to-chest. She ran her hand down from Mitch's cheek to her neck. "I'm not kidding."

Carol's absolute seriousness was clear in her glittering eyes and the soft set of her mouth, and Mitch panicked in the worst way. She struggled out from under Carol and into the chill of the room. "What?"

"Well, why the fuck not? You used to find me attractive."

"That's not the point!" Mitch found a pair of sweatpants and yanked them on over her shorts.

"What's the point, Mitch? Oh all-knowing-one?"

"That's not fair."

"Love isn't fair. And neither is sex."

"Don't you think I know that?" Mitch jammed her head through the neck of a sweatshirt then cast around for more clothes she could put on. A parka would be nice.

Carol half sat up. "What's the point, then?" she asked in an oddly calm voice.

"You're married."

That sparked a laugh. "That's not the point, and you know it."

"Jesus, Carol. What're you doing?"

"I'm trying to get close to you," Carol yelled and got to her knees on the bed, bringing her eye level with Mitch. "God fucking forbid, right?"

"But this way?"

"Yes. This way."

Mitch reeled around the room until she settled at the dresser where she opened three drawers before locating her socks.

She struggled on a pair. "No. I can't. I just…no, not after London."

Carol waved that off. "London. So some chick's hot for you over there. So what?"

"It's not some chick."

"Sorry," Carol said, employing several more syllables than necessary. "Some certainly lovely *woman*."

"His name is Reginald, and I'm in love with him," Mitch shouted in anger and relief then didn't know what to do with herself.

Carol made a strangled sound. When she spoke, her voice was hoarse but loud. "Oh, that's rich. Does Prince Charming know how much you like pussy?"

Mitch opened her mouth, but nothing came out.

"Does he know what a lying sack of shit you are?"

"I never lied to you."

"That's a fucking technicality you hide behind, Mitch. You lie all the time just by keeping your trap shut. Do you know how small and stupid you've made me feel about wanting to know you? Well, fuck that. You're nothing special at all."

"I never said I was."

"You're a huge waste of my time. And, what, now you're going to become Mitchy homemaker with this guy? You think you're so different from the rest of us, but you're just the same."

"I never—"

"You're *exactly* the same."

Mitch ran from the room then the house, barely slowing to grab keys and shoes from by the front door. She got in her truck, tore out of the driveway, and didn't slow down until she was in the next county. Even when she could finally lift her foot from the accelerator, she was still shaking.

She pulled off to the side of the road, the truck bucking across a shallow ditch and stopping inches short of a tree she didn't see until the last second. Her teeth were chattering, and there was no feeling in her fingertips. After turning the heat on high, she dragged the sleeping bag out from behind the passenger seat and unfurled it over herself.

This felt so familiar, down to the percolating rage buried under the hurt and shock in her cold chest and behind her numb face. Anger had fueled her through many frigid, dark nights like this one, had clarified confusion into a chemical compound so pure and nourishing she could practically live off it.

When she was warm again, she shut off the engine and stretched her legs out across the front seat. The night was quiet and densely dark, and she counted off the seconds between the ticks of the cooling engine. She used to do this without thinking the winter she was seventeen, used to pass the long, cold hours recalling tables of logarithms she'd memorized. She could go days without thinking of anything besides the cost of a gallon of gas and how to solve for X.

Tonight wasn't so easy now that happiness had gotten her out of practice, now that she'd learned that love was actual and desirable and not just cruelly unfair. She should have told Carol that she knew that about love, learned it long before they'd even met. She should have told Carol a lot of things before now, but habit had become comfortable, and then it didn't seem to matter. Until, really, what had she left for Carol to do but exactly what she'd done? Mitch knew about desperation and desire. She knew how an echoing feeling of isolation could fill a lonely nighttime mind with dreams of connection—not only warm and loving but violent and vengeful.

The winter chill infiltrated the cab and seduced the sleeping bag. The night blew static in her ears. She pulled the bag up to cover her head and focused on the humidity in her exhales.

Carol was right, but her accusations weren't new. They were actually so old that Mitch's reaction was like something from the primordial ooze only vaguely related to Carol and her distress. Mitch felt a small relief in not having lost this old anger, which for a while had been as essential to her survival as food and water.

Her body heat leached first from her extremities then her core, but Mitch refrained from starting the engine until she was palsied with shivers. The slow cycle of freeze-and-thaw occupied her until dawn lit the landscape in increments of chromatic relief and it was late enough that she could drive back to town and campus for the early lap swim.

The pool water felt warm against her chilled skin, and the first breath she took was so familiar and comforting she almost came to a stop in the middle of the lane. Mitch couldn't remember ever choosing to swim. Swimming had happened to her somewhat like puberty, only much earlier and without all the trauma. Concrete-and-tile-bound water had always made sense, and the buoyancy and repetitive motion of each of the four strokes was, by now, second nature.

After that long, cramped night, her shoulder's grinding ache was barely tolerable in her freestyle and backstroke but strangely absent in the butterfly, so she threw herself into laps of that, churning through the water until she couldn't gasp enough breath at the top of each stroke to keep going. Butterfly was not made for distance, was so taxing it had no use beyond showing off, and though Mitch liked its heaving feel best, she had no real technical affinity for it. Her talents in the water were as in-between as the rest of her. She'd been a middle-distance swimmer, not having either top speed or long endurance. What she had in spades, her high school coach had confided, was an enhanced tolerance for suffering. But suffering in a pool had always been easy.

She turned back to freestyle despite—or maybe because of—the fire in her shoulder. She tore back and forth across the pool, not counting laps, not checking her time, sucking in breaths every fourth, then third, then second stroke, drawing in just enough air to fuel her. She swam as she'd so rarely swum since high school, a flat-out race against consciousness she had no hope of winning.

Carol's hard words were with her at every flip turn, dogged her with every brush of thumb against thigh, but all she could do was endure it and know, absolutely, how right Carol was.

Mitch drove back to her house after lap swim ended, dry and warm but not showered, preparing herself to say whatever was needed to get through this. But Carol's van was gone from the driveway. Mitch parked and hurried inside and checked around while she called Carol's cell phone, but the place was undisturbed, empty of notes or signs of distress, and Carol didn't answer. Clean jeans, thermal, and flannel replaced her sweats, and she at least remembered her jacket this time when she slammed out of the house.

Mitch parked halfway down the block from Carol's place. The driveway was empty, but Carol's van might be hidden in the garage. She'd forgotten her watch. The dashboard clock told her James and Gordon would be off to school already, though Brian was almost certainly home. Mitch killed the engine, got out of the truck, and closed the door softly behind her. She crept up the sidewalk and circled around to the side of the attached garage that had a small window mostly occluded by dirt and dust. With her forehead against it, she cupped her hands around her face and peered inside, trying hard to see the hulking, ovoid minivan where it clearly wasn't.

Carol wasn't at The Filling Station or Dunkin' Donuts or Turning Leaves. The van wasn't in any of the town lots or in front of Abby's house. Mitch finally settled herself at the one tiny table in Loretta's Bakeshop and staked out the bookstore. But after two hours, four cups of weak coffee, and a cruller Loretta had practically shoved down Mitch's throat that had tasted like sugared cardboard, ten thirty came around without Carol showing up to work.

Mitch zipped up her jacket against the February cold for the walk to campus. Whenever the wind pushed her hair across her face, she could smell the chlorine still heavy in it. Her legs were leaden and balky—she didn't want to find Brian in his office but had to try.

His closed door and the lack of answer to her knock gave her no relief. She sagged against the dark wood and made herself stop and concentrate before running off somewhere else. Thinking was painful, standing still a misery, but she did it until her pulse slowed to almost normal and a hint of clarity returned to her mind.

Carol could take care of herself and was probably somewhere blowing off steam like Mitch had done at the pool. She was out driving or wandering the grocery store aisles eating Oreos straight from the bag or having a long, greasy breakfast at The Cracked Egg over in Moorshead. She'd be back tonight, and they'd talk. They'd work it out. There was no need to panic anyone else with their fight.

She turned around and headed down the hall. A bright, open doorway came up on her right, and when Mitch realized it was Abby's office, it tugged at her with an inverse-square pull of attraction, growing progressively stronger the closer she got. Her steps slowed then stopped when she was just short of the entrance.

From her vantage point, she could see neatly filled bookcases lining the far wall of the room and a short purple couch inside the door. The floor was bare, scuffed wood begging for a rug. When she leaned forward a few inches, the back of Abby's head came into view along with her right shoulder and upper arm, which was completely covered yet exposed by a blouse made of a sheer material the color of her hair.

The delicacy of Abby's sleeve transfixed Mitch, made her sidestep for a moment what had brought her to campus in the first place. It was deliciously unfamiliar. Carol didn't wear stuff like that, and Kim had favored bare arms whenever possible. Reginald's novelty boxers came to mind, and Mitch rapped softly on the open door to dispel the image.

A long moment passed before Abby looked up from the paper she was grading, and when she did, a breathy "oh" escaped her apparently without notice. She cleared her throat, put down her pen, and leaned back in her chair, eliciting a loud squeak.

"Hi," she said. Her knees were covered in thin tights and showed neatly between the bottom of her skirt and the tops of her leather boots. In front of her on her desk were two stacks of paper, one short, the other less so.

Mitch said, "Hi."

"Here playing another prank?"

Recalling their last meeting in this hallway took more effort than it should have. She shook her head. "Aren't you cold in that?"

Abby looked down at herself.

"Never mind. Have you seen Carol this morning? Or talked to her?"

"Carol? No. Why? Is something wrong?"

Mitch shifted from one foot to the other and shrugged. "It's fine. I mean, everything's fine. I should get to work."

"Why don't you come in? Sit down. That thing over there," she motioned to the couch, "is more comfortable than it looks."

"Really, the guys'll be wondering where I am."

"Dr. Mitchell. If you don't want to stay, just say so. Don't demean me with excuses."

The snap in Abby's voice made Mitch come to attention. A composure showed in Abby that Mitch hadn't seen before, and it made the knot in her chest unfurl a little. But she stood her ground a bit longer. "Don't call me that. No one calls me that. My name is Mitch."

Abby inclined her head a notch. "Mitch, then. Come in. Close the door behind you."

Mitch unzipped her jacket and sat down. Abby's office had all the earmarks of a hard-working university professor—stacks of journals and student papers, a well-worn leather briefcase propped against a leg of the desk, inbox piled high with a slim laptop set precariously on top. But a certain static feeling collected in the corners, a stagnation filled the cracks between the floorboards. Mitch recalled Abby's Thanksgiving distress again, letting her own slip her mind until Abby leaned forward with another squeak.

She asked, "Did something happen with Carol?"

Mitch's deep breath brought a sharp stab at its bottom. "We...well, we fought last night. And now I don't know where she is. But, you know, I'm sure she's fine."

"She's not at work?"

"No. I looked there. When I got home this morning and she was gone, I—"

Abby held up her hand. "Wait. What do you mean 'when I got home'?"

Mitch looked down at her hands and shrugged off her jacket. "I ran out. I left when things started to get … I took off around midnight, and when I got home at eight, she was gone."

"Home? Your house?"

"Yeah. She's been staying with me. Didn't you know?"

"She's staying with you?"

Mitch rubbed a hand roughly across her face. "Goddamn."

"Is she leaving Brian?" Abby rolled her chair closer.

"Yeah."

"How long has she been staying with you?" The chair inched across the floor.

"Almost a month."

"Who else knows?" Their knees were barely a foot apart.

"Abby, Jesus. Enough with the questions." Mitch assaulted her eyes with her hands.

Abby eased back. "Sorry. But you fought last night?"

Mitch sniffed twice and rubbed her nose. She looked at Abby, whose reaction gave some indication of how much Mitch's face showed the broken-up feeling that had occupied her chest since discovering Carol missing this morning. Not missing. Decisively split.

Abby whispered something unintelligible before she got up and sat down next to Mitch, taking one of Mitch's cold, stiff hands in both of her own and pulling it into her lap. Abby's fingers rested against Mitch's without motion, grounding Mitch with their surprising quiet, so unlike Abby's usual stream of agitated questions. Those fingers were like a heat sink, bleeding off just enough of Mitch's grief that she could unseal her lips.

She looked straight ahead when she said, "I lied to her. She's right about everything. And now she's gone."

"She's not gone."

"Whatever. She trusted me, and I betrayed her."

"You two have been friends a long time, right?"

Mitch nodded.

"In an old friendship, blame is rarely so well defined."

"Don't say things you don't know anything about."

"I know *everything* about it." Abby's voice was sharp again. "I know what it's like to be the one to blame, when there's absolutely no question about who's in the wrong."

"So, you're the expert, then?"

"As much of an expert as you are."

Mitch shoved some hair out of her face but didn't go so far as to take her hand from Abby's. "I've had every opportunity to change. Carol...I'm not an idiot. It's not like I don't know how I am. It's not like I'm surprised when someone tells me that I'm difficult, but they always expect me to be, seem to want me to be surprised. Or hurt. I *know*, all right? I know all about it." Mitch sat up for a few seconds then sank back next to Abby again. "Carol never did that. In the beginning, when she got me pegged, she left, didn't try to force me to change. But last night..."

The heat sink big enough to drain down the furnace of Mitch's agony wouldn't fit in this room, let alone the building. Everything she felt manifested as a searing inside her, and she was unable to speak.

Abby squeezed her hand.

"I thought everything was fine, but I forgot...nothing is unconditional. Nothing *should* be unconditional. I took advantage, and now she's gone again."

Mitch wanted to clutch at Abby's hand, to compress her flesh and ligaments and bones in an effort purely physical and violent and external. It would be such a relief, a distraction from her monumental struggle not to cry, from the twist of her mouth against the sorrow battering it from the inside. Her eyes clamped shut then drifted open to Abby's office, draped in a blurry sheen. She breathed in and out to the same stab on each inhale.

Abby squeezed Mitch's hand again. "It's okay. I understand."

Then Mitch was on her feet, her hand wrenched from Abby's and shoved deep in the pocket of her jeans. "Just tell me if you hear from her."

She was about to reach for her jacket, but Abby was sitting on its sleeve. Mitch glared at her then flung open the door and lurched out. She hurried across the cold quad, wishing she could detour to the machine shop and drill the hell out of something, lose herself in the noise and smell of the place, but that would involve questions Mitch was unprepared to answer.

She took out her phone, fumbling with it in the cold, and called Carol. Right to voice mail. She sat down on a bench in the weak sunlight, her phone resting lightly in one hand then the other. The reek of chlorine encompassed her, and she couldn't remember for a moment where she'd parked her truck. Before she could come up with any of the hundred reasons why she shouldn't, she called Reginald.

When his voice mail picked up, she disconnected fast then ran to her truck, the pavement jarring her knees and hips, the cold in her lungs shocking her back into composure.

< ≈ >

Later that afternoon, Mitch sat on a stool in the lab away from the guys at their desks and pretended to work. Her notebook was open in front of her, and a pencil dangled from between her fingers. When she sat like this, Eric said it looked like she was reading the bones. All Mitch knew was that the guys always gave her a wide berth when she did it.

She'd been sitting there a long time before she heard the office door open and close. One of them must be stretching his legs. She went back to her staring.

But Eric shouted, "Oh, Mitch. Visitor."

Mitch got up and went to the doorway. When she saw Abby standing between the guys' desks, she leaned against the metal jamb. Steve and Eric were very interested in Abby, pitched forward across their desks, faces sharp with attention as if Abby were the anticipated end to a long experiment.

Abby bounced Mitch's jacket on her arm. "You left this. How'd you get over here without freezing?"

"I hurried. Thanks for bringing it by." Mitch's shoulder had fused to the doorjamb.

"Have you heard anything?"

"No. Not yet."

Mitch was too burned out by the day to determine how she felt about Abby being here, asking questions, as usual.

Eric sang out, "Awkward."

That, at least, got Mitch in motion. "Come on. I'll walk you out." The mere suggestion of her putting her hand on Abby's arm in direction was enough to turn Abby and propel her out into the stairway.

When the glass door shut behind them, Mitch said, "I'm sorry about before. I was…distraught."

"Don't apologize." They stopped at the top of the stairs, and Abby held out the jacket. "Listen, would you like to get a coffee with me?"

"I should get home and wait for Carol."

"Do you want company?"

Mitch couldn't seem to look at Abby when she said, "I'm supposed to talk to Reginald later. We have a kind of standing date, and—"

"Fine. Of course. Some other time, then." Abby walked out the door.

Mitch was halfway down the stairs before she loped back to the top and pushed out into the cold of the alley.

"Abby," she shouted.

Abby slowed down.

"Wait. Hey."

Abby stopped and looked over her shoulder.

"My given name was Evelyn."

The thing she'd never told anyone since coming to Tilsen, that piece of information she'd hoarded for so long, elicited just a smile and a nod before Abby continued on her way.

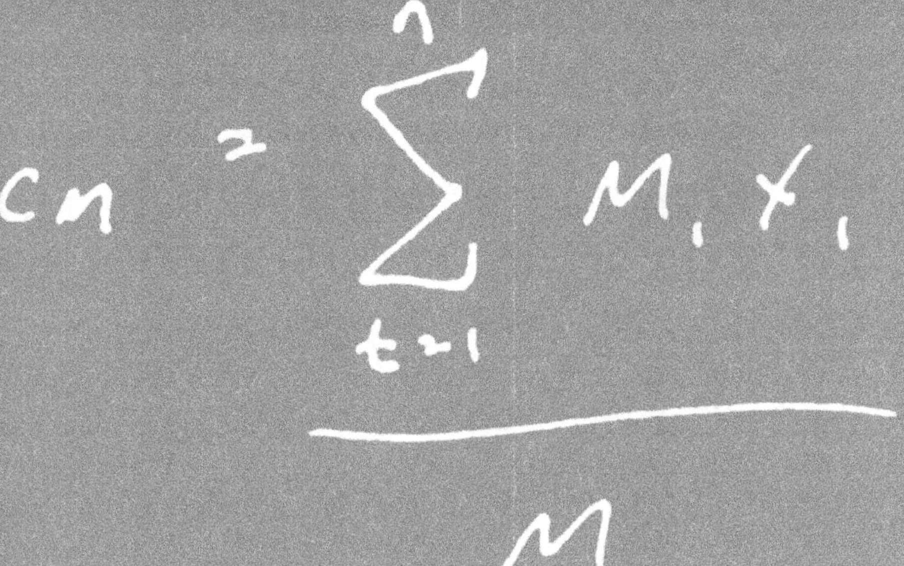

AS DIFFERENT AS WE ALL ARE, WE ARE MORE ALIKE than is sometimes comfortable to admit. We are as prone to judgment as to love. To solidarity as to strife. We are all faced with the struggle to balance individuality and conformity. Introspection and habit.

–Dr. Abigail Rosen, The F Word: Femininity in the New Century

16

WHEN MITCH ran out on their fight, Carol was left kneeling on the bed, heaving in righteous indignation and a sort of queasy triumph. Her anger was both adrenaline and anesthetic, and it took her a while to come down from the high of it. She prowled the house, cracking her fingers and running them along the backs of furniture or across the walls.

But when the cold in the small rooms seeped through her thin pajamas, reality reasserted itself, chilly and uncomfortable against her skin. She thought about the way Mitch had vamoosed, at how clearly appalled she had looked even in the bedroom's darkness. She thought about Mitch loving someone else then threw herself back on the bed, the source of every fucking evil, and cried until her eyes were puffy slits, until when she held the alarm clock to her face and deciphered the time, she panicked at the thought that Mitch might reappear and catch her like this.

Getting dressed was easy, but Carol got stuck after that. Where was she supposed to go? Who else was she going to hit up to take her in? Taking in was the best friend's job, wasn't it? Time insisted on passing, making it more and more likely that Mitch was going to walk back into her own house and ... what? Carol didn't want to find out. She packed some essentials in the smaller of her two suitcases, turned lights off, and locked the door behind her, hesitating a beat before chucking her key into the bushes.

Her parents lived over three hours away—at least with Brian behind the wheel and the boys being boys in the back. The route was marked in permanent ink on Carol's brain, but she hadn't driven it by herself since the first time she'd fled Millerton. Then, as now, she worried herself to twenty-five over the limit and a two-and-a-half-hour drive.

Fifteen years before, she had been newly pregnant, even more newly engaged, and utterly doomed. Her parents had gone through the roof at her news. Eventually, they'd all made the best of things and absorbed her fuck-ups into family history (she was a major contributor to water under their bridge), but now she was at it again, providing even more gallons for the family reservoir, and she didn't know if her parents would see her current situation as better or worse than that old one.

Her childhood home looked different without Brian or his offspring around. Layers of memory wrapped the yellow house in a soft haze that gave a hint of green to the bare bushes and a glow around the front door that felt suspiciously like welcome. She thumped the knocker and waited.

When her father answered the door, he was holding a piece of toast with half-moon bite marks around the edges. He leaned forward and squinted at Carol. She shifted her grip on her suitcase and touched her eyelids then her nose. The topography of her face gave a good hint at how terrible she looked.

"Carol..."

"I left Brian," she said, which shocked the shit out of herself. So much for a soft approach.

"Come in. Come in." Thin gray hair ringed his head in a fluffy halo. He closed the door behind Carol then took her by the arm. "Did he hurt you?"

"Of course he hurt me. I didn't leave for the hell of it." Then she saw the way he puffed up. "Not like that, Dad. Brian? He's never even hit a punching bag." She put down her suitcase, took off her coat, and looked around before she said, "He's been having affairs for years."

The waterworks started up again then settled down to intermittent for the rest of the morning while she walked her parents through the highlights of Brian's indiscretions. Perhaps the tears were the cause of her parents' surprising sympathy, but her sniffling and their ancient, familiar kitchen made her feel like a child.

After coffee and scrambled eggs and way too much bacon, her parents passed a not-so-secret signal between themselves and started talking about Gordo and James, about real and lasting remorse, about the necessity of forgiveness in all successful marriages. The catchphrases were nauseating, the low point coming with "love means second chances" followed directly by "marriage takes hard work."

Carol slapped the table, rattling the dirty dishes. "Stop it. Just…just shut up. Stop pretending that shit will make everything better. I'm not an infant. I'm not naive." She took her plate and mug to the sink and let the water run on them way longer than necessary.

Her mother said, "We just don't want you to be rash."

"Rash?" Carol laughed. "Are you serious? Do you think I've missed the lesson of the last fifteen years? Fifteen years I've paid for being rash."

"Is that how you see your family?" her mother asked, her red coffee mug halfway from table to mouth, her eyebrows so high they practically met her hairline.

"Oh, for Christ's sake. Of course not. But there's a huge difference in what Brian had to 'give up' versus what I did. And that he could…yeah, yeah, he loves me. Yeah, I'm so lucky with how things turned out. Maybe I'm being selfish, but I can't swallow it anymore."

Her father said, "We're not telling you what to do. And even if we were, you don't have to listen to us. Take as much time as you need."

The guest room she slept in was mostly occupied by a sewing table and a bulky stationary bike. The day bed was situated against a wall under neat rows of snapshots showing the brown-faced children her mother sponsored for less than the price of a cup of coffee a day—certainly less than a cup of The Filling Station's coffee. They lived in India or Africa or Central America, and her mother could tell you each one of their favorite school subjects and foods. She had a shoebox full of children who had graduated the assistance program and entered adulthood well-nourished and with a pair of good shoes. What happened after that was anyone's guess.

Carol talked to James and Gordo under the unwavering eyes of Maron and Raj and Alejandra. She pretended to the boys that she was just across town at Mitch's and felt fat with her deceit. James was different on the phone, more forthcoming, the way he'd been a few years ago but with a ribbon of maturity. Carol hadn't imagined it would be harder to be away from him than Gordo, but Gordo didn't leave the same uncomfortable squeeze in her chest.

Despite all this, Carol wasn't tempted to make everything better for them at any cost. She'd been the better-maker her entire adult life, but if she didn't do something for herself now, there'd be no her left.

In the limbo of this house, providing crossword puzzle answers to her father over oatmeal with raisins, Carol kept bumping into the ghost of her twenty-three-year-old self, who paced the hallways to burn away her terror and anger and doubt and bone-numbing boredom. She remembered that drop-stomach feeling of watching her lovely imagined future wane while her belly waxed, and she was now well aware the odds had been stacked high against that vision of herself and Sasha even without the pregnancy.

Exactly how disillusioned did she have to get to grow up? Very, evidently. But no matter how bleak the vision of her life was right now, Carol could appreciate the clarity with which she saw it. The very fact that the sight made her want to stab out her own eyeballs encouraged her to believe in her ability to identify a future direction that would be remotely attainable.

That conversation with Abby, sitting there in cocktail dresses in the dark, had been a start, an honest start. As immature as she'd been for so long, the wrinkles around her eyes and her southward-creeping ass flat-out denied the adjective "young." That said, she was also nowhere near ancient. All sorts of people changed track even later in life than this and had wildly successful careers. She'd had potential once, and as Mitch liked to say, potential isn't lost, only converted into something else. Mitch and her easy analogies.

With hopefully no illusions about the amount of work ahead, Carol used her mother's library card to check out biographies of Julia Child, Einstein, and James Joyce so she could study their slow starts and failures and how they became who they were meant to be. She looked for clues and markers and signs that her thoughts were the start of a not-moronic plan, read until her eyes hurt, then napped and read some more.

Two days into this, Carol's father strolled into the living room and sat down in the leather recliner opposite where she lay reading on the couch. He'd been lurking around, picking up these books and turning them over in his hands, harrumphing at the blurbs and cover photos. Now he fidgeted and sighed. Carol closed her book around her index finger.

He said, "I'm worried about you."

"I'll be fine."

"Carol…I know you're figuring things out for yourself, and the last thing I want to do is interfere."

"Uh-oh."

He leaned forward and steepled his fingers. "I agree that you need to find a direction you can be happy with, and if that direction is away from Brian, I would understand. Trust is difficult to rebuild."

They regarded each other. Carol replaced her finger with a more suitable bookmark and sat up. "I'm waiting for the part

I'm not going to agree with." He dropped his gaze, and Carol said, "You forget, I'm a parent, too."

"You've done wonderfully with those boys."

"Brian helped. A lot," Carol said, mostly to appear more rational and reasoned than she actually was.

He nodded. "I want you to be careful."

"Careful and not rash, okay."

He frowned then motioned at the books on the coffee table. "I see what you're thinking, but no matter how much you feel that you have unfinished business, you can't ever go back to who you were. Not really."

Carol snorted. "Dad, I love you. I really do. But I'm not an idiot, okay? Back then..." She brushed some toast crumbs off her shirt and listened to a car cruise past outside. "Back then, I'd barely stopped being a fuck-up. I wanted to work hard for once and not on diapers and teething and learning how to love a man I barely knew."

Her father sat back and listened, and she was incredibly thankful she wasn't trying to have this conversation with her mother.

She said, "Maybe I've spent too much time with Mitch, but all I want now is a chance to work as hard as I can and see what happens." Mitch, again.

"And that's admirable."

"But?"

He shook his head. "No buts."

"Bullshit. Sorry, but that's bullshit."

"You've lived fifteen more years. You have children who still need you. If you don't take your current situation into account... you could be making it impossible to succeed at all."

Carol didn't ignore him but decided to consider his concern at some point in the far future when she was at least headed in the right direction. And the first step to the right direction was getting her own place. She never should have run off to Mitch. Mitch had her own side in the whole situation, maybe even an agenda. Carol needed to look around her and think "mine." She'd seen Mitch do that. Even Abby. No matter how small and shitty, she needed her own walls and chairs and toilet. Her own rent and landlord issues and slow shower drain.

Not only was February winter's absolute bottom, it was the pit of Millerton's student-driven rental market. Even so, a shimmer grew in her belly as she used her parents' ancient computer to browse the paltry apartment listings. The source of her percolating excitement was possibility, the exact feeling her father had warned her about. She didn't care. The crappiest studios looked like boundless freedom.

She called two different realtors and set up appointments to see some places available for immediate occupancy. Then she rang up Abby for the first time in almost two weeks to make a coffee date at The Filling Station to celebrate having a new place all her own. Abby who, Carol realized, was the first thing she'd said "mine" about in ages. And who was just as flawed as these apartments were sure to be.

< ≈ >

On an unseasonably warm Saturday nearly two weeks after Carol had disappeared, Mitch sat in her subterranean office and wished she could open the small, high windows. She wanted some of the soft air that was outside but didn't have the energy to leave her desk. The white-noise hum of computers was faint and pleasing, and she'd been taking a lot of breaks from processing invoices and writing checks to sit back and listen to the almost nothing.

One of Sam's favorite phrases was "the cost of doing business," and it always came out in force when he tried to convince Mitch to expand her scope or hire his nephew or buy some equipment that, as he put it, hadn't fallen off the back of a truck. Today, even though she was crunching dollars and cents, those words seemed most applicable to how she felt about decisions having nothing to do with money. Choosing to live on her own terms meant putting some things behind her, setting sometimes unpopular priorities, hardening a little with efficiency.

A flexible ice pack nestled against the bare skin of her shoulder, and Mitch prodded at it through her thermal top. Every swim set off a throbbing in the joint that lasted for hours, but Mitch couldn't resist trying to find distraction in the water, though even if she managed to escape Carol while swimming, she was there at the tiled edge when Mitch caught her breath between sets.

When she'd finally told Reginald about the fight, she'd had every intention of spilling the whole mess to him, but she'd left a lot out, details that lodged in her throat or never even made it that far. On one point she was excruciatingly clear: she was to blame. Reginald went down the same two-to-tango road as Abby, reasonable and calm in his points, which made Mitch long to assault him with examples until he understood everything she had withheld from Carol and for how long. But either Reginald would refuse to listen or he'd deduce how Mitch's lip service to intimacy with Carol might just apply to him.

Their conversations had a new brittleness to them. Every time he asked about Carol, it was harder to deflect the question without getting ornery and short about it. He shrugged her off with jokes and non sequiturs, but that just made Mitch distrust his cheerfulness. She couldn't tell what he thought of the situation and her part in it. He had to know he wasn't exempt from Mitch's inexcusable shortcomings, but he just talked about visiting, asked how spring was in Ohio, made it clear how much he wanted to be near her. She couldn't help but believe him about that.

No matter how intent Mitch was at finding the just-right punishment for her failures, she wanted what Reginald wanted. In pockets of calm, when loitering in a warm bath or circling around sleep, she craved him. If he were close, maybe things would be different. She could lay her head on his chest and tell him those old uncomfortable things without having to see his face, without the pressure of filling transoceanic silence with her voice.

Mitch slipped fingers under her crew neck and sighed when they encountered the now-lukewarm flexible pack. After untucking her shirt, she bounced a couple times until the compress slid down her back and landed behind her in the chair. She twisted around to retrieve it, and when she turned forward again, Abby was opening the glass door. Her pulse jumped with the feeling of being witnessed in some private act.

Abby stopped just inside. "Sorry. Am I interrupting?" She wore a light-blue V-neck sweater and a long flowered skirt, her cheeks and ears were flushed from the outside, and Mitch remembered how gently Abby had held her hand the morning Carol had left.

"No, but how'd you know I was here?"

"Gee, I don't know. Doesn't you plus Saturday equal work?" Abby gave a little shrug and grinned.

"Basic arithmetic. Funny. Well, hey. Don't just stand there. Grab a seat."

Abby rolled Steve's chair to the other side of Mitch's desk and sat with her back straight and hands out of sight in her lap.

Mitch massaged the gelatinous compress and said, "I meant to stop by or call or something. I just…haven't."

"Still beating yourself up?"

"Haven't found a good reason not to."

Abby looked down. "I know exactly what you mean."

"What have you been beating yourself up about?"

"Worse things than you did, I'm sure," she said and met Mitch's eyes with the same defiant composure she'd shown the last time Mitch had seen her.

"It's not a competition."

"Lucky for you, then." Abby smiled with a hard merriment.

Mitch pushed half the compress flat, making the other half strain its seams. "I find it hard to believe, what you're insinuating."

Abby closed her eyes and shook her head. "You get mad when people decide all about you by how you look, right?"

"People think what they think."

"I'm not so magnanimous. One day the wrong person said the wrong thing about my hair and what I was wearing—and what my partner was wearing—and something in me snapped.

I thought getting that book out of my system would set things right in me, but it just set everything else wrong."

"Letting people get to you leads to nothing good," Mitch said and evened the compress back out.

"Or everything good."

Mitch nodded reluctantly.

Abby put her hands flat on the desk. "Carol called me. I thought you'd want to know."

"What? When?" Mitch jerked upright, which set her shoulder off. She clenched her teeth against the pain.

"I hung up with her and came right over here."

"Is she okay?" Mitch knew Carol had taken one of her suitcases and some clothes. She knew Carol was in touch with Brian and the boys. And she knew they thought Carol was still staying with her. But she didn't know how Carol was.

"She's at her parents', but she's coming back soon."

That didn't answer the question. Mitch clutched the ice pack, got up, and swept past Abby to the kitchenette. "Coffee? Not as good as Angel's, but I can make a pot in no time."

"That sounds nice."

After she put the compress back in the freezer and tucked her shirt in, Mitch contemplated the coffeemaker. "Is Carol going to be staying with you?"

"No. She said she's looking for her own place."

"What? With what money? Brian doesn't even know she left my— Jesus, Carol!" Mitch braced herself against the small folding table, leaning hard into her locked arms. She'd failed Carol completely. It cramped her guts so hard she thought she might vomit. Nausea rolled through her in long waves, and she closed her eyes.

Time wasn't behaving itself, and she had no way of knowing how long she stood there. Her fingers went numb from the pressure of her palms against the table's edge. She had to get a handle on herself, but before she could, Abby's hand was on the back of her neck, warm even where it was blocked by Mitch's hair.

Mitch swung from the table, grabbed Abby, and squeezed until she felt the hard press of ribs against the inside of her arms. She bent her head and pushed her face into Abby's soft neck. Breathing still wasn't the easiest thing, but the feel of a firm body against her settled her stomach. When Mitch loosened her arms a notch, she felt Abby's hands move along her back, run up the knobs of her spine and across her rigid shoulder blades. It was such a relief to lose herself in touch, in the clean spicy smell of Abby's skin and the faint whoosh of her breath, in the sweater's fine knit under her fingertips and the press of full breasts against her own chest.

She stepped back and turned to the coffee machine. "Sorry."

"For what?"

She measured beans into the grinder. "I counted. I mean, once I counted, and I went two hundred seventeen days without being touched. Not a handshake or a hand on the back. Do you take cream or sugar or anything?"

"No. Nothing."

The grinder was loud in a satisfying way. Mitch concentrated on knocking the last bits of grounds into a filter, but in her peripheral vision, she could see Abby take a step closer, then back, before saying, "That's a long time. When was it?"

Mitch put the filter into the machine before facing Abby, arms crossed. "Why are you here? You're like..."

"A bad penny?" Abby smiled but retreated another step.

"No." Mitch looked above Abby's head. "You're like rice in a salt shaker."

Abby leaned in the doorway. "I absorb water?"

"Christ. Forget it." But Mitch dropped her arms. "It was in high school."

Abby blinked.

"The two hundred seventeen days. I was a little crazy then, I think. Probably not because of the isolation, but it didn't help."

"And your parents...?"

Mitch picked up the coffee carafe but didn't want to move close enough to Abby to fill it from the water cooler between them. She looked at the cloudy glass in her hand, then at her shoes, and kept her mouth blessedly shut. Only when Mitch heard Abby shift and shuffle did she look up. Abby smiled, and Mitch spoke without thinking.

She said, "Reginald's mom called him Patty while he was growing up. It's really perfectly him, rolls right off the tongue."

"Does he ever call you Evelyn?"

Mitch's laugh was loud in that small space. "God, no. He doesn't know that name. No one does, really."

"So why'd you tell me?"

The carafe dangled from her index finger. She swung it back and forth. Abby exuded relaxation, hands easy at her sides. Mitch asked, "Are questions premeditated for you, or are they a compulsion?"

"We're both scientists, right?"

"Some would say."

Abby gave Mitch a nasty look. "Wasn't it Einstein who said, 'Never lose a holy curiosity'?"

"Ah, but what about an unholy one?" Mitch asked then lost her jollity. Carol. What was there to do but ride it out? She put the carafe down. "Let's get out of here. What do you say? Want to take a walk or something? Get some air?"

"I'll even give you the first mile free of questions." Abby brought herself to a ready attention so quickly her previous relaxation felt like an illusion.

"Deal," Mitch said, and they shook on it.

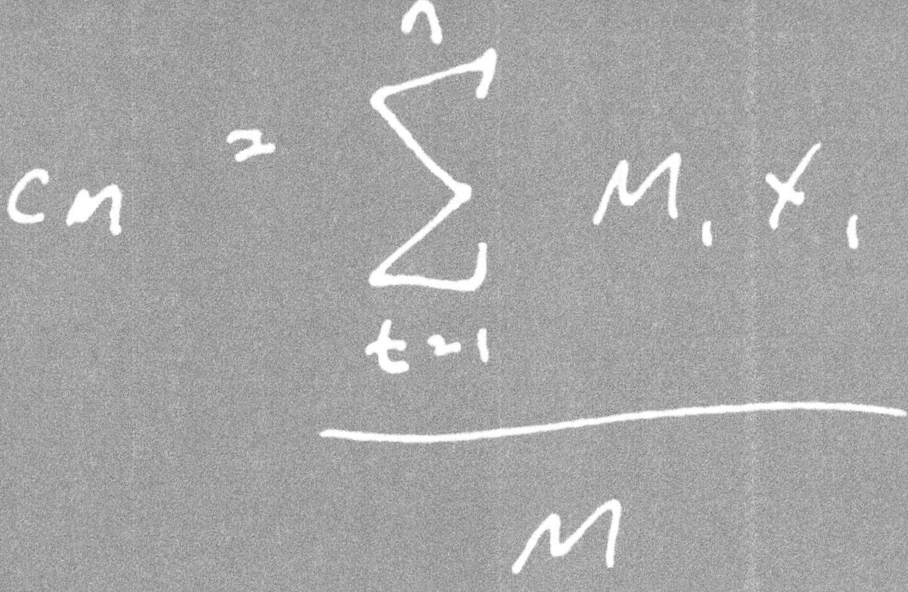

$$\frac{cn^2 \sum_{t=1}^{n} M_i x_i}{M}$$

$$\frac{W(R^3 - r^3)}{2^2 - r^3)\,\sin(a)}$$

17

AFTER LONDON, when Mitch and Reginald decided how to manage their transatlantic communication, they did so the same way they would tackle a new engineering project. They considered all the tools at their disposal—email, phone, IM, video chats—and evaluated how useful each would be in assuaging their desire for each other in comparison to usability, convenience, and cost. As a result of their analysis, the chosen foundation of their communication plan, the milestones on the open-ended Gantt chart of their relationship, were twice-weekly video dates. Thursday evenings and Sunday afternoons, they fired up their web cams and talked, complete with facial expressions and bits of their natural environments in the background.

This Thursday, Mitch left work even earlier than usual for their date, giving herself plenty of time to get settled in the hallway area between the living room and the kitchen—the most comfortable place in the house where Chester would consent to visit her. She got a glass of water and two pillows, her laptop and the bag of kitty treats. She strung the power cord to the outlet behind the coatrack then sank down onto one of the pillows, her back against the couch's back. She logged in and positioned the laptop in the perfect place in front of her crossed knees, tilted the screen at Reginald's preferred angle (low enough to see the tips of her knees, high enough to see the top of her head), and shook the bag of treats a couple of times. Chester still played hard to get, but he always joined her within seven minutes to accept a treat and curl up onto the pillow she kept on her lap.

He was purring by the time Reginald appeared on the screen. The undershirt Reginald wore glowed with such whiteness it had to be new. It picked up and reinforced the white kitchen cabinets that floated right above his head, making the picture one big eye-splitting blur. Mitch reached over Chester and turned down the brightness of her screen.

He smiled. "Am I late?"

"Chester and I are early." She lifted her hand to let Chester stretch and yawn and get comfortable again before she resumed stroking him in that just-so way she'd recently discovered.

"Does that cat have any idea how lucky he is?"

"You wouldn't fit so nicely in my lap."

"But I'd have fun trying."

He leaned forward, putting elbows to knees. His head blocked out some of the cabinets behind him, but Mitch could still see part of a spatula sticking up in his dish drainer and wondered what he'd had for dinner. He'd eaten hours ago already. With the time difference, Mitch was just getting started when he was drifting toward bed.

Tonight, even before asking about her day or Chester's day or coming out with a story from his commute home, he asked, "Have you talked to Carol?"

True, he hadn't asked this the last couple times they'd talked, but to come out with it before even a proper hello? Before she could tell him how good it was to see him? She ignored the question.

"We signed with a new turbine manufacturer today after months of pursuit. They've got a ton of units in production."

"Mitch."

"And Steve is running with a prototype of the lathe product, though I think we might have to contract with a chemist to find the optimal lubricant. Or manufacture one, I guess."

Reginald settled back against his couch, which appeared a much uglier shade of green on her screen than it actually was. His biceps bulged when he crossed his arms, bisected neatly by the sleeves of his T-shirt.

Mitch went on. "Sam's nephew is learning fast. And teaching me a thing or two. In fact, did you know—"

"Mitch. Stop." His voice was loud. And angry.

She'd never seen him mad before, heard this rough rumble in his tone, measured the visible tension in his jaw. The hardness in his face scared her, but she willed herself not to look away. She stared at his nose and waited for him to regain his usual demeanor. The furnace kicked on with a whoomph muted by the utility room door. She waited and petted Chester, her hand growing heavier and her fingers more insistent until Chester voiced an annoyed meow, got up, and gave Mitch a couple of blinks full of attitude before settling back onto the pillow.

Mitch said, "Apparently, Carol moved into her new place a week ago. It's somewhere out west of campus. Abby said she's not allowed to come by and see it, so it must be pretty slummy. I don't know what Carol's thinking."

"Abby." Reginald's cheeks softened a notch, but he was still hard to recognize as himself.

"Yeah. She called and told me." And Mitch had been insufferable on the phone in return, curt to the point of nonresponsiveness.

Reginald uncrossed his arms then draped one over the top of the couch. "The professor."

Mitch made a noise of agreement and bent her head to put her cheek on Chester's fur.

"Is she attractive?"

"Yes," Mitch said into the cat's soft side.

"Pardon?"

She looked at Reginald, who was smiling. Mitch couldn't quite smile in return, but she felt relief unfurl in her like a swallow of hot coffee. "Yes, she's attractive. And knows it."

"Married?"

"No, she's single. And since it's your next question, she's gay. And, yes, there's something in the water here. She's a career lesbian. Outspoken."

"I see." Reginald nodded with exaggeration.

"You don't see, and you know it. She's a pain in the ass, but…she's helped me out with Carol, who we were talking about, anyway." Mitch didn't want to talk about Carol, but she didn't want to talk about Abby even more. She wasn't sure why, but it had something to do with how her behavior toward Abby was unacceptable in stupid, small ways. Somehow, even her huge missteps with Carol were less embarrassing.

Reginald got up close to the screen, swimming out of, then back into, focus. "Yes, of course. Just tell me one thing. On a scale of one to ten—"

"Patty!" Abby was an eight. Maybe a nine when she was being quiet.

"Okay, okay." He sat back. "So, are you going to see Carol?"

"She doesn't want to see me."

"Are you sure?"

The viciousness in Carol's features that night still came clearly to mind in unguarded moments. Mitch had felt that expression on her own face before, and she knew the feelings behind it left marks that didn't fade for a long time—if ever. She fished out a treat from the bag next to her and set it on the pillow an inch in front of Chester's nose. She tried to find doubt in her mind but failed. "I'm sure."

"You were friends a long time." He was inching toward the screen again.

Mitch closed her eyes against his dear face. "I'm sure."

"You loved each other."

"I'm sure! Fuck. Enough." She looked at the front door then the ceiling then the yellow stove through the kitchen doorway. She took a sip of water. From where she sat, she could see one of

Carol's sweaters where it hung over the back of a kitchen chair. Carol had left it there the evening before their fight, and Mitch hadn't been able to touch it since, couldn't even go near it. In the kitchen, she hugged the countertops and cabinets so she wouldn't accidently brush against it.

When she turned back to the laptop, Reginald was waiting, his broad mouth downturned at the corners. She said, "I'm sorry. Can't we talk about something else?"

"There was a woman at the gym this morning—"

"On a scale of one to ten?"

"Eleven. She reminded me of you. She was on the treadmill. Graceful. All arms and legs and spare, sexy lines."

Mitch didn't tell Reginald that she couldn't run worth shit. It didn't matter. In the last couple months, she'd seen random men—even a woman once—who had brought Reginald to life right here in Millerton. A certain tilt of the head or timbre of a laugh or the smallest gesture, and a whip-thin old white man could steal her breath.

They talked of nothing important for an hour until Reginald started yawning then slid out of sight to the floor to do his nightly calisthenics. Mitch kept talking while he huffed his way through push-ups and sit-ups. After happier chats, he might punctuate his exertions with loud groans or predictions of imminent collapse, but he was all business tonight. Mitch imagined his strong arms and upper back and his still-soft belly. He was going to hang up soon and leave her alone with Carol's sweater, the army of her clothes still hanging in the closet, the overdue library book about Gandhi on the coffee table. This was not the cost of doing business. This was something else entirely.

The sink in Carol's new apartment dripped at the exact tempo of Tilsen's fight song. She found herself mumbling "Lead us to victory, fight, Tilsen, fight," even when she wasn't there. She'd tightened and loosened every pipe she could get a wrench on, but the dripping continued unabated. A large teardrop-shaped rust spot on the sink's white enamel indicated the epic duration of this Chinese water torture. It didn't fade with a respectful amount of scrubbing, so Carol had decided on peaceful coexistence.

A number of annoyances like this had slipped Carol's attention in her five-minute walkthrough of the four-hundred-square-foot studio. For instance, both the closet and the shower were missing their hanging rods. Even with the radiator off, Carol kept a window cracked and walked around half-naked in the heat, and the toilet practically required a secret handshake to stop running after each flush. When she'd moved in, she'd almost snapped the key off in the lock before abandoning brute force and jiggling, easing, pleading, then finally lifting up on the door knob before the bolt would slide free.

The studio came with a full-size bed, a white Formica kitchen table that doubled as a desk, and a single (and singularly uncomfortable) chair. Carol had tried to rearrange these three pieces of furniture to achieve a meager fêng shui, but she quickly gave up and moved them back to their original positions, which judging from the blue industrial carpet's heavy traffic pattern, had been their positions for a very long time.

She did, however, make one small adjustment: she scooted the table and chair toward the galley kitchen until she could reach into the half-size refrigerator when she tipped the chair back onto its rear legs.

This was the cheapest of the places she'd seen that depressing whirlwind of an afternoon, but she was still going to have to be careful with her money in a way she'd long forgotten. Sure, she'd watched what they spent as a family, taken advantage of sales, hadn't bought every little thing she wanted, but her attention to the Hollister finances was equivalent to their bank account being one of those cushy, white-collar, minimum-security prisons. If some dollars escaped now and then, it may technically have been a federal offense, but no one was going to die over it.

Carol had always had her own account at a different bank with a balance that fluctuated with her mood. She used it to "save up" for bigger purchases or to feel more independent. That account was now a state-of-the-art lockdown facility with every penny in solitary confinement—not unlike Carol.

Despite everything, she felt freedom here when she could ignore the zillion ways she was still entwined with Brian and the hundreds of things they had to settle together—not just money. The boys and the house and even their family cell phone plan.

Brian still seemed to believe this was temporary—not necessarily that Carol would come to her senses but that they would traverse this difficult period and emerge a stronger family for it. Maybe that would change when she finally told him she'd left Mitch's house for this shithole or after she moved her visits with James and Gordo from The Filling Station, where she felt sordid, almost state-supervised, to this apartment. This place would embarrass James all to hell, but Gordo wouldn't mind as long as she had some comic books lying around. Brian would surely believe the absolute permanence of the situation when he heard about where she'd rather live than with him. Yes, there was freedom here.

Though the days had been getting longer for weeks, the black of the sky outside Carol's window still looked like winter. It had an impenetrability that would fade when the temperature rose. She was happy for her prodigious heat—especially that it was included in the rent—and the drumbeat soundtrack of her dripping faucet. Pasta boiled on one of the two burners of her efficiency stove, and vegetables roasted in what she called her Easy-Bake Oven.

The table was strewn with an overly ambitious number of books, recommendations from Abby and the first step in her reeducation. No distractions now, no TV, no radio, no sexy Sasha enticing her attention just by taking up space the way she had. Sasha was surely a surgeon by now, several years a surgeon, believed in herself enough not to get sidetracked. She'd believed in Carol, too—erroneously, it turned out. Carol wanted to recapture the person Sasha had discerned through Carol's freckles. Only better this time. Focused. And with a real plan.

When Carol's cell phone rang faintly from her purse, she lunged out of her chair, clipped her side on the table, and stumbled over to the bed, her mouth still full of rotini and red sauce. She paused long enough to swallow and make sure it wasn't Mitch before she answered, not that Mitch had called her since the day after the fight.

Abby asked, "Have you eaten?"

Carol looked back at the table. "Mostly."

"Oh. So, you probably don't want to join me for dinner in town, then. My treat."

"I don't need your sympathy or your handouts."

A heavy silence on the line gave Carol time to work up some mild regret.

Abby said, "You sound like Mitch."

"Now there's a compliment. What do you know about Mitch, anyway?" What Carol wouldn't do to erase Mitch from everyone else's consciousness—at least for a little while. Bad enough that she was still so much on Carol's mind, but having Abby mention her was just maddening. "How about we start this conversation over?" Carol wandered back to the table and pushed food around with her fork. She'd bought silverware and dishes from the dollar store. She had four of everything.

"It's not sympathy. Or not that way. I know about how long the evenings can be. And I can't even cook like you."

"You've got quite the way with flattery."

"I can't tell if that means you'll keep me company tonight or not."

Carol pushed her plate away then leaned back to the fridge for a beer. "Do you know how many books you told me to read?"

"You don't have to get through them all this week."

"I have a lot of catching up to do."

"Carol—"

"If you're planning on telling me how I should be going about things, just know I'm getting really good at not talking to people." She wedged the phone between shoulder and ear and stopped short of dumping the rest of her dinner in the trash before remembering the balance in her account and scraping the food into a Tupperware.

"Okay," Abby said. "From the first time we met, you made me feel welcome. I moved here to run away, but I hadn't known how punishing it would be, so alone like this, having endless hours to go over and over things. You've been a friend I don't deserve, but you always act like I'm doing you a favor when I'm with you. What you're going through and the way you're trying to manage it…"

Carol almost hung up, actually pulled the phone from her ear and eyed the disconnect button.

"…really hard. And if people want to help, you might think about letting them."

"I can't get distracted."

"No one can be on like that all the time."

Except Mitch, Carol thought.

Abby said, "I'm not telling you what to do. I just want to see you every once in a while for my own selfish reasons."

"All right."

"There's one more thing."

"The other shoe."

"I don't remember dropping the first one."

"Whatever." Carol dumped her dirty dishes in the sink. The plate muted the dripping before accumulated water transformed each drop's landing into a small splash.

"I know you left a lot of things at Mitch's. Do you want me to go over there and help you get them? We can do it when she's at work."

Carol walked to the bed and bounced into a prone position. "Mitch. That's the second time you've mentioned her. Is there something I should know?"

After a pause big enough to throw something really big through, Abby said, "We've talked. I…she came by looking for you after your fight. She was upset."

"You talked to her about me?"

"I talked to her about *her*. She's pretty torn up. She just wants—"

Carol hung up. She lay there for as long as she could tolerate it then got up and paced a loop from the bed around the table to the sink and back. She kept it up until she was dizzy then reversed direction. Through her anger, she remembered a day when James was still an infant and she and Brian were spending his hastily negotiated sabbatical holed up in a Virginia farmhouse that had kicked around his family for a couple generations.

James didn't sleep. He was quiet and calm only when they kept him in motion. Or eating. Or eating while in motion. After two months of short, mostly fragmented sleep, Carol sat down on the steps leading up to the bedrooms and wailed along with James.

Brian ordered Carol up to bed, took the infant, and somehow shut him up. Carol slept for three hours and woke disoriented and panicked, sure she was late to a midterm or final or a date with Sasha. Reality asserted itself with both a lift and a heavy dread, and Carol sat up. It was quiet. No screaming, no hysterical meltdown, only a low murmur that had to be Brian.

At the top of the stairs, she stopped and listened then looked down at the first floor. The murmuring grew louder. Brian walked past her line of sight. He was carrying James in one arm and holding a book in his free hand. Carol crept down a few steps and sat. She watched him walk past twice more, too absorbed in what he was doing to notice her.

He was reading to James from Emile Durkheim's *The Rules of Sociological Method*. James was deeply asleep, and Carol felt freed from her dread.

"Hey," she said the next time Brian came into view. "Aren't you dizzy?"

"You're up! You look great." He swung into a figure-eight holding pattern of pacing at the bottom of the stairs.

"You're reading him Durkheim?"

"Can't start 'em too young."

"It sure put me to sleep when I read it."

"Well, yes. There's that."

"You're not dizzy?"

"I change direction every half hour or so."

"Every— How long have you been doing this?"

"Since you went to bed. It was working, and I was afraid of what would happen if you didn't get some sleep." He stopped pacing. "I've gotten pretty attached to the two of you. To you, especially."

James's wail saved Carol from having to admit the same thing.

Carol stopped her laps around the studio and zipped her phone into the inside pocket of her purse then zipped the purse shut for good measure. Temptation had to be resisted—anyone she could call would be like ice cream and hot fudge directly to her thighs. She took a book from the table and curled into bed with it.

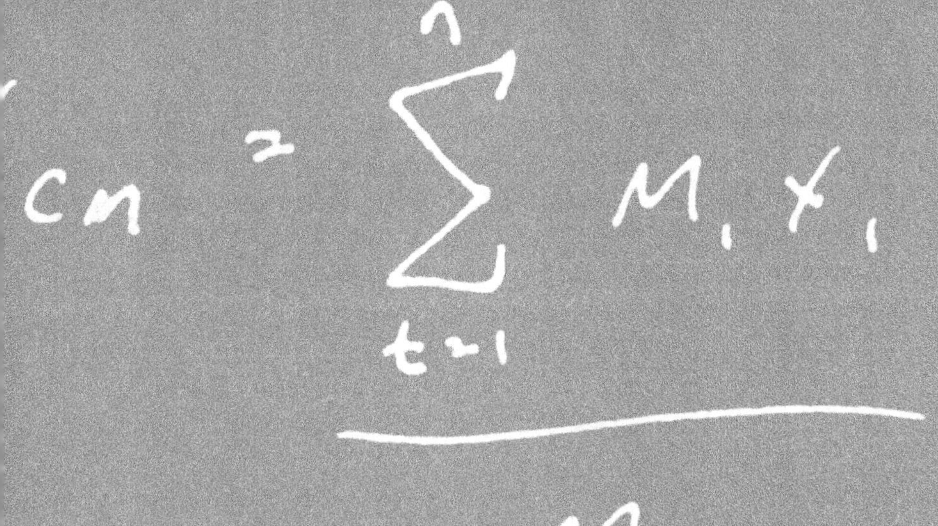

RALLYING BEHIND A SET OF COMMON GOALS IS ALWAYS
the first step in social movements, but those goals
inevitably reflect the lowest common denominator
of everyone involved. Historically, to make change,
one first has to subjugate to the larger group because it is only when the basest goals have been met
that we each have the luxury of pursuing what we
really want.

—Dr. Abigail Rosen, The F Word: Femininity in the New Century

$$\frac{w(R^3 - r^3)}{(R^2 - r^3)\sin(a)}$$

18

MITCH PUSHED a last cold bite of omelet around her plate. A bit of green pepper stuck out of the wedge of browned egg. That had been a mistake, that green pepper. She should have left well enough alone with the mushroom. Green pepper was Reginald's province. And Carol's.

After chats with Reginald, she shouldn't eat these dinners at the kitchen table, surrounded by bright cheerful colors and dead stillness. She should be at her desk, working, taking bites of this ill-conceived meal using only a small fraction of her attention, drowning her loneliness in a forced focus on data, in checking things off her list that never got smaller, no matter her productivity. She should be working, not playing with her food and giving Carol's sweater beady-eyed glances from across the table.

This rain didn't help her mood, coming down for two straight days. Sometimes it tapered off to a misty drizzle, but it was pouring now from the sound of it. A gurgle in the gutter above her kitchen window meant she had to get on the ladder and clean out last fall's accumulated leaves. Another item to add to the list. She put her fork down.

Someone knocked on her front door, and Mitch was half across the kitchen even before the short rap tailed off. If she hadn't thought for one hopeful second that opening the door might reveal Carol or if the knock hadn't caught her at lonely odds, she might have been able to determine what she really thought when she saw Abby standing on her front porch, drenched. Mitch didn't know how to wrestle her observations into either hypothesis or conclusion, couldn't tell if she was happy or annoyed or anything other than startled.

She took in Abby's blue lips and trembling shoulders. "Jesus. What're you doing out there? Come in."

But Abby stayed on the porch, dripping a puddle around her feet. She looked past Mitch, and Mitch turned, saw her living room and part of the kitchen, saw the pillows and laptop on the floor. Then, like a dog drying itself, Abby gave one big shiver and came inside.

Mitch closed the door then spent too much time trying to differentiate between the patter of drips from Abby's dark trench coat and the rain outside. This was strange. Abby was strange, always showing up uninvited and now standing here not saying anything. Mitch said, "Take off your coat and shoes. I'll turn up the heat."

She nearly tripped over her laptop cord on the way to the thermostat and knelt down to unplug it and kick it under the coatrack. Just around the corner in the hallway, she turned the dial up several degrees and waited to hear the furnace come to life. For the few years after that winter in her hatchback, Mitch had liked to keep her rooms steamy, but budgeting had taught her to get used to a little chill in the air.

When she got back to the entryway, Abby was still struggling with the buttons of her coat. The nail beds of her fingers matched her lips. Mitch knew what it was like to be cold all through and hesitated only a little before she said, "Let me." Underneath Abby's sodden coat, her thin sweater and turtleneck sported one or two dry spots, but she was mostly soaked through. Mitch bent to untie Abby's shoes, knowing Reginald or Carol or just about anyone else would know how to fill this silence with inane, calming chatter, but no words came to her.

Abby was shivering in rolling waves, but she said, "I was just walking." Mitch stopped her with a quick look.

"Come on. You need to get out of those clothes and warm up." Mitch walked down the hall to the bathroom, making sure Abby was following her. Clean towels were stacked under the sink, and Mitch grabbed the top one and set it on the toilet. "I always take a warm shower or bath when I'm chilled. Make sure not to start it too hot. Test it on the back of your hand. I can find some sweats for you, but the warmest thing I've got is that robe behind the door." Abby was standing close to her in the small bathroom, and Mitch couldn't stop talking. "It's flannel and quilted and saves me money on heat every winter. Anyway, which would you prefer?"

Abby rested her hand on the dark-blue towel draped over the bar next to her. Her fingers played over the terrycloth, and she shrugged.

"Just put your clothes outside the door, and I'll get them in the dryer. It's ancient and slow but does the job. I'll get some socks and the sweats in case you want them and leave them in the hall for you."

"Mitch," Abby said and took a half step closer without relinquishing the towel bar.

Mitch didn't know if it was just the cold, but Abby had a stiff, earnest expression that spurred Mitch into motion. She maneuvered around Abby and through the door. Breathing was easier when she wasn't penned in by all that white tile and whatever she wasn't letting Abby say. "Just get warm," Mitch said and shut Abby inside the bathroom.

Once Abby's clothes were in the dryer, she put a set of sweats and a pair of thick wool socks in a pile outside the bathroom. She cleaned up the remnants of dinner and her date with Reginald—washed dishes, tossed pillows back onto the couch, and set her laptop on her desk. The shower was still running, probably would for a while.

Back in the kitchen, she filled the kettle and set it on the stove before measuring out a loose-leaf Darjeeling into the blue teapot Reginald had sent back with her from London. He'd said that it matched her eyes, and it did—she'd taken it with her into the bathroom so she could confirm in her house's only mirror. She sat down at the table then worked hard at not conjecturing about Abby's drowned-rat appearance or dwelling over her naked presence in the shower.

Mitch considered getting up and moving Carol's sweater to her bedroom. It said too much still draped there, but by the time she decided to do something about it, Abby appeared in the kitchen doorway. She was wearing the robe, and her cheeks had color again.

"Tea okay?" Mitch went to the counter to occupy herself with the preparations she'd already finished.

"That's fine. Thanks. Mitch…"

Mitch shoved her hands in her pockets and faced Abby. A few inches of smooth skin showed between the bottom of the maroon robe and the tops of gray socks. "What're you doing here?"

"I was just walking, and—"

"Don't bullshit me."

"I wanted to see where you live. I wanted to see you, but I didn't really think you'd be here."

The kettle whistled. Mitch turned off the stove and poured the boiling water in the pot, not letting it cool down at all, just like Reginald had taught her.

Abby said, "I feel like you'll only see me if it's by accident."

"And hypothermia is a good accident?"

"Come on, Mitch. You don't make things easy. You get close, you open up, then you treat me like I don't exist."

"God, I'm so sick of being the difficult one. Whatever it is you want from me, whatever you think is in me to pry out, you're out of luck." The words came out more tired than angry, and Mitch was calm when she took the steeping pot and two mugs to the table.

"I don't have any expectations." Abby sat down with her back against Carol's sweater.

"I doubt that."

"All you do is surprise me."

"You wouldn't be surprised if you didn't have expectations."

"Okay. I don't have expectations anymore, but every time you let me see what's inside you, it makes me…" Abby ran a hand through her damp hair, leaving dark spikes in its wake.

"Makes you what?"

Instead of answering, Abby asked, "When did you change your name?"

Mitch sighed and poured the tea. She put one mug in front of Abby and wrapped her cold fingers around the other. "The day I turned eighteen. Legally, at least."

"How'd your parents take it?"

She turned away from Abby and sipped her tea, certain she should have moved Carol's sweater.

"What happened to you?" Abby asked.

"Nothing."

"Then why the mystery?"

"There's no mystery. There's just… past."

"What happened to you?"

Mitch set her mug down on the table, hard, sloshing tea over its rim. She got up and right into Abby's face. "I'm not quizzing you about catching your death to see my house, so why can't you leave me the fuck alone?"

"Because I can't. I just can't. Don't you think I want to? Don't you think this is impossible for me? I don't care how long Carol's let you get away with your silent act, I'm not her."

"Fine!" Mitch threw herself back in her chair. She picked up her steaming mug then put it down. She examined her knuckles and brushed at a ragged cuticle on her thumb with her index finger.

She told Abby everything. It came out in fits and starts at first, the clothes and the boys and swimming and math and her father. But when she got to that spring evening when she left her parents' house for good, the words gushed from her, and she couldn't look away from Abby's face. She talked about being taken in then kicked out by the Franks and living in the hatchback and the long cold winter nights alone.

Then, when the image of Lauren Tate in that locker room swam up to her attention, she stopped and eyed the lines her robe made where it lay over Abby's shoulders and chest then the vee of its edges, deep and dark between Abby's breasts. The sight brought her to some kind of sense, and she dropped her gaze and gulped down her cooled tea.

Abby dragged her chair around the table and next to Mitch. She put her warm hand on Mitch's forearm and squeezed. "I'm sorry."

"It was a long time ago, and I didn't have it that bad. Not really. I've heard of much worse."

"Being able to point at worse doesn't make a bad thing okay. Do you talk to your parents now?"

"No."

"Not at all? Do they know where you are?"

"No. I talked to them once after I moved out and before I left town. That was enough." Mitch toyed with her empty mug.

"I'm sorry."

"It was no tragedy. I was able to do everything I wanted despite it."

"Still, that kind of thing stays with you."

Mitch pulled her arm out from under Abby's hand and crossed it with the other over her chest. "Listen, just because you're probably buddy-buddy with your mother doesn't mean I'm scarred or handicapped because I'm not. Don't try to make this define me. Or explain me or anything."

"But it helped make you who you are."

"I've always been who I am. Everyone is. It's…most people…forget it. It doesn't matter. That's enough of this already."

"No, not forget it."

"What? What do you want from me?" Mitch's legs itched for motion, and her shoulder seized up with tension. She looked at Abby's wide chocolate eyes and pinked cheeks and morning-after messy hair. "What?" Mitch asked again, but softer this time, not really a question.

Abby reached out to tuck a lock of Mitch's hair behind an ear with a hand that shook like it was still chilled. Her fingers brushed Mitch's earlobe before her palm settled against the side of Mitch's neck, just like Lauren Tate all those years ago, just like Carol that horrible night. Mitch felt a flush rise up from her knees and blast through her chest. She'd been a chasm of need since getting back from London, wanted so much to lose herself in the thrumming pleasure of touch.

This desire was brought into focus by Abby's hand, and it distracted her from the discombobulation of having told her story to absolutely the wrong person. If Mitch concentrated, she could map the outline of Abby's fingers on her skin. All these dates with Reginald, all missing the heat of his body, the caress of his breath, that wordless connection Mitch had trained herself to live without but that haunted her in its absence.

She leaned across the gap between their chairs and kissed Abby. It was not chaste or warm or friendly. It said, "There, are you happy?" with a sneer. A low noise rumbled in Abby's throat. She opened her mouth wide then slid her fingers through Mitch's hair to the back of her head and pulled her closer, closer. Then even closer until their teeth struck, and Mitch snaked her arms around Abby and dragged her half off her chair in service of their kiss.

Want lodged in Mitch's throat, and she tried to swallow it down with their mingled spit. It felt huge and unmanageable, and it scared Mitch into trying to categorize the smallest details of her senses. Abby tasted of tea and, faintly, spearmint gum. Her teeth were smooth and regular under Mitch's tongue. She smelled like Mitch's soap and her own spicy musk that rose up in wafts from under the robe. The sounds she made were soft, pleading, and Mitch could almost breathe normally again.

Her observations were obliterated by a hand tugging her shirt free from her jeans then running along the curve of her lower back. It felt so good that Mitch was shocked into pulling away for a moment and grinding her forehead against Abby's.

When she could open her eyes and focus again, it was at the shadowed confluence of robe and cleavage.

Mitch ran her fingers along the cotton edging of the dark-red flannel. She watched Abby's chest rise and fall with her rapid breath, could feel her heart thudding under her fingertips. She pushed aside the robe and slid her hand under the white lace of Abby's bra. The soft, resilient skin of her breast knocked the breath out of Mitch. With her free arm, she pulled Abby's hips even closer. They were twisted in their chairs, contorting to reach and touch. Sitting here was ridiculous. She wanted to press herself against Abby, feel every inch of her firmness and give, wanted to lay Abby out in the bed, across the couch, on the floor, and lose herself in the deliciousness of having her, of being had in return. She wanted to stop time with this touching, this pleasure.

They kissed with single-minded determination, their hands moving in an oscillation between grappling and caresses. The kitchen was silent but for their huffs of breath and moany sighs. Abby's nipple was hard and her chest hot under Mitch's hand, and she wished her fingertips weren't so dry so she could feel the exact texture of Abby's skin. This was happening. This was real. It felt so good.

The dryer buzzed.

Mitch didn't stop immediately, couldn't, not while she was so intently studying the problem of how to move someplace more comfortable without reducing the energy between them. Only when the buzz tailed off into a death rattle did Mitch open an inch of space between their mouths and let her hand rest without motion on Abby's breast. Then she lurched away and was up and across the room, thought returning in small, painful increments.

"Mitch, wait." Abby's words sounded slurred, but Mitch didn't stop. She left the kitchen to gather the clothes from the dryer. When she came back, Abby was up and fumbling the robe closed. Mitch pushed the bundle of warm clothes at her.

Abby said, "Mitch, just—"

"Go get dressed, and I'll take you home." Mitch looked at her own white socks against the wide pine planks of the kitchen floor. Abby took a while to leave. When Mitch heard the bathroom door close, she lifted her head and breathed and surveyed the kitchen as if their passion must have left some visual sign, a residue or cyclonelike disturbance. But there was nothing except that Carol's sweater had slid off the chair to the floor.

Mitch bent down to get it. Tears threatened, but she sniffed them away. She draped the sweater over the back of the couch then put on her shoes and coat.

Abby appeared from down the hall, looking ready to launch into a speech she'd probably spent her time in the bathroom preparing.

Mitch said, "Your coat and shoes are still wet, but you shouldn't get too cold on the drive."

"Mitch."

"Get in the truck."

The rain was still coming down hard, and the rhythmic thunk of windshield wipers underscored the quiet between them, a quiet Mitch knew she should leave untampered with—it was structurally sound, perfect.

But she said, "I'm sorry. I shouldn't have done that."

"Don't be. Not for that."

"But I'm not…I can't…"

"I know. I know you're in love with Reginald. I know it'd be impossible for you to feel that way about me. Just don't regret what happened."

Mitch shifted in her seat but didn't look over.

"Because I don't regret it. The truth is I've wanted you in the most inexplicable way. I really hated you for it at first. And then I didn't, and now—"

"Don't say any more."

"I'm sorry you had such a hard time, but you need to know how incredible you are to have come through that like you did."

Mitch pulled them off the road and got out of the truck. The kind of confusion galloping around inside her was something she'd thought was long gone, left behind in Indiana with Evelyn. Mitch didn't know why she'd told Abby about the sordid mess of her adolescence when she'd managed to traverse almost twenty years without the urge—not with Carol, not even Reginald. The gigantic shame in this was what made her lean against the truck in the soaking rain, not her physical desire for Abby, not cheating on Reginald with their kissing.

Maybe if she could have told Carol everything back in college, if she could have let it pour out of her into postcoital darkness, maybe it would have retained its original proportions instead of both shrinking and growing until it was impossible to excise with any accuracy, until her muscles and sinews and vessels knitted it into her very cells and it became a part of her exactly as she'd tried to deny it ever would.

Mitch got back behind the wheel but couldn't manage to find the accelerator or the clutch. The ends of her hair dripped onto her coat. Abby's fingers rose to the wet skin on the back of her neck and traced out small circles that resurrected their kitchen scene and dragged it up and down Mitch's nerves.

She put the truck in gear.

Their quiet held for the rest of the ride. When they idled at the curb in front of Abby's house, the fatigue Mitch had been outrunning for weeks caught up with her. Her leaden legs sank into the driver's seat, her arms hung lifeless from the steering wheel. Her nose gurgled and dripped with her breath.

Abby opened the door and climbed out.

Mitch said, "Don't tell Carol. Not any of it."

"Okay," Abby said and shut the door.

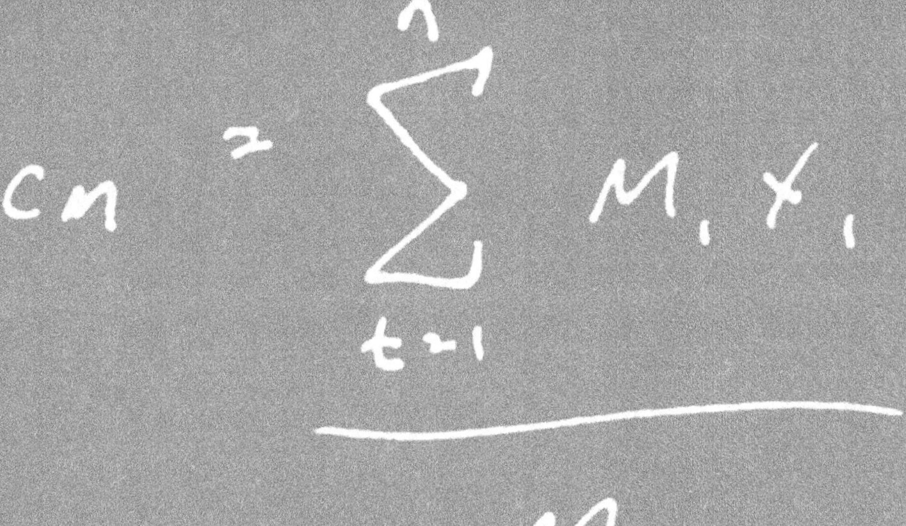

OFTENTIMES, IT IS ONLY WHEN ONE IS FORCED TO take a stand, to buck convention, to choose independently, that one finally can see clearly what is important and what is not. One can only hope the opportunity does not come too late.

–Dr. Abigail Rosen, The F Word: Femininity in the New Century

19

THREE WEEKS and two
days into Carol's stay in The Hole, as she'd come to call her studio, the morning rose clear and ripe with the moist smell of thaw. Instead of driving to the bookstore, she walked through the spring air, either to enjoy the weather or to delay getting to work, she didn't know, but when she arrived at Turning Leaves, it looked particularly charming in the bright sunlight. Inside, the familiar curved hulk of the register played on her emotions, which had not yet aligned with having pulled her head out of her ass at two that morning to confront financial reality.

Sure, power had come from finally addressing the smear of red numbers at the bottom line of her budget, but it was small, anemic really, and had no room in it for going weak-kneed at the sight of the register's round keys and pop-up numbers. If she wussed out now, it would mean the end to who she was trying to become. Melodramatic but also absolutely true.

She'd wrangled with it through the wee hours, and she'd only come up with one solution. She had to brave yet another frontier of change and find a better-paying job. In just a couple hours, she had to tell Maggie her plan to quit—if only so she'd be forced to follow through on it, and she wanted to do it without having to go into the whole situation. Yet instead of preparing her approach, she wished for some of that implicit understanding the media had brainwashed her to expect and spent her precious time farting around—cleaning muffin crumbs from the break room table, rearranging the stacks of new arrivals, and reading the first page of every book in the romance section.

She'd picked up Chastity Monroe's *Her Essential Mystery* when legitimate distraction arrived in the form of a wan-faced student who'd crept in without disturbing the chimes. He'd been lurking around the front counter for who knew how long when Carol finally noticed him.

"Can I help you?" She hastily reshelved the paperback.

He looked from Carol to the empty space behind the register. "I don't think so. I'll just wait."

"No need to wait. I'm right here."

He rubbed an eyebrow with a long index finger. "Huh?"

Carol walked back behind the counter, wondering about the caliber of student Tilsen was admitting these days. She gave the sale button on the register a push, waited for the clear ding to vacate the air, then said, "What can I do for you today?"

"Oh. Uh, yeah," he said. His Adam's apple bobbed with a swallow, and Carol knew, just knew, that he was a literature student.

His paper was on fairy tales, she finally teased out of him, and she canvassed the store to pull books he might find useful. She wondered why he wasn't bothering the research librarians at Tilsen like everyone else. Then she wondered what those librarians got paid and how hard that work could possibly be. No matter. She rang up the three books they had in stock and dismissed the student before calling in the order for the other titles. While she was on the phone, Maggie glided into the room, all smiles.

Her shining good mood had the same effect on this job that professional landscaping had on a house's curb appeal. Maggie hummed and touched her bun and looked out the front door. She came behind the counter and fidgeted, straightening the stapler and the tape dispenser then peering over Carol's shoulder at the list of books she was ordering.

Carol finished, hung up the phone, and before Maggie could say anything, held up her hand. "I can't work here anymore."

Maggie stopped humming, and the sun fell from her face. "What? Why?"

"Brian and I are separated. I need more money, and I know you can't afford it." Saying the words made Carol's mouth gummy. Why was it that letting Maggie in on this made it feel suddenly irrevocable?

"Separated?"

"I left him. And the kids. I moved out."

"Carol." Maggie reached toward her, but Carol edged away then immediately felt bad about it. "What happened?"

She shooed off the question. "Does it matter?"

"Of course it matters."

"I mean, in the scheme of things. I need more money, and you can't give it to me. What else is there?"

"You're spending too much time with Mitch. Just…mind the store," Maggie said and walked outside.

Carol heaved a sigh and waited. And waited. Then waited some more. The longer she waited, the louder Maggie's parting words became and the harder it was to ignore that assumption about Mitch's influence. Mitch, with her singular place in everyone's mind. Carol felt fucking invisible, irrelevant, and she was suddenly a little less despondent about having to find a new job.

About the time she'd gotten practically cocky with her decision to leave here, not to mention having survived this long string of nights alone in The Hole, Maggie pushed open the door with her back, her arms occupied with drinks in a carrier from The Filling Station, three unmarked paper sacks, and a small pink box from Loretta's.

She brushed past Carol, saying, "Close the store and come upstairs."

Upstairs? It took a moment for the shock of that to fade enough for Carol to flip the lock, twist the sign to "Closed," and draw the shade down over the front door. She turned off lights then walked through the back room and contemplated the steep stairs leading to Maggie's apartment. For over five years, she'd let her imagination run amok about what was up there, and she had a spasm of wanting to leave it at that before she tackled the scuffed wooden steps.

The stairway opened into Maggie's kitchen, which appeared ordinary enough, filled with the usual cabinets, countertops, and appliances. Neat but not pathologically so. A dishrag hung haphazardly over the faucet like a towel around a prize-fighter's neck, and a mug half full of murky coffee teetered close to the drain.

"Maggie?" Carol inched through a narrow white hallway, passing doors to a bedroom on the right and a bathroom and small dark office on the left.

"Up front," Maggie said.

Up front turned out to be a large living room that had been converted to a sun-filled library crawling with ivy and books. Shelves lined the walls—even the narrow strips between the windows. Not only did books jam each shelf, but they were piled in short stacks in front of most of the bookcases. A leather reading chair, big square ottoman, and very serious lamp sat in the middle of an Oriental rug. Maggie perched on a wood chair across the ottoman from her probably more habitual seat. Set out on the ottoman like some gluttonous board game was a tray full of treats: grilled cheese from Sandwichworks, scones from The Station, chowder from Lovin' Spoonful, and pink-frosted donuts from Loretta's.

Carol stood rooted in the doorway. Even given her years working downstairs, the number of books crammed together in this space was overwhelming. Such a deluge of titles would usually have distracted her from anything else, but lately she'd been missing the framed pictures of her family—both staged and silly—she'd left behind at the house. Maggie's library, in fact everywhere Carol had seen in this apartment so far, was completely devoid of this kind of memorabilia. It made her uneasy, and she began to talk.

"I'm surprised the floor hasn't collapsed under the weight of all this. Remember in college, when landlords always highlighted the part in the lease about no water beds?" She laughed then realized that this clause probably applied to The Hole. "Can you imagine? Crashing through the floor at three in the morning? Sound asleep. Or not? Anyway, I think you have almost as many books here as the Millerton Township Library. I don't know," she said from the doorway, still unable to move any closer. "I have to admit I'm a little disappointed to see that you probably are just up here reading in the wee hours, not entertaining gentleman callers or affixing tassels."

Maggie gave her a look and said, "Sit down."

She flopped in the leather chair. So many of her favorite foods, and eating seemed entirely beside the point. She finally understood Mitch's frustration with people who couldn't conduct a simple business transaction without making it personal. Why couldn't Maggie see she didn't want to talk about it? That just bringing it up had been hard enough?

Maggie didn't make a move toward the food, either, just crossed her legs and folded her hands over a knee. "You're the only employee I've ever had, but I have enough years in me to know that my odds of finding someone as capable, trustworthy, and fun are slim. If there's a way I can keep you here, I'd like a chance to find it."

Carol fought off a squirm. "I've done the math."

"There's more than one math."

"You know what I mean."

"We can talk about that later." She took a cranberry scone and a napkin and sat back. "I'm divorced. A decade ago, already. It was like the death of a thousand cuts inside our house, and I had led the way." She broke off the edge of the scone and popped it in her mouth then rubbed the napkin with her fingertips.

Carol stared at Maggie, trying to decide on a relatively intelligent response. Maggie was impassive and calm, her face practically wrinkle free. Instead of something intelligent, Carol said,

"Brian's had affairs," then took the grilled cheese sandwich. Someone should eat it while it was still warm. In fact, it was the perfect temperature—cool enough to wolf down without worrying about soft-tissue damage. The street and sidewalk noise outside was muffled by their second-story height and the closed windows, and it made their silence seem longer and more pregnant than it was.

When Maggie had made it halfway through her scone, she said, "I wonder if having a real villain in my divorce wouldn't have made some things easier. No one seemed satisfied without one, and somehow I became it. William earned, and I spent, even sat at home after the girls were gone. I volunteered all those hours at the library merely to assuage my own guilt. And now I was leaving him and probably taking him to the cleaners in the process. Wives always do, right?"

Another piece of scone disappeared between Maggie's lips, and Carol shoved the last bite of sandwich into her mouth, which had been hanging partway open, anyway. The state of affairs at the Hollister household had probably made it around the whole town by now, and no doubt Joyce considered Carol the villain for abandoning her family despite Brian's wandering prick.

"William wanted to give me the house, and I practically ran screaming. Not to be cliché, but what would the neighbors think?" Maggie put the napkin and the last quarter of scone it held back onto the tray. Carol couldn't remember ever seeing her finish anything she'd started eating.

Maggie surveyed the remaining food then looked at something above Carol's head. "I should have packed up and left the area right then, but we sold the house and each got smaller places across town from each other."

Carol imagined the kind of self-talk Maggie had surely engaged in to stick it out until her kids were grown. She imagined another ten years with Brian and felt both brilliant and hard-hearted for leaving now. She swallowed and said, "I got an apartment. A studio on the west side. Total shithole. I thought about taking off, really taking off, but I just can't. I can't leave the boys."

"I'm sure I couldn't, either. My daughters, well, my older sided with William, and the younger with me. I don't understand that. Sides, I mean. Not in this. Not in most things."

Having her way with a donut despite the grilled cheese taste in her mouth might allow Carol to avoid thinking about what Maggie said. Her fingers itched for sugar glaze and the give of soft dough, but she pushed herself back into the cushy leather. "Whatever my side is, Mitch isn't on it."

"How is that possible?"

She took one of the coffees and cradled it in both hands. "Everyone's really just on their own side, don't you think? Anyway, what happened next?"

"That's not true."

"It's true enough—at least where Mitch is concerned." Carol felt a pang at this, but she didn't know if it were for its truth or untruth. "What happened then?"

Maggie appeared uncomfortable for the first time, twisted in her chair then back, reached for the chowder but retreated. "I wish I could say I was driven from town, but is anything that clear-cut? Maybe, given things with Mitch, maybe now you know how it feels to be alone in a familiar place. It got under my skin."

Carol took half a donut and dunked it in her coffee. She wanted to say something, to agree, but she ate the warm, soaked pastry instead.

"I stood it for a long time then had to leave. I was so desperate I forced William to buy me off."

"And you came here."

"And I came here."

"And now you're independent."

"Yes."

Carol's hesitation was window dressing—she was already all-in. "I'm not taking money from Brian." The rest of the donut practically levitated off the ottoman into Carol's hand, but she started talking before she could get it to her mouth. "I don't know. Maybe it's stupid. Sometimes it feels stupid. A lot of the time, to be honest, but the rules for this…are there rules for this? I've been reading nonstop about social conventions, which are kind of vomit-inducing when I really think about them. So many apply to this, to my life, but I don't care." It came out way too loud, and Carol, feeling sheepish, took a large bite of donut then said around the mouthful, "I've always been dependent. My whole dang life. I've been insulated." She took a sip of coffee.

Carol wasn't embarrassed, exactly, but this talk—or maybe the grilled cheese—had unsettled her. Was she going to end up like Maggie? Not that there was anything wrong with Maggie and her quiet, insular life, but if this were Carol's future, she would have much rather found a trapeze hanging from Maggie's ceiling or a meth lab in her kitchen.

"Anyway," Carol said, "this has been—I really appreciate the food and the talk, but now you get it. The money. The whole room of one's own. I need a full-time job. Benefits if I can swing it, but I'll settle for rent and groceries. I'm not picky."

Maggie put down her coffee and brushed her hands across her black slacks. "I'll ask around the Main Street Merchant Association and see if anyone could use a top-notch manager."

Carol wasn't sure why she felt the need to hide the enormity of her gratitude, but she picked up a second donut and mumbled a thank you around a bite so large she ought to have been ashamed.

< ≈ >

Most people would consider Mitch's daily swims to be torture, especially given her shoulder, but the fire in her muscles and the gasp in her breath were easy compared to contemplating mistakes stacked up in front of her like lab books full of endless, damning proof. What was a little physical pain in the face of that?

After the debacle with Abby, Mitch punished herself by staying out of the pool for three long days. She anchored down the couch, didn't work, didn't email Reginald except to cancel their Sunday date, didn't even think about making a list of any kind. Instead, she reviewed every missed opportunity with Carol and considered all the very wrong things she'd said, all the taking for granted she'd done. Her conclusion was backed by fact, irrefutable: her love was too weak to find purchase on the hard exterior of her behavior. Her actions shed intentions so well they must be nearly frictionless.

On the Monday morning following this exercise, Mitch tried to deny her eagerness when she hurried into the natatorium's locker room and pulled on her suit then gave her combination lock an extra spin. The inside of her goggles tasted tangy when she tongued them. She hoofed it toward the pool through air thick with chlorine and left no break in her motion between stepping onto the deck and diving into the still water of lane four.

The first fifty meters felt so sublime she thought the pain had vanished from her shoulder. The water was silk, each stroke finished with a seemingly endless coast into the next, her breath was strong and measured, the swivel in her hips textbook perfect.

The spell held for a couple hundred meters, but then her shoulder found its voice. Mitch swam harder, hoping to drown it out with a loud chorus of effort. All four strokes hurt this morning. There was no relief from it, so Mitch pushed through toward the wrung-out physical lassitude always waiting at the end. She'd earned it, despite everything. No matter how well she could damn herself, she always ran up against her essential nature at some point, and all that was left for her to do was either erase herself or try to change.

The drag of water between her fingers and the pocket of wake she breathed in reminded her that change was possible, especially in small increments, that she would do better this time, that the pain from the consequences of fouling up with Carol would prompt her to try harder for a long time yet.

Then something snapped in Mitch's shoulder, and she screamed.

She was awash in a hot pain that seared off the ends of her other senses, and she floundered around, unable to hold on to the surface of the water until some primal part of her brain managed to get a message through to her limbs: stand up! Her feet found the pool's rough bottom, and she coughed and keened in agony, staggered with it until she encountered the tightly strung lane marker and rested there.

Mitch was still crying hard and cradling her right arm in her left when Jerry, the lifeguard, swam up to her. He was yelling something, but Mitch couldn't hear him. She couldn't catch her breath, and every time she moved even a little bit, even inadvertently, pain sparked through her.

After a while, she figured out how to breathe, which downgraded her misery from blinding to merely myopic. When Mitch opened her eyes again, another morning regular, Tim, was standing next to her. She couldn't figure out where her goggles had gotten to, but without them, the concern on Tim's face was obvious, though blurred through tears. She kept breathing and stood very, very still.

Tim said, "Jerry went to get help."

Mitch let a grunt escape on an exhale.

"The shoulder?"

Another grunt.

"Sounded like it really hurt."

Mitch started to cry again, but it wasn't from the pain.

When the paramedics arrived, they tried to get Jerry and Tim to help Mitch out of the pool, but she resisted the movement that would require, not when the press of Jerry's hand on her back made her lose her breath again. They ended up strapping her to a board as if her neck were broken then pulling her from the pool and sliding her into a waiting ambulance. The siren wailed into action, and the paramedics talked across her and shined a bright light in her eyes. It felt good to be held in place so tightly, but she was cold and fuzzy. She heard her name a few times, then "shocky," then they hit a pothole and everything went blessedly blank.

She woke in the hospital no longer strapped to the board. The pain was still there, but it had changed, had a welcome finite definition to it. Her bathing suit was clammy, but she could handle this now that it had attained human proportions.

Questions came at her too quickly to process, and she felt irrationally happy at being able to answer any correctly: she was at Millerton General Hospital, this was Monday, her name was Mitch Mitchell. But there was no end. It was like being with Abby. Who could answer all these questions while half naked on a gurney? She had no allergies, there'd been years of progressive pain, millions of meters of freestyle probably caused this.

"Is there someone we should contact?"

She'd become lucid enough to know the wrong answer to that question but not the right one. Carol would take a call from the hospital, but would she come when she found out it was about Mitch?

"Can we call someone for you, Mitch?" The man asking was thin-faced, with a beautiful smile.

She gave him Steve's name and number. An unexpected relief drowned her misgivings, and she abandoned herself to hospital process, to the welcome haze of IV painkillers, to blunt-nosed scissors making quick work of her favorite suit. She was manipulated in clinical ways, and it felt so good to be absolutely passive through everything.

After the X-rays and before the MRI, Steve stepped past the curtain drawn around Mitch's ER bed. He was carrying her swim duffel, which was overflowing with the clothes she'd worn to the pool that morning, and he looked at how her arm was strapped to her torso.

"I'm not even going to ask if you're okay, 'cause obviously you're not." He sat in the chair next to her and patted down his unruly hair. "I got you processed with the hospital then went to the pool to get your stuff. Jerry used a bolt cutter on your lock. He said he'd never heard anyone scream like that. He said he thought you were going to drown right in front of him."

The pillow was soft and cool when she dropped her head back. "Thanks for coming."

"I thought it was a crank call at first. Then, when I figured out what was going on, I panicked. They kept saying you were going to be fine, but I almost ran out of my apartment without my pants on before I remembered how cool you were when my appendix burst. Did it hurt like that?" He wrung the straps of her duffel, white-knuckled.

"I don't know. It hurt a lot."

"On a scale from one to ten?"

She closed her eyes. "I don't know."

"Just a ballpark. One to ten."

"Twelve. Listen, I have to tell you something."

"Twelve? No wonder Jerry was so freaked out."

This time she said it with more force. "I have something to tell you."

"Sure. Of course. What is it?"

But it was any number of things: how terrible it had felt not to be able to call Carol, her fear of never swimming again, her misstep with Abby. "That trip to London. His name is Reginald. I met him at that conference in Vegas last year. I'm in love with him, and I really wish he was here. Right here. So I could hold his hand or something."

She kept her eyes closed, unwilling to chart the way Steve's reaction was surely stampeding across his face. He cleared his throat, and Mitch heard him shift in his seat.

He said, "Okay. I get it. I mean…okay. But, well, you can hold my hand if you want. I can stay here all day—my boss is out sick."

Mitch opened her eyes and tried to smile. She took his offered hand in her free one and gave it a weak squeeze.

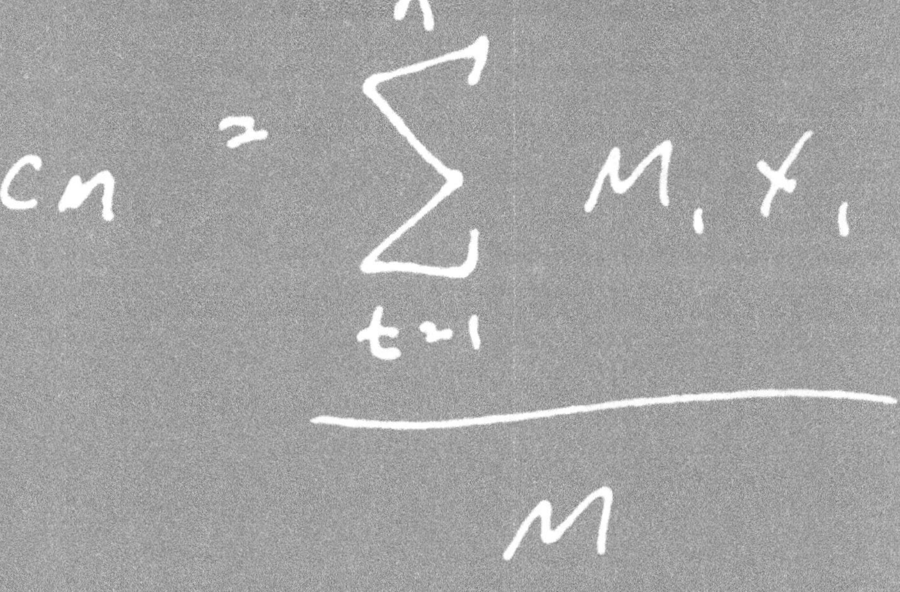

$$\frac{cn^2 \sum_{t=1}^{n} M_i x_i}{M}$$

CHANGE IS INEVITABLE. CHANGE FOR THE BETTER IS not.

–Dr. Abigail Rosen, The F Word: Femininity in the New Century

$$\frac{w(R^3 - r^3)}{2^2 - r^2)\,\sin(a)}$$

20

MITCH WOKE with a start to fuzzy queasiness that was part pain and part painkiller. Her T-shirt and the waistband of her shorts were soaked with sweat, and she pushed wet hair from her forehead while scanning the living room to orient herself. This medicine made her dreams both real and raucous. In the one she'd just woken from, her arm had dangled from her shoulder, useless but without pain, while Carol walked by her with slow deliberateness, saying something into her cell phone about a cash offer for The Device, never once looking in Mitch's direction in the eternity it took her to pass.

Her shirt was hard to peel off with only one useful arm, but she struggled free of it then used its dry spots to swipe at the sweat on her neck and the trickles that still meandered down her chest. The house was muffled in quiet, and Mitch drummed her fingers to break it. Chester's ear flicked at the sound, but he didn't move from his tight curl in the corner of the couch, next to where her feet had been.

THE MATHEMATICS OF CHANGE

Today was merely a placeholder, a needless pause between hospital visits, like the mandatory cooling-off period before buying a handgun. Only, now, the trigger was already pulled. She'd pulled it herself, held muzzle to soft tissue and bone and fired every time she'd swum another five-hundred repeat through the pain, every time she'd ignored Carol about going to a doctor, every time she thought about the "blah blah" someone in a white coat might say, someone who had no clue about her and her life, someone who thought that what they saw on film, just because it was under her skin, was something deeply her.

She balled up her shirt and started to stretch then thought better of it, just twisted her wrist to make her watch face visible. This time tomorrow, some man with hopefully very steady hands would be monkeying with bone and tendon, probably telling the OR nurse that Mitch's shoulder was a textbook example of stupidity at work. This time tomorrow, her future would take whatever trajectory was left open after tendons were stitched and reattached and bone hopefully reseeded, a trajectory mostly concerned with reducing operating stress and strain, with extending somewhat useful life and pushing out decommissioning as long as possible.

Mitch would know what to do if her shoulder were metal and rubber and lubricant; she would have been on top of maintenance and optimization, would have written a schedule of part replacements. She would have taken care of business.

When was the last time she'd taken care of business outside The Device? Addressed the areas of friction in the rest of her life? How many times had she advised clients not to wait for things to break down before learning the value of regular maintenance? Prepared or not, things break, and all that was left was to try and fix them. She'd decided to do better before this happened. A pretty low bar considering her recent track record. Doing better in any noticeable way would require more than the incremental changes she'd practiced in the pool, and not knowing if she could do it was no excuse. Before this nap, she'd called Carol twice, each time experiencing a surge of fear that had momentarily eclipsed her anticipation about tomorrow's surgery. This time, she picked out a different number with the thumb of her free hand.

When Abby answered her office phone on the third ring, Mitch said, "Abby? Hi. I'm sorry. I wouldn't bother you, but something's come up, and I need to ask a favor, however mean or coldhearted that might be." Mitch knew this was not much of a behavioral improvement, that she should address the other night, but what was there to say? They'd settled it as much as it could be settled, hadn't they?

Mitch heard a soft breath before Abby said, "It's not coldhearted. Well, maybe it is. I guess it depends on the favor." A stronger breath, then, "Not that it matters—my feelings for you aren't dependent on mutuality, so I guess you came to the right place."

"I'm sorry. I am." Mitch tossed her shirt in the general direction of her bedroom and laid back on the couch with a wince.

"Tell me what's come up."

"It's my shoulder. On Monday... it doesn't matter. The bottom line is that I need surgery."

"Do *me* a favor and don't make me ask." Abby's brisk tone made Mitch almost smile.

"All right." But words refused to form in Mitch's mind. For once, she wished Abby would layer on the questions so that any disclosure wouldn't require a force of will she possessed only in a form gummy with regret. "During my swim Monday morning, one of my tendons ripped right off my bone. My arm just stopped working right in the middle of the pool." Mitch laughed a little, finding surprise under the hurt. "I thought... I don't know what I thought. The pain left no room for that."

"Are you okay?"

"When they hit me with the test results at the hospital, I kind of wished I was still out of my mind. Physical pain, it's clean, you know? I can manage it even when I can't really manage it."

Mitch waited for Abby to ask, to pry out the shameful details of her diagnosis, not believing that now, *now*, Abby was keeping her mouth shut. Mitch ran her toes across Chester's soft side.

Abby said, "It's okay if you don't want to tell me."

"That's not it. It's just— I just—" Then Mitch rattled off the details: full tear in the supraspinatus tendon and partial tears in the other tendons in that joint and one tendon in the left shoulder due to a bone spur. Some degree of arthritis in both shoulders and the start of osteonecrosis in the bad shoulder, which meant that a small part of her humerus had died, maybe from an undiagnosed fracture that never healed and disrupted the blood flow to that area of the bone.

"I was sitting on my bed in the ER with my arm strapped to my chest, and the doctor was practically salivating over my injuries. He's fucking excited about how I could have accumulated so much damage and still retained enough range of motion to keep swimming. When he calmed down, he got serious and told me that, considering the shape I'm in, I shouldn't ever swim again, even after surgery."

"Mitch, I— I don't know what to say."

"Don't say anything. I'm calling because my surgery is tomorrow, and Carol won't answer her phone. I was hoping you could tell her." Mitch listened, trying to make out any sound around Abby in her office. Its quiet matched the quiet of her house. "I wouldn't ask, but I know she'll talk to you."

"I'll call her, of course. What do you want me to say?"

"The surgery's at ten tomorrow morning at Millerton General, and I hope she can be there. Tell her I'm sorry." The apology came in a rush and was low and husky.

"Don't hang up," Abby said, and Mitch felt exposed, her fingers caught in the act of feeling around for the disconnect button. "I don't know what to say about your shoulder or swimming or even Carol. I don't know what you think of me. If you think of me. I used to be a good person—or at least I'd like to think so. And then I wasn't. But now..."

Mitch kept quiet, continuing to stroke Chester with her toes.

"I didn't mean to get between you and Carol, but knowing both of you and watching what's happened...I didn't mean to have any feelings for you, but I do, and when you let me in the other night—"

"We don't have to talk about that."

"You don't, but I do. Maybe you told me those things to get me off your back, but what happened to you and who you are—"

"Don't."

"I have so many regrets. You have no idea. But I want to be better. I wish you could give me a chance to know you."

Mitch felt a pang that she wasn't going to invite Abby in, wondered for a moment if a friendship were possible between them. "Regrets get in the way of trying to be better. If you don't forgive yourself, nothing will ever change."

"We could both take that advice."

Mitch said, "You're probably right."

< ≈ >

Carol's cell phone jittered across the table at The Filling Station, coming to a rest against her steaming mocha. She snatched it up and checked the caller ID, sure that if it wasn't Mitch, it was the craft store to cancel her interview, to tell her they were just kidding, that she wasn't really qualified in the least.

But it was Abby, her great white hope, the one Carol had punished for liking Mitch by beating the friendship out of her like piss from a pipsqueak. "Hey, Teach, what's shaking?" The espresso machine let out a long, loud hiss.

"Not working today?"

"No." Withholding herself from Abby had gotten easier but was by no means effortless.

"I have something to say, and I want you to hear me through."

"Sure. Why wouldn't I?"

"Promise not to hang up. I'll just have to chase you down if you do."

Carol had ignored Mitch's calls this morning for a reason, and she should have anticipated this sneak attack. She knew running away from this wasn't possible, not really, not without leaving town entirely. And maybe not even then. "Oh, fine. What does she want?"

"It's her shoulder. It sounds bad. Actually, bad doesn't even approximate. She's having surgery at ten tomorrow morning at Millerton General. She wants you to be there. She said she's sorry."

"Is that it?"

Abby huffed. "No, that's not it. She's not just injured, she's permanently damaged. She won't be able to swim again. Ever."

Carol gripped her mug. Its heat burned her hand, and she was surprised it didn't shatter in her fingers. "Anything else?"

"She's *devastated*, not that she would admit it."

"What do you want from me?"

"Are you going to see her tomorrow?"

"None of your business, Abby. None of your goddamned business." Carol hung up. Only her newfound intimacy with the value of a dollar stopped her from whipping her cell phone across The Station and watching it break into a bazillion pieces. Here she was, taking a quiet half hour to drown her nerves in chocolate and espresso before her interview down the block, and now this?

Her hands and feet were freezing, and she wished she could blame it on fury—or at least a more noble emotion than fear. She was literally petrified, and trying to pinpoint exactly why just made it worse. Mitch was devastated. Sure. Might as well say she was suffering from some mild disappointment. Even Carol couldn't imagine what Mitch was feeling, but it had to be something like a fall down a bottomless pit.

Her drink was both too sweet and too bitter after that phone call, and her gut rumbled at such a high volume she coughed to cover it. She felt sick. The stubborn, crusty bits of her love for Mitch dictated that she cancel this interview and her meeting after it with Brian at the house and go to Mitch and help in whatever ineffectual way she could. But she just stared down her mocha.

This was it, then. The way she was finally going to fail Mitch, the very situation she'd been afraid of from the beginning. But wasn't it Mitch's fault for setting up this house of cards in the first place? Hadn't Mitch failed Carol first? Well, hadn't she? But even if she had, finger-pointing was useless. Carol knew damn well that if she forgave Mitch her Mitchness, they could try again. Mitch wanted to try again. Hell, Carol sometimes wanted to try again.

With the way she beat down this small desire, Carol knew that if there were ultimate blame here, she had to shoulder it. She wasn't going to Mitch not because of the possibility that Mitch would hurt her again—wasn't hurt a certainty where there was love?—but because of her own weakness. Carol couldn't trust herself to keep her resolve of real change with the comfort of Mitch's unconditional acceptance.

This was her decision, and she was going to have to pay its price for a long time.

Eventually Angel came by, carrying a rag but not wiping dirty tables. She snapped her bright green gum and said, "Something wrong with your drink?"

"Yeah. The person drinking it."

"Can't taste it right? Do you have a cold?"

"No. I'm a freak, that's all."

"Carol, if I didn't know a few freaks like you and Mitch, this town would get the best of me." Angel twisted the rag around one hand then the other, and Carol felt a brief comfort that she was Angel's destination, not the other crumbs around her.

"Mitch," Carol said and for a split second forgot why she wasn't flying to Mitch's side.

"Fighting again? But you just made up."

"Fighting for good." Angel looked set to speak, but Carol cut her off. "Can you ... will you be a friend to her? It's not about me, but she's going to be hurting for a while."

"What the hell happened between you two?"

Carol got up and put her coat on. "Nothing. Everything." She felt tears rear up. "I can't," she said. "I just can't. I have to run." Thankfully, she was telling the truth. She had to hurry the four blocks to the craft store after all that gazing into her coffee she'd done.

The interview was a welcome, nerve-racking distraction. Carol answered questions like she knew what she was talking about, which maybe she did. She had two other interviews the next day, and if either went nearly as well, her money problems might soon be over, making way for her time-management problems to begin.

After the interview, at the long stoplight on the way to the house, Carol's palms and forehead broke out in a sweat, and her blood thundered through her arteries. The steering wheel creaked in her grip with the effort of not pulling a U-turn and speeding to Mitch's house. She couldn't, she knew that, but the pain that came along with that certainty obeyed none of the limitations of Carol's will.

The light turned green, and she drove through, absolutely certain of her choice even if she were just as absolutely wrong. She steeled herself for this conversation with Brian, the laying down the law she was going to have to do, the draw she might feel to him and the warmth of their house.

He was already at the kitchen table. The strain of the last months showed only if you knew where to look. His collar was askew, his hands were chapped with winter dryness, and the wrinkle between his eyebrows was deep and unwavering. Carol resisted the urge to check the fridge and pantry, to eyeball levels of nutritional content and sugar. The lemon smell of their floor cleaner was overpowering.

"Hi," Brian said when she stood across the table from him. "You look nice."

Carol glanced down at her starched white shirt and blue slacks that she'd bought the day before. A lot of her clothes were still at Mitch's. She dragged out a chair and dropped into it. "I was interviewing. How are the boys? James okay?"

"The boys…wait, interviewing? Why? I thought you loved the bookstore."

"I do. Listen. Things have changed, but I wanted to kind of get everything settled before telling you."

Brian tugged at his collar. "Things have changed? What things have changed?"

His distress didn't move her like Mitch's secondhand pain, which was an unexpected marvel. "I left Mitch's and got my own place. Month-to-month for now, but I'm signing a longer lease if I get a new job."

"Wait." He pressed his palms against the spotless table top. "Wait. Month-to-month? When did this happen? Why?"

"I moved weeks ago."

"But why?"

Although she was determined not to tell him, his expectant gaze quickly became uncomfortable. If only they already knew the rules for this new relationship of theirs. Co-parents, yes. And maybe friends someday? That kind of forgiveness seemed impossible, but so did losing Mitch. Even if she could tell him, what would she say? "Call it a difference of opinion."

"Weeks ago?" Why was he repeating everything she said? "Did you know she called to ask if she could come over and see the boys? It sounded like she expected me to say no."

"Did you?"

He frowned, digging that wrinkle in deeper. "Say no? Why would I? She came for dinner. They've missed her."

Carol leaned back and picked invisible lint from her pants while she dealt with her relief. "Good. I'm glad she came by."

"You aren't talking, then."

"No. Can we move on?"

"Whatever you say. So, you got your own place." He looked down at his dry hands then shoved back from the table. "No. I need to say something. I know I don't deserve you, probably never did. But isn't there some way you could try again with me? To be a family? Doesn't it mean anything that I love you and hate myself and want a chance to do better?"

The kitchen was exceptionally still without the Tilsen fight song drumming in the sink. Brian's face was red, and its openness was lovely. A part of Carol was affected. It hadn't been exactly accurate, what she'd said to him that night, that she didn't love him. Of course she loved him. Just not enough.

"I'm sorry," she said. "I can't. That's why I'm here, actually. To figure out how to make this thing permanent."

Brian got up and stumbled over to the refrigerator. His forehead thunked against it, and he hid his face in the crook of his arm. Carol felt tears prick her eyes.

"Brian."

The shake of his head was barely perceptible.

She went to him and laid her cheek on his back. He sighed and sniffed.

"I don't want you to hate yourself. Just be better—for James and Gordo. They adore you. Everything's going to be okay. I know it. Just don't ask me how, exactly." She smiled and felt the short rumble of a laugh against her cheek. She wrapped her arms around him, and they stayed like that for a long time.

< ≈ >

The doorbell permeated Mitch's dream long before it roused her. She opened her eyes and felt whatever she'd been saying in her sleep clog up her throat. She was covered in sweat for the third time that day. Every one of these catnaps resulted in a need for a new shirt, and yet she couldn't stay awake.

The doorbell rang again, and Mitch went to answer it, limping with stiffness. The last time she'd opened the door, it was to Steve and Eric and two pizzas. They'd stayed with her for a few hours, artificially cheerful. They'd all smiled so wide and hard that she'd kept on smiling even after they'd left.

Reginald was outside. Mitch wondered for a moment if she were still sleeping, but the way the cool night breeze seeped through her wet shirt to her skin felt too real even for her drug-fueled dreams. He shifted from foot to foot, clenching and unclenching his hands. The small front porch was empty of any luggage, and the darkness outside hid whatever mode of transportation he'd used to get here. He seemed to have materialized out of nowhere.

"Bathroom," he said. "I need to use your loo."

"Patty."

"No. No Patty, no nothing but your bathroom. I'm not staying. Now, where is it?"

She stepped back and pointed down the hall. Reginald moved so fast a rush of outside air followed him in. The bathroom door slammed, and Mitch realized she was still holding the front doorknob. She turned it and shut the door quietly. She tried to pretend she hadn't seen Reginald's face long enough to register its expression, but she betrayed herself by not moving past the coatrack and down the hall to talk to him.

His anger and his being here could only mean that he knew about what happened and what would happen tomorrow even though she hadn't told him, had only written two short emails, pecked out with her left hand, that claimed she was too busy to breathe. Deadlines and all that, which seemed like such small lies compared to telling him what happened without also trying to explain what swimming meant to her and how its loss didn't only add to but compounded her loss of Carol. She would have to explain everything, tell him that she might be able to get a handle on all this if she could just measure it, but how could she measure things that no longer existed?

Trying to explain would only expose the enormity of the gap between the broken her and the one Reginald claimed to love, which could lead to nothing good. If losing him was inevitable, her only hope was to delay it a bit.

The toilet flush was faint, and Mitch felt the time between it and Reginald's footsteps as if she were riding on a train traveling near the speed of light, making seconds stretch to days.

He didn't look at her. "Thank you. I'll see you at the hospital tomorrow." He edged toward the door, but Mitch blocked his way.

"What's going on? You can't just—"

"Yes I can," he shouted then stared down the ceiling, the whites of his eyes glistening below his irises. "I'm making the choices here, and it's your turn to accept them." He took in a loud breath, his nostrils flared. "I'm staying at the Quality Inn, if I can ever find it with these piss-poor directions I have. I've got the bloody maps around your house memorized, but that

Quality Inn? Nooo. I'll see you through the surgery and the next two days, then you'll be rid of me."

"Rid of you?"

"Yes, rid of me. Because that's clearly what you want. What else could you want, leaving me to find out about this through Steve. Now let me leave."

No matter how much she deserved this, her left arm staged a coup and felt as useless as her right, and opening the door flirted with being a physical impossibility. All that loss she'd felt those long, cold nights in her hatchback was real and terrible and nothing compared to this horrible year where what she'd lost was only what she'd given away.

She opened the door then made herself look at Reginald's face, which crumpled from tight anger to a looseness that looked like he'd been knocked free of his wind. Mitch felt a stab between her own ribs and tried to hide a grimace.

He said, "You're unbelievable," then pushed past her. He got to the driveway before turning around. "I thought if I showed you some patience. But this. This, Mitch! I don't even care what your explanation might be, not that you'll ever offer one."

She let him take a few more steps before she said, "Wait."

"Piss off."

"I tried to call Carol."

"Good for bloody you."

Her eyes had adjusted enough to the night to see a dark car parked at the curb. Reginald was closing the distance to it in long strides.

If she let him get in the car, everything worth loving in her life besides her work would be gone. The Device might have been enough for her seventeen-year-old self, but it wasn't now. Friction presupposes touch, direct contact and force, and while she had built a career fighting it, she knew it was also the thing that enabled movement in the first place. Friction between people was uncontrolled and beyond scientific principles, but nothing in her life could compete with when she had rubbed up against others. It heated her up, changed her composition, and the fear of losing that made her cry.

She yelled in a choked voice, "Reginald."

He stopped, the door to the car open just wide enough to trigger the interior light.

Even with that yellow glow, Mitch could barely make out his face. She considered trying to steady her voice, not wanting him to think she was hoping to manipulate him even though she was. "At least come in for a cup of tea."

She thought she saw him bow his head.

"If nothing else, I can give you directions while it brews."

She heard a whisper and pretended it was her name. Her palm smeared tears across her cheeks while she waited. Her eyes closed then opened when the car door slammed. For a panicked second, she couldn't see him and was sure she'd lost him, but then she caught his shadowy figure moving up the driveway. The deep, relieved breath she took made her shoulder throb and pulse.

AUTHOR'S ACKNOWLEDGMENTS

This book might not have happened without the Great Recession, which upended me, reminded me of what was really important, and gave me the time and desperation to make different choices.

Many thanks to everyone involved in the incredible writing community Shelley Washburn has created at the Pacific University MFA program. To Claire Davis, who taught me how to deeply imagine and get my ego out of the story, and to Mike Magnuson, who hurled invectives at every wrong thing about this book but fell in love with Mitch and Carol, anyway.

Amy Merrick always finds time around freelancing and teaching and running and everything else she does to read drafts and dispense encouragement. Pacific folks Mike, Karen, Kandy, Christine, Susan, and Stephanie have all provided inspiration and high fives and priceless commiseration.

Deep gratitude to Mary Ann and Ruthie at Brian Mill Press for seeing something special in this book and putting their weight behind it.

And, as always, thank you to Anna and your unwavering support. I wouldn't be the me I am without you.

ABOUT THE AUTHOR

Amanda Kabak has had stories published in *Midwestern Gothic, Harpoon Review, Perceptions Magazine,* and other print and on-line periodicals. She was a recipient of the Betty Gabehart prize, issued by the Kentucky Women Writer's Conference, and has been nominated for a Pushcart Prize. She holds an MFA from Pacific University and is a software architect in her other life.

CREDITS

Author	Amanda Kabak
First Readers	Mike Magnuson, Amy Merrick, Rebecca Oliver
Copyeditor	Annamarie Bellegante
Cover Photography	Nathan Pearce
Cover Design	Ampersand Book Covers

www.ingramcontent.com/pod-product-compliance
Lightning Source LLC
Chambersburg PA
CBHW070824190726

48292CB00006B/2102